AF072170

138 MAIN STREET

138 MAIN STREET

GAVIN BELL

SIMON & SCHUSTER

London · New York · Amsterdam/Antwerp · Sydney/Melbourne · Toronto · New Delhi

First published in the United States by Scout Press, an imprint of Simon & Schuster, LLC, 2026

First published in Great Britain by Simon & Schuster UK Ltd, 2026

1 3 5 7 9 10 8 6 4 2

Simon & Schuster UK Ltd, 1st Floor
222 Gray's Inn Road, London WC1X 8HB

Simon & Schuster Australia, Sydney
Simon & Schuster India, New Delhi

www.simonandschuster.co.uk
www.simonandschuster.com.au
www.simonandschuster.co.in

The authorised representative in the EEA is Simon & Schuster Netherlands BV, Herculesplein 96, 3584 AA Utrecht, Netherlands. info@simonandschuster.nl

A CIP catalogue record for this book is available from the British Library

Hardback ISBN: 978-1-3985-4280-8
Trade Paperback ISBN: 978-1-3985-4281-5
eBook ISBN: 978-1-3985-4282-2
Audio ISBN: 978-1-3985-4283-9

Interior design by Karla Schweer
Printed and Bound in the UK using 100% Renewable Electricity
at CPI Group (UK) Ltd

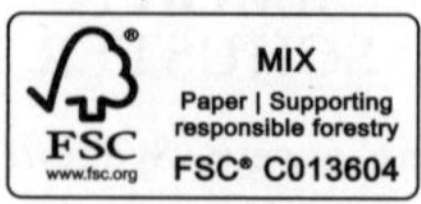

For Laura,

because I always want to be on the street where you live

History shows that today's terrorists
may be tomorrow's heroes.

Jacob W. Mendius, *A Manifesto for True Living in America*

Ain't No Love in the Heart of the City

Bobby "Blue" Bland

138 MAIN STREET

PART 1

Sunday

1

138 MAIN STREET

PEMBURY VILLAGE, LONG ISLAND, NEW YORK

"I don't know," Mrs. Dasch said when they were winding up the conversation. She was shielding her eyes from the morning sun with her right hand, squinting up at the large bay window on the upper floor of the house. The sunlight glinted off her expensive-looking nails as she tried to articulate what she was feeling. After a moment, she settled on more or less the exact words Special Agent Ben Walker had been expecting.

"This kind of thing just doesn't *happen* in a place like this."

Megan Dasch was the neighbor at number 151, the house diagonally across the street. She was in her early forties, slim and blond. Somehow, she managed to look refined even in purple velour sweatpants. With her left hand, she tugged absent-mindedly at the leash attached to the collar of her Pomeranian as it tried to continue along the wide sidewalk, obviously in no mood for this interruption to their routine.

Walker wondered what Mrs. Dasch would say if he told her he had heard a variation of the words she had just used at every violent crime scene he'd been to over the past two decades. Instead, he decided to go with the comforting approach.

"I know, ma'am. You just don't expect it in a nice community like this. But I promise you, we aim to catch the guy."

People said things like *You don't expect it here* because they wanted to be reassured that the man with the badge was going to make it all better, that this was all in a day's work and he would handle it from here. Walker had known about the case for only an hour and a half, and already he was pretty sure this one wasn't all in a day's work.

He tapped off the recording app on his phone without looking at the screen and slid it into his pocket. He thanked Mrs. Dasch for her recollections of not seeing or hearing anything suspicious three nights ago and watched as she and the Pomeranian moved off at a leisurely jog along the wide, tree-lined street. The dog yapped at her reprovingly and she murmured an apology.

Barely eight o'clock in the morning and the sun was already bathing the street in a pleasant heat. The sky was the shade of blue you normally saw only on the covers of travel-agency brochures. The leafy maple trees filtered out the noise from the highway, so you could almost believe you were in a small country town miles from anywhere instead of on one of the most crowded pieces of real estate in America. You *really* didn't expect this to happen here.

Walker turned back to the house. The Pembury PD hadn't been able to work out how to make the ornate wrought-iron gates stay open, so they'd just kept one side from closing with a sawhorse. The gates were eight feet high with tasteful spikes along the top. They projected strength, security, exclusivity. They hadn't done the house's occupants a lick of good.

Pierson was standing just inside the gate. The tall, broad-built detective had his thumbs threaded through the belt loops of his pants. Walker noticed he had buttoned his collar and straightened his blue tie since earlier. He affected a sheepish look as Walker approached.

"Listen, I just wanted to apologize if we got off on the wrong foot, Agent Walker."

The wrong foot was an understatement. On Walker's arrival, Pierson had wasted no time telling him they were good, that they didn't need any outside help here. You could almost hear the quote marks around *help*.

But perhaps Walker was being unfair. Perhaps part of the tension had been on his side. He hated coming into a case when the bodies were cold, when the most crucial investigative work had already begun and the theories had started to form, particularly when the case turned out to be connected to something bigger that the initial investigators could not have had any knowledge of.

Either way, Pierson's attitude had done a one-eighty. The motivation behind this change was not a mystery: With his keen detective instincts, he could sense headlines, national TV, maybe a book deal or a podcast.

"Not a problem, Detective," Walker murmured, making sure not to break stride.

Pierson smiled in acknowledgment and stepped into his path so Walker had to choose between stopping or knocking the detective over. He chose the former, not without some reluctance.

"Call me Steve. We might as well drop the formality if we're going to be working together, am I right?"

"Steve," Walker repeated, trying to keep the discomfort out of his voice. "Right."

"I'll be glad to go over everything we've got so far. In fact, I—"

Walker held up a hand to stop him. Spending time with Detective Steve was going to be a necessary evil, but he wanted to take another walk through the house before he submitted to that.

"That's good to know, I appreciate it." He gestured toward the house. "I'll catch up with you in a minute, okay?"

Pierson opened his mouth to say something else and then apparently thought better of it. "Got you. Take all the time you need, Agent Walker. Or do you prefer Ben?"

"Walker is fine."

Quickening his pace, Walker advanced along the curving driveway. He passed the lawn where the son's girlfriend had fallen, the spot marked with a little red flag. There was still a dark stain on the grass. He stopped twenty yards from the house and looked up at the bay window of the main bedroom again. That was where the killing had started.

The house was big, but of course that went without saying. There weren't any small houses in Pembury Village. The home sprawled in the acre of enclosed yard that surrounded it. The walls of the house were sided with whitewashed wood that gleamed in the morning sunlight everywhere except where a ladder of ivy crawled up to touch the reddish-brown roof tiles. The front door was beneath a porch at the top of a short flight of steps. Above it was a rainbow-shaped pane of stained glass with the number *138* in the center, entangled with stylized roses.

138 Main Street.

That was why the FBI was here. Because of something that had happened in two other places. Two other murder scenes, both thousands of miles from here. Different states, different victim profiles, different causes of death. *Very* different styles of home, one a modest bungalow and the other a shack that would have been bulldozed decades ago if the ground beneath it had been worth anything to anybody. The three addresses could not have been more different. Except that they were the same.

"Agent Walker!"

Walker turned around to see one of the local cops running up the driveway. She was clutching her phone in her hand like a relay runner holding a baton.

"They're trying to get ahold of you."

Walker took his own phone out and saw he had missed two calls while he was recording his conversation with Mrs. Dasch. Out of the corner of his eye, he could see Detective Pierson moving toward them as though drawn by a magnet. Walker started to ask the officer what the news was, but she was already talking.

"There's another one."

Walker felt a chill that the heat of the summer sun did nothing to alleviate. "Where?"

"Illinois. A town called Granton, outside of Peoria. One thirty-eight Main."

2

138 MAIN STREET

GRANTON, ILLINOIS

Normally, Sunday morning on Main Street was quiet. Then again, every morning on Main Street was quiet these days.

The stores that were still in business, like the Dollar General and the bakery and Penny's coffee shop, would open at various points between six and nine and cope easily with the stop-start flow of regulars. The gas station was twenty-four hours, so it didn't have to unlock the doors or roll up the shutters—not that it had shutters.

Officer Zoe Hill stood by the car and looked south down Main at the small knots of people gathering on the wide sidewalks and on front porches, gawking in her direction. It was weird to see people out on the street this early on a Sunday. But the unusual tends to bring people out, and murder was unusual for Granton.

She turned away from the onlookers, all of them keeping a respectful distance for the moment, and headed toward where her partner was talking to the jogger.

He was male, white, in his late thirties. Dressed in light gray shorts and a dark gray T-shirt, with Day-Glo orange Brooks sneakers to brighten the look up a little. On the edge of his right sneaker was a smear of dark red. He was clutching his phone in his left hand; its trailing wired earphones were draped around his neck. It reminded Zoe of a doctor's stethoscope. He lacked the unflappable calm of a doctor, though. When Zoe was ten, her parents had taken her to Magic Mountain in California and she had pleaded with her mom to ride the Viper with her. The jogger was even greener than her mom had been after that ride.

Dave Yelich, Zoe's partner, tapped the jogger on the shoulder and pointed between his feet. Zoe was too far away to hear him, but she lip-read his instruction: *Stay right here*. The jogger nodded in a distracted way. Yelich walked over to Zoe. He ignored the neat flagstones of the path and cut straight across the lawn, taking the shortest route.

"Well?" Zoe asked when he was close enough for them to converse without raised voices. She kept her eyes on the jogger, who was shuffling from one foot to the other but staying in the same literal spot Yelich had confined him to.

Yelich stopped and glanced over at the onlookers before he spoke. He was forty-five but with graying hair and lined skin that added at least a decade to his actual age. His watery blue eyes flicked back to Zoe.

"He was running by the house just after seven. Saw the door was open a crack and went to close it."

"Very neighborly," Zoe said.

"He saw broken glass. He worried that there had been an accident, so he went inside and found the body upstairs."

"He's shook up," Zoe commented.

Yelich glanced at him. He took some nicotine gum from his pocket and popped a piece into his mouth. "Yep."

"Is it bad?"

"I've seen worse." Yelich took his hat off, scratched his head, and put it back on. "You can stay out here if you want; I have to go back in."

"I'll come in."

Yelich hesitated. "There's no need. It's going to be a long wait for the coroner."

Zoe knew that was an understatement. Budgets had been cut every year for the past decade and then some. There was now a single coroner for the whole of Blackwell County.

Though murder was unusual for Granton, there would have been other unattended deaths in the county last night, maybe even other murders, so the two of them would have to wait their turn. Chances were, they would find the culprit before the coroner removed the body. Granton just wasn't that big a place, and there weren't that many people who could be provoked to lethal force. Zoe was already making a mental list of names, and she knew Yelich would have the same list in his head.

"Let's go in," Zoe said, not waiting for Yelich to argue.

The house was modest and traditionally proportioned, like all the others on the street and most in town. It was like a child's drawing of a house: two stories with a peaked roof and painted wood siding. Ground- and second-floor windows were symmetrically positioned on either side of the door.

Zoe snapped on disposable gloves and overshoes to avoid contaminating the scene and climbed the three steps to the covered porch. The porch was a triangle mirroring the larger triangle of the roof. There was a screen door, which was open, and a main door, also open. Brass numerals on the door gave the house's street number, 138. Beyond, the hallway was carpeted in gray. She could see the broken glass the jogger had talked about. A mirror had been smashed.

Dave joined her. They went in and started climbing the stairs. Zoe could smell death already.

A few hours, at least, had gone by. It had been a warm night, and the day would get a lot warmer soon. She issued a silent prayer for the coroner to hurry up and get here. Zoe half expected to feel trepidation about what she was about to see but felt only a calm detachment. They would find whoever had done this and make sure he couldn't do it again.

This was her first homicide, but it wouldn't be her first dead body. In her three years on this job, she had seen four suicides, two overdoses ruled accidental, and one fatal car wreck. She got the feeling from the jogger's pallor and Yelich's caution that this was something different.

She drew level with the top of the stairs. The landing was bare floorboards, varnished years ago and now scuffed and dented.

"Bedroom on your right," Yelich said.

Zoe didn't need the direction. Her nose was leading the way. She dug in her pocket for a face mask and put it on. The bedroom windows faced the street. The morning sun knifed through dusty venetian blinds and lit up a scene from a nightmare.

The victim had been killed in bed. He was wearing dark-colored pajama pants. Probably blue or black, but it was impossible to tell because they were soaked through with red. A white male, probably in his sixties. His naked torso was slick with blood. Zoe could see darker lines where the stab wounds were. His eyes were open, staring up at the ceiling. There was so much blood that the bedcovers had turned red. It was only around the sides that small patches of beige were visible.

"You know him?" Zoe asked when she saw Yelich appear at the door out of the corner of her eye.

Yelich shook his head. "Not really. I've seen him around town. Name's Archibald Bowman. Works at the factory. *Worked.*"

"This isn't what I was expecting," Zoe said.

Yelich moved into the room. "Me either. When we got the call, I assumed it was some kind of domestic thing."

"This definitely isn't that."

He consulted his phone. "He's a veteran."

Zoe turned to him. "Really?"

He nodded. "Gulf War. First one."

Zoe stepped around the bed, making sure to avoid the places where the blood had pooled on the rug and the wood floor. It wasn't that difficult. The sheets and the mattress had soaked up most of it.

She peered at his hands, which were splayed open, palms up, on either side of his body.

"Doesn't look like there're any defensive wounds."

"Dead before he could react, most likely," Yelich said.

Zoe suppressed a shudder, thinking of what it would be like to wake up to find your killer standing beside your bed.

"Looks like it." She continued moving around the bed and then stopped in her tracks.

She heard Yelich speak, but she wasn't listening. Something had caught her eye. There was a nightstand next to the bed with a lamp on it. The lamp had been knocked over, presumably by the killer, and there was blood spatter on top of the nightstand and running down in congealed droplets. But there was something else too.

"What is it?" Yelich said.

There was a marking on the little cabinet door of the nightstand. Deliberate, among the Jackson Pollock randomness.

At first, Zoe thought it was a circle, six inches across, with a smaller circle in the center, almost like a doughnut. She crouched and peered closer, moving carefully so that she didn't have to put a hand on the bedcovers for balance. Close up, she realized it wasn't a circle. At the bottom, it came to a point, like an upside-down teardrop. It looked like it had been made with some kind of stamp in black ink.

"What is that?" she asked.

Yelich stepped around the bed and examined the marking.

"Beats me. But it was there before this happened—the blood is on top."

Zoe had thought that at first too, but not anymore. "No, it wasn't. Look." She pointed at one edge of the stamp, keeping her finger an inch away from the surface. There was a line of dripping blood cutting over whatever it was, but she could see speckles of spray underneath the marking too.

Yelich moved closer, brow furrowed. "Huh," he concluded after a second.

Zoe stood up, glanced back at the body.

"He was stabbed multiple times. Blood everywhere. Some of it pooled on top of the nightstand and dripped down. But before that, somebody put this here, on top of the initial spray. That means the killer left it here."

Yelich stood up and scratched the back of his head. "I don't know about this. I think you're making it more complicated than it is. Maybe the spray is under that mark, maybe not. I'm not a BPA expert and neither are you. I guess we'll find out in three months when the county gets someone down here, but right now, I think this is a home invasion gone wrong."

"I don't think so," Zoe said. "Somebody broke in, came upstairs, and killed Bowman. He was the target. I don't know who did this, I don't know why they did it, but somebody came into this house for one reason: to kill."

Yelich shrugged. "Maybe you're right." He gestured at the body. The victim appeared older than his years. There were gin blossoms on his face. "Mr. Bowman here looks like a drinker. It was Saturday night, so chances are he was drinking at the Hold. A few drinks, a disagreement . . . it followed him home."

"I've seen a lot of trouble at the Hold," Zoe said.

"I've seen a lot more."

"Right. Anything like this?"

Yelich thought about it and then shook his head, conceding. "I guess not."

"We need to find this guy. I don't think this is the first or last time for him."

"Agreed," Yelich said. Zoe liked that about him. He would always push back, wasn't averse to lording his many years of seniority over her, but when she made a good argument, he conceded. "I'll call county, see if they can hurry up the coroner. With my luck, he's halfway to Chicago and one of us is going to be babysitting this scene until he gets here."

Zoe sighed. She knew which one of the two of them it would be. She wanted to be the one making inquiries at the bar. Unlike her partner, though, it would be to rule *out* a drunken grudge, not find one. She didn't think it added up, not with the little logo or whatever it was. What did it remind her of?

Yelich's phone buzzed, breaking off her train of thought.

"Who's that?" Zoe asked when he dug it out of his pocket.

He checked the screen, but from his expression, the caller was unfamiliar. "You got me." He tapped to answer and turned to look out the window at the street as he said his name. Following his gaze, Zoe saw the spectators had encroached a little, gathering around the house.

Zoe turned back to the bloodstained nightstand and the circle that wasn't a circle. And suddenly, she knew what the symbol was. She was turning to tell Yelich when she saw the look on his face. Her partner's expression said that whoever was on the other end of the phone wasn't making sense.

"Say that again?"

He listened. Zoe went closer, straining to hear the voice on the other end. Whoever it was was talking fast. She caught something that sounded like *FBI*.

"All right," Yelich said, staring at Zoe but not really seeing her. "All right," he said again. "Yeah. We'll be here."

He hung up and put the phone into his pocket, then gazed at the body as though seeing it anew.

"Well?" Zoe asked.

"The FBI is taking this."

Zoe's eyes narrowed. "The FBI?"

Yelich still had the faraway look in his eyes. He turned back to the window that faced Main Street. Zoe saw that the knots of neighbors had gotten closer still; a couple of them were standing on the lawn.

"You were right, Zoe. The killer has done this before. He's done the same thing three times in the past couple of weeks."

Zoe was still lost. It didn't entirely surprise her that this could be the work of a serial, although there hadn't been any other crimes like this reported locally. But how could the feds have linked it to other killings so quickly? The two of them had barely had time to examine the scene, much less process any evidence.

"What do you mean? Same MO? Same victim type?" Even as she spoke, she knew that didn't make sense. They hadn't even filed a report yet.

"Same address," Yelich said.

For a moment, Zoe thought he was saying there had been other murders at this house, recent murders they had somehow failed to notice in a town of fifteen thousand that hadn't seen a single homicide since 2002. But when Yelich spoke again, she understood.

"Somebody has hit one thirty-eight Main Street four times. Mississippi, Colorado, Long Island. And now here."

3

138 MAIN STREET
CHARLESTOWN, MASSACHUSETTS

Cally Principal had a lot on her mind as she rounded the last turn of the path that circled the park and broke out into the final three hundred yards of her run. She almost enjoyed this part, where a mile of undulating hills gave way to flat on the homestretch. *Almost.* Cally was the kind of runner who liked having run, not the running itself. This afternoon, she had barely noticed the grinding slog of the hills, which meant that the satisfaction of leaving them behind was dulled too.

It had been three full days now since she had heard from Melissa. Seventy-two hours since she'd spoken to her sister over the phone on Thursday afternoon. She had barely slept a wink since then.

Melissa's final words before hanging up echoed in Cally's mind: *I just think all of you would be better-off without me.*

Melissa's phone had been off since then. Cally had spent most of the past three days at home, scared to leave in case Melissa showed up. If she was going to appear anywhere, it would be at Cally's apartment.

The police officer she spoke to on Friday was nice enough, but she got the feeling he heard stories like hers twice a week.

"Seems like she struggles from time to time," he had said after he looked Melissa up in the system and found the long string of misdemeanor and felony arrests that stretched back to her teens. "You can't force it. People like your sister, sometimes the best thing you can do is give them some space."

Cally protested that Melissa had sounded different this time. That she had said they would all be better-off without her. Didn't that sound like someone contemplating . . . She didn't even want to say the word.

The officer listened and then asked, "She hasn't said anything along those lines before?"

At that moment, Cally realized she'd been outmaneuvered. Melissa had said shit like that *many* times before. But how to get across that it felt different now?

It wasn't even the first time she had disappeared for days. Her record was a month, so seventy-two hours shouldn't be making Cally as worried as she was. On that occasion, when she eventually showed up at Cally's place, it turned out she'd been shacking up with some guy in Andover, hadn't thought to check in to say she was okay. Her phone had died and she hadn't gotten around to charging it, and anyway, she always knew she could find Cally here.

"You're my rock, Cally," she said, her tone lightly mocking some line from a movie. "I always know I can come back to you."

Cally had wanted to punch her then, but last Thursday, she would've given anything to hear dumb clichés like that instead of the voice of the tortured soul at the other end of the line. Cally didn't know what it was this time. Oxy, probably. Or maybe just the latest bad breakup. Whatever it was, Melissa was in a bad way.

And so Cally had stayed home. Waiting for Melissa to show up so she could make her a pot of strong coffee and tuck her in on the couch, bail her out of whatever trouble she was in. The office had been fine about her working remotely, and she didn't have any important meetings this week. Not that she had gotten much work done; she'd spent most of the time doomscrolling through local news reports. She told herself she was being dramatic, just as the kindly but ineffectual cop had implied. If the police found someone dead, they told the family before it got to the media, right? At least, they did when they could identify the body. Melissa wasn't the most together person; Cally could easily believe she would go out without a wallet or ID. What if she had been hit by a bus or something and couldn't be identified?

She left the apartment occasionally to go to the store and once to take a check to the bank, but she thought that was okay. Melissa would stick around on the doorstep for a while. This afternoon's run had taken only a half hour, but she was apprehensive as she got close to home.

Cally slowed to a walk as she rounded the corner onto her street. It was lined with four- and five-story apartment buildings on both sides. Despite having lived here for more than eight years, she still often thought about how lucky she was to reside in a place like Charlestown—the architecture, the history all around her, the mature trees casting deep pools of shade on the sidewalks. But today, the character of her neighborhood was the farthest thing from her mind.

Her building was up ahead, and Cally could see that the bright green Post-it she had stuck to the door saying she would be back soon was still there. The only other person on the street was a man standing on the opposite sidewalk, directly across from her stoop. He was peering up at the top floor, where Cally's apartment was. He seemed to be waiting for someone. Could Melissa have sent him to ask for money? Cally took a closer look and told herself not to get her hopes up. His clothes and shoes were clean, so he was not the kind of guy Melissa usually hung out with. He wore a baseball cap and a brown jacket with a logo on the shoulder that she couldn't identify. A delivery guy or a maintenance worker.

The man turned as she approached. The brim of his hat shaded the top half of his face. He bent his head and touched a fingertip to the hat's brim as Cally passed. She smiled, wondering if he was going to ask her for directions, but he just turned and started examining the building across the street.

She climbed the stone steps to the front door and took the key out of the back pocket of her shorts.

Home, sweet home. Good old 138 Main Street.

4

GRANTON, ILLINOIS

Granton was less than ten minutes from the small airfield where the jet landed. Walker was relieved to see there were no members of the press awaiting him on the ground. He told himself to enjoy that absence of attention while it lasted.

The car that took him to Granton drove at high speed down Route 24, past long stretches of treeless fields empty of livestock or crops. The sky was a light gray. It had been clear in New York. This was like being under a thin bedsheet on a bright day. The driver left 24 and turned south, passing a sign that advertised the Crossroads Methodist Church. Walker wondered if the church was aware of the irony of its name. The crossroads was where you went to meet the devil, after all.

The houses along the road that marked the north edge of town drew nearer. Walker had spent a couple of minutes on the flight reading up on Granton: Established 1825. Population a hair over fifteen thousand. Most of the two-thirds of citizens who were of working age either commuted to Peoria or had jobs at the plastics factory on the south side of town. The latter group apparently included the victim, Archibald William Bowman, fifty-five years old, originally from Chicago. Ex-USMC, no known next of kin. There was nothing in his record to explain why he had been brutally stabbed to death in his own home. Nothing, that was, except for his address.

The homes the car passed were of generous size, the plots spaced widely apart. Walker had been a New Yorker long enough for horizontal settlements to make him feel uneasy. Too much space, too few people. Way too much sky.

There were four vehicles parked outside 138 Main Street: two late-model Ford Tauruses, a van for the forensics team announcing itself a little more clearly to the onlookers with the FBI branding along the side, and a black-and-white from the local police department that had a fine dusting of road dirt on the sills.

There were two local cops in uniform, a middle-aged man and a woman who looked to be in her twenties, standing outside the house talking to one of the agents from the Chicago field office. All three turned to watch as Walker's car drew up and he got out. The Chicago agent, a tall, bulky man with a shaved head, introduced himself as Special Agent Marvin Harper. The male cop shook Walker's hand and told him he was Officer Dave Yelich.

"Yelich," Walker repeated. "Any relation to the Brewers outfielder?"

"None that I know of, but if he wants to swap paychecks, I won't argue." Yelich turned to the other officer. "This is my partner, Zoe Hill."

Hill was of slight build, just a little over five feet, with dark hair and dark brown eyes that held a weird intensity. Something about her eyes told Walker immediately that he wouldn't want to get on the wrong side of her.

She shook his hand briefly. "No relation to Grant Hill." No smile, so Walker wasn't sure if she was maintaining the small talk or offering a rebuke.

"Thanks for holding this for us," he said.

Working with local departments was usually fraught with tension. You generally knew within the first minute if there was going to be full cooperation or not. Pierson in Pembury had been a case in point. Walker sensed Yelich was more eager to please. He hoped this wouldn't turn into a rerun of the Pierson thing. He wasn't sure about Zoe Hill yet.

More times than he could count, Walker had witnessed the first agent on the scene get off on the wrong foot with the local guys. Sometimes deliberately, more often just out of carelessness. Normally, his working assumption was that any way he could defer to the locals was worthwhile. These officers were fresh, knew nothing about the other killings as yet. He wanted their initial impressions.

He turned to face the house at 138. It was unremarkable; there was nothing to distinguish it from the others on the street except the number. It was a lot smaller than the home at the same address in Long Island. He turned back to Yelich and Hill.

"You want to walk me through it?"

Walker accompanied the two cops to the house. They climbed the three steps up to the porch, and Walker couldn't help pausing a second to look at the brass number on the door—the number that had been a death sentence for the owner.

Yelich led the way, talking as he went. "Evidently the perpetrator accessed the property via the back." He stopped in the hall and pointed through to the kitchen, where Walker could see the lock had been jimmied.

A glass panel in the door looked out on a long yard with a stand of sycamore trees over the back fence. If the killer had entered and exited by that route, it was unlikely he would have been seen by anyone on Main Street.

"We think he left by the front door," Yelich continued as if to contradict him. "It was open."

Walker didn't comment. He suspected the killer had left the same way he'd come in but had opened the front door to attract attention to the scene.

The house had the deep musty smell of a place that's been inhabited by the same owner for decades without much change in the carpets or furniture. A grandpa's-house smell, even though the victim had been relatively young in the scheme of things.

Walker wondered about the owner. The disrepair of the house and the fact he lived alone were probably hints that his latter years hadn't been a basket of sunshine. They would find out as much as there was to know about Archibald Bowman in due course. Normally, knowing the victim was one of the keys to finding his killer. It was unlikely that would be the case this time. Bowman was dead almost certainly because of bad luck, pure and simple.

They climbed a carpeted flight of stairs and Yelich stood aside to let Walker enter the bedroom first.

Walker had already seen the pictures that Yelich had sent at the Bureau's request, but a recently dead body is something that's always a different proposition in the flesh. Bowman was lying in the center of a bed that was drenched in blood. Knife wounds visible all over his abdomen, arms, and face. Overkill, just like Long Island. Whoever had done this didn't just want to kill. He wanted to send a message.

Two forensics people were in the room doing their thing. The nearer one looked up as they entered. She was female, but in the white overalls and mask, it was hard to tell anything else about her.

"Agent?" she said.

Walker flashed his ID. "Walker, New York field office."

She nodded and looked back down. "Early days; we got started ten minutes ago."

"Anything so far?"

She shook her head.

"Obviously killed here," Walker said to himself, examining the body. He heard Yelich step in behind him, and the crime scene tech put a hand up.

"Whoa—too many people. One at a time, please."

Showing only slight irritation, Yelich stepped back out onto the landing. He and Hill stood at the doorway, watching Walker.

Walker moved to the corner of the room where he could observe the scene without getting in the way of the technicians. He was looking for something that he knew had to be here. It had been at the other three scenes.

"It's on the nightstand."

He looked over at the doorway in surprise. It was Officer Hill who had spoken. She was watching him as he observed the room. His gaze went to the nightstand. The other tech was crouched in front of it, taking a sample from a wound on Bowman's head, but it didn't appear to Walker like there was anything on the nightstand other than a lot of blood and a lamp that had been knocked over in the struggle.

"What's on the nightstand?"

"It's on the nightstand door. The marking you're looking for."

"You want I should move?" the technician in front of the nightstand said. He was a burly guy with a thick Chicago accent.

Walker smiled. "Please. Just for a second."

He got to his feet with a grunt and stepped back, indicating a spot on the front of the white nightstand. "I take it you're talking about this?"

Walker took a step closer. That was exactly what he was looking for. In the midst of the blood spatters, the same mark he had seen on the bedroom carpet in Long Island.

"Was that marking at the other scenes?" Hill asked.

Walker nodded. "At least one of them." He turned to Hill. "What does it look like to you?"

"It looks like a digital pin on a map."

5

Zoe was last to descend the stairs, behind Yelich and Walker, the FBI agent with the salt-and-pepper hair. She hadn't known quite what to expect when Yelich told her what was happening. The FBI didn't generally get involved with the day-to-day activities of the Granton PD. But then again, those activities didn't generally include investigating murders. Let alone potential serial-killer murders.

Agent Harper, who, Zoe gathered, was based in Chicago, in contrast to the New Yorker, had found his way to Penny's, the coffee shop at the commercial end of Main. He arrived at the doorway of the house carrying a cardboard tray with four go-cups as they were coming downstairs.

Walker took one of the offered cups, looking like he was grateful for it. He turned to Zoe and Yelich. "You want to go outside or talk in the living room?"

"Outside," Yelich said without hesitation. Zoe was happy about that. The coffee from Penny's wasn't strong enough to overcome the smell in the house. Was it her imagination or was it getting worse?

The forensics guys had finished working on the back door, and they had left it wide open, so Yelich suggested they go out back to talk.

The pleasant afternoon sunshine felt almost indecent juxtaposed with what they had just seen. The yard was a good size, mostly grass with a paved area near the back door. A rusting barbecue was tucked into a corner. Zoe thought for a moment about Archibald Bowman stowing that away six months or six years ago, whenever it had been, not knowing that he had grilled his last burger in the open air.

The four of them stood on the paved area, staying away from the grass. That would be examined in due course to check if the perpetrator had left any shoe impressions on his entrance or egress.

Yelich blew out a puff of air and patted his pockets until he found his pack of cigarettes. He offered one to Walker. Walker held a hand up to refuse.

"Thanks. Quit fourteen years ago."

Yelich grinned. "Bet you know it to the day too." He offered the pack to the other fed, who also declined. He fit the cigarette between his lips and lit it. It took him a few moments. Zoe couldn't tell if he was deliberately holding things up to make a point or not. Walker waited, gazing up at the window on the top floor.

"So," he said after a long inhale. "What have we got?" He let the smoke drift out of his nostrils.

"This is the fourth location, as far as we can tell," Walker said.

"All at one thirty-eight Main?"

"All at one thirty-eight Main," Walker confirmed. "All this month. Courtland, Mississippi, on the first. Lyons, Colorado, on the seventh. Pembury, New York, three days ago."

"And now Granton, Illinois," Zoe finished.

"So it would seem."

Yelich let out a low whistle. "That's some spread. This guy must be racking up the air miles."

Walker didn't comment on that. He took a sip of his coffee.

"You ever see anything like this before?" Yelich asked.

The FBI man considered the question before answering. "This kind of homicide? Sure. A pattern killer choosing victims so far apart? No way. Not in a time frame like this."

"So the most recent one before here was three days ago," Yelich said thoughtfully.

Walker took a breath through his nostrils and nodded. "He killed a whole family in Long Island. Parents, teenage son, and the son's girlfriend." He glanced up at the house again. "That was worse than this one."

"Same MO?"

"He started by killing the parents with a hunting knife. Husband first, then the wife when she tried to run. We found the son downstairs, defensive wounds on the hands and arms, stabbed through the heart. The girlfriend tried to get away. Made it thirty yards from the front door. He shot her in the back, then finished her off up close with one to the head."

"And the address is the only link?" Yelich asked. "You're sure it's not a coincidence?"

Walker gave him a look that, to Zoe, conveyed how stupid he thought the question was. She wondered what the odds were of four unconnected attacks happening at the same street address in different towns in the same month. Walker caught himself quickly, though, straightening his face. "We haven't managed to tie them together with witnesses or fingerprints or DNA so far, if that's what you're asking, but yeah, we're pretty confident."

"Yelich!"

The three of them turned to see a figure at the back door. It was Matt Hensey, the only person in the department who had less time on the job than Zoe. She noticed he had been accepted quicker, though. Somehow she was still treated as the rookie. Matt took his hat off, scratched his thatch of rust-colored hair, then put it back on.

"What are you doing here, Matt?" Yelich asked, sounding a little embarrassed.

Hensey spoke fast, the way he always did when he was nervous, the words tumbling from his mouth: "Jill from the *Journal Star* is outside—Jill Masterson—and she was wondering if she could talk to me, and, well . . ."

Walker gave Yelich a look that needed no clarification.

"Excuse me a second," Yelich said with a sigh, and walked quickly toward the house. Zoe heard him mutter something bad-tempered to Hensey under his breath.

Zoe turned back to Walker. "There must be a one thirty-eight Main Street in every town in the country."

"Probably not every town, but close enough," Walker said. "That's what we're trying to work out."

"Who made the link between the murders?" Zoe asked.

"Not a person, an algorithm. It was flagged by NCIC."

Zoe had never used the National Crime Information Center database, but she knew of it. It was the FBI's central index of crime, available under certain conditions to local law enforcement as well as the Bureau. The system was developed to overcome decades of problems involving suspects who committed crimes across different jurisdictions, which meant multiple departments could be hunting the same criminal without realizing it. With NCIC, separate investigations could be more joined up. Zoe wondered how many murderers covered the kind of ground this one had in a matter of weeks.

Walker took another sip of his coffee before continuing. "The system flags patterns automatically. It doesn't wait for somebody to go looking. The problem is, there are a lot of potential patterns, and two killings at a similar address can be chalked up to coincidence, particularly when they're as far apart as Mississippi and Colorado."

"I guess a family being murdered in Long Island gets more attention, though," Zoe said.

"The first killing was in a home valued at seventy thousand dollars. The family in Pembury lived in a four-million-dollar mansion. What do you think?"

Zoe knew exactly what Yelich would have said: *That's the way of the world*. She couldn't dismiss it like that. It might be the way of the world, but it didn't feel like it ought to be.

"When the Pembury killings were reported, it made three attacks in three states all at the same address," Walker continued. "That was enough of a pattern for it to stick out on NCIC, and our analysts picked it up. Pembury PD were already deep into the investigation by the time we showed up."

"I bet they were overjoyed," Zoe said, smiling wryly. It would have been a very different dynamic there than it was here in Granton.

"You bet right. It took a while to convince them there was more to this than they thought. They had it down as a revenge attack. The husband had been involved in some kind of hedge-fund scandal five years ago. He made out pretty well; his investors, not so much. The local cops were operating on the assumption it was related. As far as we can work out, that was not the case. This wasn't payback for a grudge. It wasn't about the couple; it wasn't about their son or his girlfriend. They just had the bad luck to be in the wrong house on the wrong night." He glanced up at this house's top floor. "Just like Mr. Bowman."

"No other connection between the victims?" Zoe asked.

"Just the address."

Zoe glanced toward the back fence. If the killer had indeed left this way, he would have had to climb the fence and cut through another yard on his way to . . . well, that was the question, wasn't it?

"How long do we have until the next one?"

She saw an approving look in Walker's eyes. She could tell that he hadn't enjoyed dealing with Yelich, but he didn't seem to find this conversation as much of a chore. Maybe he thought that she was asking the right questions.

"Not long enough. Six days between the first two killings, then eight days until the third, then down to three days. The clock's ticking."

"When do you go public?"

"As soon as my boss gives me the go-ahead."

From the street, Zoe could hear the sound of a truck backing up. Main hadn't seen this much traffic in a long time. She thought about the image that the killer had taken the time to leave for them.

"What's the deal with the map pin?" she asked.

Walker looked away from her and in the direction of the street. She wondered if he would have brought that up if she hadn't. She didn't think so.

"I don't know what to think about that," he said carefully. "The address alone is enough to link these killings. The map pin tells me that whoever this is wants to make sure we get it. He doesn't want to leave anything to chance."

"Does that worry you?"

He considered for a second. "It's Hill, right?"

"That's right. Zoe Hill."

"Zoe, there isn't a goddamn thing about this that doesn't worry me. But that's near the top of the list. He's effective, he works quickly, and he definitely wants attention."

"So what's next?"

"This is the first scene we've been able to examine fresh," Walker said. "The first scene where we know from the start that it's part of a series. I'm hoping that means it'll be easier for our people to find something we can use. I'm not holding my breath, though."

Zoe nodded. "We don't want to get in your way, Agent Walker. But if you could use some help canvassing the neighbors—"

"That would be great. When I said I wanted the department to be involved, I wasn't spinning a line. Local knowledge is going to be important on this one."

"This one, and all of them," Zoe agreed. She thought about the map pin on the nightstand under the drops of blood. She thought about four pins on a map of the United States. She knew that somewhere out there, on some unsuspecting Main Street, someone was getting ready to add a fifth pin.

GEHENNA

In the Family, no one retained their given name.

Your name was the first thing that had to be willingly discarded, the first gesture of faith to demonstrate that you meant to turn your back on the Old World forever and devote yourself to something better. It wasn't a strict requirement that you had to select your Family name from the Old Testament, but most people did.

Then there were the others who were commonly known not by their names but by their place in the Family. For reasons that were perhaps more practical than any would care to admit out loud, the Family was happy for its adherents to bring with them some of the skills they had acquired in the Old World.

The Carpenter. The Doctor. The Butcher. For some reason, this unspoken convention always skewed to the older trades. The Family also counted a plumber, two electricians, and a computer scientist among their number, but they were referred to as Ezekiel, Caleb, Levi, and Esther.

He had never chosen a name, though in fact his Old World name would have fit in respectably. From the first day in the embrace of the Family, he had simply been the Professor. The Professor's career in the Old World had covered a range of disciplines, and he was able to turn his hand to others. The Family had a well-stocked library building, inherited from the community that had occupied the town decades before.

Professor had been his role in the early days; he taught the children of the Family in the dilapidated town hall where every other window was broken, and the roof creaked threateningly in heavy rain. He taught every weekday morning, Monday through Friday, and sometimes on Saturdays, but never on the Sabbath. Sometimes, the older members of the Family would sit in on the lessons, and that was when the trouble had begun. Gradually, Family members began to withdraw their offspring from the school.

That seemed long in the past now.

When Amy . . . when *Ruth*, to give her New World name, left him, there was no overt suggestion from the Family that he and the boys should follow her. But it hadn't taken long for them to do so. It wasn't that they were cast out, exactly; it was more like a mutually-agreed-upon parting of the ways.

The Professor didn't doubt the elders of the Family had been glad to see the back of him and the boys, despite their proclamations of loving all who came with open hearts. The truth was they lacked vision. They concerned themselves only with the narrow spiritual confines of their faith and with the even narrower physical confines of their New World.

He had found Gehenna by a mixture of chance and intuition, some of that retained Old World knowledge coming in handy once again. An unoccupied property with power and a water source where they would be disturbed rarely if ever. From here, they would start to build a true New World. Perhaps he had not entirely rejected the ideas of the Family. Had he not given this house a new name?

The Professor stood at the window and watched the buzzards investigate the pickings in the dead pit at the eastern corner of the field. There were four of them today. Something new to draw their attention, perhaps.

The stench from the dead pit reached all the way to the house at the height of summer, but the Professor did not mind. After all, it was the reason no one had taken on the lease on this place when the farmer gave it up. The fields were fallow; the only remnants of the working farm were the deserted pens and the remains of the animals in the pit.

One of the carrion birds turned its head and seemed to glare right at him. He stared back curiously, breaking the stare only when he heard the name he was addressed by more often than any other since they had found Gehenna.

"Father."

He turned at the sound of the voice, which was hushed, as though someone were asking a librarian a question. The two boys were standing just inside the back door. It was Aaron who had spoken, as usual. He stood in his linen clothes that had been brilliant white when the Family issued them but were now a dull, washed-out gray; his little brother, Noah, hovered a step behind him, biting one of his knuckles.

"What is it?"

As he spoke, he saw that Noah had a smear of blood on his forehead just below the unruly tangle of dark hair. He pushed Aaron roughly out of the way and swept the hair back to examine the wound. It didn't look too serious.

"Boys from the town?" he asked.

The two of them had recently begun venturing beyond the woods that backed onto Gehenna, the boundary that separated them from the nearest outpost of what passed for society in these times.

Aaron nodded curtly. "They threw rocks at us. Big ones. I think it needs stitches."

Noah winced at that but kept quiet.

The Professor straightened up and turned away from his sons. "He'll be fine. Iodine's under the kitchen sink."

"They said we were chicken."

The Professor stopped and turned. Aaron's fists were clenched; an unpleasant look in his eye.

"So?"

"Why can't we go into the town? Why can't we be like—"

"Like what? Like 'normal' people? You know there are more important things, Aaron."

Aaron kept staring at him, his expression almost unnerving. But then he dropped his gaze. For just a second there, the Professor had wondered if Aaron was about to defy him. That look he just gave him reminded him so much of his mother.

Noah was stifling his sobs. Being strong. A good boy.

He glanced at Aaron, then narrowed his eyes against the sun as he stared past him at the seven-foot-high wooden fence and the towering pines of the woods beyond. One of the boys had left a smear of dirt on the top of one of the slats as they climbed over the fence. He gestured at the smear.

"Clean it. Paint the fence again."

Aaron opened his mouth to say something and then apparently thought better of it. Which was just as well, because a dissenting word or even the observation that they had put a coat of paint on the fence at the end of last week would have resulted in serious repercussions. Aaron was a smart boy. Smart enough to take a light punishment and move on. The boy gritted his teeth for a moment and then composed himself.

"Yes, Father."

The Professor stared at him and then turned away without another word. He had work to do. He had wasted enough time today on carrion birds and children.

He moved down the hall and into his study. The television was still on. The news was showing footage of the president visiting Rome. For a minute the Professor watched the old fool glad-hand well-dressed Europeans standing in a line, then he turned the set off.

He sat down on the frayed swivel chair in front of the desk and fitted a new sheet of paper into the Remington Victor S portable typewriter, feeling the familiar tactile pleasure as the carriage smoothly drew the sheet into the machine. He wasn't averse to computers, far from it. He had used them for many years. The problem was that he knew too much about them now. The only way to be certain of security was to go right back to basics. No storage, no disks. If anyone wanted to access his writing and, therefore, the inside of his mind, they would have to come through a secure door. And anyone foolish enough to do that would certainly regret it.

He closed his eyes for a moment. It seemed to be harder to get himself into the right frame of mind lately. Perhaps it was just another symptom of getting older, or perhaps it was the sheer effort that this enterprise required.

Outside, one of the buzzards let out a cry. He looked at the window and saw it taking flight, something red and fresh-looking in its beak. Occasionally a cow from one of the other farms would stray into the field and fall into the dead pit, once even a Labrador with a pink collar. The dead pit seemed to call new material to itself, as though it were sentient and self-sustaining.

The Professor got up, reached for the string, and snapped the blinds closed, bathing the study in a dusty orange light. He sat down and closed his eyes again. It was easier to tune out the cries of the birds if he couldn't see them.

He opened his eyes and focused on the blank page in the typewriter.

Where had he been before he was interrupted?

The manuscript stack was piled to the left of the typewriter, under the heavy glass snow globe. Unlike every other surface in the house, the desk was entirely clear, apart from the typewriter and the stack.

He lifted the last page and read the final paragraph again.

> Why do we choose Main Street?
>
> We choose Main Street because it is Everystreet. It is a proxy for the whole rotten, crumbling, damned country. So we start with Main Street, but we will not finish there.
>
> Main Street is only the beginning.

6

NEW YORK CITY

Walker made it back to the building at 26 Federal Plaza by seven o'clock; he wanted to touch base before he called it a night. No—who was he kidding? He might grab a couple hours of sleep here and there, but he wouldn't be calling it a night for a long time.

He was thinking about the scene in Granton as he rode the elevator up to the twenty-third floor of the Jacob K. Javits Federal Building. Forensics had worked fast. The preliminary scene report had arrived in his inbox while his plane back to New York from Illinois was thirty thousand feet above Ohio. It would take weeks for everything to be fully processed, but the report didn't give him any cause for optimism.

There were prints and clothing fibers and hair follicles aplenty, but there was no reason to believe any of it had come from the killer. There was nothing that could have been left there only after Archibald Bowman had been stabbed to death in his bed—no fingerprints in blood spatter, no bloody shoe prints, no skin scraps beneath the victim's fingernails.

The soft chime told him the elevator had reached twenty-three. The doors parted and he stepped out into the open-plan office. It was manned at all hours, so the fact that it was busy and bustling at seven p.m. wasn't unusual; it was a twenty-four-hour-a-day operation. What was unusual was that it was a Sunday evening and there wasn't an inch of desk space to spare. Ever since Long Island was flagged, they had been gearing up for a big case, but the fourth attack happening so quickly had accelerated that process.

Enrico Ferrera was sitting at one of the desks closest to the elevator, his lanky frame making the swivel chair look child-size. He craned his head around and greeted Walker with a wave of the printout he had been examining. "How was it?"

Walker almost wanted to laugh. Ferrera sounded like he was asking a sales executive about what the hotel was like at the West Coast conference. *How was the crime scene? Were there hors d'oeuvres?*

"It was like the others. You see the report yet?"

Ferrera's mouth stretched into a pained grimace. "Not what we were hoping for."

"How's the list coming?"

"The Kid put one of the analysts on it," he answered, obviously without thinking.

Walker gave him a tired look. "You mean the assistant director in charge."

Ferrera cleared his throat and dropped his gaze for a moment. "I think the analyst's name was Brodie." He straightened in his chair and scanned the rows of desks and partitions. A lot of new faces, people not used to working in this office or on the same shift. He stood up and gestured uncertainly toward the southeast corner of the building, by the windows that faced out on the Brooklyn Bridge. "He's over there if you want to—"

Walker shook his head. "Later. I have to check in with the director."

"Good luck," Ferrera said, raising his eyebrows.

Walker made his way over to the glass cubicle that was the office of the assistant director in charge.

Billie Chapman was relatively new to the post. At forty-six, she was young to make ADIC. Naturally, that brought with it a little resentment. Walker had to admit he hadn't been immune to that feeling when he heard about the appointment. Her relative youth and her first name meant there was an inevitability to the nickname that some of the agents used when she was out of earshot: Billie the Kid.

Her track record was impressive, though. She had accomplished a lot in less than two decades with the Bureau. Having worked alongside her for the past four months, Walker respected her, even if he didn't particularly like her. A lot of the agents of his vintage still resented her, but that had less to do with her leadership style and more to do with the fact they wanted her job. Perhaps that was why Walker found it easier to let the knee-jerk antipathy go: He had never had any designs on the position. He never wanted more than to lock up bad guys, get paid reasonably well for it, and, hopefully, leave the world just a little better than he'd found it when he hung up his gun and went off into a pleasantly boring retirement. He was still a few years shy of the FBI's mandatory retirement age, but he was a long way past the halfway point.

Chapman spotted him through the open blinds on her glass cubicle before he had a chance to knock and beckoned him in. She had red hair cut in a bob and wore glasses with rectangular frames that made her look a little like an accountant.

"The Granton report is shit," she said without preamble.

Walker knew she wasn't casting aspersions on the professionalism of the team. She was just frustrated, like he was, with the lack of usable forensic evidence. He closed the door behind him and took the chair in front of her desk. "I know. I hoped he would get careless with this one. Or at least that us getting to it sooner would help."

"Well, it answers one question."

"What's that?"

"He actually *is* that careful; it's not just that we lost evidence because we didn't link the first three together until yesterday."

"We need to get this out there," Walker said. "Actually, I'm a little surprised it isn't out there already."

Chapman signaled that she had noticed the implied rebuke with the slightest narrowing of her eyes. "We're live on national television at nine tonight. I don't think either of us wanted to light the fuse on this thing before we had a firm grasp of the facts."

It was a fair point. From the beginning, he knew this would be the kind of case where the media watched every move. Even if they had still been dealing with three killings in a month, that would be true. Now that the killer was accelerating his work, the scrutiny would be all the more intense.

"Agreed. But we don't want another body before we go public. They'll say—"

"They'll say it could have been avoided if we had gone public earlier. They're going to say that anyway with four sites—you know that, don't you?"

He knew that all too well. A part of him relished being lead on any big case, but he wasn't looking forward to the media attention that went hand in hand with it.

"They'll be wrong, though," Chapman continued. "This guy isn't going to stop, no matter how much we publicize it, no matter what we do. How was Granton?"

Chapman had a habit of finishing one line of conversation and transitioning to the next without taking a breath. It took Walker a moment to catch up.

"It was worth the trip," he said. "Seeing the scene in person while it was still fresh, while the body was still there."

She nodded. "I would have done the same thing. Have you finalized the team yet?"

Chapman was referring to the task force that would be under Walker's command. The media might not have connected the killings yet, but it was already an all-hands-on-deck show. Agents across the country would work on the case, but the task force would be a smaller, core team. Walker had already filled most of the slots with a mix of reliable people he had worked with many times before and newer ones whose backgrounds made them a good fit for this job.

"I'll send you the list," he said. "Ferrera told me you gave the Main Street master-list job to one of the analysts, so if he comes up with the goods, he or she is on the team too."

"Matthew Brodie," Chapman said. "He's a little green, but I think this is right in his skill set. He minored in urban planning at Columbia, I believe."

"If you're happy, I'm happy."

"What about your police liaisons?" Chapman continued. "Thanks to our perpetrator's apparent fondness for travel, we seem to have an unusually large number of choices here. I believe there's a Detective"—she glanced down at her computer screen—"Pierson at Pembury who has expressed interest."

"Detective Pierson," Walker repeated. He folded his arms and leaned back in the chair. He wasn't consciously thinking about his body language until he saw Chapman's thin smile.

"Do I take it he wouldn't be your first choice?"

That was putting it mildly. It was no surprise that Pierson wanted in on the task force, but Walker had put away drug lords and Ponzi scheme crooks he would have worked with more readily than Pierson. He suspected part of the detective's entitled attitude came from where his department was situated. When your beat is gated communities full of multimillion-dollar mansions, you probably start to feel like you belong in such rarefied environs.

"Anybody else put in a request?" Walker asked after clearing his throat.

"Not as of twenty minutes ago. I've personally spoken to the chiefs in Courtland and Lyons. If any of the locals tried to throw their hats into the ring, it didn't get past their chiefs. We do need somebody, though. Can you live with Pierson?"

Walker shifted uneasily. The clock was ticking. He needed to lock down the task force, and a local liaison was part of that for reasons both practical and political. He knew Chapman wouldn't be happy if he held out for somebody, anybody, other than Pierson. She was asking him to take one for the team. Unless . . .

"Actually, one of the people out in Granton was impressive."

"Really?" The hint of skepticism was evident only in the quarter-inch rise of Chapman's eyebrow.

"Hill, I think her name was."

"Detective?"

"Uniform. One of the first on the scene. Sharp. Some good observations."

"A uniform. You really don't want Pierson, do you?"

"No, but I would pick Hill anyway. She noticed the map pin, knew it had been left by the killer. Her partner thought it was there before."

Chapman bit her bottom lip and thought it over. He wondered if she had already told Pierson's superior that he was in.

"Give her a call. But the press conference is at nine, and we're going to have the team locked down by then. Okay?"

"Got it," Walker said, getting up to open the door.

"Agent Walker?"

He turned around.

"As soon as this hits the news, it's going to be insane. I don't think even you or I can predict how insane it's going to get. Make sure everyone involved is aware of that."

7

GRANTON, ILLINOIS

Zoe stayed late at the Main Street scene. When Yelich reminded her to go home, it was after seven o'clock.

"I don't think there's going to be much for us to do here anyway," he had said, glancing back at the FBI forensics vehicle, a mixture of emotions on his face. "First murder in Granton in twenty years, and it's not our problem." He shrugged. "Maybe it's for the best."

Zoe wasn't sure about that. She walked the three blocks back to the parking lot outside the Granton police station. There, she picked up her personal car, a blue Toyota Corolla that had seen better days, and headed to her mom's house, stopping at the store on the way to get bread.

She tried to drop by after every other shift, just to check in. She had gotten into the routine during the pandemic, making sure her mother didn't have any symptoms of the bug and that she had enough food in the refrigerator, and the habit had stuck. But she would have made a point of stopping by today regardless, given what had happened last night a half a mile away.

Mary Ann Hill was on the porch smoking a Marlboro Light when Zoe pulled up at the curb. For as long as Zoe could remember, her dad had tried to get her mom to quit. It was a grim irony that one of the last things she heard her father say was "Those things are going to kill you" as he was opening the door to leave.

She had found herself thinking about that day more often lately: Coming home from school and seeing the police car outside the house, feeling a tug in her chest. Perhaps already knowing somehow what had happened.

Her mom in the kitchen, face in her hands. The two uniformed cops standing awkwardly in the hallway. The closer one had turned and seen her in the doorway, and his face fell. It was the first time she met Dave Yelich.

"What's wrong?" Zoe said, but the volume of her voice seemed to have been turned all the way down.

Zoe blinked the memory out of her mind's eye and gave herself a shake.

She got out of the car and opened the gate. The rosebushes at the front of the house were out of control again. She didn't think there would be a lot of time in her immediate future for helping out with the gardening, so perhaps they would keep growing until the place looked like a scruffy Midwest version of Sleeping Beauty's castle.

Her mom was wearing a loose plaid shirt over her tank top. It wasn't cold, but habit was habit, and the shirt went on when she went outside for a cigarette.

"I thought you would have called me," she said as Zoe approached.

Zoe forced a smile. There was no need to ask her mother what she was talking about; the news of the murder was all over town. This was the biggest thing to happen in Granton in years, and the craziest thing was, most people in town didn't know the half of it yet.

"Sorry, it was pretty busy."

Her mother gave a small shrug in concession. "I suppose. You coming in?"

"Sure," Zoe said. What she really wanted to do was go home and take a hot shower. It felt like the stench of the bedroom at 138 Main had been following her around all day, like it was clinging to her skin.

"I got you bread," she said, raising the bagged loaf.

"Thanks, honey. I think I've got some, but you never know."

Zoe made an effort to keep her tone light and breezy, hoping it might be contagious: "I didn't have a chance to grab dinner. I could make French toast, if you're hungry?"

"I can't have dairy anymore, Zoe, you know that."

Zoe resisted rolling her eyes. Mom's lactose intolerance seemed to come and go depending on whether she felt like eating dairy. Zoe stepped up onto the stoop. The street number was stenciled on the wall to the right of the door: 227 Pine Avenue. She thought again about the randomness of Archibald Bowman's murder. If the FBI was correct, his address had been a death warrant. She thought about how easily the killer could have gained access to her mother's house if the address on his list had been different. There were probably a lot of Pine Avenues in America too.

"Listen," she said, "I don't want you to worry, but—"

"You don't want me to worry? A maniac on the loose and you don't want me to worry?"

"We don't think there's a maniac on the loose, we—"

"What would you call it? Apparently the poor man had his head cut off. Is that true?"

Zoe shook her head. The small-town rumor mill was in full effect. "No, Mom, he didn't have . . . Look, I'll tell you what I can, okay?"

Her mother dropped her cigarette butt into the plant pot by the door that she kept for the purpose and immediately lit another one. That wasn't a good sign. She had cut down to eight a day, or so she claimed, but this didn't seem like it was an eight-smoke day. She ran her other hand through her blond hair, exposing the gray roots. "I don't know how I'm going to be able to sleep tonight."

Zoe winced inwardly. She knew what the next request was going to be; she was afraid of this. She sat next to her on the stoop, putting her hand on top of the cigarette-free hand.

"You know I can't talk too much about it, but we have reason to believe the killer wasn't from Granton."

"Well, of course he wasn't from Granton. People around here don't *do* that kind of thing. That makes it even more frightening. A stranger coming here in the night."

"We think he's long gone," Zoe said. "The FBI is involved, actually. They believe the killer has done this before. A long way from here." Technically, she shouldn't have shared this with anyone outside of the department, but she didn't think it would hurt. She doubted she was the only one talking.

"Oh, I know about the FBI," her mother said, waving a dismissive hand as though Zoe were presuming to tell her about a subject on which she was an expert. "They only bring in the FBI when it's really serious, right?"

"Like I said, they believe this individual has committed crimes in other states."

This individual. Zoe realized she had slipped into professional mode, was speaking to her mom like she was an overwrought civilian at a traffic stop.

"Would you stay here with me?" her mom said after a moment, her voice sounding more fragile.

"I don't . . ." Zoe began, then stopped as she saw her mom's face fall. "Well, I'm on late tomorrow. Maybe I could stay tonight."

Her mom's brow furrowed like she wanted to hold out for a commitment of more nights or maybe a permanent move home, but she must have decided not to push it, because she just nodded.

Zoe knew that if her mom had her way, Zoe would never have moved out in the first place. Mary Ann was always making barbed comments about Zoe's little apartment over on Commercial Street, how it was too small and the street was less than salubrious.

"Like I said, you don't have anything to worry about." Her mom opened her mouth to protest again. "*But,*" Zoe said, "I know everyone in town is a little shook up by this. Understandably. So I wanted to check the locks and so on, make sure everything's shipshape."

Her mother took a drag from her cigarette and let the smoke filter out through her nostrils as she gazed at the view. The chimney of the plastics factory was pumping out smoke too. Zoe noticed for the first time that her mother looked older than the image she had of her in her head.

Fifty-two wasn't close to old these days, but something about the news had transformed her into a scared elderly lady. Zoe supposed she shouldn't be surprised.

"God. Something like that," her mother said. "This was a safe town."

"It *is* a safe town," Zoe insisted, hoping the firmness of her voice was reassuring.

Her mother turned to face her. "Were you there?"

"At the scene? Yes."

"What was it like?"

Zoe considered how to answer. "It wasn't so bad."

"He really didn't have his head cut off?"

"No, Mom."

It had been bad enough, but she wasn't about to say that.

"You haven't had to deal with that before. I hoped you wouldn't. To be honest, I hoped you wouldn't be doing this damn job."

"Let's not go over that again," Zoe said sharply. If this went down the usual route, they would both get pissed off. Staying in Granton had been the compromise. Becoming a cop had been nonnegotiable.

"I think your father would have agreed with me."

Zoe opened her mouth to retort and then stopped herself and tried to think of a way to move the conversation to a less contentious topic. She was grateful for the distraction when her phone buzzed in her pocket. She took it out and checked the screen, which read *No caller ID.*

"I have to take this."

Zoe's mother went inside. She answered the call with a cautious hello.

"Is this Officer Hill?"

The voice sounded familiar, and it took Zoe a moment to realize who it was. She had talked to a lot of new people today.

"Speaking."

"This is Ben Walker with the FBI. We talked at the scene this morning."

"Of course," Zoe said. There must have been some kind of development in the case. "Are you trying to get ahold of my partner? He plays basketball at the Y on Sunday evenings, so he may not have—"

"No, as a matter of fact, I was looking for you."

"Me?"

"Yes. Do you have time to talk right now?"

Zoe threw a glance at the house. Mom was in the kitchen, lighting her third cigarette in twenty minutes.

"Of course—what can I do for you?"

"We're holding a press conference at nine. We're going to tell people what we know so far. At the moment, everyone who lives at a one thirty-eight Main Street is potentially at risk. We don't know who's doing this or why, but these people have a right to know."

"No argument from me," Zoe said. Was he calling to ask if the story had leaked yet?

"This is going to be a challenging case," Walker continued. "I don't know if you've been involved in many federal operations . . ."

Zoe wanted to laugh at that. In Granton? Then she remembered Yelich telling her about busting a teenager on Jefferson Avenue four or five years ago, a kid who had been running some kind of nation-spanning Bitcoin scam from his bedroom in his parents' house. That would have been a federal investigation, but that was the closest the Granton PD had come to the big leagues recently.

"No. I've been on the job only three years, and Granton is a pretty quiet town. Normally."

"Okay, sure. Well, we're putting together a task force specific to this case. For things like this, it's useful—vital, I should say—to have somebody from one of the local PDs on board. I was wondering if you would be interested in taking the spot. Assuming your chief is okay with it."

Whatever Zoe had been expecting, it wasn't this.

"I . . . I mean . . ." She was temporarily at a loss for words. What she wanted to say was *Why?* "I'm very flattered you would think of me, but I'm not sure I would be much use to you."

There was a pause, and she expected him to politely thank her, hang up, and move on to the next name on his list.

"Zoe . . . can I call you Zoe?"

"Sure."

"I have eight open homicides on this already, four distinct scenes across four states. I have a press conference in an hour. Do you think that I would be wasting my time calling people I didn't think would be useful?" He spoke quickly and directly, but his tone betrayed no irritation. He sounded as though he was just stating a fact.

"Right. Of course."

"You knew what you were doing this morning. If that was your first homicide, I couldn't tell. And the map pin—your partner didn't notice it, did he?"

Zoe cleared her throat, feeling a weird urge to defend Yelich even though he had dismissed the symbol when she pointed it out. "I think he would have noticed it. It just so happened I was on that side of the room first."

"Sure. Anyway, I'm not talking to your partner, I'm talking to you. What do you say?"

"I, uh . . ." She looked back at the house, thinking about the conversation that would have to happen if she took Walker up on his offer.

"If you're worried about your chief, don't be. The process is straightforward, and the local department usually ends up doing pretty well. I'll call him next—unless you want to speak to him first."

Zoe wanted to slam on the brakes. Walker was talking like she had accepted already. He was persuasive, used to getting his own way. But was part of it that she wanted to be persuaded? Her thoughts went to the scene at 138 Main this morning. The way Yelich had been so overprotective, like he was expecting her to faint or something.

Yelich couldn't have known, but it was the opposite: She finally felt at home, like she was doing the job she was made to do. The job her father had done.

And that again made her think of her mother. She was still there in the kitchen, watching her with a warning eye, like she already knew.

"Zoe, are you still there?" Walker prompted.

"Can I think about it?"

There was a hesitation, and Zoe knew that the real answer to that question was *no*.

"Could you let me know your decision tonight? I appreciate this is out of the blue, but these things have to move fast."

"Sure. Give me your number and I'll let you know as soon as I can."

"Thank you. If you decide in favor, we need you in New York tomorrow. Or Tuesday morning, at the latest."

"I understand."

"Okay. And, Zoe?"

"Yes?"

"I hope you decide to join us."

Zoe took Walker's number, then hung up and looked at the house that had been her childhood home. The last place she had seen her father before he went to work on the final day of his life.

She knew at that moment that Walker's offer might be something like a last chance—stay on her childhood stoop or venture out beyond her comfort zone. Were she advising a friend, it would be an easy decision.

But here and now, it felt like there was no right answer.

8

138 MAIN STREET

CHARLESTOWN, MASSACHUSETTS

The FBI lady on television looked like a politician. She had red hair and wore a dark suit over a white blouse. Cally had barely been paying attention. She had the news on in the background as she worked. But then she had heard her own address read out by a voice on the TV, and she forgot all about work.

"And we are advising residents to be cautious. We believe these murders are premeditated. We can't say for sure whether other attacks are planned."

Cally stared at the screen, trying to make what the FBI assistant director was saying and the text on the bottom of the screen coalesce into meaning. She didn't know what was going on, but she didn't think it was anything good.

The banner on the screen read *Main Street Killings*, and underneath that: *FBI assistant director in charge, New York City, Billie Chapman.*

Main Street killings? Which Main Street? A little box in the corner of the screen showed aerial footage of a residential neighborhood with police vehicles and officers clustered around a small house.

The FBI woman kept talking as Cally watched, her eyes glued to the summary on the chyron at the bottom of the screen. She caught up fast: four murder scenes in different parts of the country. All four with just one thing in common.

Cally perched on the edge of the couch and watched the rest of the briefing. For the first time in days, she forgot about Melissa. The speaker took questions from the media. The clamor of voices was such that it sounded like a scuffle was about to break out among the assembled members of the press.

The questions for the woman came fast, almost as fast as the questions Cally was frantically asking herself. Without consciously thinking about it, she got up, went over to the window, and looked outside.

She didn't know what she had expected. A crowd staring up at her, perhaps, but so far there was no one down there. Parked cars lined the sides of the street. A bicycle courier weaved past, staring at the screen of his phone.

She stepped back from the window and hurried to the front door. Hesitantly, she peered through the peephole. The landing was as empty as the street outside.

She snapped the second lock on the door and then stopped. The FBI agent on the TV had said that the intruder gained access to his victims' homes and murdered them in the night. Cally felt a shiver travel the length of her spine.

The people on the news channel chattered away in the background. Standing at the door triggered a memory. It reminded Cally of when she was left home alone for the first time. She was a kid, about eight, and her mom had to take Melissa to the hospital. As soon as the door closed behind them, she became suddenly convinced that she was not alone.

She went from room to room in their house in Lexington, kneeling to check under beds, opening all the closets, and going up on her tiptoes to see the shelves at the top. She finally steeled herself to go down into the basement to confirm it was all clear.

Now, thirty years removed from that scared little girl, she found herself doing the same thing.

This apartment was smaller, at least. Not as many places for someone to hide.

Not as many places for you to run, the voice in her head added unhelpfully.

The bedroom first. She knelt on the floor by the bed and lowered her head, tensed for a gnarled hand to shoot out. But there was nothing there other than dust bunnies. The closet was full of her clothes and unpacked boxes from her last move. She opened it, but someone hiding in there would have had to do a lot of rearrangement. The window was always jammed shut, but she tried it anyway to make sure.

Kitchen. The only place she couldn't see from the doorway was the nook behind the row of cabinets. She walked slowly into the room until she could see that it too was empty.

The window on this side actually opened and allowed access onto the fire escape. She looked outside. The fire escape was empty, the ladder at the bottom pulled up. She knew that the ladder made a hellish noise when it was pulled down, so if anyone tried to come in that way, she would have some warning, at least.

Cally pushed the window down and fastened the catch, letting out the breath she had been holding. She took a moment to gather herself and then, with an effort, forced herself to move back to the television. As she returned to the living room, a reporter from one of the networks was asking a question: "How can people be sure you'll keep them safe?"

The FBI woman hesitated for a split second before answering. The answer was bland, but Cally wasn't really listening.

She was too busy thinking about that hesitation.

Monday

9

NEW YORK CITY

"First question: How many Main Streets are there in this country?"

Assistant Director Billie Chapman didn't like to waste time—she got straight to the point. Walker leaned back so he could see down to the bottom of the conference table, shielding his eyes against the morning sun streaming through the floor-to-ceiling windows. The room was packed. Twice as many people as there were chairs. It took him a second to find the analyst in the crowd.

"I guess that's as good a place as any to start," Walker said to the room. He looked across at the analyst. "Brodie, do you want to go ahead?"

Matt Brodie cleared his throat and his eyes surveyed the room nervously. He was in his late twenties, with curly brown hair and glasses. He was wearing a blue shirt and a tie but no jacket; there seemed to be some kind of unspoken tradition that the analysts didn't wear one. He looked as though he would have been much more comfortable in an unbuttoned plaid shirt over a T-shirt with the name of an obscure metal band on it. He stood up, glancing at the pile of the morning's newspapers on the table as though they held his lines.

"Introduce yourself," Chapman said. The assistant director's words were abrupt but her tone was neutral. She didn't believe in burning twenty minutes with general introductions, even when the matter at hand was less urgent.

"Good morning, everyone, I'm Matt Brodie. I know some of you, but I'm still kind of new, so . . ." He had a British accent, and his voice was a little shaky. Walker guessed he wasn't used to speaking in front of a roomful of people.

"And what do you have for us?" Chapman asked.

Brodie's eyes met Walker's.

"I asked the team to look into the question you just asked," Walker said. "Brodie came back with some quick results." He gestured at the large screen at the front of the room, hoping Brodie would take the hint to get on with it.

Brodie walked hurriedly around the table and tapped the side of the screen to select his presentation. The first slide was a map of the Lower Forty-Eight.

"How many Main Streets are there in the United States?" Brodie began, waving a hand at the screen. "Actually, it's not as straightforward a question as it sounds."

He tapped on the screen and the map stayed there, but a series of red dots started to appear in every state on almost every inch of the map. Thousands of them, each one representing a Main Street. There were audible groans from around the table. Walker had had the same reaction.

"Jesus, every goddamn town in the country," someone said.

Matt Brodie shook his head at the source of the comment. "Not quite." He tapped the screen again, and a blank slide appeared, followed by numbers. Big numbers.

"Okay, so, according to census data, we have over seven thousand Main Streets in the United States. Seven thousand, six hundred and sixty-four, to be exact."

Chapman was seated in front of the screen. There was a smaller screen built into the table that showed the same presentation so she didn't have to crane her head around. Her brow was furrowed. "That's why whoever is doing this picked Main Street—because it's the most common street name. How do—"

"Technically, it isn't," Brodie said, evidently comfortable enough to interrupt the big boss now that he was on his own territory.

Chapman blinked behind her glasses. "It isn't?"

Brodie tapped the screen again to bring up more numbers. "Actually, Second Street is the most common street name in America. That's because not every main street is named Main Street. Some of them are called First Street. Do we count those?" He opened his hands in a *Your guess is as good as mine* gesture. "We don't know. It depends on if the killer counts them. So far, every killing has been on a Main Street, but four sites is too small a sample to draw a definitive conclusion from. Once we have—"

"If it's all right with you," Chapman said, interrupting Brodie this time, "I think we'd all be happier if this sample doesn't grow any bigger."

"Of course," Brodie said, chastened. Walker thought that was a cheap shot. He wasn't under the illusion this was going to stop at four attacks, and he didn't think Chapman was either.

"So if we're including First Streets, that number grows. A lot."

The number 17,542 appeared on the screen to a reaction of more groans and a couple of exclamations of *Shit*.

"If we're including Main, First, and any street that counts as the primary thoroughfare of any town or city, it grows even more. It's difficult to say what's in and what isn't. In fact, at that point, you might as well assume there's one in every town in the country."

Brodie tapped on the screen again and the map came back with an even larger number of purple pins augmenting the red ones.

"So what you're saying is," Chapman said, looking at Walker, "we already have the address that the perpetrator is going to strike next, but it's on a list of thousands of other locations."

"That's about the size of it," Walker said.

"Sorry, this doesn't count Alaska and Hawaii," Brodie said, tapping the screen again and widening the scope to show the noncontiguous states. It didn't make the picture that much worse, but it also didn't do anything to lighten the mood in the room.

"Thank you very much, Mr. Brodie," Chapman said in the tone of someone who'd been handed a garbage bag full of rhino shit. Brodie nodded an acknowledgment and walked quickly back to his seat.

"Why?" Chapman asked, addressing the room. "Who is doing this and why?"

"I know you're not going to like the answer we have now," Walker said, "but it's the same thing Brodie just told us. We don't know, because the sample size is too small. We're confident this is the same perpetrator, and we know he wants attention, but beyond that, we just don't have enough information yet."

Walker reached for the clicker so he wouldn't have to go stand by the screen. He preferred to present from the table; standing up in front of people always made him feel like a substitute teacher.

He brought up his own slide deck and quickly ran through the exterior photographs of the four 138 Main Streets, pausing to identify each location as it appeared.

"First one: Courtland, Mississippi. One victim. June first. Then Lyons, Colorado, on June seventh. Two victims. Pembury was on the fifteenth, four victims. Then Granton, Illinois, on Saturday the seventeenth. One victim."

Ferrera said from across the table, "That's one piece of good news."

"Eight murders is good news?" Chapman asked incredulously.

"No, but breaking that pattern is good news. Technically, the body count doubled each time up to Granton." Ferrera cleared his throat. "We thought that might have been part of the pattern."

"Thank heaven for small favors."

Walker had never bought into that particular theory. Unless the killer had been planning to stop with the next address, there weren't that many homes where sixteen, thirty-two, or sixty-four people lived. "Victim profile is apparently random, as you would expect," he said. "Cause of death varies between blade and gunshot. But he isn't making mistakes. No survivors so far, although one victim got close to getting away in Pembury."

He started to scroll through the crime scene photographs from each house. The Mississippi and Colorado locations had been processed by local cops, who had no reason to suspect that their apparently random home-invasion killings were part of a series linked to addresses thousands of miles apart.

The address in Mississippi was a small shack in a town with a population of under six hundred. The picture showed a male victim, forty years old and about a hundred pounds overweight. The shack was just two rooms, neither one defined enough that you could tell which was the bedroom and which was the living room. The victim was wearing boxer shorts, no shirt. His torso was covered with blood; it had drenched the shabby couch he was sprawled on.

"Clarence Wood. The killer walked into his house sometime between midnight and two. The door was unlocked. The pathologist says he was stabbed twice in the chest at the start of the attack. He tried to struggle. Defensive wounds on both hands. Another stab to the heart here, which would have been fatal, but the killer cut his throat for good measure."

Walker tapped the button again. The slide changed to the Colorado victims. An elderly couple. Separate photographs, because they had been found in separate rooms. "Marjorie and William Kent. They had three children, seven grandchildren. Marjorie was a night owl, liked to watch TV late most nights. The killer broke into the living room through the French doors and shot Mrs. Kent. Mr. Kent woke up and was coming to help. The killer met him halfway."

Then Pembury. Four victim pictures this time. The first scene showed an opulent bedroom. White sheets that were now mostly red and a well-preserved man in his late fifties with stab wounds to his chest.

"And this is where we came in. Pembury, Long Island. Homeowners were Christopher and Lisa Jameson. Christopher was a hedge-fund manager; Lisa worked in finance before she quit to raise their two kids full-time."

He tapped to show the next slide. A woman face down on a carpeted floor, curled in on herself. The bottom of a framed painting was visible at the top of the image.

"Their daughter lives in a dorm at college, which is why she survived. The son, Chris Junior, was smoking weed with his girlfriend in the pool house. Working theory is they heard the mother scream and came into the main residence."

New slide. A young male dressed in loose shorts and a black T-shirt face down in a pool of blood on a tiled floor.

"Ed Junior was stabbed like mom and dad. His girlfriend, Millie, tried to run."

New slide. Female victim, around the same age, cutoff jean shorts and a tank top, barefoot, face down on grass. Visible gunshot wounds, one in the center of her back, one in the back of her head.

"The killer pursued, shot her in the back from a distance of at least eight yards, then made sure with one to the head."

New slide. The only victim Walker had seen with his own eyes.

"Yesterday morning, we got the word there was another. Granton, Illinois. Victim was Archibald Bowman, United States Marine Corps veteran, fifty-five years old. The killer broke in through the back door, stabbed him to death."

He clicked on the close-up of the map-pin image.

"He's left this symbol somewhere at every crime scene to date. A map pin."

"Why?" Chapman prompted.

"Signing his work," Walker said. "The killer is proud of what he's done. He obviously didn't want to take the chance that we'd miss any."

Walker tapped to go on to the final slide. Like Brodie's images, it showed a map of the United States. On this map, there were only four pins, marking each of the kill sites.

"Eight victims, four sites," he said, pausing to look at the faces of the people around the table. Nobody interrupted. Everyone knew what this meant. The air in the room was still. "We don't know what the motivation is yet. All we know is that this individual is ruthless and prepared and efficient. These crimes are thousands of miles apart, and they've all taken place this month. It's possible, likely even, that the perpetrator killed before

Courtland, but we haven't been able to find any other historical murders at a one thirty-eight Main before this month. There will be more, and soon."

The silence was broken by Chapman. "It's our job to prevent that."

A barrel-chested agent in a blue tie at the end of the table cleared his throat. "Is anyone going to ask the obvious question?"

"Which obvious question?" Walker asked.

"How the hell do we protect seven thousand addresses? He only has to get it right once; we have to get it right every time."

"We don't," Walker said. "Not by ourselves. It's going to take cooperation with state and local law enforcement on an unprecedented scale."

"What can we do?" a youthful agent sitting diagonally across the table from Walker asked. He was skinny with hollow-looking eyes and slicked-back dirty-blond hair. "I mean . . . we have no idea where he's going next."

"Sure we do. I can give you the address," a voice from the other end of the room shot back. There was no laughter.

The agent with the slicked-back hair ignored the crack and pressed on. "I mean, what? Do we put everyone in a Holiday Inn for the night?"

Walker shook his head. "This is why going public last night was the right thing to do. Yes, there was a danger of causing panic. But as of now, the people at each one of these seven thousand addresses and all their neighbors are on alert. Some of them will go stay someplace else. We're developing a register of every one of those addresses so we can keep tabs on the people who live there, look after the most vulnerable. We're talking to local police departments about coordinating surveillance."

The woman sitting beside Walker looked alarmed. Walker vaguely recognized her—Ellie something. "You think they're going to put a round-the-clock stakeout on those addresses? Even if you're just talking night shift, that's gonna run to—"

"It's going to be a challenge," Walker agreed. "Which is why we can't just rely on a defensive strategy. We need to go on the offense. We need to find out who this guy is, and we need to stop him."

"What's the motive?" Chapman asked. "It can't be a personal thing. The victims are only related by the address."

Walker looked over at Dr. Edgar Holland, who was seated across from him. The behavioral-science specialist wore wire-rimmed glasses and a pensive expression. Walker was interested to see what the rest of the room would make of Holland's theory on motivation.

"We don't know yet," Holland said. "This could be a particularly organized and motivated serial, or it could be something else."

"Something else?"

Holland glanced over at Walker before answering, as though checking he still wanted him to go ahead.

"It could be terrorism," Holland said.

"Terrorism?" Chapman repeated. "This isn't like any terrorism investigation I've been involved in."

"Well, quite," Holland said. "It's not a single attack or a coordinated, synchronized series of attacks. No one has claimed responsibility after three weeks, although you have to assume they would know we wouldn't have picked up the pattern until the third location, so . . . but, yes, it's not some kind of disorganized lone-wolf thing, and it's not what the bin Laden types used to call a 'spectacular.' At least, not yet."

"So what about this says terrorism?" Chapman asked. Walker could tell she was interested. Holland was holding her attention.

"What is terrorism for?" Holland replied. Before anyone else could speak, he answered his own question. "To strike fear into your enemy. Have you seen the front pages this morning?"

He gestured at the pile of newspapers fanned out on the table. Big headlines. The *Post*'s "Terror on Main Street" popped out from the rest.

"People are scared. They don't think we can protect them. Not just the six thousand–plus people living at a one thirty-eight Main—"

"Seven thousand," Brodie cut in. "Seven thousand–plus."

Holland raised a hand in acknowledgment. "Not just them. Almost everyone lives in a town with a Main Street. You said this wasn't like any terrorism you had seen. That's because we think of terrorism as something that happens in the cities. New York, Washington, DC, LA. This does something subtler but maybe more troubling. It hits close to home. Somebody creeping into your house at night and killing you for no reason."

Walker watched the room. Most were hanging on Holland's words. Holland had briefed him on this scenario before the meeting, and he had a point. Walker had spent more time in the Bureau than most in this room. He had been in the city on 9/11 and was involved in the aftermath. But right now, he was thinking about September 11 of the following year. The nation had been braced for something big on the one-year anniversary. Holland's theory was close to one of the scenarios that had been gamed out by the doomwatchers: small, coordinated attacks on the heartland, planned and enacted in the knowledge that the big cities and national monuments would be under tight security. Law enforcement hadn't known what to expect back then. Even with the warnings of attacks on nuclear facilities and dirty bombs, Walker remembered that heartland-attack scenario had touched a nerve.

Was that because of the relatability Holland was describing? That was part of his apprehension. But the other part was the logistics. If ISIS or whoever showed up in a one-stoplight town in the middle of nowhere and started executing people, how the hell could you have predicted that? And how the hell did you stop it?

Chapman looked at Walker as Holland finished speaking. "He makes a good point. What do you think, Mr. Walker?"

Walker took his time replying. "I think it's possible. If he's right, we'll know soon. If not, it doesn't make any difference to what we do here and now. We know what this person or people have done so far. We know they're ruthless, effective, and well resourced. And we know they'll want to strike again. Maybe tomorrow, maybe in a couple of days, maybe tonight. They've already planned their next move." He finished by slapping his hand down on the table.

"Let's get in the way."

10

GRANTON, ILLINOIS

After a few hours to think about it, Zoe reflected that the conversation over breakfast with her mother hadn't been as bad as she had anticipated. It had been worse. By some measure.

Anger first, then tears, then more anger. That had been effective at inducing guilt but hadn't managed to achieve her primary objective of changing Zoe's mind. But then she made a strategic mistake: She tried to belittle her daughter.

"All right. You know why you shouldn't go? You're going to make me say it, aren't you?" she said, wiping the tears from her eyes with the heel of her hand. "It's too big."

"What's too big?"

"This case. New York. The FBI. All of it. You don't know what it's like out there. It's not like Granton."

Zoe couldn't help herself. "I don't know what it's *like* out there? And whose fault is that?"

Those were the last words they exchanged. Mary Ann Hill had pursed her lips, then turned and walked quickly upstairs, leaving Zoe alone in the living room.

One of Walker's people contacted her to say that she was booked on the first flight out of O'Hare tomorrow morning. They would catch up when she got to New York, but in the meantime she had been added to the task force's online work group. There were dozens of names on the screen, and she had access to several other groups as well as the core task force team of eight. Periodically, her phone lit up with new notifications, unfamiliar names sharing updates and asking questions using terms she recognized maybe five times out of ten. She could see there was going to be a steep learning curve.

That left her a few hours to tie things up here in Granton. She would be based in New York City for the next two weeks, Walker said, and they could review things then. She didn't think Walker meant it this way, but she couldn't help but look at the two weeks as a probation period. After that, assuming they hadn't caught the Main Street killer by then, he would have his pick of local police liaisons, most of them more qualified than her.

Yelich greeted her with a grin that was ever so slightly tight around the eyes as she walked into the station.

"Special Agent Hill. To what do we owe the honor?"

"Knock it off, I'll be back soon enough."

"I'm sure you'll have Mr. Main Street locked up by sundown tomorrow. Is that what you're calling him? Or is it all 'the unsub,' shit like that?"

Zoe smiled dutifully and waited a moment before trying to move the conversation on.

"I'm going to pick up my stuff, but I need to give you a list of where I'm at with the Miller assault and the thing with Joe Remmy." The first was an altercation that had taken place on Frankie Miller's porch last week in which each party claimed the other had assaulted him. Joe Remmy was due for a slap on the wrist for flouting the open-burning ban that had been imposed a week ago. Her mom's words came back to her as she considered these cases: *It's too big.*

Yelich waved his hand dismissively. "We'll cope."

"Just the same, I'll leave you a one-pager. After that, I was thinking of swinging by the Bowman scene. If you don't mind."

"It's your case, Zoe. It's not ours, not anymore."

She didn't rise to the bait, just cleared her throat. "Okay. Who has the keys to the house?"

"Your buddies. Sorry—your new coworkers. I don't think they stuck around, though."

"All right." She turned to go, then looked back at him.

"What?" he said.

"It's only going to be a couple weeks. And it wasn't my idea."

He stared at her for a moment, then down at some paperwork. "We'll be here when you get back."

11

138 MAIN STREET

GRENVILLE, PENNSYLVANIA

Patrick Massie sat in front of the television with a single-malt Scotch on the rocks in his hand that had edged up to body temperature as he watched the latest press conference. It was earlier than he usually started drinking, but he figured he had a good excuse.

The doorbell rang, snapping him out of his thoughts. He watched as the anchor picked over the meager information the FBI had provided, then turned off the news and sank the last of the Scotch in one gulp before moving to the window and looking down at the street.

It had been raining hard for the past hour, the low clouds making it much darker than it ought to be this early in the evening. There was a marked police car parked across the road. A uniformed officer was standing in the street staring up at him. He raised one hand to wave at Patrick and shielded his face from the downpour with the other.

Patrick took his walking stick from where it rested against the bookcase and made his way down the stairs to the entrance hall, where he could see the silhouette of another officer through the stained-glass panel. He opened the door but kept it on the chain.

The officer was already holding up her ID. She was about five foot five, relatively young; late twenties, perhaps. Long hair tied up underneath her hat. The other cop, the one who had waved from the street, was standing at the bottom of the steps that led up to the town house.

Patrick leaned closer to the gap in the door to inspect the photo above the badge and read the text that identified her as Officer Catherine T. Semple, Grenville Police Department, badge number 1812. The brown hair, blue eyes, and freckles matched the photo. She was smiling in the picture. Perhaps the photo had been taken on an easier day than this one.

"Patrick Massie?" she asked.

"That's me." Patrick offered a grim smile. "I suppose I don't need to ask 'Is there a problem, Officer,' do I?"

"You know why we're here. Good. Do you mind if we come in?"

Patrick looked beyond Officer Semple to the other cop. "I'm sorry, I hate to be rude, but could I see his ID as well?"

"Of course, not a problem. I'm Officer Semple, this is Officer Blatch."

"Semple and Blatch. You sound like a law firm."

Blatch chuckled good-naturedly as he stepped up next to his partner and pulled his own ID out. "I guess we are, in a manner of speaking."

Blatch's picture didn't look a lot like the man holding it. It was a few years out of date. The hair protruding from under his hat now was a little longer and wet from the rain; there were more lines on his face. But the gray eyes and the shape of the jaw were right. This was the man in the ID photo, but in his fifties rather than his late forties.

Satisfied, Patrick closed the door, took the chain off, then pulled it wide open.

"Sorry about that. I'm a little on edge."

"I don't blame you," Semple said. "We just wanted to check in, let you know what we're doing to keep you safe."

"I appreciate it," Patrick said.

Blatch was eyeing Patrick's walking stick. Patrick had picked it up in an antiques shop in the city a couple of months ago. It was fashioned of polished mahogany with a stylized duck's head for a handle.

"What'd you do to yourself?" Blatch asked.

Patrick wondered if this was Officer Blatch's idea of polite conversation. It probably was. "Old injury."

He turned and led Officer Semple and Officer Blatch across the tiled floor of the hall and into the living room. It was a huge space, almost three hundred square feet, with varnished floorboards and a bay window that looked out onto the street. There was a fire in the hearth, although it wasn't the season for fires, and two large couches and two armchairs positioned around a low square oak coffee table. Patrick sat down on a couch.

The two officers waited for Patrick to ask them to sit, which he did. Semple sat in an armchair and took out a notepad, but Blatch stayed on his feet, surveying the floor-to-ceiling bookshelf that took up most of the north wall.

"You sure do have a lot of books."

"Most of them aren't mine," Patrick said. "They belong to my landlord."

"He didn't move them out before he rented the place to you?"

"No, the books and the furniture come with the house. I kind of like them."

"What do you do for a living?" Blatch said as he came over and perched on the edge of the couch. "You a professor or something?"

Patrick laughed. "Actually, I'm retired."

"Little young to be retired, aren't you?"

"Not when it's from the US Marine Corps."

His visitors exchanged a glance, and Patrick realized they were operating on less information than he had expected.

"You were a Marine?" Blatch said, a slight edge of suspicion in his eyes and his voice.

Patrick wondered if he had lost the air of a soldier. Or perhaps it was like that line from *Mad Men*: A man is whatever room he is in. This room didn't feel like the room of an ex-Marine. Well, perhaps a retired sergeant major, but Patrick had never had any designs on climbing that far up the ladder.

"For almost twenty years. Mostly Iraq and Afghanistan."

Semple raised her eyebrows and made a note on her pad. "Thank you for your service."

"You see any action?" Blatch asked.

Patrick let the question hang in the air long enough for Semple to shoot her partner a pained look, but it seemed to bounce off him.

He gripped the handle of the walking stick. "Enough to last me a lifetime, yes."

"Sure," Blatch said. "I guess it was rough over there. Speaking of which . . ."

Semple took her cue, clearing her throat. "You've been keeping up with the news?"

"I just watched the latest briefing. Hell of a thing. I don't know if I feel sorrier for myself or you guys. Has to be a real pain in the ass, logistics-wise."

Semple nodded. "Everyone is taking it very seriously. And, first off, we wanted to assure you that there's probably nothing to worry about."

Probably. "Easy for you to say," Patrick said. "What's *your* address?"

The two of them exchanged a glance, and Patrick detected the hint of a smirk at the corner of Blatch's mouth.

"Fair point," Semple said. "What I meant was, we're taking the threat seriously, but statistically, it's unlikely you're in any real danger."

Patrick sat back on the couch and scratched his head. "Do you have any idea if the FBI are close to catching this nut?"

"They have several lines of inquiry open," she said. "Part of that is coordinating with local PDs, which is why we're here."

"Doing the grunt work," Blatch said.

Semple didn't acknowledge her partner's interjection. "We just want to run through a few things with you, check that your home is secure, ask you a few questions."

"Questions?"

Semple reached into her jacket pocket and took out a folded piece of paper. She glanced down at it and back up at Patrick. "They gave us a list. You want me to go through them with you first?"

Patrick told her to go ahead.

Semple glanced down at the paper again. "Have you received any unexpected visitors over the past few weeks?"

"No unexpected visitors," Patrick answered. "No visitors at all, in fact. My ex-wife lives in Seattle."

"What about maintenance people? Anybody come to do any work for you?"

Patrick thought about it and shook his head. "Nobody has come through my door recently apart from the two of you. I'm afraid I don't get out much at the moment."

Blatch stared pointedly at his walking stick. "That because of . . . your injury?"

He hesitated before replying. "I feel safer inside, I suppose."

Semple considered that for a second and then moved on without further comment. "Have you noticed anybody unusual hanging around outside the building?"

"Define *unusual*."

"Anybody who doesn't fit in. People who don't live around here. Unfamiliar vehicles."

"I don't know any of the neighbors, really; I've been here less than a year. I wouldn't know who fits in and who doesn't. And as far as vehicles go, the street out there is always lined with cars. Some belong to residents, and some people park there to catch the train to the city. And obviously, there are delivery people all day every day. Amazon, Whole Foods, UPS . . ." He opened his hands in apology. "If I stood by that window for an hour, I would see a dozen faces I've never seen before."

Semple scratched some comments in her notebook.

"Anyone suspicious, then? You know, people hanging around in doorways, sitting in parked cars."

"I haven't seen anyone who stuck out. Of course, now I'll be seeing bad guys everywhere."

"Might not be the worst thing," Blatch said. "Better safe than sorry."

"Do you have someplace else you could go for a while?" Semple asked. "Could you stay with family, maybe?"

"No family left, really. No one I'd want to impose on."

"Well, as I said, it's a long shot he's going to show up here," Semple said.

"I certainly hope it's a long shot."

Semple looked around the room as though sizing it up. "Besides, if this guy is as smart as we think, he isn't going to go out of his way looking for hard targets. You were a Marine—you know how to handle yourself. Do you have a gun in the house?"

"Uh, yeah. Been a while since I fired a gun even on the range, but I can handle myself."

Blatch tapped his own holstered weapon. "Like riding a bike."

Semple leaned forward and handed Patrick a sheet of paper. It had the words *Resident Safety Program* at the top and a series of bullet points going over the same questions she had just asked him. There was a phone number and a website at the bottom.

"You got any concerns at all, call that number. Anything urgent, make it 911 and tell them your address. You'll get preferential treatment." She caught Patrick's raised eyebrow and smiled. At that moment, he noticed that Officer Semple was quite pretty. "All the Main Streets get priority until we catch this guy."

Patrick examined the piece of paper. The stock was flimsy, and he could see a couple of typos at first glance. Clearly a rush job. Like this whole operation, by all indications. "Priority. Like a platinum club, huh?"

"Right," Semple agreed. "And unless you have any objections, we're going to be checking in with you once a day."

"No objections at all. I appreciate it." He looked beyond them, out the window at the falling rain. "You don't expect something like this. Something so . . . targeted. It almost feels personal, you know? Does that sound stupid?"

"Not stupid at all, Mr. Massie."

He waved a hand in dismissal. "Call me Patrick."

"Patrick. I'm Cat."

"Ray," Blatch added.

There was an awkward lull. Just three new friends on a first-name basis.

"Let's not get too worried about this," Semple said after a moment. "You take reasonable precautions, and other than that, just live your life as normal."

"Right. Is there any chance we could get someone stationed out there to watch the place?" Patrick gestured at the street where the police car was parked.

The two cops exchanged a glance that Patrick recognized from his time on the front line. It said: *Pigs will fly.*

"We don't believe full surveillance is necessary at the moment," Semple said, snapping out of the informality and back into the rehearsed lines. "We want to make sure we minimize any disruption to members of the public who are residing at these addresses."

"Disruption," Patrick repeated. "I get it."

"We'll take your suggestion under advisement," Semple said. She glanced over her shoulder, as though expecting to see her captain lurking in the doorway, and lowered her voice. "And to be completely honest with you, Patrick, those decisions are above our pay grade. Like I said, we're not looking at full surveillance right now, but that could change tomorrow. Best I can do is promise you that if I hear anything new, I'll let you know. Good enough?"

"Sure."

Blatch was looking around again. "Big place for one guy."

"My wife and I divorced last year. You know, that old thing about needing space. Well . . ." He shrugged. "This had space."

"You can say that again," Blatch said. Massie could read his thoughts like one of the books on the shelves: He was thinking that there were a lot of places to hide in a house this big. He was pleasantly surprised that Blatch was tactful enough not to give voice to that thought.

Semple snapped her notebook shut and stood up. "Let's take a look at your security."

Patrick gave the two officers a brief tour of the town house: The ground floor with its two spacious reception rooms and an eat-in kitchen, the second floor with the library and the primary bedroom, and the top floor with four more rooms. Patrick had set up his office in the bedroom on the west side; the one on the east was empty. They checked every window in the house, making sure they locked.

The yard out back was a long, paved rectangle enclosed by brick walls. Beyond it was a service alley, and the gate in the wall was locked. Patrick told them he couldn't remember if there was a key for it. Semple suggested installing a motion-activated security light.

Last, Patrick took them down to the basement, which smelled of damp and was all but empty other than a small stack of boxes in the corner. The cops decided that the basement was secure enough but recommended he install bars on the window, as it was just about big enough for an intruder to squeeze through. Semple told him they would type all the recommendations up in a report and email it to him.

"That all sounds good," Patrick said as he led them back up the stairs to the ground floor. "But I'll need to speak to my landlord about the extra security. He's, uh . . . not too responsive."

Blatch looked up at the high ceiling of the hallway. "You don't mind me asking, what's a place like this run you a month?"

Patrick told him, earning a whistle from Blatch.

"I sold my house after the divorce and I wasn't ready to think about buying a new place yet. I thought there had been enough upheaval, enough drama." He smiled wryly. "Who knew, right?"

"For that kind of rent, your landlord should be a little more helpful," Semple said.

"Those precautions you talked about—is there any kind of government funding for this?"

Semple looked apologetic. "Not that I know of."

"Okay. I thought it was worth asking. My lease is up at the end of October anyway. I expect I won't be renewing for another year."

"Probably a good thing, with all this," Semple said.

"Good thing for me, maybe, but not for my landlord."

"You got that right." Blatch grinned. "I wouldn't want to have to find a tenant for this address for a while."

12

138 MAIN STREET

CHARLESTOWN, MASSACHUSETTS

Cally thought she was managing her anxiety pretty well up until the moment the siren screamed to life, making her jolt upright on the couch.

She moved to the window in time to see the blue lights of the police car reflecting off the windows at the intersection of Eden and Main. The piercing sound became distorted and then quieter as the car moved at speed away from her. She let out a long breath and looked down. The streetlight closest to the building had been broken for a week. She barely noticed it before, but now the uneven stretch of inky darkness on the sidewalk seemed full of malevolent purpose. Anyone or anything could be hiding down there.

She walked into the hall and made sure that the door was locked.

She thought back to the police officers who had visited earlier in the day. A man and a woman. She couldn't remember their names, but she had the card they'd left in the kitchen drawer, along with their little fact sheet. It hadn't actually been titled "Helpful Tips for When You're Marked for Death by a Psycho," but it might as well have been.

They had given the apartment a once-over, which didn't take long, given the size of the place, and discussed security. They told her she was in a pretty good position, although now she wondered if they just told everybody that. They said the risk, if there was any, was split three ways, since there were three apartments at 138 Main. Then again, the duplex on the second and third floor had been unoccupied since the old man who owned it died last year. So perhaps the risk was split only two ways. But there was a single front entrance, and anyone coming in had to get through that door before they made it as far as her apartment. Besides, it was statistically very unlikely that Cally's would be the address this guy showed up at next.

The female cop had seemed a little cold. The male one had been nicer. "Don't lose sleep over it," he said. "The odds are way in your favor. It's like lottery odds."

Cally wanted to correct him on that. First, the Massachusetts Lottery odds were more like fourteen million to one, not seven thousand to one.

Second, somebody won every week.

She opened the door of the aging refrigerator and stared at the contents for a while before deciding she didn't want anything. As she closed the door, she noticed it had moved a little away from the wall. She pushed it back into place and went into the living room.

Her phone screen had lit up. She rushed over and picked it up, then sighed when she saw that it was just a text from a friend at work asking if she was okay, if she needed anything.

"Goddamn it, Melissa," she said out loud. She tried her sister's number again, expecting the message, and was surprised when she heard it ringing. By the fifth ring, she had resigned herself to the fact that her sister wasn't going to pick up. Eventually, it went to voicemail.

"It's Cally. Again," she said, trying and failing to keep the weariness out of her voice. "I guess you charged your phone. I would really appreciate you getting in touch to let me know you're okay. I don't know if you've been watching the news, but I don't need . . ." She stopped and rephrased: "It would help a lot if I didn't have to worry about you as well. Anyway, you know where I am."

Cally hung up. She was so tired. She had gotten maybe an hour and a half of sleep last night, total. She went to the door again and looked out the peephole. The landing was empty. She made sure the chain was on securely, then unlocked the door and opened it a couple of inches. The hinge creaked as it always did. There was no one out there.

Then there was a soft patter of paws, and the tabby from apartment A stuck his head above the top step, summoned by the creaking noise.

"Sorry, buddy, back to your own place," Cally said, then closed the door and locked it again.

She went into her bedroom and undressed. She made sure the notifications on her phone were on, just in case Melissa called in the night. If she got in touch—*when* she got in touch, Cally corrected herself—it could be at any hour of the day or night. As usual, Melissa wouldn't waste any time worrying if other people kept different hours than she did.

Cally usually left her bedroom door ajar at night. After a moment's thought, she closed the door fully and positioned the back of a chair underneath the doorknob.

She lay down in bed and closed her eyes. A moment later, she heard the exterior door slam closed downstairs, and her eyes snapped open. She tensed, then heard a peal of laughter. The bartender who lived in apartment A bringing a girl home.

She closed her eyes again and tried not to think about the shadows.

And then she remembered the man she had seen outside yesterday.

Tuesday

13

NEW YORK CITY

Zoe's flight left O'Hare in darkness at six and touched down at LaGuardia just after nine, having gained an hour on the trip east.

New York was ten degrees warmer than Chicago had been, but there was a light rain as she left the terminal. She took a cab into the city, and when they crossed the Williamsburg Bridge, she saw the skyline laid out before her like a scene from a movie or an implanted memory.

It wasn't her first trip to New York, and its grid system, like Chicago's, meant it wasn't difficult for her to find her way around. Big cities always instilled in Zoe a strange mix of exhilaration and anxiety. All these people crammed into the same small patch of land. The intermingling smells and sounds and the way the air tasted of burned electronics.

She had asked for accommodation as close to the FBI building as possible, and they'd booked her into the Wallace Hotel in Tribeca. Her room was on the eleventh floor; it was small but had all the necessities. She showered and changed into the new suit she had bought, then took the elevator down and walked the four blocks to her temporary place of work.

The FBI's New York field office was based in the Jacob K. Javits Building on Federal Plaza. Zoe had googled Javits after receiving the meeting request from Walker's people. He'd been a congressman and a senator, apparently.

The building looked a little like a cheese grater and rose forty-one stories into the congested Manhattan airspace. A building this tall would dominate most other cities on the planet; here, it just blended in with the crowd. There was a guard at the door in a dark blue uniform, but he didn't challenge Zoe as she went through the revolving door and into the foyer. She saw a row of turnstiles arched with metal detectors and a reception desk. The floor was tiled in white with a marbled effect, as were the walls. The signs were tastefully illuminated. To say it was a contrast to the station back in Granton would be like saying a Mercedes A-Class was a contrast to Zoe's five-year-old Toyota.

Zoe showed her ID to the receptionist and said she had an appointment with Special Agent Walker. The receptionist tapped on his keyboard, then searched for something underneath the overhang of the desk. His hand came out clutching a pile of lanyards and he sorted through them until he found the right one.

He held it out, and Zoe took it. It had her photograph and all her details on it. There was a light blue *Visitor* watermark over it, and she noticed the lanyard ribbon was red, unlike the white one worn by the receptionist and the woman she'd seen making a call by the door.

The receptionist stood up and pointed past the turnstiles to the elevator bank. "Go through security and up to twenty-three. Somebody will meet you there."

Zoe put her purse and her badge and her gun on the tray and walked through the metal detector. The gray-haired security guard there didn't respond to her *Good morning* and didn't offer anything other than a curt nod once she had passed through the machine.

She rode up in the elevator and took a deep breath when the tone pinged for the twenty-third floor. The doors opened, and a guy who looked to be in his mid-twenties was standing there. He had short, dark brown hair, glasses, a leather-bound notebook under one arm, and a cardboard coffee cup in his hand. He wore a blue shirt and a tie but no jacket. For a moment, Zoe thought he was just waiting for the elevator, but when she stepped out, he smiled and offered his free hand.

"Officer Hill, right?"

She shook it. "Zoe. Then I've got the right floor."

He swept his hand around. "You're early—welcome to hell." He turned back to her. "Matt Brodie." Zoe was surprised to hear what she thought was a British accent.

"You're an agent?"

"Analyst. It's my job to work out where this guy is going to hit next."

"That's all, huh? Maybe they don't need me."

Brodie flashed a grin and beckoned for her to follow him. He talked as he walked. "You picked a great time to join us. I've never seen anything like this, have you?"

"No," Zoe said, though she could have been talking about her immediate surroundings rather than the case.

The floor was open-plan, divided into cubicles. People were seated at their desks, working the phones, talking on video calls. Brodie led her down the aisle that cut through the center of the floor. There was an incredible view of the city to the south, though no one seemed to be hanging around appreciating it. Zoe could see the buildings of the Financial District, One World Trade Center towering above the rest. And beyond, the Statue of Liberty in the bay. Wisps of cloud threaded between the buildings like floating cotton candy.

"Great view."

"Yeah, it is, isn't it?" Brodie said, following her gaze. "You get used to it."

Brodie led her to one of the few unoccupied desks, in a corner where the view was blocked by a support pillar. There was a pile of papers and folders on the desk and a power cable but no computer.

"Shit." He cleared the stack of documents off the desk and placed them on the floor. "Sorry about this—you were supposed to have a laptop. Give me a second."

Brodie jogged back the way he had come, leaving Zoe alone amid the chatter and clatter of keyboards. She looked around at the people seated nearby, wondering if anyone was going to question whether she belonged here.

"Hey."

She turned toward the source of the voice and saw a dark-haired man wearing slightly tinted glasses sitting at a desk. He had on a headset with a mic and was evidently in the middle of a conversation. Zoe looked away, deciding he hadn't been talking to her, then looked back when he snapped his fingers.

He pointed at the stack of papers Brodie had moved from the desk and covered the mic on his headset. "Red folder. Quick."

There was a red folder a couple of items down. Zoe slid it out, careful not to topple the rest of the pile, held it up, and mouthed, *This one?*

The guy kicked his swivel chair forward so he was within arm's length of her, snatched the folder out of her hands, rolled himself back, and snapped it open.

"Let's see," he said, addressing the person on the call again as he leafed through the documents in the folder. "Okay, I got it. You got a pen?"

Zoe tuned the conversation out and hesitantly sat down at the desk in front of the pillar. Aside from the guy on the phone, no one seemed to have noticed her presence. She took out her phone and checked her emails. There was a meeting invite titled simply *Briefing*. The meeting had started half an hour ago in someplace called the Stipe Room. *Shit*. She got up and looked around for a sign or something.

"You okay?"

A woman with blond hair and red-framed glasses was walking past and heard Zoe curse.

"Yeah. I'm late for a meeting. You know where the"—she checked the message again—"the Stipe Room is?"

The blond woman pointed along the aisle, past the elevator banks, to the center of the floor. Zoe could see a wall of glass split into rooms. Some of the walls were transparent; some had opaque glass. "Second from the left."

Zoe started to move but stopped when she felt the woman's hand on her arm. "You're on the one-thirty-eight case?"

"I'm on loan from the Granton PD."

"Never seen anything like it," she said, echoing Brodie's words from a minute before. "That meeting doesn't start until noon, though. Did you lose an hour?"

Zoe realized the woman was right. She breathed a sigh of relief. "I guess my phone is still on central time."

The woman flashed her a quick smile. "You're not in Kansas anymore, huh?"

"Illinois," Zoe said, but the woman had already moved on, weaving nimbly past the seated agent on the phone.

GEHENNA

The Professor finished typing the last line, pulled the sheet out of the typewriter, and placed it next to the nine other pages he'd done today. It was still early. Some days the work dragged out until the wee hours of the morning; some days, like today, he was done before lunch. He resisted the temptation to keep working. The task was almost complete, and there was no point in rushing the job.

The sound of an engine overhead drew him to the window. He pulled the blind up and saw a small prop plane climbing from the west, about to pass over the house. Seen from up there, this would seem to be a deserted building, not worth anyone's attention. He wondered how long that would last.

He released the blind. The slats snapped back into place, cutting out the shaft of morning sunlight and plunging the room into its usual perma-twilight. The grandfather clock in the hall quietly chimed eight. Time for breakfast.

The Professor shuffled into the kitchen and prepared his usual breakfast: a single boiled egg with a pinch of salt. He made two mugs of black coffee and consumed everything quickly and efficiently at the small table with its single chair.

When he was done, he wiped his mouth with the back of his hand and deposited the dirty plate in the sink with the four others that had built up this week. When the sink was full, he would wash them. It was a simple system, like everything in his life.

The grandfather clock chimed the half hour as he was pushing his chair back in. He passed through the hallway again and returned to the back room.

The map on the board had four black pins in it. The Professor reached into the container on his desk and carefully selected a white pin.

He stopped moving when he heard a floorboard creak in the bedroom above. Noah, walking around in his room. The boy had been quieter than usual lately, but the Professor couldn't pretend that was a bad thing. There was too much work to be done; he didn't need any distractions.

The footsteps above moved across the room and then there was a bump as the boy settled in the chair in front of his window. There was no further sound.

The Professor traced his finger right to left across the map. The West Coast. He squinted until he found the name of the town.

Cresta Ranch, California.

Carefully, making sure he had just the right spot, he pushed the fifth pin in.

14

NEW YORK CITY

Managed to find something to keep yourself busy?"

Zoe looked up from her screen in surprise and forced a smile. "Special Agent Walker, hi."

Walker was dressed in a different suit than the one he had worn Sunday. Dark gray rather than black. He appeared to be relatively unharried, given the pressure he must be under.

Zoe was seated at the desk. Someone had found a laptop and she was navigating her way through account setup.

"I'm sorry I wasn't here to meet you," Walker said. "It's been a little hectic."

"Sure. I can imagine."

"You got five minutes before the meeting?"

There was a cafeteria three floors down, almost empty. Walker got them both coffee and they sat at one of the tables lining the east-facing windows. She could see the traffic crossing the Brooklyn Bridge from here, the cars looking like toys from this distance. Despite what Brodie had said, she didn't foresee a time when she would get used to the view. Walker paid as much attention to it as he would have a brick wall.

"Thanks for coming on board," Walker said.

She tore her eyes from the toy cars on the bridge. "What do you want me to do?"

Walker let out a short laugh. "That's a dangerous question to ask someone with more jobs to hand out than he has people to hand them out to. Right now, you're useful because you're a blank slate. What are your thoughts on this thing?"

Zoe froze for a second. Was he really expecting her to walk in with some kind of fresh insight into a case this unprecedented? And then she remembered Brodie's words—it was unprecedented for all of them.

"No one's seen anything like this," she said.

"That's for sure," Walker said.

"Maybe there's something in that, though," she continued. "Whoever's doing this got the idea somewhere, so maybe it's not so unique. I'd like to see if there's anything similar on the books, maybe not on the same scale, but . . . I don't know."

Walker's expression was hard to read, but he was listening. When he saw Zoe had finished, he said, simply, "Interesting." He checked his watch and looked back at her. "Any questions before I introduce you to the AD?"

Zoe asked the question that had been on her mind since eight o'clock Sunday evening. "Why me?"

He sipped his coffee and grimaced. "You want the cynical answer or the one that's going to make you feel wanted?"

"I want the answer that's true."

"Any case like this—not that there have been cases exactly like this—we need to make sure we have people from local police departments on the team. In theory, there are solid practical reasons for that. This killer is working across state lines, targeting relatively small communities so far. We need local knowledge, and having somebody who's worked one of these murders on the ground is going to be useful."

"In theory?" she repeated.

"To be completely honest, it isn't always useful, because it depends heavily on the person you get. Often, the kind of people who put themselves forward for the task force aren't the right candidates."

"In what way?"

Walker smiled. Zoe suspected he would have been happier if she hadn't asked for details.

"You didn't put yourself forward. The other guy did, your partner."

"Yelich?" Zoe was surprised. He hadn't said anything to her about that. But it suggested it hadn't been her imagination that he acted a little weird when she told him the news. "He's a good cop. You might have been better-off going with him."

Walker nodded. "More experienced, maybe more confident, right?"

"Yes."

"That's the problem. The guy who puts himself forward—and it usually *is* a guy—is confident and ambitious. You have to be to want to attach yourself to something this high stakes. But I've gone through this a lot of times, and confidence is important, but it's not the most important thing. I want someone who questions herself, who comes up with ideas, thinks out of the box. Someone who takes her time and notices things."

Zoe understood now. "The digital map pin."

"Yes. Your partner dismissed it when you showed it to him. The cops at both of the first two scenes missed it. That was understandable—it didn't really stick out, and they didn't know they were dealing with a series of killings. You spotted it, though. You knew it was important. Why?"

She considered. "It didn't fit with the rest of the room. It was too neat. It didn't look like something that the victim would have chosen as decor."

"There you go. That's both answers to your question. We needed to take somebody local for the task force because of politics. But we had a choice of somebodies, and you were at the top of the list."

Zoe filled her cheeks with air and blew out. "No pressure."

"Oh, there's enough of that to go around, trust me. You ready?"

"Let's go."

They went back upstairs, got Brodie, and made their way to Chapman's sparsely furnished office. There were only two chairs in front of her desk.

Walker took one of them. Brodie and Zoe exchanged a glance, then both stayed on their feet. If the other two noticed, they didn't comment.

"It's been three nights since Granton," Walker said. "I think it'll be tonight."

Billie Chapman straightened her jacket before she responded. "Not necessarily. The playing field is completely different now than it was on Saturday night. The publicity, the way security has been stepped up visibly—"

"He's factored it in," Walker said. "You read that report. He's not trying to do this under the radar. He knew it would be picked up at the third scene, so he made sure to carry out the fourth attack while we were still getting up to speed. He'll want to throw us another curveball to let us know who's in charge."

"You really think that, Ben? That he's in charge? Maybe I need to find somebody with a less defeatist mindset."

Walker didn't rise to the bait. "I'm talking about *his* mindset. He's controlling this game. That doesn't mean he gets to keep controlling it. I think we can use that cockiness against him."

"But in the meantime, we just sit on our hands and wait?"

"Of course not. We need to lock these targets down. Properly."

Chapman did not react to what sounded almost like an order. "I've taken a look at Brodie's list. He's going to have to be a little more specific. There are over a thousand apparently high-priority targets here, according to Mr. Brodie."

Brodie cleared his throat. "That's not an exhaustive list. We have . . ." He trailed off at a sharp look from Chapman.

"I'm not talking about the priority list," Walker said. "I'm talking about all of them."

"All of them? All seven thousand?"

"All of them," Walker said. "We need to evacuate people where possible. We need round-the-clock surveillance on every Main Street."

Chapman started to laugh, then left her mouth open as she realized he was serious.

"You know we can't do that. Even if I directly controlled the budget of every police department from here to Honolulu, we couldn't do that."

"We need to find a way to do it. You don't want to wait for another body? Well, that's what we need to do. Regular check-ins aren't going to cut it. It doesn't take a criminal mastermind to stake out a house and wait until the police car has driven around the corner. You need people parked out front and somebody else on the back door. At all these addresses. Until we narrow down where this guy is going to be next, we have to assume he can be anywhere."

Walker and Chapman locked eyes for what seemed like an eternity. "I'll see what I can do, but I can tell you now, I'm not going to get authorization for a full-court press. In the meantime, *you* need to see what *you* can do."

15

Walker looked like he wanted to punch a wall when they walked out of Chapman's office. He didn't raise his voice; he didn't say anything at all, in fact, but Zoe saw his hands clenching into fists as she tried to keep up with his long strides down the corridor.

They convened with some of the other members of the core task force in the ops room, which was on the southwest corner of the twenty-third floor. Walker got those in the room to briefly introduce themselves for Zoe's benefit. She nodded at each one, knowing she didn't have a hope in hell of remembering everyone's name.

Walker updated them on what Chapman had said in the meeting, putting it more diplomatically than Zoe sensed he wanted to, then started allocating tasks. He finished up by asking Zoe to talk through the crime scene at Granton from her perspective.

She described the scene as they had found it. She knew they had all read the full report and examined the photographs, but they would be interested in her impressions.

The other members of the task force asked some questions after she finished. The first was from a tall guy in an immaculately pressed shirt who introduced himself as Enrico Ferrera. He asked for clarification on the killer's entrance and exit routes. Zoe told him she agreed with Walker's theory, that the perpetrator had entered and exited by the back door and the front door had been deliberately left open to attract attention to the house. Without that, the body might have lain undiscovered for days.

Zoe answered some more questions and warmed a little as she realized they were taking what she said seriously, treating her as a peer, as someone who had something to offer.

"Bowman didn't have anything out of the ordinary in his history, did he?" Ferrera asked.

Zoe shook her head. "No, nothing that stuck out. Why?"

One of the other agents answered before Ferrera could. "It's Ferrera's theory. He thinks there's a targeted vic hidden among the random ones."

Ferrera shot him a look that had an edge of defensiveness. "It makes sense, right? You want to hide a book, you put it in a library."

"All of the victims are getting full background scrutiny," Walker said. "If there's a reason they might have been targeted other than the address, we'll find it."

When Zoe was done, Walker thanked her, handed her a file, and told her to work on what they had discussed earlier—finding similar cases, anything with an echo of the current case. She was pleased he had listened to her suggestion, but a part of her thought it seemed like the kind of job you handed to the newbie because there were limited opportunities for screwing up.

"There were six days between the first two killings," Walker said, wrapping up. "Eight days between the second and third. Only three days between the third and fourth. The next one is coming soon. I want us to be there to stop it. Go to it."

The meeting broke up. Zoe left with Brodie.

"You did all right in there," Brodie said.

"I don't need a pat on the head. How old are you anyway, twenty-five?"

"Twenty-nine," he said immediately, looking wounded. "In October," he finished. "Just saying, I know what it's like to be the new guy, so, you know . . ."

"When were you the new guy?"

He furrowed his brow as though thinking hard. "Sunday afternoon?"

She laughed despite herself.

"I've been with the Bureau for eighteen months now," he continued. "I worked trading-desk support for an investment bank before that. This seemed like it would be more interesting."

"How's it working out for you so far?"

"Well, sometimes I think you can get too interesting."

"So what exactly does an analyst do?"

"I'm looking for patterns, trying to predict the most high-risk targets."

"So I heard. What makes a particular target higher risk?"

His wince told Zoe that he hated being asked this question.

"It's not an exact science, but we take into account factors like population density, proximity to major highways, transport hubs. Normally, we'd like to assign higher risk to targets in the vicinity of confirmed prior incidents, but with the spread so far . . ."

"Doesn't sound like it's been easy to narrow down."

Brodie smiled, warming to his subject. "That's why it's so perfect."

"Perfect?" Zoe repeated, making a face. It wasn't the word she would have chosen.

"Yeah. The pattern is completely rigid, but the sheer numbers mean it's difficult for us to make any progress. Normally there are obvious reasons why a serial picks a particular location or victim, and the challenge is working that out. On this one, we know exactly why all of these victims were picked, but it doesn't get us anywhere. It's a really impressive setup."

"You sound like you're a big fan of this guy."

"Come on. You don't have to condone what he's doing to appreciate the design work here. And you have to admit, it's original."

"Seventy-six hundred Main Streets, huh? I never would have guessed there were that many."

"How many would you have guessed?"

She thought about it for a moment. "I don't know. You don't think about Main Streets, but they're everywhere."

"It's fascinating when you start to dig into it. Do you know that Main isn't even the most common street name in the country?"

"It's Second Street, I looked it up," Zoe said, pretending not to notice his disappointment. "But let's hope he sticks to Main."

"I think he will. It's the symbolism. I think that's the key aspect here. He's sending us a message. You know, striking at the heart of America. One of the symbols of America. What's more American than Main Street, USA?"

Zoe took a moment to savor the irony of a Brit lecturing her on American symbolism. "So what do you think he's trying to say? Maybe he's just some tourist who had a real bad day at Disneyland?"

"Maybe. It runs so deep through the culture. Disneyland, movies, literature, music . . . do you know how many songs there are named Main Street?"

Zoe considered. "I don't know. I can't think of any."

"Over three hundred. I put together a Spotify playlist. I like the Bob Seger one."

"You're really enjoying this, aren't you?"

He looked puzzled. "Of course I am. This is why I signed up. Why did you sign up for the police force?"

"Because I wanted to put bad guys away."

He considered this. "Whatever floats your boat, I guess." He pointed at the file in Zoe's hands. "What did Walker put you on?"

"Putting bad guys away."

"Really, though."

Zoe hesitated, then decided to open up. They were part of the same team, after all. "Actually, it was my suggestion, and it was inspired by something you said."

"Something *I* said?"

"I know; doesn't seem likely, does it?"

"What did I say?"

"You said you had never seen anything like this. I'm looking into cases that might be a little like this."

16

138 MAIN STREET

CRESTA RANCH, CALIFORNIA

It had been a hot day, so hot that the chrome guardrail on Chester Frohoff's balcony was still warm to the touch, though the sun had long since dipped beneath the tops of the trees on the other side of the park. The air was still redolent of citrus. On nights like this—most nights, in fact—he missed having someone to sit with in the open air.

Chester had welcomed the policeman and the lady from the security company into his house earlier in the day. He had read about the killings in that morning's *Orange County Register* and noted the coincidence of the address with mild interest before flipping to the crossword.

He was a little surprised to receive a personal police visit. After all, the murders had happened a very long way from here, and even if this person was targeting people who happened to live at the same address as he did, there had to be a million other Main Streets.

Chester ordered out for dinner. He had never been much of a cook, and he knew his late wife, Barbara, would probably disapprove of how often he picked up the phone and ordered pizza from Mario's.

Around ten, Chester made his last rounds before the evening's movie.

He opened a beer and set it on the kitchen counter, his one beer of the evening. Any more than one and he would be pissing like a racehorse all night. He put some popcorn into the microwave, went out into the yard, and turned on the light. Barb's chickens clucked at the interruption to their routine. After he'd changed their water and scattered some seeds around, he went back to the house to drink his beer in front of TCM. Tonight's movie was *In the Heat of the Night*, followed by the original *Thing from Another World*.

He watched both of them, fighting sleep to make it to the end of the latter.

Widowerhood wasn't so bad, really. Barb would have talked all through the first movie, and she hated horror flicks. A good book was more her speed. No, it wasn't so bad, except for the loneliness.

Chester checked all the locks, as the police had told him to do, then turned off the lights. Through the window, he saw one of the security company's black-and-red SUVs drive by, slowing a little as it passed his house. He climbed the stairs, reminding himself that he should really get somebody in to see about that fifth stair, which always creaked.

He brushed his teeth, changed into his pajamas, got into bed, then turned off the lamp and closed his eyes. In the distance he could hear the low hum of traffic on the parkway, just far enough away to be soothing.

In the yard, one of the chickens clucked at something. Probably next door's cat, testing the chicken wire again. It was secure; Chester had checked that just as carefully as he had checked that his own coop was secure.

Typical—now that he was in bed, he didn't feel tired anymore.

Chester knew better than to try to sleep when his mind was still working away. Thinking about Barb, about the visit from the cops earlier. He switched the light back on. Barb's to-read pile was still in her bedside drawer. Mysteries and historical romances, mostly. He picked up one with a black-and-white cover that looked intriguing. *Shroud for a Nightingale* by P. D. James. He started reading. He was a slow reader, but it was a ritual he had gotten into on those nights when he didn't feel tired enough to sleep. He thought Barb would approve of him working his way through her unread books.

He had just finished chapter 2 when he heard a sound closer than the parkway. Closer even than the chickens.

It was the sound of the fifth stair creaking.

PART 2

Wednesday

17

NEW YORK CITY

"The victim was the homeowner, Chester John Frohoff. Seventy-six years old, widowed. He lived alone."

Walker rubbed the bridge of his nose and took a moment. The agent on Walker's laptop screen, Jason Wozniak, was more than two and a half thousand miles away in an affluent planned community in the south of Orange County.

Five years ago, Walker would have been in the air on the way to the scene by now. This was the first time he had run the task force on a major investigation where new crime scenes were popping up so far apart from one another, it made sense for the local field office to get agents on the scene early and report back. There might be cause for him to travel to California later on, but in the meantime he knew he could rely on the people on the ground.

"Where the hell were the local cops? Did this guy just fall through the cracks?"

"I just talked to the local PD," Wozniak said. "They visited the victim yesterday afternoon around two. Went through everything with him, did the security checks. This is a gated community, so I spoke to the local security outfit as well."

Walker understood immediately. "So we had two sets of people responsible for looking after Mr. Frohoff, which means that—"

"No one was responsible," Wozniak said at the same time as Walker.

"Shit."

"Yeah. The local cops say the company got a little territorial and wanted to keep it to themselves. The manager I spoke to at Max Security says that's bullshit. She thought they were both stepping up patrols."

"He said, she said."

"I don't know that it would have made a difference," Wozniak continued. "I took a look at the logs, and both parties made more runs than usual on Main last night. The gates have license plate recognition; no unauthorized vehicles came through. The killer must have come in on foot and picked his moment carefully. There are cameras but nothing like blanket coverage."

Walker could picture the killer finding a vantage point to watch the patrols, biding his time. "Patrols aren't going to do it, are they?"

Walker had suspected as much when he spoke to Chapman yesterday. An increased visible police presence on the street was effective in preventing opportunistic crime but not something as carefully planned as this. The killer would have anticipated the extra patrols and simply watched and waited for a gap. Hell, he could have been inside the house when the cops or the security company drove past and there would have been no outward sign of anything wrong.

"We need round-the-clock surveillance," he said, thinking aloud. "Somebody watching, not just a patrol."

Wozniak's pained expression told Walker that he was glad he wouldn't be the one trying to explain that to whoever controlled the budgets. "That would be my recommendation too, sir."

"Let's hope they listen to us," Walker said, knowing it was a vain hope.

He looked at the other people in the room. Zoe Hill, Brodie, and Ferrera were standing behind him, eyes fixed on the small screen. They had two people en route to California. Walker wanted to make sure at least one member of the core team was at every scene. For now, they would see it via Wozniak and the video feed.

"Okay, take us through the scene."

The image tilted as Wozniak picked up his phone and started walking. He flipped the camera direction, held the phone in front of him, and progressed slowly. It reminded Walker of the opening Steadicam shot in *Halloween*. Except that scene showed the killing in progress, not the aftermath.

These virtual walk-throughs had become more common in recent years. It was no substitute for actually being there, for using all five senses and seeing it in three dimensions, but it was a hell of a lot better than just a report and photographs. Wozniak's disembodied voice came from off-screen as he walked across a neatly kept street lined with citrus trees and approached a house flanked by police vehicles.

"I'll take you up to the primary scene first, but this isn't the route the perpetrator took. He got in via the back."

Wozniak passed a uniformed cop, who gave him a mildly resentful glance, and climbed the terra-cotta-tiled steps that led up to the front yard of 138 Main. The plots on the street were about ten feet above the level of the road, presumably to provide the houses with a better view of the park. The house was large, though not ostentatiously so.

"The security company carried out a welfare call at eight a.m. There was no answer, so they sent an officer down to knock on the door. No answer again, so they went around the back and found the lock busted and the alarm disabled."

Walker made a mental note to consider the possibility of inside involvement on this one. The killer knew what he was doing, managing to bypass several layers of security.

Wozniak was inside now, approaching a staircase. The camera became less steady as he started climbing. There would be a more professional recording later done by a field photographer, but this would give Walker a good feel for the layout of the house. He heard Wozniak's shoes clicking on the bare wood of the stairs; one of the steps creaked. At the half landing, he turned around.

"The victim is in the bedroom," Wozniak said.

"Nice place," Zoe remarked as Wozniak's camera caught some artwork on the wall and an expensive-looking bronze sculpture on the spacious landing, which was floored in parquet with a Persian rug over it.

There was a king-size bed. The bedroom was large enough that the bed wasn't against a wall but in the center of the room. The victim was half under the covers. Chester Frohoff had a thin face with wispy gray-white hair on his crown and a neat beard that was a darker gray. He wore checkered pajamas. One arm was dangling over the edge of the bed and the other hand was resting on his chest, as though he were recovering from a sudden shock. Walker guessed there had been a sudden shock but not the kind you recover from.

Slowly, deliberately, as though he were a movie director composing one of the key shots that would be in the trailer, Wozniak panned down so the camera was pointing at the floor immediately in front of the bed.

The carpet was thick and light gray. There was a bloody print on the carpet—in the shape of a digital map pin.

"His signature seems to be getting bigger," Walker said. It looked as though this print was three or four feet in diameter.

Wozniak moved the camera to focus on a blood-drenched pillow that had been tossed onto the foot of the bed. "He must have brought some kind of stencil with him, then used the pillow to make the print."

"A stencil?" Zoe asked, leaning closer to the screen.

"It's bigger than the mark in Granton," Walker commented. He raised his voice so the agent on the scene would know he was addressing him. "I don't suppose he left the stencil on the scene?"

"We haven't found anything like that so far," Wozniak said.

Interesting. And a potential opportunity. The killer might have tossed the stencil after leaving the house or he might have kept it on his person. Walker didn't think it would be the latter. It was too much of a risk, keeping something heavily stained with the blood of the man you had just killed.

"It's not garbage day today, is it?"

Wozniak answered immediately. "It's tomorrow. We're checking Frohoff's trash, the neighbors', all the street cans."

"Good work. Can you get in closer to the body for me?"

Wozniak complied. There were two gunshot wounds. "One in the chest, one in the head," Wozniak said.

Walker noticed there was a rip in the fabric of the pajama shirt. He asked Wozniak about that.

"Looks like a strip has been removed," Wozniak said. "No sign of the strip here, so we think the perp took it with him. A trophy or something."

That was new. Or perhaps it wasn't. The killer could have taken less obvious items from the other scenes. Walker watched as the camera panned back up to the body. He had been shot in the middle of the forehead.

Wozniak answered a few more of Walker's questions. Zoe hadn't asked anything, but she was listening intently. After that, Wozniak took them downstairs and out into the backyard, retracing the killer's steps. The side yard had a locked gate, and the security camera out front hadn't picked up anyone coming in that way. It was likely the killer had accessed the property via the backyard of the house behind this one.

The back door had been opened using a snap gun, a tool used by law enforcement and locksmiths. It wasn't a finesse job. The gun had destroyed the lock, rendering the door incapable of closing. The use of the tool showed that he had come prepared, once again. As did the fact that the killer knew how to disable the alarm.

Walker thanked Wozniak, ended the call, and looked at the other three.

A protracted silence filled the conference room. Walker noticed Zoe glancing at Ferrera to see if he was going to say something. When he didn't, she spoke.

"I don't think we were ever going to stop this one, boss. He's been planning a long time. We're still playing catch-up."

"I told you, you don't have to call me boss, Zoe. We're a team."

Walker looked up at the television on the wall, which, as usual, was tuned to CNN. The sound was muted, but they could see a blond female reporter standing outside the California house on Main. She was speaking as the ticker rolled by at the bottom of the screen.

At least one confirmed dead in latest Main Street attack. FBI says . . .

"This thing is going to go nuts," Ferrera commented.

"He was making a point," Zoe said. "He knew we were hoping the surveillance would scare him off. He's telling us he's not scared."

"He's also telling us he can be anywhere," Walker said. "He found a Main Street about as far west as he could go—"

"Actually," Brodie cut in, "there's a—"

"Yes, I'm sure there's a bunch farther west than that," Walker snapped. "The point is, he's making sure we know just how big the playing field is. How's he traveling? If it's by air, we might get somewhere. We can look at passengers flying out of airports within a hundred-mile radius of Cresta Ranch, cross-reference those with anybody who's been in Illinois or New York recently."

"If he's smart—" Zoe began.

"Yes, if he's smart, he won't be flying. Or he'll drive out of the locale and fly from there to wherever he's going next. But we check everything: planes, trains, and automobiles. Look at rentals. Let's come up with a match somewhere. Five times now. He's leaving a trail even if he doesn't know it. We just can't see it yet."

18

138 MAIN STREET

CHARLESTOWN, MASSACHUSETTS

The officer who conducted Cally's follow-up security visit was named Franklin. So far, he had tested Cally's newly installed alarm, examined her locks and windows, and made a couple of recommendations. He went out back and examined the retractable ladder on the bottom of the second-floor platform of the fire escape and made sure the mechanism to drop it could be accessed only from the platform, not from ground level. He noted the plastic drainpipe that ran up the height of the building and passed one of Cally's windows but decided it was too flimsy to support the weight of anyone heavier than a child. He didn't seem worried at all, which made Cally feel a little better. And then he spoiled it.

"They'll pick him up next time he tries anything. Unless he's smart enough to quit before he gets caught."

That idle comment unnerved Cally in a way she couldn't quite explain. The cop must have noticed something in her expression, because he broke into a reassuring grin.

"I really wouldn't worry. We're going to be watching, because better safe than sorry, but this isn't the kind of place that's going to be a target."

"How do you mean?"

"I have ten years of experience working B and E. You learn to think like these assholes, pardon my French. They go for easy targets. Ground-floor or basement apartments, unlocked doors, old locks. This place?" He looked around her modest living room. "This is pretty safe. You're on the top floor."

"So you think the guy who lives downstairs has more to worry about?"

Officer Franklin looked awkward and cleared his throat. "Ah, I was meaning to tell you."

"Tell me what?" Cally asked, bracing herself for more bad news.

"The man in apartment A moved out yesterday. He's gone to stay with his girlfriend."

"Oh," Cally said. "So . . . that makes this the only occupied apartment in the building?"

Franklin spoke quickly, realizing the effect the news had had. "Trust me, this place probably isn't on the list."

She thought about telling him that she had read up on the other murders and apparently had paid more attention than he had. She knew that security systems seemed to be no barrier. That poor family in Long Island had had their security system disabled, and so had the latest victim in California.

As the cop was leaving, she remembered the guy she had seen across the street the other day. At the time, she had barely noticed.

Franklin listened patiently as she told him about returning from her run and seeing the guy who might have been staring up at her apartment window, though she couldn't be certain.

"What did he look like?"

This was the frustrating part. "I wish I had paid more attention. I'm kind of face-blind—I don't really remember things about people unless they're really distinctive. This guy wasn't."

"You remember if he was white? Black? What was he wearing?"

"He was white. Clothes . . . I don't know." She closed her eyes and tried to dredge up an image. "Oh, it was a uniform. Like a baseball cap and a brown jacket with a green logo on the shoulder. I think the logo had a number in it. He looked like a maintenance guy, I guess."

"Any idea of age?"

"Not old, not young. Sorry, I know this is really vague."

"Sounds like it didn't make much of an impression. 2Gen have uniforms like that, so he was probably just on a job in the neighborhood."

"I mean, he made enough of an impression for me to notice him, but it just didn't feel important at the time. I only really thought about it later."

"It was probably nothing. I don't blame you for worrying, though. You know how many Main Streets there are in the Boston metro area?"

"No."

"Sixteen. Who knew? There's a one thirty-eight on all of those Main Streets, and in all of those homes, there's someone who thinks they saw somebody suspicious in the past couple of days."

Cally's face burned with embarrassment. "I'm sorry, forget about it."

Franklin grinned, misunderstanding. "It's no problem. All I'm saying is, it's natural to jump at shadows."

When he left, Cally checked her locks and tried calling Melissa again. There was no answer.

19

NEW YORK CITY

The core team spent the next few hours cooped up in the relatively spacious ops room on the twenty-third floor. It was a lot more comfortable than the cramped office back at the station in Granton, but Zoe had to suppress a nagging feeling of claustrophobia.

They went over the five kill scenes again, looking for . . . something. Any clue to the motivation behind these senseless acts—138 Main Street times five. What message was the killer trying to send?

"Maybe it's some kind of childhood-trauma thing," Ferrera suggested. "Like something happened to him at that address somewhere, and this is his way of . . . I don't know, punishing the world?"

"I read that scenario from the profiler too," Walker said. "I don't know. The killings aren't rage-fueled. He makes sure they're dead, but he doesn't stab them four hundred times and burn the house down. They're more like targeted hits. Except that we know for sure the victims are random because they're chosen purely by address."

But they would keep the theory in mind, because every theory had to be considered. They had people looking for past crimes tied to that address. So far, nothing. Widening it out to include crimes committed anywhere on a Main Street gave them too much to work with. What if the theory was right, though, that something had happened at a 138 Main, but the crime had never been reported? What if the subject had no direct connection to the address; what if it had belonged to a relative or a friend?

Ferrera's book-in-a-library suggestion was getting some play too. They were looking into the backgrounds of all the victims. This morning had added another name to the list, but so far, it didn't look like Chester John Frohoff had made any notable enemies in his seven and a half decades.

"Maybe the real target hasn't been hit yet," Zoe suggested.

Walker shook his head. "No. If you're trying to disguise a targeted murder by hiding it in a series, you make sure it's one of the early ones. Not the first, but in the first few."

They went back to the master list of Main Streets in the USA. Brodie put it on the big screen and scrolled down. He sorted it alphabetically by town. He sliced the data by population size and by voting patterns and by date of founding and a multitude of other characteristics. Nothing seemed to differentiate the five targets from any of the others.

"The genius of it is," Brodie began, sounding a little more impressed than Zoe thought was appropriate in the circumstances, "that you've got one common detail. Apart from that, everything else is up for grabs. It cuts across geography, social class, demographics . . . You've got people on welfare and you've got millionaires, and the only thing they have in common is they all have the same first line of their address. And so far, we've seen only residential places hit. Most Main Streets are commercial. On this list there's bookstores, delis . . . a police station in Minnesota."

"Maybe we should hope he picks that one next," Zoe said.

"If he sticks to the nighttime routine, most of the nonresidential addresses are safe, because nobody's there at night," Walker said. "We can focus on the homes. We need to find a way to stake out these places twenty-four hours a day. Maybe we can move some of the higher-risk residents."

"What if we move them and he goes after them someplace else?"

"I don't see it," Walker said. "The game has rules. It's always one thirty-eight Main. I don't think the victim is important to him. They aren't people, they're . . ."

"What?"

"Materials. Like an artist. He's using them in his design. Who they are doesn't matter. *Where* they are is everything."

GEHENNA

The Professor awoke to the sound of the birds. Morning feeding time? No, twilight. How could he have slept so late? Time seemed to pass so quickly these days.

He took a moment to completely come to, then sat on the edge of his bed, waiting for the grogginess to subside. He used the bathroom, then realized how dehydrated he was. He went to the kitchen, filled a glass from the faucet, and drained it in one gulp. It was lukewarm and failed to provide the refreshment he wanted. He filled the glass again and took it with him to the study.

The completed pages were in a neatly squared stack on the desk next to the typewriter, an oversize snow globe sitting atop it as a paperweight. The sheet in the typewriter was half-finished. He didn't like to stop in the middle of a page like that, but last night the exhaustion had overcome him. He read the last few lines.

> Some will call us terrorists. History shows that the elites will use every trick to smear, besmirch, and deny those who threaten their world order. History shows that today's terrorists may be tomorrow's heroes. Will we be judged thus? Perhaps it is too early to say.

The rest had done him good; he knew what had to come next. Before he sat down, he laid a hand on top of the stack of pages and closed his eyes, enjoying the tangibility of what he had created.

People today had no appreciation for the tangible. Everything was ephemeral. Insubstantial. Unreal.

Something about that made him think of those who had stood on this spot before him. All the people who had lived in the house before he and the boys had found it, before it had become their Gehenna.

Most people never thought of a home's previous occupants beyond vague antipathy for the prior owner who had chosen that wallpaper or those kitchen appliances. The Professor had a full list of everyone who had occupied this house since it was built in the spring of 1892. Their names, their occupations. Birth and death dates. Where they lived after moving on from the house. People were ephemeral too. Soon he would also be gone, and there would be no more caretakers.

20

NEW YORK CITY

Zoe had finished going through the list of historical cases she had pulled from NCIC and come up with nothing but dead ends. The most promising lead had been the Wheeler case in Detroit, but even that had gone nowhere.

In the late 1990s, four women and one man had been murdered over a two-year span. The killings were home invasions, like the 138 Main killings, and there was also a strong specificity to the locations. Every one of the victims lived on a numbered street. The first victim had lived on Twelfth Street. Victims two and three were found dead a few months later in their home on Fourteenth Street. The last two had been killed on Tenth Street and Thirteenth Street, respectively, seven months apart. The killings hadn't made waves in the media at the time, probably because they were spaced out over a long period and because they hadn't been linked until a suspect—a transient named Luther Wheeler—was arrested.

Zoe followed up but found the detective who worked the case had died a few years back. Even if he were still around, talking to him would have been a waste of time, because she had been able to establish that Luther

Wheeler, now in his late seventies, was still incarcerated and therefore had a solid alibi for the current killings.

And there were still hundreds upon hundreds of Main Streets that had to be checked out in the vain hope that something useful might present itself. She wondered how much time anyone had for doing more than a cursory check of each one.

Walker had asked the analysts to break down the gigantic list of 138 Main Streets into four-page segments, each segment was assigned to a team of two. The teams would work through each list, gather as much intelligence on each address as possible, and try to thin out the numbers by identifying higher-risk targets.

Zoe's brain was well and truly fogbound by now. She had to get out of the building. Maybe a change of scene would help.

Walker told her it was fine to go. "We don't chain people to their desks anymore. That practice stopped around 2015, if memory serves."

Zoe printed out her assigned portion of the master list and took it to a small coffee shop on Worth Street with dark blue subway tiles and wood tables. The rich scent of arabica made a comforting contrast with the scentless, conditioned air of the office. Zoe took a booth by the back wall and laid her paperwork out.

She spent the next hour going through the list, checking details, making notes in the margins. When she completed her first pass, she glanced at her phone and saw that there was a text from Brodie asking where she was. She tapped out a reply. Five minutes later she saw him through the window; he tossed a milkshake cup into the nearest trash container and entered the coffee shop. He had a laptop satchel over one shoulder.

"Get done with your homework?" he asked as he approached the booth where Zoe was sitting.

She laughed. "Ask me again in about forty years. You have a smudge." She touched her hand to her top lip in the place Brodie had a smear of chocolate milkshake. He wiped it off with the back of his hand and sat down opposite her.

"They checked the trash around Frohoff's place. No sign of any stencil. They turned up something else, though. A phone."

Zoe leaned forward. "A phone? Like, a burner? You think—"

"We don't know. They processed it in double time. No prints, which is suspicious in itself, and it was only used once as far as they can tell. It made a call to a number three days ago, and that number is no longer active."

"Nothing to say it's his, then," Zoe said. "I bet if you subject the trash cans on most streets to that kind of intensive search, you'll find a burner or two."

"Yeah, that's what they said. There's only one thing that makes me think it could be the killer's."

"What?"

"It was switched on only twice. Once yesterday, when it pinged a cell tower a couple miles from Frohoff's place. The other time was a week ago in Kansas City, Missouri."

"Kansas City," Zoe repeated. "Pretty far from SoCal. There hasn't been a killing in Missouri, though."

"Not yet," Brodie said. "I don't know, could be nothing to do with our guy, but . . . I think it's worth looking at. I don't think you get many people chucking their burner phones in the bin in a neighborhood like that."

"In the bin," Zoe repeated, smiling.

Brodie shrugged. "You can take the boy out of Blighty, et cetera."

That reminded Zoe of a question she had been meaning to ask him. "How did you get here, anyway? I thought you had to be a US citizen to join the FBI."

Brodie shot her a wounded look. "I'll have you know I'm as American as apple pie and country music."

"Really?"

He nodded. "Naturalized citizen. My parents moved us over here when I was fifteen. My wife—ex-wife, actually—is a New Yorker. Thought I might as well become a Yank when we got married. In for a penny, in for a pound, right? Anyway, as it turned out the citizenship lasted longer than the marriage, but the FBI was happy enough to let me in."

"Must be weird, though, being an outsider." Immediately, she wondered if that was the right word, but Brodie didn't seem to take offense.

"I think it helps," Brodie said. "I see patterns you might not because you've lived with them your whole life. I'm a fresh pair of eyes, relatively speaking. Though, to be honest, I feel that advantage is waning a little. The other day I even used the word *faucet*."

Zoe laughed. She knew what he meant, too, even though her own outsider status was a little less obvious. "So the burner was used in Kansas City. Do they have a one thirty-eight Main in KC?"

"Yep," Brodie said, looking vexed. "But it's an office building, not the kind of place he's been hitting so far. Nobody's going to be there at night."

"We know he likes to mix things up. Maybe there's a janitor or somebody who always works late there."

"I'm going to talk to the police out there," he said. He didn't sound too hopeful, and Zoe knew why. Even *if* the phone had been discarded by the killer and *if* he had been in Kansas City and *if* he was planning to strike there, the target didn't sound like a strong possibility. A lot of ifs in that chain, and every lead they chased down was more time burned.

The waitress drifted over, a different one from the one who had served Zoe at the counter when she came in. Zoe ordered another coffee and Brodie opted for a chocolate milkshake.

"Another?" Zoe said, raising an eyebrow as the silent waitress turned and departed.

"I don't drink caffeine," Brodie said. He waved a hand at his throat. "I get a swelling."

"You're going to be getting a swelling around your waist if you replace it with chocolate."

He tapped a finger to his temple. "The white heat of intellectual exercise. Burns calories."

"Whatever you say. Where are you at on the list?"

Brodie considered. "I have a few that stick out, but most of them . . . most of them you can't rule out. Even setting aside the most geographically isolated ones doesn't help, and I'm not sure we can rely on that as an indicator anyhow. Part of the problem is it's easy to see patterns where there aren't any; it's hardwired into us as humans."

The killings had ranged far and wide, but they were all in the contiguous United States and all had occurred within thirty miles of a major airport or interstate, so addresses that fell within similar distances were assigned higher priority.

The problem, as Brodie quickly pointed out, was that the thirty-mile rule didn't exclude all that many addresses. Sure, there were towns in rural Wyoming where every street but Main Street was a dirt track, and a person would have to drive a hundred miles to get a cell phone signal, but the overwhelming majority of Main Streets were within a thirty-mile radius of an airport or an interstate or both.

"I never really thought about how connected this country is," Zoe said. "Everybody talks about how big America is, and, yeah, that's part of our problem. But another part of it is how small it is too, if you know what I mean. How easy it is to move around."

"That's what I was talking about earlier. You don't think about that kind of thing because you're so used to it. Where I come from, it can take you a couple of hours to travel fifty miles in the countryside. You can thank President Eisenhower for this country's connectivity," Brodie said. "That's what the interstate program was about. Spreading out. Being able to move troops anywhere in the country if you needed them in a hurry."

"For real?" Zoe asked.

Brodie nodded. "Suburbanization too. Urban sprawl. People talk about it like it's an accident or an organic thing, but it was deliberate policy."

"Why?"

"Think about it. You want to attack a country as big as this one, how do you do it?"

She considered. "Back then, if we're talking about the Soviet Union, they'd use nukes, right?"

"Right. And where would they drop those nukes?"

Zoe caught up. "Cities. The interstates were to spread people out."

Brodie nodded again. "The people and the infrastructure."

"Makes sense."

"It does make sense if you're trying to ensure that a nuclear war is survivable and that you're able to move ground troops from place to place quickly. But it means Mr. One Thirty-Eight has a lot of easily reachable targets from which to choose."

Brodie searched around in his satchel, pulled out a map, and flattened it on the table. It was covered in fine pencil annotations. "I mean, think about it. Let's say for the sake of argument that this guy can fly and isn't worried about being tagged on too many of the wrong flights. Say he bases himself here." He stabbed his thumb down in the bottom right of the map. "Atlanta, Georgia. Atlanta International is the busiest airport in the world. From here, he can reach any state in the union within a matter of hours."

"I don't think he's flying," Zoe said. "You need ID, you can't carry weapons. It's too regulated."

"You need ID, but it's not like you need a passport. You can pick up a convincing driver's license for a few hundred dollars. That doesn't go through the same checks. As long as the picture looks like you and the name matches the one on the booking, Bob's your uncle. If this guy's smart, he has a pile of fake driver's licenses."

"But he isn't necessarily flying. Three days minimum between each killing so far. He could be driving."

"And the interstate makes that easy. All he has to do is rent different cars outside of the hunting grounds, and he doesn't even have to worry about toll roads or security cameras at gas stations. There's too much noise. Too much traffic, literally."

Zoe's phone buzzed.

"Your boyfriend?" Brodie asked, craning his head to see the name on the caller ID.

"My mom," Zoe said irritably.

She took the phone outside before she answered. "Is everything okay?"

Mary Ann Hill's voice sounded strained, weak: "I barely slept a wink last night worrying about you."

Zoe sighed and tried to be patient. "I've spent the past day and a half between a hotel room and a desk. A couple of hours ago I got *really* adventurous and went to a coffee shop."

"I'm just concerned for my daughter," she said, bridling.

"I know, Mom."

"Beth from next door came around last night. She says Randy is getting worked up again. He slept in a lawn chair out front with his gun last night."

"Are you serious?"

"Deadly serious. He was out there from dusk till dawn."

Randy Lawler was an eighty-two-year-old retired National Guardsman and basically the town drunk, despite some stiff competition. She made a mental note to call Dave Yelich later so that he could politely advise Randy not to drink and carry weapons.

"He doesn't need to worry, really."

"Everyone's worried," her mother said quietly. "It's all anyone can think about. A thing like that happening here."

"I know. But the one thing we know is whoever is doing this is targeting Main Streets across the entire country. He's already been there, so Granton is just about the safest town in America right now."

She kept talking, and by the end of the conversation, she sensed she had managed to calm her mother's nerves a little. She wound up the call by telling her mom that her boss wanted to speak to her.

They said their goodbyes and she hung up. What she said was true, wasn't it? There was no way the killer would go back to Granton. Even if he did, there was no one to kill at 138 Main Street anymore. It was a hollow shell. Spent. Discarded.

Safe. Was it really true? Was it true for any of them?

21

As Zoe walked back to her hotel, the sun burned down through the pollution. A WABC-TV helicopter passed high overhead, the chatter of the rotors drowned out by the traffic noise. She felt a pang of envy, thinking about how nice it would be to be up there, above it all. At street level, the city was an assault on the senses—the people, the noise, the clamminess. She could feel the heat radiating up from steel drain covers, and the sweet scent of garbage hung around the mouth of every alley she passed. She took her jacket off, already feeling sweat gather in the small of her back barely a block after she had left the air-conditioned bubble of the coffee shop.

Her phone buzzed in her pocket as she was approaching the hotel. She quickened her pace and stepped into the welcome chill of the lobby as she answered.

"Is this Special Agent Hill?" The speaker had a husky voice with a Midwestern accent, and somehow she could tell from five words that he was a cop.

"This is Zoe Hill, but actually, I'm not—"

"This a good time to talk?"

"Sure. Who am I speaking to?"

"This is Lieutenant Perlenbacher, Detroit PD. I understand you were looking to speak to Detective Carlson about the Wheeler case."

The Wheeler case? It took Zoe a second to figure out what he was talking about. She had made a lot of calls over the past day and a half, run up against a lot of dead ends. Then she remembered: the serial killer who had targeted random victims living on Detroit's numbered streets in 1997 and 1998.

"That's right," she said. "I was sorry to hear Detective Carlson passed."

"I have his former partner here if you'd like to speak to him."

Zoe wasn't sure that would do any good, but it probably wouldn't do any harm either. "Sure, that would be great."

"Actually, do you mind if we do a video call? I'd like to sit in."

Zoe told him that was fine but asked him to give her a couple of minutes to get to her room. She rode up to the eleventh floor in the elevator, rushed into her hotel room, and hurried to her desk as she pulled her laptop out of her backpack. When she opened it up, she saw an email with a link from Lieutenant Perlenbacher. She clicked on the link, shivering as the AC chilled the sheen of sweat on the back of her neck. A minute later, she was looking at two male cops sitting in front of a cinder-block wall. They were both in suits, hunched close together to fit into the camera frame.

The one on the left was in his early forties and was slim with sandy-colored hair and glasses. The man on the right was a little older. He had dark hair that was going gray around the sides and a wide frame. Zoe knew to look beyond the surface with cops, and the vibe she got was an administrator and a bruiser. They all exchanged the obligatory small talk, and the older cop introduced himself as Perlenbacher and the other one as Detective Edward Stoll, who had been the late John Carlson's partner.

"Right, John Carlson was primary on the Luther Wheeler case," Zoe said, glancing at the notes she had made the previous day.

"I didn't work the case," Stoll said. "Before my time. I'm afraid John passed two years ago."

"Yeah, the guy I spoke to yesterday told me. I was sorry to hear that."

"Too young," Perlenbacher said. Stoll didn't add anything. Even through a screen, Zoe could sense he didn't want to be there. He was sitting back a little compared to his superior, his hands clasped on the desk in front of him. His whole manner reminded her uncomfortably of the way Yelich had acted the last time they spoke. Like her membership to the club had been revoked.

"So, we wondered how we could help you," Perlenbacher said. "Like Ed says, the case was before his time, but John told him a lot about it."

"Okay, well, like I said, it's not exactly glamour city on this one-thirty-eight thing. You know all about it, I don't need to tell you—"

Perlenbacher cut in, waving his hand. "Oh, no, you can tell us."

She guessed that answered one question; they wanted to know about the case. Whatever; it wouldn't do any harm to humor them. Maybe a couple of fresh pairs of ears would help.

"They've got the analysts working on it. We got seven thousand Main Streets, which means about seven million lines of inquiry. This isn't the kind of thing I'm used to, and between you and me"—she leaned in, hoping to get them on her side with a conspiratorial lowering of her voice—"it's not the kind of thing *they're* used to either. The feds handle complex crimes and homicides with a wide geographic spread but not usually in one case. One of the things they've been looking into is historical crimes that bear some kind of relation to this one."

"Which is why you were looking at Wheeler."

"Right," Zoe said. "Very little chance this is related, but I got a list to go through and—"

"Wheeler isn't unsolved," Stoll said, interrupting. "Tried and convicted. Been cooling his heels in Ionia since 1999." He folded his arms and stared at the camera.

"I know," Zoe said. She hesitated, trying to choose her words as carefully as possible. "I just wanted to ask you guys if—"

Stoll's facial expression hardened. "If John got it wrong?"

"She doesn't mean that, Ed," Perlenbacher said. Stoll shot a look of mild irritation at his superior.

"Oh God, no," Zoe said quickly. "Not at all. I spent some time reading up on the case and the trial." An exaggeration. She had skimmed it. "It was solid. Your old partner killed it."

"Appeals were struck down in record time," Stoll said, not unfolding his arms.

"Right. I have no doubt he got the right guy. And there isn't any kind of link between that and this. Different MO and all the rest. That's not why I wanted to talk to Carlson. And you, of course."

Perlenbacher put a hand on Stoll's arm. "I don't think she was casting any aspersions on John. What do you want to know, Zoe?"

"I just have a few questions."

She ran through a series of questions about the case, clarifying details. Stoll and Perlenbacher between them had a pretty good grasp of the case, though the latter was far more forthcoming than the former.

She hesitated before asking her final question.

"One other thing I was wondering. The psychiatrist at the trial said Wheeler had some kind of obsession with numbers, and that explains why he targeted those streets, why he took trophies. I'm thinking about the victim at Tenth Street. You said part of his shirt was torn off, taken away. A strip of clothing was taken from the victim at one of the scenes recently."

Zoe was going slightly out on a limb here. That detail had not been released to the press, but she hoped she was keeping on the right side of things by omitting the specific location from where the clothing strip had been taken.

Stoll shrugged. "That's in no way unusual. Wheeler took trophies from all the scenes."

"I read that," Zoe said. "Door numbers, keys, things like that. The clothing seems different. More personal, maybe."

The two men exchanged a glance.

"I just wondered if maybe that suggested a second person was involved."

"There was no accomplice," Stoll said shortly.

"Wheeler was a drifter," Perlenbacher added. "He had no friends, no associates. Only relative was his mother, who he was estranged from."

"So no reason to suspect he didn't act alone?"

"None," Stoll said with a tone of finality.

After the call finished, Zoe sat back in her chair and massaged her eyelids. Perhaps she couldn't blame Detective Stoll for the frosty reaction to her questions. How would she have reacted to an outsider trying to pick holes in a long-resolved case on her turf?

She stood up and went to the window. She could hear the sounds of horns from eleven floors below. Always the horns. She wondered why drivers honked their horns so much in big cities, what they thought it achieved.

It appeared Luther Wheeler's crimes were unrelated to the current ones. Wheeler was in jail, the cop who had caught him was dead, and it didn't sound like anyone else had picked up the baton. The clothing strip in California had to be a coincidence. One more thing crossed off the list, though, and it had been good to talk through the process of finding Wheeler.

In the end, it was a lucky break that nailed Luther Wheeler, just like the parking ticket that had ended Son of Sam's reign of terror. She hoped that was a good sign for their case. With thousands of people working this, surely they had to get lucky sooner or later.

22

138 MAIN STREET

GRENVILLE, PENNSYLVANIA

The doorbell rang just after eleven p.m.: the antique chimes echoed through the house. Patrick Massie peered out of the window of his living room. The police car was still parked across the street.

The department had suddenly found room in the budget for a full-time police presence after last night's murder and the subsequent injection of cash from the federal government. It had to be one of the officers at his door. They didn't let anybody else get close enough to ring the bell.

Just in the past few hours, he had seen some rubbernecking college kids firmly escorted away from the stoop, and the Korean food he had ordered for dinner had gotten cold while the officers outside interrogated the delivery guy to within an inch of his life. He hadn't much liked the two cops who had visited him in the early evening. Both had a brusque manner.

The silhouetted figure behind the glass in the front door shifted position as Patrick approached, his walking stick tapping on the tile floor. The shape was slighter, didn't look like either of the tall, heavyset men from earlier.

"It's Officer Semple, Mr. Massie." She raised her voice to carry through the glass. "You can open the door."

Patrick guessed Semple and her partner must have relieved the other two sometime after nine, when he had last looked out. He unlocked the door, removed the chain, and pulled it open.

"I told you, call me Patrick. Everything all right?"

Semple was alone this time. Looking beyond her, Patrick could see an arm resting on the open window of the car across the street, everything above shoulder height in shadow.

"Everything's fine. I wouldn't have disturbed you this late, but I saw your light was on."

"That's okay, I don't sleep much," Patrick said, then, with a grim smile, added, "Particularly not at the moment. Can I help with anything?"

Semple glanced back at the car. "You wouldn't have a phone charger I could use, would you? I don't want to impose, but . . ."

"Of course, come on in."

Patrick led Semple to the kitchen at the back of the house and rooted around in the junk drawer until he found a USB cable.

"Thanks, appreciate it," Semple said as she took it.

"I was about to make myself a coffee, you want one?"

Semple glanced at the clock on the wall above the doorway. "You really *don't* sleep much. Sure."

Patrick made two cups of coffee with the machine and offered Semple cream and sugar. She declined both, took the cup, sipped, and nodded in approval. "That's good. This'll help get me through to seven."

"That's when your relief comes?" Patrick asked. "Shitty assignment, huh?"

Semple shrugged. "I've had worse."

"You've had more exciting too, I'll bet."

Semple laughed. "Come on, Patrick. You were in the military, so you know a boring shift is a good shift."

"I hear you."

Semple was looking at him with a focused gaze, as though studying him. "You ever miss it?"

Patrick considered for a second. Decided there was no reason not to tell the truth. "Absolutely not. We were an occupying force. Half the time we were getting shot at or blown up, and the other half we were trying to mediate between different groups trying to massacre each other. All the time we'd see civilians killed because they went to the market at the wrong hour or just because they looked at the wrong guy in the wrong way. You get tired of it, the sheer pointlessness. It eats away at you, like acid, you know? Makes you think about what kind of world this is."

Semple didn't say anything. He could tell she was thinking about some of the things she had seen herself. He sensed that she was in no hurry to get back out to her vehicle.

"You want to ask your partner in? He could probably use some coffee too."

"Nah, Ray doesn't drink anything but water and Coors. Besides, we can't leave the post. Technically I shouldn't even be here."

He gave a short laugh. "I won't tell if you won't. Besides, I have to be safer with you here with me, right?"

She narrowed her eyes and gave him an appraising look that bordered on the flirtatious. "I think you can handle yourself."

"Maybe five years ago. Any word on how it's going?"

"You've probably seen more news than I have today, so you know as much as I do."

In fact, he hadn't watched much news today. But there was only one real salient fact: another dead body.

"California was a curveball," Patrick said. "He wants to stretch you. He's showing how big the canvas is."

Semple nodded. "Hard target too. Gated community, police presence, and local security. You're right, he wants to send a message."

"You think it could be an inside job?"

Semple raised an eyebrow. "You mean like a cop? Do I need an alibi for last night?"

Patrick laughed. "I think California is a little outside your neighborhood." He stopped and acted like he was considering it. "Although, it's, what, a five-hour flight from LA to Philadelphia? You could have been back here early afternoon. What time did your shift start?"

"I don't like to fly, Patrick," she said, giving him a playfully stern look.

"You would say that, wouldn't you? Seriously, though, whoever it was knew what he was doing out there."

"All I know is this thing is big. The manpower is insane. They'll get him before the next one."

"I'll drink to that," Patrick said, raising his cup.

Semple finished her coffee and looked around for the sink to rinse it out. Patrick took it from her. She sighed and rubbed a kink in her neck.

"Well, I guess I better get back out there before my partner sends in a search party."

"Feel free to drop in anytime," Patrick said.

He went to the window as Semple walked back to the car. Her partner's arm was still resting on the sill. She stopped when she reached the vehicle, looked up, and flashed him a quick smile before she got into the car.

Just doing the job, Patrick told himself. She was putting the customer at ease, letting him know they were on top of it and there was nothing to worry about. Or was there more to it? He shook his head, chastising himself. Someone in the situation he was in didn't need distractions. Even if the distraction came in as pleasing a form as Officer Cat Semple.

He caught a flicker of movement at the edge of his vision and raised his gaze to see someone hurriedly stepping back from a third-floor window on the opposite side of the street. So this was what it felt like to be in a fishbowl.

He sat down and turned the television on to CNN. Jake Tapper was interviewing a Republican congressman. It didn't take long for the 138 Main killings to come up.

23

138 MAIN STREET

CHARLESTOWN, MASSACHUSETTS

Cally must have fallen asleep sometime during *The Tonight Show*. The last thing she remembered was Jimmy Fallon doing a bit about the 138 Main killings. Some black humor she was pretty sure would attract complaints. She rubbed the sleep out of her eyes and massaged an ache in her shoulder, then turned off the television and got up to go to bed.

She glanced at her phone. Nothing from Melissa.

She went to the kitchen for a glass of water. When she turned the faucet off, she thought she heard a sound that had been muffled by the running water. She stood at the sink, listening. Ten seconds passed. Twenty. It was quiet at three o'clock in the morning. Quieter than at any other time of the day. She could hear far-off sounds in the city, the low hum of traffic, a siren, but nothing close by. Then she heard a creak.

Not from outside. From inside the apartment.

She took a sharp breath and put her glass down. Gingerly, so as not to let it clunk on the counter. She looked around the kitchen. The knife block was on the opposite side of the room. She moved across to it and plucked the largest carving knife from it.

She waited, holding her breath. There was no sound but the pulse thudding in her ears.

Probably nothing, right? It was an old building. Its aging joints creaked all the time during bad weather, like an old man's.

But the weather was fine. The rain had stopped and she could see a clear starry night through the window. The kitchen was at the back of the apartment. The police would be outside, but she would have to go into the living room to look out the window. What if someone was in there?

Steeling herself, she gripped the knife tighter and stepped into the hallway.

Her bedroom door was ajar. She hadn't left it like that, had she?

She decided to head for the living room. She walked slowly through the doorway, wishing she hadn't turned off the light and the television. She ran her free hand along the wall, feeling for the light switch, and screamed when something brushed against her leg. She raised the knife and turned the light on.

An orange tabby shot between her bare legs and dashed into the bedroom.

She let out a sigh of relief and tried to make herself laugh. She couldn't.

The goddamn cat from downstairs. Either her neighbor hadn't bothered to take it with him to his girlfriend's or it had found its way back home. How the hell had it gotten in here? She thought about it. The cat must have snuck in earlier when she came back from the store. She had left the door open for a minute because her arms were full. It'd probably been napping under her bed since then.

It just went to show, even though she was being careful to the point of paranoia, it was possible for an intruder to get in.

She walked to the living-room window, not wanting to let go of the knife just yet. The police car was down there. One of the officers had gotten out of the car, perhaps wondering why a light had been switched on in the middle of the night. He took out a phone and dialed.

Her phone lit up on the couch.

"Everything all right, Ms. Principal?" The voice wasn't Officer Franklin from earlier. She didn't recognize this one, another new guardian.

She cleared her throat and hoped the breathlessness wouldn't be audible in her voice.

"Everything's fine, I just, uh . . . needed a glass of water. And stop the 'Ms. Principal' thing. Call me Cally."

The cop didn't say anything. He was looking back up at her, his face shadowed by the brim of his hat.

"Are you okay out there?" she asked, just to break the silence.

"We're fine. Nice, quiet night."

"All right, well . . . I'm going back to bed now. Thanks for checking in."

"Not a problem, ma'am. Cally. You rest well."

As Cally slipped beneath her covers a minute later, the bedside lamp on, she thought about how ridiculous that suggestion was.

The neighbor's tabby meowed from the corner. She'd get in touch with Tommy from apartment A tomorrow and tell him to come pick it up. In the meantime, she had to admit it was a little comforting to have it there.

"Yeah, yeah. Good night to you too, shithead."

24

138 MAIN STREET

PORT ANTHONY, ALASKA

Miriam Yorke had changed into her nightgown and was about to retire to bed when she heard the soft knock at her door.

She padded through the hallway in her slippers and then remembered her new routine. She went back to where the shiny new tablet was hooked up on the kitchen counter and tapped the screen to wake it. The feed from the little camera positioned above the front door appeared. It showed Officer Llewellen staring straight at the camera. She tapped the button for the speaker.

"Is everything all right, Phil?"

"Everything's fine, Miriam, just wanted to ask you—"

"Hang on a second."

Miriam closed the window, went to the hallway, and opened the door.

Phil Llewellen was still on the doorstep, one hand braced on the doorjamb. He was in his mid-fifties, and his bushy mustache was more salt than pepper. There was a slightly disapproving look on his face.

"What'd I tell you about answering a knock on the door in the middle of the night?"

She gave him a mock-wounded expression. "I'm sorry, you know I live on the edge."

"Famous last words." Phil kept his face straight, but there was a twinkle in his eye. Miriam suspected he was enjoying this detail as much as she was. She had been a widow for more than a decade, and it was nice, if unexpected, to have a gentleman take enough notice of her to flirt. "I just wanted to ask one thing, you didn't need to come all the way outside."

"You know I hate talking through that thing. What's up? Isn't this past the end of your shift?"

"Well, that's exactly it." For a moment, she wondered if he was angling for an invitation inside for a nightcap. She was surprised at her disappointment when she found out that wasn't why he had knocked on the door. "My relief had some car trouble. Some jerk slashed all four of his tires. He lives all the way out on Cedar. I could tell him to call a cab and get his keister down here that way, but . . ."

Miriam knew the *but*. There was one taxi driver serving Port Anthony, and that was probably more than the town warranted. If he wasn't asleep or drunk, he would charge fifty bucks for a pickup out at Cedar Road. Miriam didn't know how much police officers made, but she suspected it wasn't so much that you could blow that kind of money on a ride and not feel it.

"You're not going to tell the captain, are you? You're going to go out there and bring him over. Has anyone ever told you that you're a soft touch, Officer Llewellen?"

He sighed. "I just wanted to see if you'd be okay with it. We'd be back in twenty minutes, but if you'd rather—"

"Don't be silly. I'm perfectly fine."

He hesitated for a second, but she could see relief in his eyes. "All right, I'll see you soon."

Phil stayed there as she closed and locked the door. She went back to the kitchen and turned the dishwasher on. She wasn't worried, and she didn't believe that Phil was either. Yes, it was technically a concern that she had drawn the short straw by living at 138 Main Street. Funny that a decision made thirty years ago when she was a young schoolteacher with a spring in her step could have such dark potential consequences so many years later. But it wasn't as though she was in one of the high-risk areas. The FBI man on the news had talked about treating every address equally, giving everyone the same protection, but she didn't believe that and didn't think it was necessary either.

Up here, you got used to things that were apparently of great importance in the Lower Forty-Eight not being of particular relevance. That went double when you were out on the bottom tip of an island off the coast. These murders were terrible, of course, but so were terrorist bombings in the Middle East and shark attacks in Australia. The distance lessened the sense of threat.

If anything, she felt a little guilty that the past few days had been sort of exciting. The police visits, the interview with that polite young lady at the local paper, then the security being ramped up further at the behest of the FBI. It was an odd feeling to have your own twenty-four-hour security detail, like you were a head of state or something.

She felt bad for Phil and the other guys. Even though she hadn't asked for this, she couldn't help but feel like she was imposing. The department had only six officers covering more than eight hundred square miles of the southern half of Baranof Island. She knew they had better things to do than babysit someone who was likely in no danger whatsoever. The last killing had been in California, after all. She didn't see this maniac coming all the way to Port Anthony when there had to be hundreds of other locations that were far easier to reach.

More than hundreds, actually. The FBI man had talked about *thousands* of addresses. It was odd to think about. She had lived in Port Anthony all her life, and the image of her own Main Street was always the one those two words conjured in her mind's eye, even when she heard people using the term in a metaphorical sense, like Main Street versus Wall Street.

Miriam checked the back door lock again and turned to go to bed, then stopped, one foot on the first stair and her right hand on the banister.

The noise seemed to come from outside in the yard. Sounded like a boot heel tapping on one of the paving slabs.

She went back to the kitchen and looked out the window at the yard. Everything looked okay. The grass stretched to the line of bushes at the back. Beyond that was the timber fence her late husband had built more than twenty years ago to replace the one that had blown down in the storm of '02. Above the fence, she saw the water of the bay stretching out to the line of dark hills on the opposite shore. The surface was perfectly still and reflected the stars in the clear sky.

The tall spruce in the corner cast its usual jagged shadow. Nothing looked out of place. But still . . .

She went to the back door again and flicked the switch for the yard light, just to be safe. She wanted to roll her eyes as she did so. What had she just been thinking about? Feeling perfectly safe?

She went back to the kitchen and saw that the yard was lit up brightly. Nothing untoward. She turned the light off and checked the lock one more time. As she was walking through the kitchen, she cast one more glance out at the darkened yard.

And jumped.

There was a man out there. At least, she assumed it was a man. A figure in a dark raincoat with the hood up, standing in the yard.

It had to be Phil or one of the other policemen. She took a step forward to look more closely and raised a hand.

The figure raised his own hand.

There were three flashes and suddenly Miriam was on the floor, staring up at the ceiling, with a fleeting moment to wonder what had happened before the darkness closed in.

Thursday

25

NEW YORK CITY

Elliot Westerberg arrived at the Times Building on Eighth Avenue a little later than usual. His thoughts were divided between the 138 story, the unfolding scandal surrounding the city trade commissioner, and at what exact point he should have stopped drinking last night. He was on his way to his desk, trying to look less hungover than he felt, when his editor stepped out of the conference room. He could tell by the expression on her face that something was happening.

"What's up, Kelly?"

Kelly Kaminsky was in her early forties with platinum-blond hair and a good line in icy stares. She inclined her head in the direction of the conference room and stepped back in without a word.

Elliot followed. There was only one other person besides Kelly in the room: Dan Fortino, one of the managing editors. He was dressed in his usual throwback-newsman attire: chinos and suspenders over a white shirt. He had taken his jacket off and had his sleeves rolled up, which was unheard of for him at nine in the morning. It was so unusual, in fact, that it took Elliot a second to register the other unusual thing: he was wearing thin surgical gloves.

And he was looking down at a stack of paper on the table.

The stack was book-manuscript-size. Beside it was a large manila envelope that had been ripped open. It was closer to Elliot than the stack of paper, so he glanced at it. The address of the *Times* was printed on a plain label. No return address. There was another sticker in red that said *Urgent* affixed to the package. A California postmark.

Elliot glanced across the table at the stack of paper. The first few pages were face down on the table. The one he could see was a wall of text in Courier font. Or was it? He leaned closer. No, that wasn't a font.

"Is that *typed*? Like, on a manual typewriter?" Elliot looked at the other two. "What is this?"

Fortino cleared his throat and carefully picked up one of the sheets of paper that was face down on the table. He held it by one corner and read from it.

"'To whom it may concern. Who I am is of no consequence. What I am doing is of very great consequence.'"

Elliot looked from Fortino to Kaminsky, then down at the stack of paper. He noticed something else beside the envelope: a strip of gray checkered fabric with a dark stain on it. It appeared to be dried blood.

"What the hell is this?"

26

NEW YORK CITY

"We never thought it would happen here. I don't know what to tell you."

The Alaskan sergeant sounded shell-shocked on the phone. Walker couldn't help feeling a stab of sympathy. A tiny settlement at the tip of an island in an archipelago on the edge of the Gulf of Alaska. Not so much the middle of nowhere as the outermost edge of nowhere.

"If it's any consolation," Walker said, "I don't think anybody thought it would happen there. And that's exactly why he chose it. Did you know the victim?"

"Not personally, but a couple of the guys did. She was a nice woman. Went to church every week, volunteered with old folks. She didn't deserve this."

"Of course she didn't. We know these people aren't being targeted because of anything they've done."

The sergeant cleared his throat. "I know this is your case, Mr. Walker, but anything you need from us . . ."

"Thank you." The field office in Anchorage was sending some agents to the scene, but they wouldn't arrive in Sitka for another two hours, at least.

"Just tell me how things are going so far. It's your case too, and I know you'll be doing everything you can."

"We left the body in place, as requested. Shooter fired from the backyard through the kitchen window. He spray-painted the map-pin symbol on the window, right around the bullet hole. Mrs. Yorke was killed between midnight and twelve thirty, when my officer got back on the scene. He blames himself."

Walker declined the opportunity to say that Officer Llewellen shouldn't blame himself, because he thought he absolutely should. Okay, given that the perpetrator came in from the back, he probably couldn't have saved Miriam Yorke's life even if he had been there watching the front of the house, but he might have had a chance to see her killer.

"We don't know if he used a silencer or what, but the closest house is five hundred yards away. Neighbors heard nothing, but one reported that their dog started barking around twelve fifteen. We think the guy was parked nearby and came into the yard on foot."

"How's the door-to-door going?"

A resigned sigh. "It was late, and people go to bed early in these parts. Nobody saw anything around the time of the shooting. You could fit the population of the town in a phone booth, so we're asking if anybody saw anyone unfamiliar. So far, zilch."

"How does somebody get out there?" Walker asked. "Say they flew into Anchorage yesterday."

"If they came via Sitka, they would need a car for sure. We're talking to the rental outfits at the airport, the cab companies—we'll make sure you get the list."

"Thank you."

Walker said he would be back in touch later. He ended the call and chewed over the conversation for a minute. The lack of eyewitnesses to the killing or even reports of a stranger in town was disappointing, but Walker couldn't help hoping that the killer had overreached.

"Alaska," Zoe said, watching him from across the table. "Nobody saw that coming."

Walker scratched the back of his head, thinking. "Maybe he boxed himself in this time. He didn't drive there from California. He didn't walk from the airport. That means he rented a car or he got a ride from somebody."

"An accomplice?"

"Maybe. Maybe an unwitting one. Point is, we can narrow those possibilities down pretty easily. We trace anybody who arrived at the airport yesterday. In the meantime—"

He was interrupted by a knock on the door. It was Ferrera.

"We have another development."

27

The package from the killer had been delivered to the *New York Times*. The manuscript it contained ran to over five hundred pages. To allay any doubts as to its authenticity, the sender had enclosed a strip of blood-drenched fabric that looked like a match to the missing piece of Chester Frohoff's pajama shirt. It was with the lab being checked out, but Walker had no doubt the blood would also be a match.

The document was titled *A Manifesto for True Living in America.* It had been manually typed out, single-spaced, with occasional handwritten corrections in red ink. The manuscript was at the lab too, but every page had been scanned and circulated. Walker had teams of readers going through it.

Zoe Hill was seated at the table, leafing through a printout of the full document. "This is deranged. You think it's on the level?"

"I think it has to be," Walker said.

"It's like reading a serial killer's diary crossed with the Unabomber manifesto. I've been reading this shit for an hour and I can't work out what it is this guy wants."

"He wants attention."

"Well, he's got that."

Walker had skimmed some of it on his computer. If the samples he had looked at were representative of the full document, it was a long, rambling tirade against modern life, the erosion of American values. It was written in an academic—or maybe pseudo-academic—style. There were occasional words that weren't quite right but would probably sound impressive in a lecture if you weren't paying much attention.

The closest thing to a coherent ultimatum, though it was not explicit, was a list of stipulations at the end. Outlandish, millenarian stuff, like banning tech companies, shutting down the banks, closing all borders; there was a long, particularly dense section on removing the cell phone infrastructure and scaling the internet down to bare bones. It amounted to rolling back fifty years of modernity, maybe a hundred. If these were the killer's demands, he was going to be disappointed.

The world is getting worse, day by day, hour by hour. It must get worse still before it gets better. Our country requires shock therapy.

The debate between the FBI and the *Times* editors on the advisability of publishing the manifesto hadn't lasted long, because at exactly 9:30 a.m., it had appeared in full online at 138main.com, a domain that had been registered in January. It was out there for all to read, as the author intended.

Just looking at the pages gave Walker a headache. The manifesto was dense, walls of text, single paragraphs going on for two or three pages.

As though reading his mind, Zoe shook her head. "I know, right? I think we can rule out John Grisham as a suspect."

Walker smiled grimly. "Makes you appreciate the Zodiac killer. Short, concise—a puzzle."

Zoe raised an eyebrow. "Maybe don't open with that comment at the next press conference."

Walker picked up the stack of paper, weighing it in his hands. The manifesto bothered him. It didn't fit with everything else. It was obtuse, impenetrable. Much as he hated to give credit to a psychopathic killer, the killings seemed the opposite of that. They were well thought through. Well executed—no pun intended. There was a fleetness about the operation that was the antithesis of this thing. It didn't feel like the work of the same mind. And yet, the bloody rag had been included to make sure the two were linked.

"There's more than one of them," he said. "More than one person involved here."

Zoe looked up from the papers. "Because of Alaska?"

"Not just that. The guy who neatly circled the bullet hole with his logo in Alaska isn't the same guy who spent thirty pages talking about the evils of mega-malls."

"So why send this?"

"I don't know yet."

Zoe looked back at what she was reading. "It's weird. It's political, I guess. Sometimes he sounds like he's a Communist, sometimes like he's a true-blue soldier of the alt-right, and then he'll turn into a revivalist preacher for ten pages. I think the profiler might have been right about this being domestic terrorism. This guy has some very strong beliefs—they just don't make any goddamn sense."

"Sounds like every other terrorist," Walker remarked. He looked at the big wall map again. Six pins on the map now.

"This new one is another escalation. We thought California was him taunting us, showing us his reach, but this one is *really* sticking it to us. He had to know that if there was any prioritization at all, a speck on the map in Alaska would be low on the list."

"But there are places just as low on the list that would be easier to get to, that would be less of a risk."

"Exactly. He's playing with us. He's arrogant."

"So what do we do?"

Walker thought for a minute.

"I know we resisted putting too much stock in predictions, but I don't see any other way. We need to draw up a new list and try to outguess this asshole. He's methodical and he's planning these out. We have six scenes now. That ought to be enough for us to come up with some possibilities."

He slammed his hand down on the desk and looked back at the map.

"He's just given us a phone book's worth of his thoughts. There has to be something in here that helps us get inside his head. Let's go through it in teams. By tonight, I want a list of the top ten potential targets."

GEHENNA

The room had grown much colder after darkness fell, but the Professor hardly noticed it. The bone-deep chill barely registered. The work was all there was. Nothing else mattered.

The house was silent, as it always was now. The Professor tried to remember how long it had been since he had crossed the threshold and could not. It was of no consequence. Time was an illusion. Changing seasons were an illusion. All that was important now was the work. The work and the map.

The map covered most of one wall of the study. To hang it, he had had to dismantle the shelves after laboriously moving piles of books to the kitchen, the only room that still had enough floor space to accommodate them.

It was a necessary sacrifice. It was too big now. He had to see his canvas in one piece.

He stood back and stared at the map for a long time. Target selection was an inexact science. It was of paramount importance that the sites be selected in the right places and in the right order. Much of that was dictated by logistics, but it always began in the same way: emptying his mind and waiting for inspiration. Sometimes it was immediate; sometimes it took hours. Tonight was somewhere in between, but when the mist cleared and an area of the map revealed itself like an island in a fogbound ocean, he knew it had always had to be.

"We strike at the heart," the Professor said.

28

NEW YORK CITY

Zoe didn't know what a normal day at the office was like at the FBI, but so far it felt like working in the middle of Grand Central Station. A never-ending stream of personnel filed in and out of the office, hot-desking, taking calls, handing out or being given assignments. She tuned the background noise out and focused on the manifesto.

She had grimly persevered for a couple of hours when Brodie pushed his tablet roughly aside and stood up. "Calling a time-out. This is like swimming through treacle."

Zoe looked up from her printout of the manifesto and shrugged. She removed the pen that she had been chewing from between her teeth. "That's why they pay you the big bucks."

Brodie raised his eyebrows. "Do you even know how much I get paid?"

"Sure. Sixty-eight thousand dollars a year."

Brodie looked surprised but amused. "How did you know that?"

"It's the entry-level salary for an analyst posted on the Bureau's website. You know how much I get paid a year?"

"I don't—does your department publish entry-level salaries?"

"Less than sixty-eight grand a year. Get me another soda."

"Guess it's on me," Brodie said, and took off. He would be gone for at least fifteen minutes, the time it took him to go down to the ground floor, stand outside for a few moments to get some "fresh air"—although Zoe wasn't sure how fresh the air was in Lower Manhattan in the middle of the afternoon—go to the nearest store, a bodega on Broadway, and return.

She liked Brodie, but she appreciated not having to listen to him thinking out loud and tapping on the table as he scrolled through the manifesto, pausing only when he had to scratch down some notes, which was frequently.

Zoe reached for his tablet and turned it around. Brodie was deeper into the document than she was. The screen displayed a wall of text about air quality, how a hundred thousand people a year had their lives cut short due to pollution. Zoe wasn't sure what murdering innocent people in their beds had to do with air pollution, but then, she wasn't sure what it had to do with any of this shit. Brodie had underlined the figure giving the number of deaths in green, and there was a squiggly notation next to it.

She looked back at her printout of the manifesto. It had been ten pages since she had made a mark anywhere. The latest chapter started with a lengthy section on why it was noble and right to kill innocent people to make a point.

```
Some will call what we do terrorism.
```

The manifesto's author always used *we*. Maybe it confirmed Walker's assertion that there were multiple people involved, or maybe he was simply using the royal we.

```
So be it. Because there is a civilized case for what
one might call terrorism. If, by delivering hard les-
sons, we might better educate the populace and there-
fore galvanize meaningful, lasting change, would said
terrorism not be justified? Would it not be more akin to
discipline enforced to promote responsible behavior?
```

Zoe sighed and rubbed her eyelids. She hadn't found anything useful so far. Maybe this was all one big distraction, a way to get them chasing their tails and wasting time while Mr. Main Street set up his next hit. The tip line was flooded thanks to the author's decision to post the manifesto on the website. Perhaps that could work in their favor, but it was just as likely they would miss something important in the noise.

She wondered, not for the first time, what it would be like to be one of those people on a seven-thousand-name-long hit list. What would she do? Get the hell out of her house, she supposed. She didn't know why any of them were sticking around.

But then she realized she was Monday-morning-quarterbacking. It was easy to talk about a simple solution when you weren't the one facing the threat. She thought about what she would really do.

She could stay with her mom, of course, though that wasn't exactly the most attractive option. There was no one else in town she really felt close to, no one she could ask about staying in a spare bedroom. And even if there were, she wasn't talking just one night, was she? This would go on until they caught the guy. And maybe they would *never* catch the guy.

For the same reason, booking a hotel room was not a long-term solution. A night? No problem. A week? The cost started adding up, even in an out-of-the-way place like Granton. A room at the Keystone Inn was eighty or ninety dollars a night. At that rate, even somebody on Brodie's salary would struggle after a while.

It wasn't so straightforward when you put yourself in that position. And then there was the human impulse to assume it wouldn't happen to you. It was a pretty safe bet, odds-wise. Seven thousand to one. You had better odds of being hit by a car or slipping in the bathtub and breaking your neck. Last night, thousands of people had gambled on those odds and only one of them had lost.

Those who had the means to get away had done so, of course, but it was a surprisingly low proportion. If their figures were right, it was under 17 percent of the total. The 17 percent who could afford an indefinite stay elsewhere or who didn't break out in a cold sweat at the thought of forced extra time with their extended families. She had seen a TV interview with a tattooed, bearded guy in Davenport, Iowa, who actually bridled at the suggestion he might want to find alternative accommodation. "Nah, this jerk doesn't scare me. I'm a stayer."

A *stayer*. More than four-fifths of 138 Main residents were stayers, whether they wanted to be or not.

She heard the elevator ping and Brodie rushed over, almost knocking a pile of papers off someone's desk, offering an absent-minded apology in his wake.

"You're back fast. Did you get my soda?"

He didn't answer, just picked up his tablet and started scrolling through it.

"What is it? Did you come up with something?"

He stopped scrolling and stared at the screen, deep in thought.

"Hello? Earth to Brodie?"

He blinked. "Sorry. Did you say something?"

"What is it?"

"I don't know yet."

He made notes on the pad beside his tablet. Zoe waited patiently. After a few minutes of scribbling, he looked up.

"Shit, I forgot your drink."

"It's cool. What did you find?"

"I don't know yet, not for sure. But it's like he's hinting at the different locations in one of the mismatching sections."

"Mismatching sections?"

Brodie took a minute to collect his thoughts. "That's right, you were on a call. Some of the sections seem like they were added later. Different style, different reference points. Even the pages themselves look different on the scan."

"Okay, so you think he went back and changed something?"

"It's possible," Brodie said. "I think he added them after he had decided on the targets. Maybe that came later or he changed his mind or . . ." He turned his tablet around and indicated something on the page. "Here, he talks about 'suffering on the Long Cross.'"

"What's that, another Bible reference?"

The manifesto was shot through with religious imagery. They already had a couple of agents checking out faith groups and places of worship in the murder locales, just in case there was some kind of link.

"I thought so, but there's no reference like that in the Bible."

Brodie tapped on the screen again and brought up the map of killings so far. He swiped two fingers dexterously to zoom in on the first four sites: Colorado, Mississippi, Long Island, and Illinois. They made a rough cross formation, with the east and west arms spanning a longer distance than north and south. He looked up at Zoe expectantly.

"Like a cross that's wider than it is tall?" Zoe said doubtfully. She had noted the formation of the first four murder scenes herself, but she wasn't sure that it meant anything. Perhaps Brodie had been staring at nothing long enough to see something.

"A long cross," Brodie agreed. He dragged the map over to the Alaska site. "Right after that line, he writes something about New Archangel. That was the old name for Sitka, back when it was still part of Russia. It's got to refer to the Alaska target."

Zoe looked from the map to the paragraph Brodie had highlighted, her interest piqued now. If they knew one thing about this perpetrator, it was that he was cocky, confident. Could he be telling them where he was going to strike next?

"And right after that," Brodie continued, the hint of a smile at the corner of his mouth telling Zoe he knew he was slowly reeling her in, "he talks about 'the Heart of the Matter.' Capitalized."

"The Heart of the Matter," Zoe repeated. "Main Street is the heart of every town, so I guess every one of these strikes at the heart."

"Right, but I think he's talking about the heart geographically."

"So . . . he's saying it's somewhere in Middle America? The heartland?"

"I think so. He's playing with us. Hinting at the next target, like he's calling a shot in pool. When it happens, it will be another data point to verify the provenance of the manifesto. If that's right, it narrows the possibilities down."

"It doesn't narrow them down all that much," Zoe said. "What do we count as the heartland?"

Brodie thought about it. "Has to be the Midwest. Let me see . . ." He brought the map up on his screen and zoomed in to the middle. "Okay, leave out Alaska and Hawaii for sure this time. Nothing on the coasts. Nothing too far north or south. Let's look at region two."

"Slow down. What the hell is region two?"

"The US Census Bureau has four regions—region one is the Northeast, three is the South, four is the West Coast. Region two is the Midwest."

"What states does that give us?"

He rattled them off without having to think about it. "Region two has two divisions: The first is Illinois, Indiana, Michigan, Ohio, Wisconsin, and Iowa, and the second is Kansas, Minnesota, Missouri, Nebraska, North Dakota, and South Dakota. Twelve states."

Zoe snapped her fingers. "The burner they found at the California scene. You're thinking about the call that was made in Kansas City."

Brodie nodded. "Yes, but I don't think it's Missouri." He tapped a couple of times on the key at the side of the map, and the map turned gray. He tapped on the twelve states he had just mentioned and they colored again. Another tap brought up the locations of the Main Streets.

"Still a lot," Zoe said.

"A lot, but not as many," Brodie said. "We know he must be casing the addresses ahead of time, right? The cell tower he pinged was near the Kansas City airport. He could have been flying out of there after surveilling a target. If that was our guy, I think we should be focusing on this region, especially division two and the most central states within that: Nebraska, Oklahoma, and . . . and Kansas."

He stopped and swiped the screen. He found a couple of lines of text at the opening to the chapter, an unattributed quotation from something, and read them aloud.

"'No matter how dreary and gray our homes are, we people of flesh and blood would rather live there than in any other country, be it ever so beautiful.'"

"What's that from?" Zoe asked. "It's familiar, but I can't place it."

"I thought so too. I meant to go back and check it, but I remember now. It's missing the end of the line, which is the part you'd know from the movie. The quote finishes, 'There's no place like home.'"

"*The Wizard of Oz*. You think he's saying it's going to be Kansas?"

"I think that's got to be what this means."

"What if this is a bluff? Then we're taking our eye off the ball again, like with Alaska."

"It's a risk," Brodie agreed. "But a bigger risk is it's not even intentional. Like I said, it's human nature to impose patterns on randomness. I might be way off here, so I don't think we should go to Walker yet."

Zoe was silent for a minute. Thinking.

"What?" Brodie prompted. "You agree, right?"

"I think we should take it to Walker. Maybe you are seeing something where there's nothing, I don't know, but . . ."

"But?"

"But we're not imposing order on chaos here. The hits so far haven't been picked randomly. The spread has been too even. There's a plan behind this, a design. You might not be right about it, but what does your gut tell you?"

"It tells me there's something here."

29

Mississippi. Colorado. New York. Illinois. California. Alaska."

Billie Chapman didn't look down at the report in front of her as she listed the names of the states visited by the 138 Main killer so far. She just held Walker's gaze, leaving a meaningful pause between each name.

"Six states, ten victims. And we are no closer to finding the person who is doing this. Why is that?"

Walker set his jaw and forced himself to keep his temper. His team had been working flat out on this, and she knew it. If there weren't as many good leads as either of them had hoped, it wasn't for lack of trying.

"We're making progress on a number of lines. One of the big problems is we still don't know if we're dealing with one person or a hundred."

"The manifesto suggests it's one. Our analysts confirm it's all typed on a single typewriter. You can ID manual typewriters like a fingerprint, imperfections in some of the heads and so forth."

Walker resisted the urge to say that he knew that because he was just old enough to remember when that technique was often useful in this line of work. "I don't know about the manifesto."

"What don't you know? Its provenance is undeniable. The blood from that strip of cloth is a match for Chester Frohoff's."

"I'm not questioning that."

"Then what?"

Walker considered his answer for a moment. "I don't know yet. All I know is the guy who typed out that phone book is not the same guy who slipped in and out of Port Anthony, Alaska, last night to kill Miriam Yorke without leaving so much as a footprint. We're dealing with more than one person."

Chapman pointed at the tablet on her desk that had the manifesto on its screen. "But the person behind this is the brains of the operation."

"Perhaps. That's why I have people going over every last word of it to find something we can use."

"But nothing so far," Chapman observed.

"We need time."

"Then let's stop wasting it in here."

Walker got up and headed for the door but stopped when Chapman said his name.

He turned back. "Yeah?"

"We need a win. If this guy hits somewhere else and gets away clean again, I'm going to have to make some changes. I'm sorry, I know it's not your fault."

Walker nodded. "Do what you have to." He didn't add what he was thinking: that being kicked off this case, public embarrassment aside, would feel like a blessed relief at this point.

When he got outside, Brodie and Hill were waiting for him. He could tell from their expressions that they had something.

"It's like he's playing with us," Brodie said, sweeping a hand to indicate the eight selected pages he had put up on the screen in the conference room.

"What am I looking at?" Walker asked. He glanced from Brodie to Hill and back again.

"These are pages I've pulled from the full manifesto. They don't fit the rest."

"What are you talking about? The analysis says—"

"That it all came from the same typewriter. But I don't think it all came from the same *writer*."

Walker sat back and waited for him to go on.

"The people in linguistics agree with me. I ran it by Holland, and he thinks so too."

Walker didn't interrupt Brodie, but he thought that if he had managed to get Dr. Holland to agree, it must have been pretty cut-and-dried. The behavioral specialist was notoriously contrarian. He didn't like any idea that wasn't his.

"Same typewriter, same paper, but there are a couple dozen individual pages that stick out. The formatting is a little different, to begin with. What do you notice about these eight pages?"

Walker examined the pages. "A little lighter on the text. More paragraphs."

"Right. I read through this entire thing, and every time I hit one of these pages it felt like it was moving faster. They're just better written."

"So there are two authors?"

"Maybe," Brodie said. "The paper was typed on at a different time too. It's the same stock, probably the same batch, but these eight pages are a little cleaner. The creases are fresher."

"So another person helped on this."

"Right. And the other person wanted to send a message."

Walker leaned forward in his chair. "A message?"

"At first glance, the content of these pages doesn't deviate from the rest of it. It's this kind of long scream of frustration at the modern world. It's like distilled internet rage. But if you take these eight pages in isolation, they all refer to the six scenes so far. And maybe a seventh."

He tapped on one of the pages to enlarge it. There was a line two-thirds down the page that Brodie had highlighted in red. He tapped on the highlight and the single sentence popped out to take up the whole screen. The Heart of the Matter.

"That's what it's all about, though, right?" Walker said. "He's striking at the heart. Main Street is the heart of every town."

"Right," Brodie said. "If we think of this like a work of art . . ." He stopped when he saw Zoe roll her eyes. "I know, I know, but stay with me. Think about it like a symphony or a novel. Striking at the heart of America is the overall theme of what he's doing here. It's referred to over and over again, it's implicit in the choice of address he's targeting. But this line doesn't refer to a broad theme. I think this is specific."

"The next one is going to be in the heart of the country," Walker said. "So . . . the Midwest?"

"We think Kansas," Zoe said. "He quoted *The Wizard of Oz* a couple of pages before, so it ties in with that."

Walker considered that. He thought about telling them that some people believed Pink Floyd's album *Dark Side of the Moon* synced up with *The Wizard of Oz* too, but he wasn't sure either of them had heard of Pink Floyd. Instead, he went with the other problem that jumped out at him immediately.

"Even if you're right, Kansas is a big-ass state."

"Population of three million, but they're spread out. Almost two thousand distinct settlements," Brodie said. "Maybe a hundred big enough to have a Main Street. It's going to be tough to narrow it down."

"Tough, but not impossible," Walker said. "Let's get on it."

30

138 MAIN STREET

CHARLESTOWN, MASSACHUSETTS

Cally had never wanted to leave her apartment more.

The morning news about the woman in Alaska had hit her like a physical blow. If it could happen there, it could happen anywhere. All of a sudden, the bland reassurances from Officer Franklin the other day rang even hollower.

She had been sitting in front of the TV since this morning, occasionally wandering to the kitchen and back, even getting as far as switching the damn thing off a couple of times but always being lured back. The police and the FBI agents who had been interviewed on the news looked similarly shell-shocked. The criticism of the FBI from the pundits had turned from qualified to overwhelming. How could this be happening? The president was asked a question about it on TV earlier today, and he responded with vague comments about being in close touch with the investigation but finished with "We expect to see some results very soon." His tone left no doubt that there was a silent *or else* at the end of that sentence.

She hadn't eaten all day. There was a sick feeling in her stomach that told her she wouldn't be able to hold anything down. Melissa or no

Melissa, she had to get out of here. She couldn't imagine sleeping here tonight.

The more information that came out about the Alaska murder, the more anxious Cally felt. The killer had planned carefully. He had managed to get in and out of the area without being seen by the police watching the house or by any of the people living in the small town. His job would be ten times easier somewhere like Charlestown, a bustling neighborhood in a big city where most people wouldn't be able to pick their own neighbors out of a lineup.

In fact, it sounded possible that the only person who saw the killer in Alaska was likely the victim herself. That thought reminded Cally of the guy she had seen on Sunday morning, the man in the uniform across the street who seemed to be looking up at her window.

When she mentioned the man to Officer Franklin, he hadn't seemed too worried. But now the facts suggested that these killings had been planned in advance and the targets had been surveilled ahead of time. That made sense. It wouldn't have been as important for the first few killings, but it would be vital for the killer to slip through the net later.

The latest news told her that perhaps what she had seen on Sunday meant something.

She went to the window and looked down at the spot where the man had been standing. It was barely ten feet from where her surveillance police car was parked. And the reason the car was in that spot, of course, was that it provided an unobstructed view of her apartment.

The Alaska victim had been shot through her kitchen window by someone in the backyard. That would be a more challenging shot to make through her top-floor window, but . . . she hesitated. Her gaze lifted from the street to the building opposite. There were dozens of windows facing her, some of them lit up, some of them dark.

Cally pulled the drapes closed.

She had been holding off calling the FBI's priority 138 Main residents' line, part of her still fretting that she was imagining things. The number was on the bottom of the information sheet the officer had given her the other day. She closed the blinds in the kitchen, even though it didn't face any buildings on that side, sat on the stool at the counter, and dialed the number.

The call was immediately answered by an operator, who delivered her well-drilled lines brightly, with no indication that this was likely her hundredth call of the day.

"Hi, my name is Cally Principal. I'm calling from . . . well, I guess you know where I'm calling from."

There was a rattle of keys in the background. "Yes, ma'am. We have your number tagged to one thirty-eight Main Street, Charlestown. That's in Boston, is that correct?"

"Yes."

"Is everything okay over there?"

"Yes. I mean, I think so. I just wanted to let you know about something I remembered from a few days ago."

She told the operator she'd seen someone the other day when she returned from her run, but she was distracted at the time.

"It's my sister—she's missing," she explained.

"I'm sorry to hear that, Ms. Principal. Have you made a report to the police?"

She sighed. "They know I'm concerned, but . . . well, this isn't the first time she's gone dark for a while." *Never for this long, though*, Cally thought. "Anyway, just as I got back, I saw a guy I didn't recognize across the street from my building. I didn't think too much about it, but I think he was looking up at my window. You know, like, checking the place out. I think he was wearing a 2Gen uniform, but they're not my supplier."

The operator's fingers had been tapping on keys as Cally spoke. Now the tapping stopped. "You had never seen this man before?"

"No, never."

"What about since?"

"No, just that day."

"Can you describe him for me?"

Cally felt reassured by the professionalism of the FBI operator. She was listening, taking Cally seriously, and, if the rapid key tapping was anything to go by, taking notes.

"He was white, maybe in his forties or fifties. Average height, average weight."

"Hair color?"

"He was wearing a hat. Glasses too."

"Sunglasses?"

"No, just regular glasses."

More tapping.

"Did this man do anything else that seemed suspicious?"

Cally thought hard. She had barely noticed him at the time, her thoughts consumed by Melissa's vanishing act. "I don't think so. I don't know how long he stayed there. I went up to my apartment and showered, and he must have been gone when I looked out the window next."

The operator asked a few more questions, then thanked Cally for calling and assured her she would log this information in the database. She suggested giving the police outside the description of the man, just to make sure they were on the alert.

"It's probably nothing," she finished. "But better safe than sorry."

Cally hung up, feeling mildly reassured. She had half expected the operator to blow her off or just humor her. She put her phone down and it buzzed; the screen read *No caller ID.* Maybe the FBI calling back. She answered with a hello and waited.

There was silence on the line.

"Hello?"

No response, but the caller was still there. She could hear traffic noise in the background.

"Melissa?"

Five more seconds of silence, and the caller hung up.

Cally stood with the phone in her hand, looking down at the police car and the spot where the man in the uniform had stood. The feeling of reassurance she'd had after her call to the FBI line evaporated.

She thought about Melissa out there in the night. Crashing on the couch of one of her flaky friends, perhaps, or maybe sheltering beneath a bridge somewhere. Cally needed to know where she was, soon.

31

NEW YORK CITY

Walker got back to his sixth-floor apartment on West 112th just after eleven. He dropped the usual pile of junk mail and flyers from his box straight into the trash. He removed his jacket and his gun, stopped to think for a moment, then did something he didn't ordinarily do.

He picked up his gun again and walked from room to room, checking each space: the bedroom, the bathroom, the small galley kitchen that was separated from the living room by a counter.

He found nothing unusual, of course. The apartment was the same as it had always been. He'd lived here three years, since he and his wife had divorced, and it still felt a little like a hotel room. Traffic noise and the sound of distant sirens drifted in from the tiny balcony outside his window.

He took a shower, standing under the hot water and wondering if he could just stay there for a month or two. Eventually, the water became cold enough to make getting out a slightly more appealing prospect than staying in.

He toweled off and shaved so he could save five minutes in the morning, then changed into loose shorts and a T-shirt. His belly was rumbling but he didn't feel like ordering from the Thai place downstairs for the fifth night in a row. The refrigerator was practically empty, nothing but eggs and a loaf of bread that had gone moldy in its unopened plastic. He dumped the bread into the trash with the mail and turned on the news while he made an omelet.

That was one good thing about having such a small apartment: The kitchen and living room were in the same space, separated by a small island, so he could keep an eye on the TV while cooking. By the sound of it, he hadn't missed anything while he was in the shower. The anchors were experts at making you think things were constantly happening when in reality, they had been recycling the same updates for the past four hours. They kept playing the interview with Llewellen, the cop in Alaska. Walker couldn't help feeling sorry for the guy. Yes, he had screwed up by leaving his post, but Walker was under no illusion that Llewellen was the only one to do so. Dozens of cops in his position had probably done the same thing last night, but for them it hadn't mattered.

He remembered Ferrera's words at the briefing the other day. *He only has to get it right once; we have to get it right every time.*

Walker was still hopeful that the killer had overreached himself in Alaska. There was simply no way to do what he had done and leave no trace. It would take time, but the FBI would find those traces. If they had to interview every man, woman, and child who had flown into the state the previous week, then that was what they would do. They would find someone who was worth looking into.

In the meantime, he was cautiously optimistic about Brodie and Zoe's theory. There was a lot to do before the team committed to it, but he was already glad of his decision to pair the two up. Hill's groundedness helped balance Brodie's ebullience and vice versa. There were a few other avenues of inquiry suggested by the manifesto, but his gut told him the Heart of the Matter line was significant. If nothing else, it evened out the distribution of killings on the map.

He scooped the omelet out of the skillet and onto a plate, wishing he had bread to make toast. He dropped a waffle into the toaster for carbs. Close enough. He was carrying the plate over to the couch when his phone buzzed.

The screen read *No caller ID*. Somebody who had his number but who was not known to him. Perhaps an agent from another field office or a cop in some small, unremarkable town that had a population of three hundred and a Main Street. He had a bad feeling about what the caller was going to tell him.

He answered with a hello, not with his name the way he usually did. There was a long pause and then the caller spoke.

"Special Agent Benjamin Walker." It wasn't a question. The man on the phone said his name like he was welcoming him into his office.

"Who is this?"

There was a short laugh, as though the question were ridiculous, and Walker lost all doubt about who this was. Or at least, who the caller wanted him to think he was.

"If you need a name, why don't you call me Lewis."

Walker noticed that there was very slight distortion in the voice, like it had been put through some sort of subtle modulator. It didn't sound robotic or anything; more like the speaker was talking through gauze. It was fuzzy around the edges with the hint of a digital crackle. There was no background noise. The caller was inside somewhere.

Walker put the phone on speaker so he could look at the screen and tapped on the recording app.

"Agent Walker? Are you still there?"

He cleared his throat. "You said your name was Lewis."

"I didn't say that. I said you can call me Lewis."

"That a first or a last name?"

"It's whatever you want it to be. And you can spell it however you want to too. I'm not calling at a bad time, am I?"

"I wouldn't say there's a good time for somebody to call and threaten me."

"Threaten you? What have I said to threaten you?"

"Look, pal, I get a hundred of these calls a day. Cranks like you who get their kicks from inserting themselves into high-profile cases."

"I don't think that's true. It wasn't easy to get your direct number, Ben.

And that's for a reasonably smart, resourceful guy like myself. I don't think a *crank* would get past the first hurdle."

"Okay, you're very smart. I'm impressed. I'm watching Jimmy Kimmel with some company and a glass of wine, so you better get to the point before I hang up."

"I'm not sure you're being frank with me, Ben. You're watching the news. Alone. Maybe you're eating pizza from that place on the corner. Alfredo's, isn't it?"

Walker felt a chill settle at the nape of his neck. He went to the window and snapped the blinds shut. "Who is this?"

"You know who this is."

"I know who you want me to think it is."

"Did you like the map pins? That information has been withheld from the media so far, I noticed."

"Plenty of people know about the map pins. You can find anything on the internet."

"You can find anything, but very little of it is true. Even some of the accounts in the mainstream media are flat-out wrong. The *Times* reported that the husband and wife at Pembury were both killed in bed, but that's inaccurate. The woman tried to run. She died on the landing, right next to where that very tasteful Gauguin print was hanging. The one with the two Tahitian ladies."

Walker felt his sinuses clear. He had suspected already that this wasn't some random wacko, but he was sure of it now. "Okay, I was wrong. You're a good crank."

"Let's not waste each other's time."

Walker tried to think. The longer he could keep this guy on the line, the more chance there was of him revealing information that could be useful. He didn't hold out much hope that the call could be traced, but perhaps they would get lucky.

"All right. Say you're who you claim to be. What do you want?"

"I thought I explained that quite clearly in my communication to the media."

"You and I have different definitions of *clearly*."

"How typical. It's all in there. But you might say I'm making a statement."

For the first time, Walker heard irritation in Lewis's voice. Was he getting to him?

"Killing people isn't a statement. You know what Samuel Goldwyn said? If you want to send a message—"

"Use Western Union," Lewis finished, sounding amused again. "I always liked that piece of advice. But Goldwyn was an idiot. The message is everything. All you need is a little imagination."

"It doesn't take imagination to kill people, pal, trust me. I've been dealing with guys like you for my whole career. This does not make you special. All you're doing is telling us Rand McNally made you do it instead of *Catcher in the Rye* or the Bible."

"I can give you the Bible, Ben. How about Genesis, chapter forty-two, verse five? 'And the sons of Israel came to buy grain among those that came: for the famine was in the land of Canaan.'"

"Oh, good, a religious nut. I get all the best cases."

There was a brief snort of amusement. "How about I give you some information that will let you relax for tonight? It must be hard being in your shoes."

"How are you going to relax me?"

"I'm not going to kill anyone tonight. You can tell your people to stand down."

Walker laughed. "Right. I'll do that. Maybe we'll tell everyone not to bother locking their doors while we're at it."

"I can't promise about tomorrow, but tonight, no Main Street call. At least, not one I'm involved with."

"Why not?"

"Honestly? Because I'm in a kayak paddling home from Alaska, and my arms are getting a little tired."

"So what do you want? Why call me at all?"

"I just wanted to hear your voice. Talk to the competition, man to man. And one other thing: I want you to know you're helpless, Ben."

"Big talk."

"I've done more than talk. What have you done? Make a few achingly predictable moves and let me kill another two people. No, I mean it. You're helpless. You can't stop me. And this is going to keep happening until I decide to stop."

"What do you want?"

"You'll know in good time, but not yet."

"People like you always get caught unless they stop. That's the only way you're going to get away. If you quit now, we'll still look for you and we'll probably find you, but maybe not. It's your last chance."

There was a long pause, and Walker wondered if he was actually thinking it over.

"We'll talk again, Ben. But not before the next one. Good night."

There was a click, and Walker was suddenly alone in the silence.

Friday

32

NEW YORK CITY

But not before the next one. Good night."

Zoe raised her cup to her lips and found her coffee had gone cold as she listened to the recording. They were on the twenty-third floor, burning the midnight oil. Or the 2:30 a.m. oil, actually. They weren't alone. If she closed her eyes and listened to the activity on the floor outside, it sounded like it was ten in the morning on a Monday.

"You think it's really him?" she asked Walker.

"Yes. He knew too much. This wasn't a crank."

"How the hell did he get your number?"

"It isn't that difficult. I'm available to a lot of people; he could have gotten it anywhere."

"Just as long as he doesn't have your address too."

"I'm pretty sure he does," Walker said, thinking about Lewis's reference to Alfredo's on the corner. "I'm not worried. He's not interested in apartments on One Hundred Twelfth Street." Walker pointed at the laptop where the audio clip had just played. "Thoughts?"

"It's him," Brodie said. "I'd bet my paycheck on it. And this is all consistent with him wanting as much attention as possible. *Lewis* probably refers to Sinclair Lewis. He wrote a novel called *Main Street*—it was a bestseller in its day."

"Really? I've never heard of it," Zoe said.

"Well, that's because its day was a hundred years ago," Brodie said. "He won the Nobel Prize for Literature later on. I read the book the other night."

"Any good?"

"It was more of a page-turner than *A Manifesto for True Living in America*, put it that way."

"The guy on that recording doesn't sound like the guy who wrote the manifesto," Zoe said. "He's confident, chooses his words carefully. Not like the word salad in that document."

"Some people talk better than they write," Walker said.

"He did refer to the manifesto," Brodie said. "You could be right, though, maybe he didn't write it."

"It's always been a strong possibility there's more than one guy here," Walker said. "The area covered alone makes that likely. And he doesn't say anything about being the only person involved."

"So we're no farther forward," Zoe said. "It could be one guy, two guys, or a busload of guys and gals."

"Let's work on the assumption that there's more than one person but the one on the phone is definitely calling the shots. He wants us to know he's in charge," Brodie said.

"That's what I thought too," Walker said. "He thinks he's smarter than us. Hell, he's probably right. I can't shake the feeling he was dangling information in front of me with that Bible quotation."

Brodie skipped back to the section of the conversation where Lewis showed off his biblical knowledge. "And the sons of Israel came to buy grain among those that came: for the famine was in the land of Canaan."

"What do you think it means?" Zoe asked. "You think he has some kind of religious background? A priest or something?"

Walker shook his head. "I don't get that vibe. He's not a Bible scholar, just the kind of asshole who knows everything. No offense, Brodie."

Zoe noticed Brodie didn't react to the dig. His brow was furrowed in concentration, like he was trying to come up with a quiz answer.

"What is it?" she asked.

"Something I checked out earlier that turned out to be a dead end. One of the quotations in the manifesto sounded like it had come from the Bible, but when I googled it, I found out it wasn't in the Bible. The only hit was an old newspaper article about one of these weird Christian sects."

"Oh, yeah?" Walker said.

"That's what I thought too," Brodie said. "It was promising, until it wasn't. The sect was called the New World Church. They owned fifty acres of land in Southern California, based themselves in some ghost town out there. They wanted to bring about a new world order via the fall of Babylon, aka the USA."

Zoe and Walker exchanged a glance. Brodie kept talking.

"The only problem is the church doesn't exist anymore. The founder died years ago and it looks like the church died with him."

"You think Lewis could have been part of this sect?" Walker asked.

Brodie shrugged. "Maybe. Or he could have just picked up one of their pamphlets someplace. Either way, it doesn't get us anywhere. The New World Church is gone. It doesn't have a base or any remaining adherents as far as I was able to find."

"There's other religious-sounding stuff in the document," Zoe said. "Sometimes it's straight Bible quotes, sometimes it's just a vibe." She looked at Walker. "Maybe he's going to hit a church next. Do we have any churches at a one thirty-eight Main?"

Walker thought about it. "I think there are a few; we can check them out. Or what about the Bible reference? Genesis, chapter forty-two, verse five—does that tie in somehow?"

"Wait a second," Zoe said. "Maybe we're overthinking it. There's got to be a town named Canaan somewhere. Could it be that simple?"

"I don't think so," Brodie said quietly.

They looked at him. His hands were raised a little off the table, like he was a pianist getting ready to play a concerto.

"No town called Canaan?" Zoe prompted.

"There are a couple dozen towns called Canaan all over the map. But he's not going to any of those."

Walker cleared his throat. "We're not paying you by the word, so cut to the chase."

"Canaan was situated in modern-day Lebanon."

Zoe saw a change in Walker's expression as soon as Brodie said *Lebanon.* But he didn't say anything, just watched as Brodie pulled out his laptop and started typing.

A couple of minutes later, Brodie sat back and examined his work for a second. Then he turned the screen toward them and brought up the map with the Midwestern states highlighted, the coastal states grayed out. He tapped on Kansas to isolate it. Then he tapped at a spot in the north of Kansas, and a single pin appeared. Walker had noticed that that innocuous digital-pin image triggered a Pavlovian reaction in him lately. It was one of those symbols that were so common, you didn't even think about them. But now it was the mark of the enemy. And it was planted somewhere in the heart of the state at the heart of the country.

"That's the middle of America, isn't it?"

Brodie had opened his mouth to start speaking, but that made him pause. Walker saw Zoe grin at the look of disappointment on Brodie's face.

"That's right . . . it's actually—"

"It's a town named Lebanon, Kansas," Walker said. "The geographic heart of America. They have a Main Street."

"You've heard of it?" Zoe asked.

"My kid had to do an assignment on this in fourth grade—find the center of America. It took her about five seconds on Google. Technically, there's no true center of America, because you get a different location depending on whether you count Alaska and Hawaii, but if you take the contiguous forty-eight states and balance them on the head of a pin, you get a spot just outside Lebanon, Kansas. Since day one, this guy has been one step ahead of us, and he's been cocky about his target choices. This fits right in with that pattern, like he's gone as far east and west as he could, and now he's hitting the middle. How do you know that one's next, though?"

"We don't," Zoe said. "Not for sure. But we've been over these pages, and aside from references to the six original murder scenes, we can't see anything that looks like it refers to another location. In the absence of any other signposts, I think we have to assume this one is coming up, even if it isn't the next one. It doesn't mean we have to ignore anything else, but—"

"But we definitely don't want to ignore this," Walker finished. "Agreed."

Brodie was still hovering by the screen. His expression showed a mixture of delight and disappointment.

"Anything else?" Walker asked.

"Uh, no. I kind of had a whole spiel to explain that, but you got it."

33

36,000 FEET ABOVE KANSAS

Eighteen hours later, they were in the air, and the Midwestern skies were unsettled. Zoe wasn't a great flier at the best of times, and now she gripped the handrests and quietly resented Walker's and Brodie's seeming obliviousness to the turbulence.

In fact, she was genuinely grateful when Brodie sat down across from her and started telling her what seemed like every piece of information he had gleaned on their destination. It didn't take long, and that was no reflection on Brodie's research skills. Lebanon had been founded in the late nineteenth century and named after a town in Kentucky. Half a century earlier, the Kentucky Lebanon had been given the name as a reference to the biblical region. There were forty-seven cities, towns, and villages named Lebanon across the United States, but no one had any doubt that this was the one that Lewis had in mind.

Brodie spoke about their destination with his usual nerdy glee. The town was almost a perfect square on the map, the northwest corner of the square nestled at the intersection of Routes 281 and 833. Lebanon's Main Street was almost exactly in the center of the settlement in the center of America. It bisected the town north to south, with east–west avenues branching off at right angles, each named functionally or geographically: School Avenue, Railway Avenue, Kansas Avenue. The north–south streets parallel with Main were mostly named for trees: Pine, Walnut, Maple.

"It's like the platonic ideal of a Main Street," Brodie said with enthusiasm. "If I were creating a microcosm of a town to represent the whole case, this is what I would design."

Zoe looked at him with raised eyebrows. "I'm very happy for you."

A sudden drop sent Zoe's stomach lurching downward in tandem. Brodie smiled at her reaction.

"Relax. Do you know—"

She cut him off by holding a hand up. "If you're about to tell me the statistics on air crashes versus car wrecks, don't."

Brodie wisely decided to close his mouth.

The plane descended through clouds to Phillipsburg Municipal Airport, and Zoe was grateful to see elusive snatches of solid ground start to appear.

At the landing strip in Phillipsburg, there was a silver SUV the size of a tank waiting for them. The driver wore dark glasses and an earpiece, and Zoe thought, not for the first time, that she had stepped into a different world. She, Walker, and Brodie climbed into the back of the SUV, which was configured with two rows of seats facing each other. There was another agent in a gray suit already in the back. He was slim with short hair and dark eyebrows, and he reached out to shake Walker's hand as they climbed inside.

"Ted Winters, KC field office."

Walker introduced himself and the other two and asked Winters to give him the lowdown on preparations so far. Lebanon was a straight forty miles ahead on Route 36, so they had plenty of time.

"Operational base is a town named Smith Center, fourteen miles from Lebanon," Winters told them. "Lebanon itself has a population of under two hundred people, so we're going to have to be a little more discreet than normal."

"So just two or three FBI-branded Humvees?" Zoe said, straight-faced. She was feeling a lot more human now that she was back on the ground.

"We're not going to have any vehicular presence within Lebanon at all, ma'am. We think that would be—"

"She's joking, Ted," Walker said.

Winters looked relieved. "Of course. We have people on the ground already, and the address at Main Street has full surveillance, front and back."

"You haven't pulled the police guard that was already there, though?" Walker asked quickly.

Winters shook his head. "Don't worry. Everything that was in place is still in place. The Kansas staties have had a car outside the property for the past four days, and that's continuing. They're the only visible presence on Main Street."

"Good. Tell us about the residents."

Winters consulted the tablet in front of him. "The owners are Jane and Harold Furman, sixty-eight and seventy-two years old, respectively. They live at the house with their adult son, Nathan, who's developmentally disabled."

"How are we going to evacuate them?" Zoe asked.

"We already had a full schedule of their normal movements from the standard door-knock visit earlier this week. On Friday evenings, they always go for a walk after dinner. They're doing that now, as usual. When they get back, they'll enter through the front door. The backyard has cover on either side."

"That's another reason this is a strong target," Brodie commented. Zoe glanced at him and saw he was looking at the satellite image of the house on his phone.

Winters continued. "We have people inside the neighbor's place to the south, and the north and west sides have the line of sight blocked by trees. We take the Furmans out through the back, and there'll be an unmarked vehicle waiting for them under the tree cover. We sit tight for a while as our people in the house turn on the lights, close the blinds, and so on, and then we drive the Furmans back to Smith Center."

Walker nodded his approval. "Any sign of surveillance that isn't ours?"

"Obviously we can't be as thorough as we'd like without drawing attention, but it doesn't look like it," Winters said. "The population size is a problem for us, but it'll be a problem for the subject too. We've got names, addresses, and DMV photographs for every adult resident of Lebanon. So far, everyone we've seen has been on the list."

As she listened, Zoe gazed out the window at the unending panorama of fields. The sun was beginning to set on the horizon, which seemed so distant it felt like it should be in a different state. She was used to flat, featureless landscapes in Illinois, but Kansas was a whole different kind of flatness. The land seemed to go on forever. She saw a worn sign for a town called Troublesome. She wondered what was going on in Troublesome tonight and whether it was any more troublesome than what they were likely to encounter.

Winters's phone buzzed and he held it to his ear.

"Yeah, we're ten minutes out. Good. Good. I'll let them know."

He hung up and looked at Walker. "The Furmans are on their way back from their walk."

Zoe dwelled for a second on the absurdity of a regular evening walk suddenly being subject to more intense and expensive surveillance than your average presidential meet-and-greet.

"Who's going to be in the house?" she asked.

"I am," Walker said.

They reached Smith Center twenty minutes later. Winters had given them a brief background. Compared to Lebanon, Smith Center was a thriving metropolis, with a population of over fifteen hundred. Even here, the FBI footprint was as light as possible. No marked vehicles, no swarms of agents in FBI-branded jackets and ball caps. The ops center had been set up in the local elementary school. The silver SUV pulled up outside the sprawling redbrick building and parked next to three black SUVs. Zoe thought that these would be incongruous enough in a town like this, a town not so very different from her own. The rumor mill would already be working.

Winters led them through corridors lined with bulletin boards adorned with informational posters and student art to the gymnasium. It was hot and clammy. The AC was either shitty or nonexistent. A couple dozen agents in shirtsleeves were working on laptops at fold-out lunchroom tables and chairs. Large screens were set up at the far end of the gym, some of them blank, some showing aerial views of the terrain.

The bleach-and-rubber smell and the echoing chatter of the space took Zoe right back to high school. She had been a quiet student for most of her academic career, surrounding herself with a small, tight group of friends. She had come to the attention of the teachers and the wider student body only after her father was killed. That had led to a few weeks of overattention, and then the school had settled back into its routine, except that now, everyone knew who she was. Most people avoided her, as though tragedy were contagious.

Zoe sat down at a clear space at one of the lunch tables opposite a woman who looked to be in her early twenties and wore glasses with thin frames. Zoe opened her laptop. While she waited for it to come to life, she looked around at the hive of activity.

"You think we'll get him tonight?"

Zoe glanced at the bespectacled woman. She had light brown hair and a little gap between her front teeth.

"Alison," the woman said, offering her hand. "I'm not with you guys—they tapped me from the local PD."

"I'm not with us either," Zoe said, shaking her hand. "Not really. Zoe Hill, Granton PD."

Alison took a second to think about that. "Granton—the Saturday-night case?"

"That's the one," Zoe said. "I'm on the task force. For the moment."

"What was it like?"

"You've seen the pictures?"

"Yeah, pretty gruesome. I mean, I'm sure it's different in real life. I've never been at a homicide scene."

"It was my first."

"Quite a debut."

Zoe decided to change the subject. "So have you been out to the house?"

Alison nodded excitedly, reminding Zoe a little of Brodie, and swiveled her laptop around so that she could see. The screen was split into six squares, each showing a live feed of a different room in an unremarkable family dwelling. Right now, it looked like nobody was home.

"I was out there this morning when they set up the cameras. One in every room. I had to dress as an RN. They come every morning to help the Furmans with their son."

"The Furmans were home when you were there? What are they like?"

"They're sweet. They're a little confused by all this. I expected them to be, you know, freaking out. I mean, wouldn't you be?"

"Yeah, I guess."

"But they seemed totally chill. Like, they've seen it on TV, but they don't think this guy would come anywhere near them. Unless your people are right, huh?"

"Right."

Time passed quickly. The sky outside the long, narrow windows near the ceiling of the gym darkened. Evening elided into night. The Furmans were successfully evacuated as per the plan, and their arrival at a motel three streets away from the elementary school was confirmed.

Around eleven, Zoe looked up and saw Walker approaching across the parquet floor of the gymnasium.

"Everything okay?" she asked.

He raised his eyebrows like he didn't want to commit to an answer to that question. "The Furmans are safe. We have two agents in the house already, and there's about to be a third. I'm headed there now."

Zoe swallowed, suddenly feeling a lot more anxious than she had before. All signs pointed to this being the next target for a killer who hadn't missed yet. For the first time, someone she knew was heading into danger.

"Good luck, boss."

He opened his mouth, probably to tell her not to call him boss again, but then closed it again. Finally he said, "Thanks. Hold the fort for me here, huh?"

She pointed at Alison's laptop. "We'll be watching."

Walker turned and headed for the door. Zoe watched him go. It seemed to have gotten even hotter in here. She took off her jacket and opened up her notes. Not that there was anything she could usefully contribute from here on in, of course.

All there was to do was watch and wait.

34

SMITH CENTER, KANSAS

A half an hour later, the hustle and bustle had abated, and the majority of the personnel had dispersed to locations in and around Lebanon. Zoe was sitting with the remaining personnel in the gym watching the house on Main Street—the feeds from the twelve cameras arranged around the interior and exterior of the house were showing on the big screens at the back of the gym, along with a live static satellite image of Lebanon with the house at the center and another angle from a high-altitude drone circling far above town.

One of the cameras, the one in a laundry room at the back of the house, was a little fuzzy, blurred due to interference. The technicians had tried a couple of things to sharpen it up, with mild improvement, but it was still a little grainy in contrast to the others.

Picture quality wasn't an issue at the moment, since there wasn't much activity on any of the screens. There were two agents in the house, one in the kitchen at the back and one upstairs at the front. The streets of the town were quiet, but Zoe assumed that was normal. An outsider would stand out like a vegan in a barbecue joint, so if their killer really was planning to hit this place next, it was a ballsy move, even if he did keep to his routine of striking between midnight and four. Speaking of which, they were almost in that zone now. The clock on one of the screens was ticking toward midnight and currently showed 23:37 local time.

The voice of one of the agents transporting Walker to the scene sounded from the speakers and echoed off the walls of the gym:

"We're approaching the edge of town now."

The agent who was running the ops room acknowledged the update and told him they could see them. It wasn't hard to spot them on the satellite image—there was only one set of headlights on 281. Zoe watched the small twin dots of light pass out of the darkness of the country, and the car became visible under the streetlamps on Elm Street, which marked the eastern boundary of Lebanon. The car proceeded north, passed North Railway and Kansas Avenues, then made a right on Chicago Avenue.

The car continued past the intersection with Main Street, then made a right into the darkened alley between the houses on Main and Maple. It disappeared when the driver turned off the lights.

Zoe shifted her gaze to the square on the screen that showed the backyard. A moment later, the gate opened and Walker appeared, walking quickly toward the house.

She followed him to the next square, the back door that opened into the kitchen. He met the agent there and they exchanged a few words.

Everything going according to plan.

The clock read 23:42.

And then the first surprise of the evening landed.

"Oh, shit, are you sure?"

Zoe looked in the direction the raised voice had come from. An agent standing by the climbing bars on the wall was on his phone. Suddenly, he became conscious that every eye in the place was on him. He took the phone away from his ear and raised his voice to address the rest of the room:

"Sarasota. One thirty-eight Main in Sarasota, Florida, has just been hit."

35

There was an immediate reaction: synchronized curses. The scraping of chair legs on the polished gym floor. Zoe took her phone out and checked the news sites. Nothing yet, but if the FBI had only just heard about it . . .

She checked Twitter, or whatever it was called this week, searched *Sarasota,* and saw there was already a stream of speculation. There were pictures of a single-story house. Video showing multiple police cars, lights flashing. Not a lot in the way of facts, other than there was substantial police activity on the 100 block of Main Street, Sarasota. And by now, everybody on the planet knew what that meant.

Her eyes went to the segment of the screen showing the living room in Lebanon. There was no sound, but it was clear Walker and the other two agents were having the same conversation the knots of people here were having.

"Shit, this doesn't look good."

Zoe turned her head from the screen to see Alison from earlier. "Let's wait and see."

Slowly, the details began to filter through. As more of a picture started to emerge from Sarasota, the tension in the room seemed to dissipate a little. There had been an incident at 138 Main, but so far, it looked like it was different from what had happened at the other sites.

Shots had been fired, at least one person wounded. But it sounded like he had been shot outside of the house. Within twenty minutes, they had enough information to say that this shooting did not appear to be the work of the Main Street killer.

Ten minutes later, it was on all the networks. The technicians kept the camera feeds from the house up on the big screens, but almost everyone was ignoring those in favor of the news channels playing on their computers and the smaller screens dotted around the gymnasium.

Zoe felt her phone buzz in her pocket and read the text from Walker.

False alarm. Let's keep our eye on the ball.

"Poor guy."

Alison was staring at her phone.

"Hmm?" Zoe said, still staring at Walker's message.

"The victim in Sarasota died. He was a pizza guy, got the wrong address. The owner heard somebody at the door and shot him through it."

Zoe shook her head. "People are going crazy," she said. "We'll be damn lucky if this is the only time that happens."

"I guess it's another thing for the security people's list," Alison said. "No unescorted visitors."

"It's already on the goddamn list," Zoe snapped, letting her frustration out. "Those assholes should have walked him up to the house."

Alison blinked, and when she spoke there was a frostier tone: "Maybe the department out there doesn't have the same kind of generous budget that you do."

Zoe ignored the pointed *you*, meaning the FBI. She was damned if she was going to apologize, even if Alison here thought it was bad manners to criticize their brothers and sisters in blue.

"Whatever. The big problem right now is that every cop on one-thirty-eight detail is going to be on their phone or their radio right now instead of . . ."

"Instead of?"

Zoe didn't answer. Her eyes were on the screen. The static satellite view. A single vehicle was moving south along the highway, approaching Lebanon.

"Instead of keeping their eye on the ball," she said, then raised her voice. "Car! Approaching north of town."

There was a murmur as the other people in the room put aside their phones and looked up at the screen. The car was a few miles out, taking its time, in no hurry, but there was only one destination on that road.

A moment later, the guy with the headset put his hand to his ear and listened, then addressed the rest of them. "North Unit has eyes on them and we have a license plate. Whoever this is, it's not a local."

Saturday

36

138 MAIN STREET
LEBANON, KANSAS

Midnight passed, but there was a long way to go. The Furman house reminded Walker a little of his youth, specifically his weekend visits to his grandpa's place in Newark. The furniture and carpets were all good quality and well maintained but had clearly been there for decades. The son's bedroom on the ground floor was the only exception. It had been refurbished recently, the door widened to accommodate his wheelchair. This house felt like a real home, though. It was clean and comfortable and . . . safe.

Or at least, it should have been safe. Not for the first time, Walker felt an almost primal anger at the transgressions of this killer. The people in these homes would never feel entirely safe again. The FBI might catch him tonight, but he had already taken something from thousands of people that they would never get back.

Walker was in the living room at the front of the house. They had a man in the kitchen and another upstairs in the main bedroom. Per the plan, they all stayed away from windows. As far as anyone watching was concerned, the Furmans had kept to their usual Friday-night habit, returning home just before nine o'clock. All families tended to have a routine—usually a more predictable one than they thought—but the Furmans' was particularly regimented due to Nathan's requirements. They ate an evening meal, went for a walk, and then watched television until eleven, at which point they helped Nathan get to bed.

The Furmans hadn't been able to relocate from 138 Main because of the difficulty of finding suitable accommodations for the three of them for an indeterminate period of time. Tonight, they would be staying in adjoining rooms at the motel in Smith Center with an aide to help Nathan. Walker wondered what would happen if Brodie's theory was wrong or even just wrong about tonight. How many more times could they concentrate so much manpower on one town?

He wondered how Zoe and Brodie were getting on at the command center. The false positive in Sarasota had ruffled a few feathers. Walker could understand that.

The anticipation was intolerable. Would they get another report from somewhere else on the map? Or nothing at all? Walker wondered for a moment which would be worse and then chastised himself. Of course a night of unbroken tension would be better than the report of another murder.

At 12:07 a.m., Walker got the first indication that he wouldn't be waiting all night. A two-word message from Zoe: Vehicle sighted.

Walker put the headset on and spoke to central command. "What's happening?" He went to the kitchen and signaled to Agent Manning, who was sitting at the dining table. He brought the feed from the high-altitude drone up on his laptop screen. Walker could make out a vehicle traveling top to bottom on the screen. Just a dot on the straight line of the road.

One of the agents back in Smith Center responded to Walker's question in his earpiece. "North Unit has eyes on. It's a gray Dodge Challenger, two miles from town. Male driver, no passengers. License plate matches a rental picked up in Wichita earlier tonight. You want them to stop it?"

Walker considered. He wanted to see where this driver was going. The vehicle was a rental, so couldn't be linked to any of the residents of Lebanon. That didn't necessarily mean the driver *wasn't* a resident, of course, and Walker was wary of showing his hand too soon. Once he made the decision to go in, there was no way to hit the reset button. If it turned out to be a false alarm, the cat would be out of the bag on their surveillance, and their quarry would be alerted.

There was only one way to be sure this driver was the man they wanted, and that was to see where he went.

"No. Tell North to sit tight. If they can get some video without breaking cover, do it."

Manning was following the progress of the car on the laptop. "He's past North Unit now, approaching the town limits," he reported.

Manning brought up a closer image of the car. Walker could see the headlights moving down the screen. Manning tapped and zoomed in closer still, tracking the vehicle. It reached the edge of Lebanon, and they could see the gray Dodge clearly under the streetlights. It slowed a little along School Avenue, the route the car that had brought Walker here had taken. Walker held his breath as the Dodge slowed for the intersection with Main and then turned right.

"He's coming our way," Walker said. He looked up from the screen and checked the room. The blinds were closed, the lights were off. From outside, it would appear there was nobody awake. He tapped on his communicator to put him through to the agent upstairs.

"He's on Main, headed in our direction," he whispered. "Stay alert."

"Copy that. I can see his lights."

He had to be at the window to do that. Walker hoped he wasn't too close.

He contacted the op center and told them to coordinate the roadblocks on every road out of town. Now that this guy was inside the zone, he wasn't getting out.

Walker took his gun out and saw Manning do the same. He told him to go to the back, watch the door. As Manning got up, Walker put a hand on his shoulder. "We want him alive, but don't put yourself in any danger. If he comes in shooting, we put him down."

There were four agents positioned at cover points with a line of sight on 138 Main. As soon as their suspect approached the house, they would move. But they knew the suspect wouldn't approach from the front, not with the state police car parked outside.

The vehicle passed the intersection with Oak Avenue, crossed onto the 100 block, and slowed again. Walker tensed. The Dodge was in the line of sight of the police car parked out front now. It passed by the police car and 138 and continued along Main.

"He's casing the place," Walker said. "He's going to circle around to the alley."

They watched the Dodge carry on to the next intersection and turn left on Grove Avenue. It slowed when it reached the mouth of the alley, and Walker held his breath. But it kept going, picking up speed again.

It traveled another two blocks, slowed again, turned onto a narrow street, and drove under the cover of a shed or outbuilding.

"What the hell is that?" Walker asked. "Where is he?"

"That's a row of garages," Manning said. He looked up from the screen. "Maybe it's a local after all?"

Walker kept watching the dark rectangle that had swallowed the car. He became aware that he was holding his breath. There was still no movement. "Manning, go to the back door; keep an eye on the yard."

He tapped the button on his earpiece to talk to one of the guys in the alley out back. "Anything?" he asked quietly.

"Negative."

Another voice chimed in, someone at the ops center. "He's parked in a garage off Grove Avenue. We're going to take another look."

An interminable wait, and then the voice spoke again.

"It's definitely a garage. Shutter's down; he must still be inside."

Walker kept his eyes on the backyard. The gate was still closed. There was no movement in the gaps between the fence slats. The seconds drew out into minutes. He checked the time. It had been eight minutes since the Dodge pulled off Grove Avenue and into the garage.

He looked down the short flight of stairs that led to the laundry room and the back door. Manning was down there, crouched beside the dryer. Manning met his gaze and shook his head.

Walker tapped the button again to talk to the command center. "What's happening?"

"Subject hasn't moved since he parked. Vehicle's still inside."

"You're sure the driver's still inside?"

There was a slight hesitation. "No one came out. Nowhere else to go."

Something was up. There was no reason for the driver to park and wait. If this was an innocent resident, he would have exited and walked to his home. If this was Lewis, he would want to get in and out, do what he'd come here to do. Had he intuited that something was wrong?

"Agent Walker, do you want us to approach the garage?"

Walker considered. He wanted to catch the bastard in the act. Maybe this was close enough. Parked near a 138 Main Street, no doubt with weapons. That would show what he had come here to do. He was in the net; that was all that mattered. Then again, they could move only once. If this wasn't their suspect, there was no way to pretend nothing had happened.

"Agent Wa—"

"Okay," he said. "I'm coming out. Units Delta and Echo, seal the jar."

Walker ran to the back of the house. He motioned for Manning to stay put, opened the back door, and stepped out into the night. There was a lingering warmth from the paving stones and the faint smell of jasmine from one of the other yards. Cicadas chirped, the only sound other than the distant hum of the engines of the two cars blocking off the alley. Their suspect had to know he was in a box now. How would that make him react? Walker knew better than to play around with a cornered animal.

As he moved toward the alley off Grove where the garage was, he heard the two SUVs move, closing off either end of the alley. The agents in each car called in their positions.

He reached the alley and saw one of the other agents already outside a low-slung garage with a corrugated-steel door. The garage was at the end of a row of six. It didn't stand out from any of the others in any way. They were neat, well-kept storage units.

Another agent took up a position on the far side of the door; Walker could see his silhouette in the headlights. The three of them faced the door in a loose triangle formation.

"We got cover on the back?" Walker said into his earpiece.

"There's a door, we've got it covered."

Walker had a sinking feeling at the news there was a back door. A back door that could have been used while they waited. He signaled to the nearest man, who moved toward the shutter and then, hesitantly, tugged at the handle on the bottom. It was locked.

Walker didn't have to tell him to fall back immediately after he had rattled the shutter. If their suspect was cornered in there, he had nothing to lose by shooting through the door.

But there was no sound, no sign of life whatsoever. Walker tried to picture the drone view in his mind's eye. They had definitely gotten the right garage, the last one on the row. That was the one the car had gone into.

Another man appeared with a crowbar. His eyes met Walker's; he was waiting for the go-ahead. Walker gave him the nod.

He approached the garage side-on so he wouldn't present a target even if whoever was behind the door possessed X-ray vision and quickly and efficiently slid the chisel end of the crowbar underneath the door. He pulled the bar up and the lock snapped, the door rising an inch or two.

Still no sign of movement.

The agent dropped the crowbar, put one hand under the edge of the door, and threw it up. The corrugated steel rolled up into its housing with a screech of metal. Flashlights lit up the rear of a gray Dodge. The vehicle's lights were extinguished, and it was too dark to determine if there was anyone inside.

"FBI—get out of the vehicle with your hands raised," Walker called.

He heard voices from behind him as two more agents approached from the direction of Grove. Walker held his gun with both hands, his eyes locked on the car. He tightened his finger on the trigger and moved forward.

37

SMITH CENTER, KANSAS

"What's happening?"

Zoe ignored the breathless question from Alison, who was no longer giving her the silent treatment; they had both been watching the same screen, they both had the exact same information. She looked around for Brodie. He was on the other side of the room, watching one of the other screens.

She pulled her jacket on. Forget holding the fort, she was going out there.

Zoe glanced at the screen in front of her. It had been almost ten minutes since the Dodge Challenger had turned into the alley and disappeared into a garage. Now they were watching the bodycam video from the agents as they approached the car.

One of them crouched down, shone his flashlight beneath the chassis.

She saw Walker on the other side of the vehicle. The driver's door was slightly open. He reached out with his left hand, keeping the gun in his right hand aimed at the car, and gripped the door handle.

38

LEBANON, KANSAS

Walker tensed and yanked the door all the way open.

The car was empty.

Walker looked up at the agent approaching from the rear. "Check the trunk."

The trunk was also empty.

"You still out there?" Walker said, addressing the agents covering the back door.

"Yep. Nothing here."

"I'm coming out. Try not to shoot me."

Walker moved beyond the car and played the flashlight over the back wall of the garage to find the door. It had a push bar, like a fire exit. Using the back of his hand to avoid smudging any prints, he pressed down at the far side of the bar. The door popped open on the blinding glare of two more flashlights. Walker shielded his eyes and looked around. The garages backed onto a small wooded area that was only about twenty feet across but ran the length of the two rows of backyards it divided. From here, a man could exit onto either street at virtually any point.

They had miscalculated with the allocation of manpower; they had expected the perpetrator to park as close as possible to the target house, the better to make a fast getaway.

He cursed and checked his watch. Fifteen minutes had elapsed since the Dodge pulled into the garage. More than enough time for the guy to make it over to Main on foot.

"Where the hell did he go?" the bald agent on the opposite side of the Dodge said. "He was only out of sight for a second."

Walker took out his phone and called Manning in the house. "You still inside?"

"Yes, sir, no change here."

Walker lowered his gun and looked around. The driver of the Dodge Challenger had somehow vanished into thin air.

And at that moment, the thin air was broken by the sound of two gunshots.

Walker yelled to one of the agents to stay with the vehicle, and the rest of them ran in the direction of the shots, toward Main Street.

They rounded the corner to see one of the two officers from the car out front approaching a thick stand of bushes in the yard of a house on the opposite side of the street. Residents of the houses were coming outside in robes and pajamas. Walker yelled for them to go back inside.

He called out to the two cops that there were agents approaching from the rear. He drew level with the nearest, who had his gun trained on the shadows.

"What happened?"

"We saw something moving over here." He cocked his head at his partner. "We started to approach and somebody fired on us. We returned fire."

"You hit him?"

"I don't know."

"Get some more light on this," Walker ordered.

They lit up the bushes. There was nobody there. Behind the bushes there was a low fence with horizontal slats. The top one was broken. Walker took the flashlight and played it over the broken slat. Fresh wood gleamed in the light.

He got on his phone and alerted all units to look out for an armed man in the vicinity of Main Street.

"We'll get him," the cop beside him said. "He's not going anywhere."

Walker wasn't so sure about that.

39

SMITH CENTER, KANSAS

A tall, shaved-headed agent named Schmidt asked Zoe if she wanted to drive them out to Lebanon while he finished speaking to his boss on the phone. He was big enough to be a wrestler. She could have used his jacket as a tent and taken a couple of friends camping.

Schmidt finished the call as they were passing the town limits. Periodically, he tried to engage Zoe in conversation as they traveled the fourteen quick miles along US 36, but the best she could offer was monosyllabic responses as she kept her eyes on the GPS, wondering if it would be too late to help when they reached the destination. After what felt like a century, she turned north on 281, and an endless moonlit sea of corn whipped by on the right side.

The southern perimeter line was a roadblock beside a row of low, broad grain silos. Zoe had just pulled onto the side of the road when she saw headlights approaching. A dark-colored pickup truck was moving toward them at a leisurely pace.

They got out of the car. Schmidt signaled to the uniformed officer at the barrier that he would take this one. "You stopping everybody?"

"Yes," the officer said, sounding a little testy. "We let them through if they check out. Unless you want an orderly line?"

Schmidt took his gun out and held it down by his side as he walked into the middle of the road in front of the barrier. He held his left hand up to instruct the driver to stop, even though Zoe was pretty sure the lights and the barrier across the road had done that.

As the vehicle got closer, she could see it was a dark-colored four-door Chevy Silverado, a flatbed at the back. She relaxed a little when she saw a lone female driver. Then she reminded herself that she shouldn't be lowering her guard no matter what. They had no idea who was behind this. She had seen too many bodycam videos of routine traffic stops that ended in somebody getting killed.

The Silverado rolled to a stop and Zoe could hear music from within. Something vaguely familiar. Schmidt closed the distance, his left hand still up, as though he were holding the vehicle in place using willpower alone.

He called out the license plate without turning around. The cop beside Zoe checked her tablet screen.

"On the list. Registered to Michael Sandberg, two-oh-four Chicago Avenue."

Zoe took three paces forward, moving closer to Schmidt as he approached the driver's window. It buzzed down and she recognized the music: "Green, Green Grass of Home."

The driver was a woman in her late thirties. Dark hair, a haggard look in her eyes. The piercing wail from the back seat gave Zoe an indication of what that was about. She ducked a little to see in the back. There was a baby in a car seat, screaming loud enough to put a heavy-metal front man to shame.

"Is there a problem, Officer?" the woman asked, looking past the agent to the barrier and the lights. Her voice was low, tentative. The sound of the helicopter overhead was almost loud enough to drown her voice out.

"Special Agent Schmidt, FBI," Schmidt said, not bothering to show her his ID. "Can I see some identification?"

She reached over to the passenger seat for her purse. Zoe noticed

Schmidt slightly raise his gun below the level of the sill. But she pulled out her driver's license and handed it over. Schmidt took it in his left hand and looked from the card to the woman. "This is you? Lara Sandberg?"

"Yes." The baby's wailing seemed to step up a pitch, and the woman reached her right arm between the seats to soothe the infant. "It's okay, baby, we'll be moving again soon." She looked back at Schmidt. "It's the only thing that calms her down. Keeping moving."

"We'll let you get on your way in a minute. Is this your car?"

"It's my husband's."

"What's his name?"

"Mike. Mike Sandberg."

Schmidt examined the ID again, then glanced at the baby. "Which one of you is the Tom Jones fan?"

"It's the only thing that makes her settle," she snapped.

Schmidt handed the license back. "You still live at this address?"

"Yes."

"You drive by Main Street on your way out here?"

"No. Just came straight from home." She glanced at the screaming kid, exasperated. "Is this going to take long?"

Schmidt looked back the way she had come. The road was empty. "You happen to see anybody suspicious?"

"Suspicious? Suspicious how?"

"Somebody running. Or maybe hiding behind parked cars."

She shook her head.

"Mind if I take a look in the back?"

She glanced at the wailing baby and said plaintively, "If we don't get moving again, she's going to get so worked up that she—"

"I'll just be a moment, ma'am." His tone said that he would take as long as he wanted. The baby was her problem.

She sighed and drummed her fingers on the wheel.

Schmidt moved around the back with his gun pointed toward the flatbed and peered over the sill. Zoe couldn't see what was in it from her position, but evidently, there was nothing of concern there.

Then, in the distance, the sound of gunfire rang out.

Schmidt froze. He and Zoe exchanged a glance.

Three gunshots. Then answering fire from at least two different sources. It came from the center of town.

Schmidt lowered his gun and walked back around. He glanced at the baby with a pained expression as the crying got even louder. He stepped to the driver's side again and bent to address Ms. Sandberg. She didn't seem to have registered the gunshots; maybe she hadn't heard them over the noise of the engine and Tom Jones.

"Sorry to hold you up. I hope it calms down."

"She," the woman corrected.

"We'll need you to wait here at the barrier when you come back, ma'am."

"Sure," she said, and rolled her window up.

Schmidt waved at the cop, and she lifted one of the sawhorses out of the way. The Silverado drove through.

"Was that what I think it was?" Schmidt said, looking in the direction of town.

Zoe didn't answer. She was listening. There hadn't been any further gunshots.

She flinched when the phone lit up in her hand, buzzing against her palm unexpectedly. It was Walker.

"You got him?" she asked breathlessly.

Walker sounded composed. "I don't know. We think we have someone holed up in a trailer on Kansas Avenue."

Just then, Zoe heard more gunshots in stereo—in the distance and louder in the background of the call.

Then the line went dead.

40

LEBANON, KANSAS

The trailer was a long single-wide on a vacant lot between two houses on Kansas Avenue. The paint job was a faded light green. The windows were all dark.

Two agents were sheltering behind a boundary wall when Walker reached the scene at the corner of Kansas and Pine, a block from Main Street.

"He still in there?" Walker asked, crouching behind the wall.

The agent nodded.

"You get a look at him?"

"No. We saw movement in one of the backyards and told him to come out, and he opened up on us. We came after him and he made it to the—"

His words were cut off by another two gunshots from the direction of the trailer. A chunk of brick popped off the top of the wall near where they were crouched.

"FBI," Walker yelled. "You are surrounded. Lay down your weapon and come out."

There was a pause and then one more gunshot in response.

Walker could hear and see other agents converging on the scene from all angles. They had stationed people all over town, though most had been clustered around Main. The helicopter was overhead, the searchlight picking out the trailer like it was the headline act at a rock concert.

Walker shouted into his headset, struggling to hear himself over the sound of the rotors. "Tell the pilot to back off a little, we don't want—"

As though to demonstrate exactly what they did not want, the person inside used a chair leg to clear the broken window glass out of the way. Walker saw a skinny arm reach out holding a handgun, a pale face looking up at the light. Blond hair.

He yelled something unintelligible and started firing at the helicopter. Just what Walker had been worried about.

"Fuck it," the agent next to him said, standing up. Before Walker could say anything, he was taking aim at the upper body leaning out of the trailer window.

The shooter was firing up into the sky; the beam of the helicopter's searchlight spun away as the pilot took evasive action and tried to gain altitude fast.

The agent beside Walker opened fire.

At least two of his first three shots found their target. The sound of his shots was joined by others as more of the agents surrounding the trailer opened up.

The shooter slumped across the edge of the window, the gun dropping on the dry grass. He was shirtless. Dark blood ran down his back from multiple wounds. Walker yelled for everyone to hold their fire.

"We got him?" the agent beside him asked breathlessly. Then, more triumphantly: "*I* got him."

Walker watched as two men moved in, not rushing, keeping their guns on the motionless suspect. The first one kicked the gun away from the body, then reached out and put a hand on the man's neck. He waited for a moment and then turned to Walker with a look that said everything.

Walker holstered his gun. Over twenty years on the job, and this was the first time he had been present at an agent-involved shooting. He almost didn't feel the slap on his back from the young buzz-cut agent beside him.

"We got him."

Walker didn't share the younger agent's certainty. "Something's wrong."

Buzz Cut started to say something, but Walker was walking toward the trailer. The door was open, two agents already inside. The shooter's bottom half was visible now. He wore gray sweatpants and no shoes.

"Where are his clothes?" Walker asked. He wasn't addressing anyone in particular, but the agent standing by the body frowned. "He didn't drive out here like that," Walker said. "Is he carrying any ID?"

"Nothing."

Without another word, Walker turned and went back outside. He approached the limp body of the shooter. His blond hair was long enough to partly drape over his face. Walker crouched a little to get a better angle and used his phone to take a picture of the face. He uploaded it to the system and waited. They had DMV photos for every adult in Lebanon. A moment later, it pinged with a match on one of them.

"What is it?" the agent next to him asked.

"Shit."

Before he could say anything else, an unholy shriek sounded from across the street.

A middle-aged woman in a nightgown was being held back by two agents on the opposite side of the road. Beyond her, the door of the single-story house from which she had presumably emerged was wide open.

"Billy! Oh my God, you killed my Billy!"

Walker turned away from the screaming woman, wincing. He held his phone up so the agent beside him could see the resident profile with which the deceased shooter had been matched.

"His name was William Colby Skerritt. Lived in that house over there. He's not our guy."

41

Zoe grimaced when she heard the latest update. One civilian down, and they were still hunting the bad guy.

She had to fight the urge to leave her post at the boundary and venture into the heart of Lebanon to join the hunt. It was frustrating being just on the edge of things, knowing that the killer was somewhere inside this perimeter. Hiding, perhaps biding his time. Maybe planning to go down in a blaze of glory, taking as many cops and feds with him as he could.

More Lebanon residents were starting to emerge from their homes, drawn by the sound of the gunfire, the helicopter, and the general commotion. Mostly, but not exclusively, they were men. A guy in a blue silk robe strolled across the neat grass of his front yard as though he were on his way to pick up the morning paper. Agent Schmidt yelled, "Sir, please go back inside your home and stay in place."

The man glanced at him with an irritated expression. "Who in the hell are you? What's going on?"

Schmidt turned away from him and jutted a thumb toward the three luminescent letters on his jacket. "Three guesses, buddy." He turned around. "Get back in the house. We have an active shooter in the neighborhood."

Silk-robe guy thought for a second and then complied, though he didn't seem pleased about it. When the man had closed the door behind him, Schmidt turned to Zoe and saw her expression. "What?"

"Nothing."

"We don't have time to play nice. They're going to bitch about it anyway. Last thing we need is another one of these idiots getting themselves shot." He looked up and down the street for more wandering townsfolk. "The woman with the screaming kid was pissed at us too. You think she's gonna file a complaint?"

"Had to be done," Zoe said. "She'll understand when she finds out what—"

"What?" Schmidt asked when Zoe stopped abruptly.

Zoe turned and looked past the barrier at the road the woman had driven down several minutes before, right as the shooting started.

"The woman in the Chevy pickup. Did she ask what this was about?"

"No. Why?"

"Don't you think that's a little weird? You're in your car in your small town in the middle of nowhere at midnight and suddenly there's police and FBI and helicopters and a roadblock . . . What's your reaction to that?"

Schmidt's face drained of color. He took out his phone. "Put me through to whoever's at the three-mile line on 281 South."

Zoe was already running to the car.

A minute later, she was following the road the Chevy had taken out of town. She joined 281. The last few buildings on the outskirts of Lebanon melted away and the landscape opened up.

Maybe she had gotten this wrong. Sleep deprivation meant people didn't function properly. That could explain why the woman hadn't reacted normally.

How much of a head start did the Chevy have? Fifteen minutes? Twenty? With nothing else on the road, she could be twenty miles away by now. Way beyond the range of their surveillance. She slowed as she got to the parked Bureau cars at the three-mile line and held up her ID.

"Did Schmidt reach you?"

The agent was a short woman wearing a blue baseball cap. She nodded.

"Woman in a gray Chevrolet. We'd gotten the plate from the team at the town boundary, so we let her through right before he—"

Zoe pressed the gas pedal to the floor, and the woman and the last outpost were gone. Her headlights lit up the road ahead, and she saw the speedometer climb above eighty. The darkened landscape flashed past. She glanced at a sign for Sweet Home Cemetery and almost missed something on the opposite side of the road. She looked in the rearview mirror, saw some kind of dark bundle by the roadside. She slammed on the brakes, and the car skidded to a halt a hundred yards down the road. She got out, took out her gun, and dug her flashlight from the other pocket, thinking that if this was a bag of somebody's garbage, she could say goodbye to any possibility of catching up with the Chevy.

But a part of her hoped it was just a bag of garbage.

She ran back along the side of the road, the beam of her flashlight strobing up and down as she moved. In the distance, from the direction she had come, she heard sirens.

Getting closer, she could see the bundle was someone sitting on the side of the road with their back to Zoe, unmoving.

She covered the distance quickly, gun trained on the figure.

"Don't move," she said.

She came within five feet and started to circle the figure, keeping the gun trained on its center mass. She let go of the breath she was holding when she saw that it was the woman from the Silverado, cradling the baby in her arms.

She didn't look up at Zoe, didn't seem to be aware of her presence. She was murmuring something over and over, like a mantra. As Zoe got close, she was able to discern the words.

"It's okay . . . it's okay . . . it's okay . . ."

It felt as though the woman were talking to herself as much as the infant. Zoe lowered her weapon and looked north along the highway. A couple of feet away she saw tire tracks in the dirt. The flat landscape extended into the darkness. Would a car that had taken off from here a few minutes ago still be visible? Maybe not, if its lights were doused.

A sharp intake of breath told her that the woman had finally noticed her presence.

Zoe kept her gun low and raised her other hand in reassurance. "It's okay, ma'am, I'm a police officer. Is everything okay?"

The woman began hyperventilating. The baby shifted position and started crying again.

"He—he said he would kill my baby unless I did what he told me."

"Who said that, ma'am?"

"I stopped at the corner of Main to check she hadn't slipped out of her straps. Mike is always telling me to keep the doors locked when I—"

"Ma'am, did somebody get in your car?"

She nodded. "He was all in black. He lay down in the back seat. He had his gun pointed at Molly. I was so sure the cop back there would see him and then, and then . . ."

"Shh," Zoe said, realizing she was talking to the woman as though she herself were a baby who needed soothing. "You're okay now. I'm sorry to ask you, but this is really important. Did the man have another car?"

A shake of the head.

"So he's still in your Chevy?" She pointed south. "He went that way?"

Another nod.

She saw lights approaching from the way she had come. Most likely Schmidt or one of the others, but . . .

She told the woman to hunch down, but Zoe kept her eyes on the approaching lights. A moment later, she saw that she had been right—it was a Kansas state police car, Agent Schmidt in the passenger seat.

He got out before the car came to a full stop, his face pale. He had the expression of a man who knows he's fucked-up.

"What happened?" he said.

"Our guy was hiding in the back seat. He's headed that way."

"What? You mean—"

"Just go; I'll stay with her."

Schmidt didn't need to be told twice. He got back in, and the car took off, its wheels spinning; the driver swerved onto the highway and floored it as the car straightened out.

How long was the head start? Twenty-five minutes now? She knew that 281 crossed Route 36 less than a mile away. Three points of the compass to choose from, and there were multiple minor roads peeling off from the highways in all directions from there.

They'd had him in their hands and let him go.

GEHENNA

The Professor opened the door and stepped out into the night. There was an unseasonal chill in the air.

He looked west to where the sun had sunk below the horizon a few hours before. There was still a slight glow. There was no sound from the dead pit.

He thought about the mission. He thought about the map.

He closed his eyes and found himself doing something he hadn't done for more than ten years.

He began to pray.

42

138 MAIN STREET
LEBANON, KANSAS

Walker was still absorbing the fact that not only had they shot the wrong guy, they had let the right one get away. He was standing on the sidewalk outside 138 Main Street when he saw Zoe get out of the black SUV that had pulled up to join the dozen other vehicles.

The place had come to life like somebody had called a surprise block party. Police cars and FBI SUVs everywhere; residents outside their houses in robes and pajamas, gathering in knots to trade rumors. The body of William Skerritt had been removed from the scene on Kansas Avenue. His distraught mother had been taken to the hospital in Jewell County. Preliminary interviews with some of the neighbors had sketched a picture of a troubled soul in and out of jail on assault and drug charges. *Never seemed quite right in the head.*

Those who had spoken to Skerritt said he had been worried for years that "they" would come to get him. A phalanx of armed federal agents suddenly appearing from nowhere had thrown gasoline onto the already burning bonfire of Skerritt's paranoia. He had struck out, wounding two agents and ending up dead. Another guy in the wrong place at the wrong time.

Pretty soon, the media would be here in force. There was already a helicopter making slow circles above them. The FBI's own helicopter had long since departed to make so far fruitless runs up and down the highways looking for a trace of the Chevy Silverado.

"He knew," Walker said. "He knew it was a trap."

"He must have spotted one of the lookouts," Zoe said. "Or maybe the drone?"

"No. Something tipped him off at the last minute. He got all the way to Grove Avenue. If he had known before that, he would have turned back. Something happened."

Walker looked back at the house, mentally running through the minutes leading up to the gray Dodge Challenger parking in the garage. He had been in the bedroom at the front of the house; Manning in the little office at the back. They got the update that the car was en route and followed its progress in real time via updates from the command center. What had changed?

Then he knew.

"Son of a bitch," he said as he started striding toward the house.

"What?" Zoe called after him, hurrying to catch up. "What is it?"

There was a youthful agent standing by the door. He got out of Walker's way so fast that Walker half expected to see a cartoon cloud of dust appear in the space. Walker moved quickly through the hall and down the short flight of steps to the laundry room at the back of the house. The room was only about ten feet square, with a washer and dryer, some shelving, and the electricity box. On the wall was a novelty sign with faux-vintage advertising art of a 1950s housewife in a blue dress with black polka dots and a slogan reading *Make Yourself at Home—Clean My Kitchen*. He opened the electricity box and examined the switches, looking for anything out of place. There was a panel in the metal box, screwed shut.

"What is it?" Zoe asked.

"Right after the driver parked, Manning came down here."

Zoe looked at the little glass window in the door that led out to the backyard. "You think he could have seen him?"

Walker shook his head. "No, he was a quarter of a mile away." He dug in his pocket for his keys, used the edge of his door key as a screwdriver, and loosened the screw holding the panel closed until he could get it off with his fingers. He pried the cover off.

"I don't get it."

Walker examined the wires inside. Nothing. But there had to be something. He took a step back and the sign caught his eye.

"Make yourself at home," he said under his breath.

Then he reached out and pulled the picture off the wall.

Behind it was a small pinhole camera, no bigger than a cigarette lighter. Walker looked back at the picture. The camera had been positioned behind a tiny hole drilled in it, right through one of the polka dots on the 1950s housewife's dress.

Ten minutes later, they were in the Furmans' kitchen. Zoe had found a jar of instant coffee in the cabinet, and she and Walker were sipping the brew she'd made from matching Disneyland mugs. The forensics guys had already bagged and removed the camera. They had everything they needed to process it in a rush back at Smith Center. Fingerprints were probably too much to hope for, but analysis of the camera might prove fruitful.

"Well, it explains a lot," Zoe said. "He doesn't just case the targets ahead of time, he keeps tabs on them too."

"Neither of us had been in the laundry room until Manning came down here at the end," Walker said. "The perp must have checked the camera and seen him, knew it was a trap."

"Why didn't he see anyone before?"

"He can't be watching all the time," Walker said. "He didn't know anything was wrong until the last minute. He's approaching the target, decides to check in on his spy camera, sees Manning, and knows he needs to get out of here."

"I can't believe we missed the camera," Zoe said. "Didn't they check the house earlier?"

"Yeah, but it wasn't an invasive search. We couldn't rip the place apart while trying to make it seem like nothing had changed. We didn't know we were looking for this—it wasn't part of the MO. Or not a part we knew about."

"There were no cameras at the other scenes," Zoe said. "We would have found those, no question."

"There were no cameras by the time we got there," Walker corrected. "But he could have removed them after doing the job. It makes sense. Especially for the last few kills—he would need to be sure his target was home. What better way to do that?"

"Okay, so this could be how he keeps tabs, and if you're right, he's removing the surveillance after the kill." Zoe thought for a second, then looked at Walker. "But how did he get a camera in here in the first place?"

43

138 MAIN STREET

LYDCOTT, NEBRASKA

Officer Samuel Wynn needed to piss.

This was his third straight night on Main Street detail, and the attraction of a posting that had been sold as a chance to be part of the biggest case in the country or at worst an easy few nights away from paperwork had quickly began to pall.

The briefing with the FBI task force had covered the main points of the case and what they required from local police departments. Not surprisingly, what they required was the grunt work. Sitting in the car staring at an unremarkable split-level house inhabited by a standoffish young couple and their toddler, a family recently transplanted from Lincoln.

Wynn was supposed to make a circuit of the house and the backyard every half hour, but after Mrs. Boorman asked him if he could "step quieter" on the gravel underneath their kid's window, he had scaled that back to once an hour.

It looked like the whole family had gone to sleep early tonight. The house had been in darkness since just after eleven, the blinds closed on every window. Wynn had heard that the killer often approached houses from the rear, but in this case, that was unlikely. The house backed onto a drainage gully. There was a nine-foot-high chain-link fence that rattled in a strong breeze. If someone tried to scale it, Wynn would hear it, even if he weren't sitting with the window down.

From the hourly news on the radio, it sounded like it had been a busy night elsewhere. A pizza guy killed down in Florida, and some big operation seemed to be going on a little closer to home, just over the Kansas state line. No excitement here in Lydcott, though, as usual.

He yawned and checked the Cornhuskers score from the previous evening on his phone. Minnesota had won by three points. It was 3:14 a.m. O'Leary wasn't coming to relieve him until seven, and he would be late, as always. Wynn got out of the car and rubbed a crick out of his neck. He could combine a piss break with a quiet circuit of the house.

The night air was cold. It had rained in the afternoon, the first time in two weeks, and the ozone smell was still hanging above the asphalt. There was a word for it. His girlfriend, Jayce, had told him it a while ago, but damned if he could recall what it was.

He walked toward the darkened house. It was one of those soundless Lydcott nights when it was quite possible you were the only human being awake in a five-mile radius. The only sound he could hear was his own breathing. No night birds, no barking dogs in the distance.

Access to the backyard was via the side of the house. There was a light, but the Boormans must have forgotten to switch it on tonight. He would take pleasure in reminding them of that in the morning. *It's a team effort, folks. Everybody has to do their part to keep you safe.*

Wynn took his flashlight out and snapped it on, lighting up the passageway at the side of the house like a ballpark during a night game. Everything was exactly the same as it had been a couple hours ago and every time he made this trip. He moved around the back, making sure to step off the gravel and onto the patch of grass as he passed the kid's room, and stopped to play the beam of his flashlight over the windows of the house. They were all dark around this side too.

The bark of a dog from down the street made him pause. He stopped and listened, but there was no other noise. He looked over at the chain-link fence. It was silhouetted against the night sky. For a second, he had the claustrophobic sense of being inside a cage. He turned away, looked back up at the dark windows, and felt a chill.

The killer had been able to move in and out of houses seemingly at will. Sometimes the victims had lain undiscovered for hours. He was a man, but he operated like something that wasn't a man. Something supernatural.

Wynn shook his head. He didn't believe in any of that shit. It was just too easy to scare yourself when you were awake and alone on a dark night. Just him and the mutt down the street.

He gave the yard a cursory check, making sure to go behind the woodshed, then glanced back at the house before unzipping himself and pissing into the darkest corner of the yard. He tried to direct the flow into a thick patch of grass while keeping an eye on the top-floor windows.

When he was done, he sighed in relief, zipped himself up, and walked back out front the way he had come.

He was digging in his pocket for the keys when he caught a hint of movement in his peripheral vision. He stopped halfway across Main Street and looked in that direction. A moment later, a jet-black Labrador rounded a corner, stopped, and stared at him as though evaluating the stranger who had unexpectedly joined him in this solitary midnight world. His eyes glinted yellow in the streetlights.

Wynn grinned and approached the dog. He liked dogs.

"Hey, buddy, out late tonight, huh?"

This was the dog he had heard bark earlier, he guessed. He'd gotten out from one of the neighborhood houses, clearly. The owner forgot to tie his leash in the yard, or maybe a gate had been left unlatched.

Wynn squinted as he got closer, trying to see if the dog had a collar. It was all microchips these days, but perhaps he would be wearing a tag with his address. Returning a missing dog to his owner would be the most useful thing he had done in three nights of this misbegotten detail.

As he got closer, he saw that there was a collar, and streetlight was glinting off a shiny tag attached. "All right, let's see who your human is."

Something passed between Wynn and the streetlight fifty yards away. He saw a man approach unhurriedly, hands in the pockets of his coat.

"Rocky, don't bother the nice man." The voice was deep, confident. It didn't sound like a local accent. East Coast, maybe.

Wynn scratched the dog behind the ears and smiled. "This guy yours?"

He felt the tag under his fingers and something made him glance down at it. There was a name and a phone number.

But the name was *Cooper*, not Rocky.

Wynn looked up and the man paused, hands still in his pockets, ten feet away. And then he moved forward, taking his right hand from his coat.

Wynn reached for his gun, fumbling at his holster as the man in shadow stepped forward, pointing his own gun at him. The dog scampered away with a whimper.

Wynn finally got his hand around the butt of the gun and pulled it loose, but it was already too late.

44

138 MAIN STREET
LEBANON, KANSAS

The techs processed the pinhole camera quickly. Unfortunately, it didn't tell them anything they didn't know already. It had a battery with a life of six months. No memory card; it just piggybacked on the home Wi-Fi and streamed a live feed to a single-page website with no links elsewhere. There was no way of tracing who checked the feed, because the site was publicly accessible. Anybody with the URL could have looked in on the Furmans' laundry room at any point. It was a reasonably high-end camera, but prices for tech had dropped so much in recent years, you could pick one up for under a hundred dollars. The person who had placed it almost certainly had other cameras out there feeding to other anonymous URLs.

The technician who told Walker all this suggested that police and field teams should make discreet searches for cameras at Main Street properties. Perhaps they would get lucky, but Walker knew it wouldn't be that easy. This camera in Lebanon was hidden so carefully that the team that had checked out the house had missed it. They could knock holes in walls and rip up floorboards from coast to coast, and they might find a few of these cameras, but they wouldn't get all of them. The killer would know exactly which targets they'd found and, worse, which they had missed.

The Furmans had gone through the usual checks when the initial surveillance was put on their home, and they answered a lot more questions after Brodie identified them as a high-risk target. They reported no visitors in the past few weeks, had seen no evidence that anyone had entered their house while they were out. But when Walker told them where he found the camera, Jane Furman had nudged her husband. "What about that rude man?"

"What rude man?" Harold asked, and then he remembered.

A while ago, maybe two or three months back, a worker from the power company had visited to check on a problem with their electricity. Actually, Jane Furman corrected, the company had sent *two* workers. The first one fixed the problem, and the second one said there must have been a screwup with the appointments system but he acted like it was the fault of the Furmans.

"Did they both go down to the laundry room?" Walker asked.

"No, only the first man. The second one didn't even come inside the house. He was the rude one. The first man was so nice."

Walker asked them to describe the first guy. They struggled, because it had been a long time, but they remembered he was white, thirties or forties, about six feet tall. His uniform was brown with a green logo that featured a number. When Walker pushed them, they agreed it could have been the number two.

They established that the Furmans were supplied by Kansas Electric and called the company. It took a while to get somebody who could answer their questions in the middle of the night, but eventually a sleepy-sounding supervisor came on the line. He confirmed the company had been called on April 12 and their engineer had visited the next day but found the problem had already been resolved. There was no record of the first visit.

Walker thanked him and asked one last question.

"What do your uniforms look like?"

The guy at Kansas Electric sounded puzzled but told him their uniforms were orange and blue. Not brown with a green logo.

Walker hung up and was opening his mouth to tell Zoe when he saw she was on her own phone, and her face had drained of color.

45

138 MAIN STREET

LYDCOTT, NEBRASKA

Officer Samuel Wynn's body had been found face up on the short lawn outside the house at 138 Main, in Lydcott, a scant twenty miles across the Nebraska state line. His killer had used a can of fluorescent survey spray paint from the trunk of Wynn's patrol car to daub the map-pin symbol around his body on the grass. The stolen pickup from Lebanon was found burned out at the side of the road just outside of town. It was one more surprise on a night that didn't need any more of them.

Zoe looked on as Walker examined the body. His expression was composed, but the way his jaw was set told her his blood was boiling.

"This is a fuck-you," Walker said as he straightened up. "He had already gotten away clean. All he had to do was clear out of the area and come back in another state in a day or two. But he wanted to pay us back for anticipating Lebanon."

Zoe didn't know what to say, so she looked away from Walker and down the street, beyond the taped-off perimeter. A flag on a pole outside one of the homes at the intersection moved in the light breeze. Farther down was a small redbrick church, the twenty-five-foot steeple towering above the other buildings. Every Main Street was different, and yet every Main Street was the same after one of these killings. Faces at windows, some people openly gawking on the sidewalk. She felt their eyes burning into her, and while she knew the stares were mostly prurient curiosity, she couldn't help but feel a weight on her: *You let it happen here. What are you going to do about it now?*

One of the crime scene people had marked a circle on the asphalt around the spot where Officer Wynn's gun had fallen, an unintentional echo of the bigger marking around the body. Wynn had been shot three times at close range, twice in the chest, once in the head. His own gun had not been discharged. He had managed to draw it but not had time to fire.

The shots would have been immediately fatal. Several of the neighbors were woken up by the gunfire, so the killer hadn't used a suppressor. But he had still taken the time to grab his victim's heels, drag the two-hundred-pound deadweight of Officer Wynn thirty yards down the street, and leave him in the middle of the lawn outside 138.

Zoe closed her eyes, and clear as day, she could see Yelich on that summer afternoon years ago.

Your father was involved in an incident earlier today. The suspect was armed, and . . .

Zoe felt like she wanted to vomit, but she gritted her teeth and tightened her fists and willed the moment to pass.

When she turned to Walker, she saw concern in his eyes. "Are you okay? You look like you saw a ghost."

"I'm fine."

One of the local uniforms walked by. He was slim and wiry with a sharp jawline. As he passed, he made eye contact with her and glared.

"What?" she asked, too pissed to let it bounce off her.

"Easy," Walker said quietly, putting a hand on her shoulder. The cop with the sharp jaw shook his head and continued on his way. "He's looking for a fight. Let him find one someplace else."

Zoe nodded. She gestured at Wynn's body. "You think he planned all this in advance?"

Walker gave her an uncertain look before answering. "Yes and no. I think this was a backup target, which he took advantage of."

The jingling of keys drew their gaze to the local police chief as he approached. He was moderately overweight, probably in his mid-fifties, but the tiredness in his eyes made him seem more like eighty. Zoe braced herself for another hard stare, another cutting aside, but when he spoke, the chief just sounded defeated.

"Anything else we can do?"

"No, but thank you. I'm sorry about your officer."

He looked over at the sheet-covered body, regret in his eyes. "Kind of typical, in a funny way."

"How do you mean?" Walker asked.

"If it was gonna happen to someone, it was gonna happen to Sam. Guy was the unluckiest son of a bitch I ever knew. Seven thousand addresses and he had to be outside the one that got hit." He raised his eyes from the body. "I hear you fellas chased him away from his intended target."

"We didn't want to chase him away," Walker said. "But yes. Sorry."

The chief took a deep breath through his nose and nodded. "You got close, though. Nobody'd been able to lay a glove on this prick until last night. I'm just sorry Sam had to pay the price."

Walker said nothing. Zoe knew there was nothing to say. The chief wasn't blaming them. In his line of work, he knew all about the weight of expectation. The law of unintended consequences.

"You going to be sticking around long?" the chief asked.

"We'd like to do some more house-to-house inquiries."

"My men will help you out on that." He looked up at the windows of the house across the street. "Somebody saw your suspect, I hear."

Zoe consulted the notes on her phone. The elderly lady who lived in that house had been the best of the three witnesses they spoke to. "She went to the window when she heard the gunshots. Saw him as he was dragging Officer Wynn's body."

"Definitely a him?"

Zoe nodded. "She was sure of it. Pretty much had to be. Not many women have the upper-body strength to drag a body that size easily. She said he was wearing dark clothing and a hood, but he was about six feet, average build. Then he took a minute to spray the pin shape around the body."

"The other two witnesses only saw him as he was leaving the scene," Walker said.

That was the part that gave Zoe the creeps. All three of the witnesses who looked out to see the killer walking away from the body of the man he had just killed told the same story. He walked briskly but made no attempt to run. He stopped just before he got to the corner and looked up at the single lit window. Jerry Rawlson, a fifty-two-year-old plumber, had been the first one to switch on his light. He said he couldn't make out any features or provide any identifying information beyond corroborating the other witnesses' descriptions, but he said he could feel the eyes burning into him.

"Jerry's the dramatic type," the chief said. "He'll be down at the station asking for a round-the-clock guard tonight."

"You should be able to reassure him," Walker said, gazing at the horizon across the expanse of flatness to the south. "That's the one good thing about being hit by this guy. He doesn't come back."

The chief thought about this for a moment and nodded. "Not so far."

MAIN STREET

138 MAIN STREET
WESTFIELD, MASSACHUSETTS

Christopher Sawyer herds his family out to the driveway and hurriedly loads as many of their belongings as will fit into their gray Honda Odyssey. Then he drives the four of them at speed away from the five-bedroom house that has been their home for the past decade. His brother Joel lives in Salem. They haven't spoken in fifteen years, but after an awkward phone conversation, Joel agreed to let Christopher's family stay in the two-bedroom apartment he runs as an Airbnb. He can give them a week. After that, no promises.

As they merge onto the highway east of Springfield, eleven-year-old Olivia gasps in the back seat. Kate Sawyer snaps at her, telling her not to make sudden noises like that. Olivia tells her she left her science project in her bedroom. It's almost finished and the fair is next week.

Christopher says they're not going to make it to the fair.

138 MAIN STREET
WILMINGTON, ILLINOIS

Lauren Erdmann hasn't been able to stop thinking about the man who she's sure is coming for her in the middle of the night.

Her father called the other day, offered to let her stay in his spare room, but she can't go back there, and she doesn't have the money to stay in a hotel, not even a bad one. No real friends here in Wilmington, and her acquaintances at the store where she works the checkout counter are all very sympathetic, but no one's offered their spare room or even their couch. Every night, she thinks it will be her turn. More than that: She *knows* it will be her turn. Her turn to hear the footsteps on the sidewalk outside, the creak as someone tries the door handle. The fact that it hasn't been her turn yet does not reassure her.

Part of her almost wants the Main Street Man to come. At least then it would be over. She has fentanyl in the bathroom cabinet. She finds herself thinking about the pills almost as often as she thinks about the man who'll be coming to her door in the middle of the night.

138 MAIN STREET

LOS ANGELES, CALIFORNIA

It's a beautiful morning. The sun is glinting off the windows on the top floors of city hall. The art deco tower juts into the indigo sky a quarter of a mile from this unremarkable stretch of sidewalk, just down the road from a restaurant called Señor Fish and across from the Caltrans Equipment shop.

Zak Salguero was hoping for a handful of people to show up to the event he posted on Facebook an hour ago, but there are already two dozen or more people here. Some of them have brought signs. There's a party atmosphere with an undercurrent of tension, like a buzzing dive bar ten minutes from the first fight. Three feet to his right, an attractive girl of about twenty in a lime-green halter top is conversing with an overweight, bearded fortysomething man wearing khaki shorts and a black T-shirt that says *Proudly Unpoisoned.*

"At first I was like, who is this guy?" the girl says. "But you read his work and you realize it makes a lot of sense." Proudly Unpoisoned says he's been talking about the same things all his life, and he's glad people are finally taking notice.

Zak examines his own sign. He's pleased with it. He thinks it's simple and to the point.

FUCK THE SYSTEM
START OVER
138 IS RIGHT

138 MAIN STREET
NAZARETH, PENNSYLVANIA

Travis Streeting hasn't slept a full night in almost a week. The front door is barricaded with the tires he brought home from the garage. Every night he sits in the armchair in the corner of the living room. He's moved it out of the line of sight of the window, and the blinds are closed night and day anyway.

He keeps the Glock in his lap. When the man comes around, he'll be ready. It was hard to stay awake the first few nights, but now it's a breeze. The boundaries have blurred; sometimes he finds himself dreaming while he's awake. He's ready.

GEHENNA

The old house lies empty. The doors are locked and the windows shuttered. The only sound is the clock ticking in the hall.

PART 3

46

NEW YORK CITY

The return flight to New York was almost as turbulent as the previous one, but it didn't affect Zoe as badly this time. Walker was silent. He sat staring out the window, ignoring his files for once. She used the time in the air to grab a nap. It had been a long night. Brodie had skipped Nebraska and returned ahead of them. She wondered how he felt about the night's events.

When they landed at JFK, it was after four o'clock. It took another hour to fight through traffic and get to the FBI building. They went straight into a meeting with Chapman. Brodie was at his desk watching them as they went in. Zoe didn't like the look on his face.

Chapman was standing at the window looking out at Lower Manhattan. She didn't turn around as Zoe and Walker entered. The two of them stood as the door swung closed behind them, waiting for Chapman to speak.

"What happened?" she eventually said.

"We lost him," Walker said simply.

Chapman didn't turn around. "You let the car through, is that right, Officer Hill?"

Before Zoe could say anything, Walker answered.

"It's not right at all. An agent on the scene let it through, nothing to do with Zoe. I'll take responsibility. I know what you have to do, and I understand."

Chapman turned to them at last. She gave Zoe a suspicious look and then addressed Walker. "You're telling me what I have to do?"

Walker cleared his throat. "I know how this goes. We fucked up. *I* fucked up. We had him, and we lost him."

"You also got closer to catching him than anybody else has, as far as I can see."

Zoe looked at Walker. He resisted her attempt to catch his eye and kept talking to Chapman.

"That's down to Brodie," Walker said. "He called it right."

"He may have called it right, but you listened to him. Maybe you didn't nail him this time, but you and your team were right. You're still on."

Walker considered this. Zoe found his expression hard to read. Perhaps a part of him wanted to be relieved of this case.

"Okay," he said after a moment. "I appreciate it."

"Don't," Chapman said. She sat down at her desk and peered over the rims of her glasses at a report in front of her. "I don't do anything out of the goodness of my heart. There's very little goodness in there." She picked up the report and put it into a drawer before looking at them again. "Go home, get some rest. Then rally and get back to it. He underestimated us. Keep it up."

47

Brodie was waiting for them when they came out, an expectant look on his face and an iPad under his arm. The evening sun flooded through the office windows behind him.

"How'd it go?" he asked Zoe. She shot a glance at Walker. Walker consulted his watch, then looked at Brodie.

"Why are you still here? You should have gone home a couple hours ago."

Brodie scratched the back of his neck. He looked as rough as Zoe felt. "Just finishing a couple of things. We might have something on Alaska." He held his hand up before either of them could say anything. "Don't get your hopes up, it might be nothing. We managed to whittle down the list of passengers on flights into Anchorage and found one we can't identify. The ticket was booked under the name John Newman. The phone number on the booking is out of service, and the credit card was used once only. The billing address is a vacant apartment in Santa Fe."

He tapped on his tablet and brought up grainy security footage. It showed a man at the check-in desk wearing a baseball cap, his face in shadow.

"Is this the only video you have?" Walker asked.

"Yeah. You can tell he's definitely camera shy. Look at the way he keeps his head down the whole time."

"This could be him," Walker said. "But it doesn't do us a whole lot of good unless we can follow the trail."

Brodie sighed. "And despite our best efforts, the trail seems to lead to a brick wall."

"Keep on it. We'll find cracks in the wall." Walker turned to Zoe. "You need to get some rest. You didn't sleep last night."

"Neither did you. I'm too wired to sleep anyway."

Walker considered that. "Let's all go get a drink—we can catch Brodie up on the way."

The three of them walked to a quiet bar a few blocks south of the office. It was hip-ly dark and dingy, with a long steel-topped bar lit by a red neon strip that ran along the ceiling and wood-paneled walls festooned with vintage signs.

Walker ordered three beers from a sullen bartender with a lip piercing and carried them over to the nook at the back where Zoe and Brodie were sitting. He passed a quartet of stylishly dressed young women, caught a fragment of a conversation in progress.

"I mean, you can't have twenty-one-year-olds at speed-dating. They're *fetuses*."

Walker couldn't help but smile. At least somebody was talking about something other than the case. He reached the nook and pushed the beers across the table toward the other two.

"I thought she was going to can us for sure," Zoe said, taking hers. She clinked it against Walker's once he had taken his seat beside her. Brodie sat opposite, regarding his own drink with disinterest.

"I didn't," Walker said.

"No?"

"No. She has a lot of flaws, but she's not a politician." He reconsidered that and then said, "At least, she's only as much of a politician as she has to be. She knows we got close, and while taking us off the case might get the heat off her, the investigation would lose ground."

"The cop he killed in Lydcott," Brodie said. "What do you think happened there?"

"It was an improvisation," Walker said. "But it was an improvisation based on background prep. I think he always has alternative targets lined up in case something goes wrong with the primary."

"And last night, we were what went wrong," Zoe said.

"His turn to have a bad night on Main Street," Brodie commented. "About time too."

A fire truck blew by on the street, siren blaring, horn blasting at the traffic. The bar's quiet ambience returned in its wake.

Zoe blew out a puff of air. "Main Street. No wonder it's so effective. You say the words and you get a picture in your head. Everybody's got a Main Street."

"Not me," Brodie said, finally picking up his beer and taking a sip.

Zoe shot him a skeptical look. "You don't have Main Streets in the UK? Where do you put the post office?"

"We have some. In England we have High Streets, mostly."

Walker repeated the term. "*High Streets*. Fancy."

"You had at least one High Street over here until Georgetown was absorbed by Washington, DC, and they renamed the streets. High Street became Wisconsin Avenue."

"You missed your calling as a game-show contestant, Brodie," Walker said.

"So what was your High Street like?" Zoe asked.

"Same as every other one. Lots of shutters and To Let signs. People shop on the internet or at retail parks now, just like here."

"No, really," Walker said, putting his beer down and leaning across the table. "What was Main Street in your hometown like?"

Brodie hesitated, then relaxed against the leather upholstery of the booth. He looked pleased to be asked about something unexpected after the intense focus on one case.

"I grew up in a place called Brockworth, in Gloucestershire. You won't have heard of it, but nobody else has either. It's about a hundred miles from

London." He took a long drink, wiped his lips, and put the bottle down. "The High Street was all right, I suppose. Post office, butchers, the Co-op, a pretty good chip shop. I used to meet my mates at the fountain at the end of the street before we went off to drink Strongbow in the car park behind Woolworth's."

Zoe blinked. "Was any of that English?"

"Fuck off." He laughed, waving a hand. "Go on, what was yours like, Zoe?"

She shrugged. "You know it already. My Main Street is still my Main Street. About a hundred fifty miles from Chicago and about, oh, twenty years behind."

As she spoke, she thought about the scene at Archibald Bowman's house. The knots of people out on their lawns, some neighbors talking with one another for the first time. Farther down, there were the shuttered stores. The vacant, weed-infested lot where Dino's ice cream parlor used to be. That made her think about the Main Street in Granton that Brodie hadn't seen.

"It was better when I was a kid. Or maybe I just remember it being better. You know, like how summers used to last forever and it never rained? There used to be a video-rental store called Ritz VHS. Now, VHS was a little before my time, but they still rented DVDs until they closed a few years back. My dad and I used to walk down there on a Friday night after he picked me up from track. We'd get chocolate sundaes at Dino's—that burned down ten years ago, probably an insurance job—and then we'd pick up a DVD to watch at home. I saw a lot of great movies I was probably way too young for." She smiled, basking in a memory that had been tucked away at the back of her mind until now. She looked at Walker. "How about you, boss?"

Walker had been smiling as he listened, waiting his turn. "My family moved around a lot, so I saw a lot of different Main Streets. Then I signed up for the army straight out of high school. Frankfurt at first, then we were in Kosovo for a while. You know what they call the PX and BX stores on US military bases?"

"Main Street," Zoe and Brodie answered as one.

Walker raised his beer in acknowledgment. "I suppose that's what I think of when I think about Main Street. Or it *was*, at least."

The young women at the neighboring table departed, leaving half-finished cocktails. The jukebox cycled from an Aerosmith ballad to Bobby Bland's "Ain't No Love in the Heart of the City."

"Everything's getting worse, isn't it?" Brodie said after no one had spoken for a minute. "Maybe he's right about that part."

"I don't believe that," Walker said.

"Seriously?" Zoe asked. "The world is going to hell in a handbasket. We've got recessions, war, pandemics. We have a maniac killing people because they live at the wrong address . . . What more evidence do you need?"

"We've always had those things. The world has always been going to hell. But that's why it's important to have people who try and fix it."

"Wait a minute," Brodie said. "Aren't we supposed to be the naive youngsters trying to convince the grizzled realist to be more optimistic?"

"Grizzled?" Walker repeated sharply, straightening in his seat.

"Sorry, I meant—"

"He meant distinguished," Zoe said.

Zoe noticed Walker appeared very tired all of a sudden. Then again, she probably did too; she hadn't looked in a mirror in a few hours. All of them were running on fumes.

"I don't know," he said. "Sometimes I wonder if I've made any difference. Then I think about some of the people I've put away and I figure the world has to be a little better without them walking around free in it, right?"

"I guess," Zoe said.

"And for now, there's cold beer, soul music, and, if we're lucky, some good people around to keep us company while we complain about the state of the world."

No one spoke for a while; the only sound was the music playing low at the front of the bar. For a moment, it was possible to imagine they were three office workers at the end of a long day and that tomorrow held no greater threat than the server crashing.

"Anyway," Walker said, straightening in his seat and putting the beer down. "Back to work. He got away this time, but we know some things we didn't know last night. Let's run through them."

"Okay," Zoe said, arranging her thoughts. "We have a partial description from the woman with the baby in Lebanon. She says he was male, average height, white. She didn't get a good look at his face. That's backed up by the witness in Lydcott, who also didn't get a good look at his face."

"We know for sure that he cases the targets first," Brodie said. "I mean, that was all but certain after California. He has to be sure there's somebody home."

"And we know how he does that now," Walker added. "Or at least, how he did it this time."

"I think he's used surveillance like this before," Zoe said. "Maybe not for the early kills, but if he means to continue, he needs to be certain of his targets. If we find any cameras, we know for sure we've found a potential target. Maybe we can even lay a trap."

"Don't get your hopes up," Walker said. "First off, that camera was tiny and well hidden. A dozen agents missed it when they gave the house the once-over. It's going to take time to do a thorough search of every property. Even if we get lucky, we won't find everything. And as to your suggestion—"

"It won't work," Zoe finished, seeing it now. "Because we'd have to search seven thousand addresses, but our guy only needs to keep tabs on a handful of camera feeds. And he'll know that we've found a camera even if we don't disrupt the feed."

"Yep," Walker agreed. "What we need is a way to find one of these things without tipping him off that we've found it. Then we can think about setting a trap."

Zoe scratched an itch on the back of her neck. She hadn't slept properly in thirty-six hours, and all of a sudden the adrenaline was wearing off and the fatigue was catching up with her. Her head felt as though it were stuffed with packing peanuts. Perhaps she would be able to think better in the morning.

"It's a pity we can't sweep for the cameras somehow or trace where the feed's going. Brodie, I know you said—" She stopped when she turned to Brodie and found his seat empty.

She turned to Walker, who was equally taken aback. "Don't look at me."

Sunday

48

NEW YORK CITY

"Charlestown, Massachusetts."

Walker looked up from his third cup of coffee of the day. Brodie was standing in the doorway of his office holding a crumpled printout. He had finally picked up his phone the previous evening the fifth time they'd tried. He apologized for disappearing and told them he had an idea and was working on something. Now it sounded like he had gotten somewhere.

Walker said, "Talk."

Brodie seemed out of breath. He put the paper on the desk, flattened out the creases, and pushed his glasses straight on his nose.

Walker glanced at the printout. It was a map of the Boston metropolitan area. An *X* was scrawled at a location in the top left quadrant of the map.

"This is a target?" Walker asked.

Brodie nodded. For a moment his mouth formed the start of different words, as though there were a traffic jam in his brain and he needed to maneuver things around to clear the gridlock.

"I think so. I mean, I'm not a hundred percent, maybe seventy, seventy-five—"

"What have you got?" Walker prompted, failing to keep the impatience out of his voice.

"The guy the Furmans told us about at Lebanon, the one who we think planted the camera. What was weird about that?"

Walker thought about it for a minute. "He was posing as a power-company employee, but the uniform was wrong. He should have been from Kansas Electric, but they wear orange-and-blue uniforms, and Mr. Furman said the guy was wearing a brown jacket."

"Brown with a green logo with a number two on it," Brodie said. "The Furmans couldn't remember anything else about it, so the guy could have picked up the uniform anywhere. But I figured it was worth following up. We think he has cameras in some or all of the target homes. He probably used the same pretext to access some of those addresses. Why bother matching the uniform exactly to the location? If your power goes out, you don't care if the guy who comes to fix it is wearing blue or brown."

"Right," Walker said. "So?"

"So I had to work out who had a matching uniform. The Furmans' recollection didn't give me a lot to go on, and it's not like you can just search a list of power companies by color scheme, so it took some digging. I found three companies with a brown uniform and a green logo. One of them is 2Gen Energy. They operate in the Northeast. Then I took a look at leads from anyone mentioning a maintenance worker visiting their place. We got one hit."

Brodie jabbed his index finger on the *X* he had drawn on the map. "One thirty-eight Main, Charlestown. It's a neighborhood on the north side of Boston."

Walker was examining the map. "It's an apartment building."

Apartments were a headache. In the absence of a set of rules provided by the killer, they had to assume that any apartment in a building at a 138 Main was fair game. Fortunately, apartment buildings represented a reasonably low percentage of the list, but it meant more sub-addresses to cover for each location.

"Apartment C, top floor," Brodie confirmed. "We got a tip to the main line two days ago," he continued. "It was lost in the noise, but it was the only thing that came up when I used *2Gen* as a keyword."

He took his phone out and tapped on the screen to play a sound clip. It was just under two minutes long. Walker kept his eyes on the screen as the progress bar moved smoothly from left to right. The sound was tinny and compressed. A woman's voice, young, soft Boston accent:

"Hi, my name is Cally Principal. I'm calling from . . . well, I guess you know where I'm calling from."

The woman sounded embarrassed, like she expected the call handler to roll their eyes and tune her out. That would have been almost optimistic, because the truth was the backlog was so big that this call had not been evaluated yet. If it had, there wasn't much to separate it from all the other reports of suspicious visitors the FBI was receiving every hour of the day.

"Just as I got back, I saw a guy I didn't recognize across the street from my building. I didn't think too much about it, but I think he was looking up at my window. You know, like, checking the place out. I think he was wearing a 2Gen uniform, but they're not my supplier."

The call handler asked, "You had never seen this man before?"

"No, never."

"What about since?"

"No, just that day."

"Can you describe him for me?"

They listened as Cally Principal gave a description that sounded a lot like the man the Furmans had described. Neither man spoke as the recording played to the end, finishing with words of reassurance from the call handler that sounded very hollow: "It's probably nothing. But better safe than sorry."

"What do you think?" Brodie asked, his eyes eager.

Walker stood up and took his jacket from the back of the chair. "Call Boston PD, get them to send the officer watching the place up to the apartment. If she's in, tell him to stay with her." He glanced at the clock on the wall. "We can be there this evening."

"I looked up the route already. We're never going to make the five-forty American flight, and the next available is eight o'clock. It'll take us three hours and forty-seven minutes by car," Brodie said.

"Call it three and a half," Walker said. "We'll get Zoe to drive."

49

138 MAIN STREET

CHARLESTOWN, MASSACHUSETTS

It had been a weird weather day. Torrential rain one minute, clear blue skies the next. Cally sat in the living room of her apartment and watched the rainbow that hung in the air over the roof of the building opposite. The shadows were lengthening on Main Street. She had started to resent the onset of darkness, knowing she would more than likely spend another night divided between jumping at shadows and waiting for the phone to ring.

She went to the window and looked down at the police car outside. She did it unconsciously now, the way she would put her hand in her bag to check her boarding pass was still there at the airport. The boarding pass always was there, of course, and so was the police car.

She peered up and down the street. No traffic, no pedestrians. More than eight million people in the Boston metropolitan area, but standing here, she felt like she was the only woman on earth.

The soft buzzing of an incoming call drew her away from the window. She walked over to the couch and picked her phone up; the screen read *Unknown caller.*

"Hello?"

There was no answer. She heard only the unmistakable sound of the interior of a moving car. She repeated her hello, and a male voice responded.

"Is this Caroline Principal?"

"Yes, this is Cally."

"This is Special Agent Ben Walker, FBI, with the New York field office. Are you at home right now?"

"I am."

"That's good—we're coming to you. We're about two hours away."

"Is something wrong?"

"No, ma'am, I don't want you to be concerned. You made a call to the information line a couple days ago and we'd like to talk to you a little more about it. I just wanted to let you know that we're on our way and I've asked the officers outside to come up to your apartment."

Cally felt a chill. They were driving all the way from New York. They had asked an officer to be in the apartment with her. Despite Agent Walker's reassurances, it sounded as though there might be a great deal to be concerned about.

"Nobody's come up yet."

"Okay, let me check on that for you," Walker said. His voice was relaxed, calming, like an airline pilot's. "When they get there, I'm going to ask them to take you to the station so we can—"

"No. I can't leave."

"What do you mean, you can't leave?"

As though in answer to the question, Cally heard a soft ping from the phone. She took it from her ear and saw there was a incoming call. A call from a local number. Could it be . . .

"I have to call you back, Agent Walker."

She ended the call, hoping the caller wouldn't give up before she could answer. She stabbed at the button to answer the second call.

"Hello? Melissa?"

There was a long pause. Cally could hear a radio playing in the background.

"Hey, sis."

From two short words, Cally detected at least a bottle of vodka in her sister's voice.

"Melissa, my God, where have you been?"

"Havnbnanywhere." Slurring. Confrontational. "Wherevyoubeen."

"I've been in the fucking apartment waiting for you to show up, wondering if you were lying dead in an abandoned crack house, Melissa. *Jesus*. Have you even *seen* the news?" She slapped her forehead. "Of course you haven't seen the news."

"Well . . ." There was a long pause, and Cally knew that her sister had forgotten that she had started a sentence. That happened a lot.

"Look, where are you now? I'll come get you."

There was a long silence. Cally heard street noise in the background but nothing distinct.

"Melissa? I have to know where you are. The FBI is coming to see me in like an hour."

"I'm *lookin'*."

Cally gritted her teeth in frustration and forced herself to wait. The chime of an incoming call sounded in her ear. Probably Agent Walker again, thinking, not unreasonably, that his call was more important than this one.

"Veence sore."

"What? Oh, a convenience store? Where?"

"Ye. Lissen. Need a loan."

Cally sighed. "Then you need to tell me where you are."

"Hey—hey!" Melissa called to someone. "Whrsthis?"

Cally heard some unfortunate passerby responding, reluctantly, to Melissa.

"Copsil," Melissa said.

"Copsil?" Cally repeated, then her brain managed to process it. "Copp's Hill? You're at a convenience store in Copp's Hill?"

"Swhatised."

"Can you see a street name, Melissa?"

"Sure, see you."

The line went dead and Cally let out a grunt of frustration.

50

As soon as Cally saw the Uber turn onto Main Street, she stepped out onto the landing and pulled the door shut behind her. As she turned the key in the lock, she heard footsteps on the stairs and took a sharp breath, holding her keys in her hand, wondering whether there was time to unlock the door and go back in again.

But then the stair climber rounded the last corner and she saw the familiar face of Officer Franklin.

"Ms. Principal," Franklin said, slipping back into using her last name as he always did. "I don't want you to be alarmed, but the FBI has asked us to—"

"To come up and check if I'm okay, I know. I'm fine. I just need to step out for a half hour."

Franklin had stopped on the third step down from the landing, his hand on the rail. "I don't know if that's a good idea. The FBI are on their way."

"I'll be back soon," Cally said, walking forward and forcing Franklin to choose between stepping aside and physically barring her exit. He chose the former.

"I think one of us should come with you."

That was new. She had always been allowed to leave the apartment without question before—not that it had happened often. Had the FBI told Franklin something they hadn't told her? Either way, she couldn't risk Officer Franklin or his partner scaring Melissa away.

"The agent I just spoke to said there was nothing to worry about. I really have to go. Why don't you stay here?" She gestured at the door. "That's what they asked you to do, right? Watch the place?"

From outside, she heard the Uber blasting his horn. Twice.

Franklin opened his mouth, and without giving him time to think of a response, Cally hurried down the stairs.

When she reached the ground floor, she had to take a moment before pushing the door open. Suddenly, she was aware of how much the past week had changed her. She was actually apprehensive about stepping out of her building. She took a deep breath and willed herself to do it.

The Uber driver was a gaunt-looking man with hollow eyes and a dusting of stubble on his cheeks. He didn't respond to Cally's apology for taking so long. She slid into the back seat and realized she hadn't checked to see if the license plate of the car matched the one on the app.

Before she could say anything, the driver said, "Cooper and Salem?"

It took her a second to remember that was the address she had put in. There were two convenience stores close to that intersection, and one of those was likely the store her sister had called from.

"That's right."

He pulled away from the curb with a jolt, and Cally checked the photo on the screen. The guy looked exactly the same in the picture: hollow eyes, stubble, pissed-off expression.

Copp's Hill was only a mile south. The driver followed Main to City Square and then past Paul Revere Park and onto the North Washington Street Bridge. This was farther from home than she had been for over a week. It felt alien but also freeing at the same time. If she could just find Melissa, both of them could go someplace else, get the hell away from 138 Main for a while.

The driver dropped her at the corner of Cooper Street and Salem Street and drove off. Too late, Cally realized she should have asked him to wait.

She walked briskly along Salem Street. It was lined with four- and five-story redbrick buildings on either side, framing the wispy clouds of the evening sky above. She passed a quiet-looking café and saw the first convenience store up ahead. Small neon signs in the window advertised *Beer and Wine, ATM, Samuel Adams Lager.*

She pushed through the doors and went in. It was cramped inside, the shelves spaced narrowly apart and stuffed full of produce, a central aisle leaving barely enough space to squeeze by. A large woman at the counter wearing a purple smock was perched on a stool peering down at a magazine. She raised her eyes as Cally approached.

"Help you?"

"I'm looking for my sister—she might have been in twenty minutes ago?" Cally said, digging in her pocket for her phone. She showed her the picture of her sister. The woman shrugged.

"Maybe she used your pay phone?"

"No phone." The woman leaned across the counter and pointed to her left. "They got one at the Seven-Eleven down the street."

The sky clouded over as Cally ran the three blocks. It would be dark soon. As the illuminated *7* of the logo came into view, Cally slowed and reached for her phone again, hoping the clerk in this place was a little more observant. She had pushed the door halfway open when she stopped and looked farther down the street.

A familiar figure was shuffling along the sidewalk, thirty yards ahead, wearing a shapeless gray hoodie. Was it . . .

Before she even thought about it, she yelled, "Melissa!"

The figure flinched and quickened her pace, and Cally knew she had found her sister.

51

COPP'S HILL, BOSTON, MASSACHUSETTS

Cally suggested they get an Uber, but Melissa didn't seem sure about that, so Cally lied and told her she had left her purse at the apartment and they could just walk back.

Melissa looked all right. Well, as all right as she ever looked. She apparently hadn't eaten in a while, and she *definitely* hadn't showered in a while, but the fresh air seemed to have sobered her up a little. She was slurring her words less than she had on the phone.

"Didn't need to come out here," Melissa said as though her sister were imposing on her in some way. "Could've just sent me it on your phone."

"If you want money, fine. But I had to see you to know that . . . that you're all right."

"Well, mission accomplished. You can see I'm fine, right?"

Cally didn't take the bait. "So where the hell were you? I called and called and I—"

"Jesus. I *said* I was sorry."

Cally bit her tongue. Melissa had been like this even before she had problems. She had always been a pain in the ass.

They reached the bridge and started walking across. Instinctively, Cally put herself on the water side. Then she started worrying about the traffic on the other side.

"I don't know if you've seen the news, but . . ." Cally started. "Well, I've been having a little trouble at the apartment, you could say."

Melissa stopped dead in her tracks. A familiar expression came over her face. Cally knew it like she knew her own heartbeat. It was the same expression her sister had worn when their mom asked, in a tone of quiet fury, who had spilled Cheerios on the living-room carpet.

"Is this about the guy?"

Cally put her hands on her sister's shoulders. "What guy?"

"He said he would just be five minutes. I mean, he had ID, I think . . ."

With an effort, Cally wrenched the story from her on the rest of the walk to the apartment. The man from the power company who had showed up when Melissa dropped by on the day she had gone missing. Cally remembered she was in the office that day. Melissa said she had dropped by to see if Cally needed anything (translation: to borrow money), and the man in the uniform had appeared when she was on the landing using her key to get in.

The man said he was from the power company and he had been called out to check on a wiring problem. He said it would take a little time, so Melissa could leave her key and he would put it under the mat when he was done.

"Melissa, what did you do?"

"I had to meet somebody and, well . . ."

"He gave you money, didn't he?"

Melissa was looking at her sneakers. "Twenty bucks."

Cally felt her fists clenching. Patience, she reminded herself.

"You didn't stop to ask why a guy from the power company *paid* you to get into a job?"

"I just, I don't . . ." Melissa waved her arms helplessly as though it were all beyond her control. "Did he . . . take anything?"

They approached her building. All of a sudden, she was pretty sure why the FBI were coming to see her. Her apartment was on the list. They climbed the front stairs and Cally took her keys out.

"Listen, Melissa, I'm not blaming you, but you have to tell me everything. The guy you let in, was he in a brown uniform with a 2Gen logo?"

But her sister wasn't paying any attention to her. She had stopped halfway up the steps and was looking across the road at the police car. *Shit.*

Cally didn't hesitate. She grabbed her sister roughly and managed to push her up the stairs to the door, blocking her escape route. She couldn't—wouldn't—go back to square one now that she had finally found her.

"They're not looking for you, Melissa, for Christ's sake. But I need you to talk to them, tell them about—"

Melissa was shaking her head. She tried to push past Cally. Cally grabbed her arm, grateful that she was physically stronger than her sibling. "Okay, okay, you don't need to talk to them yet. Let's just, let's go inside and you can get changed, eat something, okay?"

Melissa looked over at the car and back at her sister, then reluctantly nodded.

They climbed the stairs, Melissa first, Cally following two steps behind. Not wanting to take her eyes off her sister for a second, Cally unlocked the door to her apartment and gestured for Melissa to go in first, then closed and locked the door behind them.

"Can't stay here," Melissa said.

Cally swallowed and tried to look reassuring. She dragged up the *Everything's fine* voice from somewhere: "Why don't you take a shower and I'll make you something to eat?"

Melissa thought about it and hesitantly accepted the offer.

Cally heard the shower starting to run and went to the kitchen, wondering if she had anything Melissa would eat. She forgot all about that when she heard a knock on the door.

52

138 MAIN STREET

CHARLESTOWN, MASSACHUSETTS

"Ms. Principal?"

Cally hesitated, then stepped closer to the door, trying not to make too much noise. She put her eye to the peephole, thinking about all the movies she had seen where the bad guy chooses that moment to put his silenced gun to the other side and blow the peeper's brains out.

There was a uniformed officer standing a little back from the door. He was wearing his hat, and the light directly above him cast his face in shadow. It wasn't Officer Franklin. He was a little taller and broader. But then, the officers on duty changed all the time. From her regular trips to the window to check her guardians were in position, she knew that. Some were familiar faces; some she saw only once or twice. She wasn't sure she had ever seen this one.

She looked down at the phone in her hand and tapped 911, ready to call if whoever was out there started kicking the door down. Not that the police would get here in time. She took the chair from beside the door and braced it under the handle. Excellent. That would ensure she was dead nine minutes and thirty seconds before help arrived instead of the full ten.

She cleared her throat and tensed. "Who is it?"

"It's Officer Moore—we want to make sure someone's with you while we wait for the FBI to get here."

That was reassuring. Part of the script, as she knew it. Except . . . she tried to think. The past hour and a half had been a blur. Not enough time to process everything that had happened.

How did she know the guy who had called her was who he said he was? She knew Walker was the name of the agent running the Main Street task force, but who was to say the caller was really him? What if this was all part of the killer's plan?

She hesitated and put her eye to the peephole again. Officer Moore hadn't moved. The shadow covered two-thirds of his face, leaving only his mouth visible.

"Could you hold your badge up, please?"

Cally thought she detected hesitation. Or did she? Anyway, he held up the badge. She squinted. It looked real enough.

"Okay? Can you see it, ma'am?"

His voice sounded weary, like he was making an effort not to tell her to open the goddamn door.

"Thank you," Cally said. "Can you wait a second?"

"Take all the time you need."

She moved away from the door, keeping her eye on it, and went to the back of the apartment. It was noticeably darker and cooler here, on the east-facing side of the building, away from the sunset pouring through the front windows. This time of evening, it felt like crossing time zones.

Cally slipped the big carving knife from the block and started to go back and answer the door. If the officer outside was on the level, it would be a little embarrassing for her, but surely understandable. And if he wasn't, she would have worse things to worry about than embarrassment.

As she turned, she caught something out of the corner of her eye. She turned back, but everything appeared normal. She thought she had seen movement outside the window where the fire escape was.

Behind her, she heard the water hitting the tray in the shower, where

Melissa was still ensconced. The kitchen window looked out onto the platform of the fire escape, but you couldn't see the whole space without getting right up close.

She heard another knock behind her, and Officer Moore called her name.

She moved closer to the window.

And found herself staring at a masked face separated from hers by three inches and a single pane of glass.

53

Cally screamed and flinched back, dropping the knife.

The man outside was on the fire escape. He was dressed in a dark blue jacket and he wore a gray ski mask. His lips were red against pale white skin. He raised his hand, and Cally saw that he had a gun.

Dimly, she heard Officer Moore bang on the door. He had heard her scream.

She wasn't paying attention to that. Her eyes were glued to the man in the ski mask. As she watched, he pointed the gun at her. She was frozen, and there was nothing she could do. He was going to pull the trigger and she would be dead by the time Officer Moore managed to get in.

And then something clicked in her mind, and she hurled herself to the side just as she heard a snapping sound and the glass broke. The bullet smacked into the wall right behind where she had just been standing.

She heard hammering on the door, then a loud crack as the back of the chair she had wedged against it gave way.

At the same time, she heard a smash from the opposite direction as the man in the ski mask used the butt of his gun to clear away the broken glass. Cally looked around for something, anything, to defend herself with. Her eyes alit on the fruit bowl. It was heavy ceramic, twelve inches in diameter. She picked it up, scattering apples and bananas, and heaved it toward the window just as two hands gripped the edges of the frame.

The bowl glanced off one of the gloved hands and she heard a yell of pain and a curse, both muffled by the fabric of the ski mask. At the same moment, the front door slammed open.

Officer Moore charged across the hall and into the kitchen, the gun in his hand. He looked around, saw the broken window.

"He's out there," Cally yelled, pointing at the window.

Her warning had the opposite effect from what she'd intended. Moore took his eye off the window. When he turned back, the man in the ski mask was at the window with his gun outstretched. He was big, with thick, powerful arms. He didn't need the gun. He could probably break her in half with his bare hands.

Three rapid shots. Officer Moore jerked and fell back, blood blossoming on the front of his shirt. He managed to get a shot off, but it went high, hitting the ceiling.

She immediately knew Moore was dead. His head bounced off the floor and he came to rest with his eyes open, staring sightlessly at Cally. She scrambled away from him, trying to run for the door. Out of the corner of her eye she saw the man in the ski mask raise his gun again and she ducked left into the hallway at the last moment.

The shot missed, but she was cut off from the front door now; she couldn't reach it without running across his line of fire. So instead, she ran for the bedroom.

Behind her, she heard more glass breaking. Boots on the floor as the intruder's substantial weight landed on them. She slammed the bedroom door and braced a chair against the handle. But this chair was lighter, flimsier than the one she had used on the front door, and Officer Moore had managed to break that down. She backed into the room. She was cornered.

Unless . . .

She pulled the window up. It was a four-story drop to the yard, but there was a drainpipe within reach. The cop who did the security walk-through had been a little concerned about that but decided it wouldn't hold an adult's weight. Cally prayed he had been wrong.

She hadn't opened the window more than a crack for air since she'd moved in. It lifted four inches and then stopped. She looked up at the frame. There was a wooden catch preventing it from traveling any farther.

She heard a shoulder or a foot slamming against the bedroom door. It rattled in its frame and the chair bracing the handle jerked out of position but held for now.

She looked around the bedroom for something to move the catch with and her eyes landed on her laptop. She picked it up and smashed it edge-on against the catch. The catch cracked but did not give.

An answering smash from the direction of the door gave her next swing added urgency. The catch snapped, splintering part of the window frame with it, and the laptop casing cracked. She pushed the window up again and this time it traveled another few inches. It would have to be good enough. She climbed onto the ledge and put her legs through the window, then she turned around so she was facing the room and let her legs dangle outside. Moving a lot faster than she wanted to, she maneuvered the rest of her body out until just her forearms and her head and shoulders were inside.

Suddenly she remembered Melissa was in the shower. She froze for a second. She couldn't leave her. But she knew the only chance was to get help.

At that moment the door gave way. A final kick had cracked the door-jamb and bounced the bracing chair across the room.

Cally slid farther out, trying not to think about how little time she had left. She had misjudged the distance to the drainpipe. She braced her feet against the wall and reached out. It seemed very far away. She brushed it with her fingertips, dimly registering the man bursting through what was left of the door and entering the bedroom.

She almost slipped and went back to gripping the ledge with both hands. It was no good. There was no way to reach the pipe.

And then she heard another sound. It took her a second to realize it was a chuckle. She turned her head and saw the man in the ski mask leaning out the window above her. Through the holes of the mask, she could see that the skin around his eyes was crinkled with amusement.

"Jump."

The sick bastard was offering her a choice: kill herself or wait for the bullet.

She glanced down. A forty-foot drop. It seemed a lot farther with her whole body weight suspended by her fingers. Nothing soft down there, just concrete.

She shook her head. "No."

The man in the mask didn't answer. He just raised the gun and pointed it at her.

54

Main Street again," Brodie said, not addressing anyone in particular as Zoe made the right turn off Union.

Main was lined with four- and five-story Victorian brick buildings, occasionally interspersed with smaller wood-sided structures. They passed coffee shops and boutique stores, a restaurant with tables out front, bustling with Sunday-evening diners. At regular intervals, trees sprouted from the red-paved sidewalks on either side, their leaves caressing the tops of the tallest buildings. The setting sun bathed the road in an orange glow.

Zoe found a space fifty yards down the street from Principal's building and parallel-parked the Chevy Tahoe. She got out and walked around the hood to the sidewalk, which was spotless as far as the eye could see. Not for the first time this week, she thought about how every Main Street was different. This one felt almost European in character. That made sense, since this was the oldest part of Boston and therefore one of the oldest parts of America.

Walker and Brodie joined her and they walked southeast. There was a Google Street View screenshot of every 138 Main on the task force's online workspace, so the three of them didn't have to hunt for building numbers. They knew what the place looked like. The entrance for 138 was between a café and a pet shop. The Boston PD car was parked right outside, but it was empty.

Brodie was opening his mouth to say something when they heard a muffled bang. It sounded like it had come from above.

As though choreographed, the three of them froze for a second, then started moving more quickly toward the building. Zoe passed Walker and took out her gun as she reached the door. It opened onto a high-ceilinged Victorian lobby, subway tiles lining the walls and wrought-iron railings on the stairs ahead.

They moved inside and toward the stairs. Walker stopped before they reached the first step and put a hand on Brodie's shoulder.

"Brodie, stay here and make sure nobody comes down."

Brodie nodded gratefully and took up a position at the foot of the stairs. Walker called to Zoe as he picked up his pace to catch up with her: "What floor?"

"Four," Zoe said, moving quickly up the stairs. When they passed the third-floor landing, they heard the sound of wood cracking above them. A door being broken down?

They didn't need to say anything. Zoe started running, hearing Walker's steps quicken behind her. As she gained the top floor, she saw the front door hanging off its hinges. That hadn't been the sound she had heard, though. That had been an interior door.

As soon as she stepped in, she saw a body sprawled on the floor and felt her chest tighten. She followed her training, kept her eyes up, started to cover the space.

"Oh, shit."

Walker arrived at her side. Zoe took the opportunity to glance down at the body. It was a Boston PD cop. He was on his back, one arm outstretched, his gun a short distance from his hand. They would check for vital signs in a minute if they got the chance.

"FBI," Walker called as the two of them advanced into the apartment. They heard something smash inside one of the rooms and moved faster. Walker made it to the doorway first.

"Freeze! FBI!" he yelled, and in the same instant, Zoe heard a gunshot.

Walker jerked back from the doorway, and for a second, she thought he had just ducked instinctively. But then he stumbled against the wall and she saw blood on his chest.

She pulled him out of the way of the door as another bullet smashed into the wall.

Walker collapsed to the floor. Zoe backed against the frame.

"Throw down your weapon!" she yelled.

There was no response except scuffing noises and a grunt of exertion. Zoe glanced around the door, ready to fire, and saw the figure of a man clad in a dark blue jacket and a ski mask halfway through the kitchen window. She fired three times as he gripped the frame and pulled himself the rest of the way out.

Zoe looked down at Walker. He was crumpled against the wall, his gun lying on the floor beside him. He was still conscious, but he was in a bad way. He had managed to get his phone out of his pocket, but it had fallen to the ground. Zoe picked it up, put it in her pocket.

"Can you talk?" she asked him.

Walker started to speak, and immediately winced. "Call for backup."

Zoe ignored him, moving his jacket aside so she could see the wound. There was a lot of blood. He had been hit in the shoulder or the upper right side of his chest.

"Zoe," he said, more firmly this time. She looked at his eyes—they were utterly focused. "I'm fine, I just need to keep pressure on. Call it in."

She hesitated, and before she could say anything, she heard a scuffling noise from another room. The bastard was coming back in. She went to the room, already starting to squeeze the trigger, then stopped as she saw a slight, dark-haired woman crawling in the window. It took her a moment to recognize Cally Principal from her file pic. She was wearing jeans and a tank top.

At the same moment, she heard a latch snap and a door on her right opened inward. Zoe spun, tightening her grip on the gun. A woman with a blue towel wrapped around her, her skin reddened, her hair wet, threw her hands up and screamed.

Zoe turned from the newest arrival and rushed to help the woman climb through the window. "Ma'am, are you okay?"

Principal said that she was, though her pallor told Zoe this was pretty far from the truth. “He tried to kill me.”

Zoe looked over at Walker. He had straightened up a little, was leaning back against the wall. He held his bunched-up tie against the wound. She should wait with him, call it in herself.

Zoe looked at Cally. “There’s another agent downstairs—tell him we’ve got two men down and I’m going after the shooter.”

55

Zoe got to the kitchen window and looked out in time to see the shooter descend the ladder at the bottom of the fire escape and start running. The sky was already darker on this side; it was hard to tell exactly where he was in the shadows down there.

"Stop or I'll shoot!"

The man in the ski mask turned as he ran and fired up at Zoe. She ducked behind the window frame and then returned fire. He kept running.

Zoe climbed through the window and onto the fire escape and descended the narrow, creaking steel stairs as fast as she could, keeping her eye on the running man as he took off across the yard. She reached the ground just as he made it to the wall at the far side. She fired twice and saw one of her shots kick up brick dust next to the shooter's leg as he scrambled over.

Zoe cursed and started running in pursuit. She reached the boundary of the yard. It was a seven-foot-high brick wall that looked like it had been there for a hundred and fifty years. The runner had used a storage box to climb up, and Zoe followed his example. She hesitated as she stuck her head over the top of the wall, but the shooter was running down the narrow alley, more interested in escaping than in bagging another cop. From the speed he was moving at, she guessed that her other shot had missed.

Zoe holstered her gun so she could use both hands to climb over the wall and drew it again as soon as her feet hit the pitted concrete ground of the alley. She ran full tilt along it, then slowed when she got to the corner and glanced around, ready for an ambush. The shooter was still moving, though, crossing the busy street. Cars were swerving to avoid him. There was a park across the road, the streetlamps there lighting up the leaves of the closest trees but giving no hint as to how big the dark space beyond was.

She followed him across the street, holding up her free hand to halt the oncoming traffic and keeping her gun raised, hoping for a clear shot at him but not getting one with so many cars and people around.

As fast as she was moving, her mind was moving faster. This was all wrong. They hadn't expected to encounter the killer. It was too early in the evening. How the hell had he known they were coming? How had he beaten them to the scene?

Zoe forced herself to focus on the now. She called out for him to stop again, but even if the running man had been in a mood to obey, he wouldn't have heard her over the noise. He ducked through the gates into the park.

Zoe followed, knowing she should stop and call for backup like Walker had told her to. She compromised, taking her phone out as she ran and calling Brodie. She could give him the information she had and trust him to coordinate.

"Zoe, where the fuck are—"

"Brodie, suspect is heading . . . east?" She tried to picture the map of the area she had looked at earlier. This shit was a lot harder when you were the away team. East, yes. Through the leaves of the trees, she could see the traffic moving along the raised section of the Northern Expressway. That was east. "Heading east through the park. I'm in pursuit. Get somebody to intercept, okay?"

"Zoe, what the—"

"In pursuit," she repeated and passed through the park gates, jamming the phone back into her pocket. There was a long path lit by streetlamps made to look like old-fashioned gas lanterns. The path was straight and flat, like a runway. She poured on the speed. The guy was big, but he wasn't a runner.

She had closed the gap by half when the shooter reached the gate on the opposite side of the park. He hadn't looked back. Zoe wasn't close enough yet to take a shot, and she didn't want to stop to aim. She wanted to run him down.

Beyond the park was a busy six-lane highway, and here her quarry caught a break. There was a gap in traffic that let him push straight through without breaking stride. When Zoe made it to the road, there was an eighteen-wheeler bearing down, too close for her to risk running in front of it. She cursed and waited for it to pass, then stepped out into the road, holding a hand up and hoping for the best. Horns honked and at least two cars had to quickly change lanes to avoid hitting her, but she made it to the other side.

She had lost twenty seconds. The shooter glanced back and saw her at the edge of the highway. She saw two muzzle flashes but barely flinched. He wasn't aiming, just trying to dissuade her from following. He was going to have to try harder than that.

She kept running, through an open gate in a chain-link fence and across a large parking lot. He weaved between the cars trying to lose her, but she kept him in sight. The attempt to lose her slowed him down, so she had almost caught up to him when he reached the opposite side and sprinted beneath the Northern Expressway. Traffic rumbled above, tires thumping off the expansion joints. Zoe followed.

The shooter had vanished.

The lights over the railroad tracks on the other side of the fence were bright, creating long black shadows behind the thick concrete supports of the expressway.

Zoe slowed and approached the nearest pillar. He must be around here somewhere. He hadn't had time to scale the fence in front of the railroad tracks, and he couldn't have doubled back without Zoe seeing.

Her pulse was thudding in her ears, almost as loud as the eight lanes of traffic roaring fifty feet above her head. Joining the other noises was the whir of helicopter rotors. She saw a searchlight swing around the railroad tracks. Brodie had evidently gotten the message through. But air support was no help underneath here. It was just her and him.

There was an abandoned car parked up against the fence, all four wheels gone and every window smashed. She approached it, looking for movement. It was empty.

She stopped and forced herself to tune out the noise from above. Listen for a giveaway. She heard it after a moment: labored breathing. The shooter was out of shape, not accustomed to running flat out for a mile. She followed the breathing, zeroing in on one of the concrete pillars. Carefully, keeping her eyes and her gun trained on the pillar, she bent and picked up the bottom of a broken Thunderbird bottle. She weighed it in her hand, then tossed it into a patch of shadow twenty feet away, equidistant between herself and the pillar.

As soon as it hit the ground, she saw movement at the edge of the pillar. She adjusted her aim and fired three times.

She heard a cry, and the shooter disappeared behind the pillar. Zoe kept her gun trained on it. Was it a bluff? She waited. There was no sound except the traffic overhead.

Gradually, she advanced, keeping the pillar ahead of her and slowly moving around the side. Finally, she cleared the line of sight and saw . . .

Nothing.

Actually, there was something. Drops of blood on the ground, glinting in the meager light.

At that moment, she heard movement behind her and instinctively dived out of the way. The shooter fired from behind the abandoned car fifteen feet from the pillar.

Three shots, and then a very audible click. He was out of bullets. She got up and fired again. He clambered up onto the car roof and used it to scale the fence. He tumbled over the top with a cry of pain and managed to land clean. Now he was running again, crossing the brightly lit gravel yard between the overpass and the railroad tracks.

She had him now.

She could see blue lights flashing on the road on the other side of the tracks. The helicopter was circling above. All she had to do was keep him from doubling back.

She yelled for him to stop again, but the shooter wasn't listening. Her words were lost under the rumble of a particularly heavy truck passing overhead. The shooter was weaving, expecting her to fire. He reached the shelter of a row of parked train cars and darted around the front.

Too late, Zoe realized that the rumbling wasn't coming from above. It was coming from straight ahead.

A passenger train, heading north out of Boston and picking up speed.

She yelled out again, but it was too late.

The shooter sprinted out from behind the car and directly into the path of the oncoming train.

Zoe flinched as she saw him look up at the last second, too late realizing his fate.

The train hit him and passed over him and kept going. It took ten seconds after the impact for the driver to pull on the brakes.

56

When Zoe finally got back to Cally Principal's apartment building, she was relieved to see Brodie standing outside, just within the perimeter tape. She had been trying to get through to him on his cell for the past half hour in between answering questions from cops and paramedics at the scene of the train strike. Information coming from the apartment on Main was patchy. She hadn't been able to learn anything about Walker's condition.

He saw her and hurried over. "He's at the hospital. No word yet."

Zoe bit her lip. "How was he when they got there?"

"He was conscious the whole time. Tried to get me to leave him and come after you."

"I'm glad you didn't listen to him."

"What, are you kidding? I'm a fucking analyst—they don't pay me enough to dodge bullets."

Zoe attempted a smile. It didn't come. "You think he'll be okay?"

Brodie hesitated, and the lack of an immediate reply made Zoe's heart sink. "They got here fast. They worked on him for a little while up there, stabilized him, then took him away in the ambulance." He looked up at the apartment building. All the lights were on in Cally Principal's apartment. He looked back down and, as though to reassure himself as much as Zoe, repeated what he had said a moment ago. "They got here fast."

Zoe nodded, not trusting herself to speak for a moment.

"That was stupid, going after him," Brodie said. "You could have gotten hurt."

"I wasn't the one who got hurt," Zoe said.

"So I heard. Do we know who he was yet?"

"No ID on the body. He took the eight-thirty-one to Reading full in the face."

Brodie winced.

"I won't be sending flowers," Zoe said, looking up to the lit windows of Cally's apartment. She could see the forensics team moving around in there. "How's Ms. Principal?"

Brodie pointed at the mobile command center parked at the edge of the sealed perimeter. "She's talking to Agent McKenna. She's okay. Sounds like we got here just in time."

"Kind of a coincidence, isn't it?" Zoe said. "Him showing up right before we did."

"I've been thinking that too," Brodie said. "Seven thousand potential targets, and he happens to hit the one we're heading to. And way outside of his normal midnight-to-four window. He knew we were coming."

"How is that possible?"

"We found the camera already, in the kitchen. There was also a bug for sound, so he probably heard her talking to Walker on the phone. He must have been close by to get here so fast."

"So why risk it? Why not just write this target off?"

"Maybe he thought he could get in and out quickly, leave us another fuck-you message. Or . . ."

"Or?"

"Or there was something important about this one. Maybe he wanted to stop us from talking to her or finding out something he didn't want us to find out."

Zoe nodded. "My thoughts exactly."

"They're still searching," Brodie said, looking up at the top floor. "Plenty of time to get to the bottom of it, now that it's over."

"Hmm," Zoe said. Perhaps it was her small-town pessimism, but she couldn't believe it was over. She gestured in the direction of the mobile command center. "You want to come with?"

"Sure."

They walked over to the hulking truck that was blocking one whole lane of Main. There was an agent in a gray suit outside. Zoe hung back, wondering if they needed to get permission to go in, but Brodie breezed past him with an offhanded wave. The agent didn't question them. She guessed it was because they were all inside the tape already, and besides, everybody on the scene knew who she was: the cop on loan who had chased the bad guy into a fatal rendezvous with a train.

The inside of the truck was a little more spacious than Zoe had expected. There was a bank of video screens and narrow desks with chairs and power outlets. Cally Principal was sitting at the end of the truck talking to a jacketed female agent with brown hair whom Zoe vaguely recognized. Brodie had called her McKenna. Cally had a blanket draped over her and was holding a mug of coffee in both hands. She looked up as Brodie and Zoe entered.

McKenna followed her gaze and acknowledged Brodie with a wave. "Any word on Walker?"

"Nothing yet," Brodie said.

McKenna turned her attention to Zoe. "You're Hill, right?"

"Yes."

"You were with Walker when he was hit?"

"Yeah. Guy got off a lucky shot; I don't think he was planning on us showing up at that moment."

"Sounds like his luck didn't hold," McKenna said. She took her phone out and looked at a message on the screen. Her expression gave no hint of what it said. She put the phone away and turned back to Cally Principal. In a softer tone, she said, "Listen, I just have to check on something outside, can I leave you with these two?"

As McKenna left, Cally stood up and put her mug down on the nearest surface. She took a step toward Zoe, hands clasped in front of her. The look on her face made Zoe feel uneasy, like she was a celebrity being approached by a nervous fan at a meet-and-greet.

“Agent Hill, I am so grateful to you. If you hadn’t gotten there, I would be dead. I feel so bad about Officer Moore and Agent Walker.”

“They were doing their jobs,” Zoe said. “Same as I was. Could just as easily have been me who got shot, and I’m telling you, I wouldn’t want you to feel guilty about it. The only person who should feel guilty is the man who caused all this.”

“They said he was . . . that he was killed.”

“That’s correct. I was pursuing him and he was struck by a train.”

Cally grimaced, but she didn’t look like she would be shedding any tears over it. “Who was he? Why was he doing this?”

“We don’t know yet. We were on our way to talk to you right before this happened.”

“Of course. With everything . . . I forgot. What did you want to talk to me about?”

Zoe glanced at Brodie. He took the cue.

“We’ve been analyzing his patterns. We managed to predict he would be in Lebanon, Kansas, on Friday night. He got away, but it highlighted one of his techniques. He cases addresses as a power-company worker, and sometimes he plants cameras. We took a look at reports from one thirty-eight Main Street addresses that tied with that, and—”

Cally’s skin had turned white. “My sister let him in. You’re saying he planted a camera?”

“We found it in the kitchen,” Brodie confirmed.

“Jesus. So he was watching me the whole time?”

Zoe said, trying to sound reassuring, “It’s unlikely anyone was monitoring it the whole time. We believe he used the surveillance to make sure his targets were home, when he . . .” She trailed off. Cally Principal looked like she was about to be sick. So much for reassurance.

“I called the tip line days ago about the 2Gen guy. They said they would look into it.”

"We had a lot of calls," Brodie said. Then he cleared his throat and tried to change the subject. "Why didn't you leave?"

Cally blinked. "I couldn't."

Zoe put a hand on Brodie's arm and physically moved him aside. "He didn't mean that as an accusation. We know it's not a simple thing. Even with the support package, having to leave your home for an indefinite period—"

"I couldn't leave because of my sister."

"What do you mean? Does she live here?"

"No. I mean, sometimes. Look, Melissa has some issues. She went missing ten days ago, right before all this started. I knew this was where she would come back to."

"And you wanted to be here."

"Yeah."

Zoe looked out at the street through the open doors of the truck. The flashing blue lights lit the place up like a club. "Melissa was the woman in the shower, right? Where is she now?"

"They took her to the hospital; she was having a panic attack." There was only the slightest hint of an eye roll when Cally said this. Zoe thought that showed restraint. Her sister hadn't been the one hanging out of a window.

Agent McKenna appeared at the door. The expression on her face said there was news.

"Walker?" Zoe asked.

"Nothing, sorry. But we have an ID on the guy you ran down. Prints were in the system."

"Who is he?"

"The suspect's name is"—Agent McKenna paused and corrected herself—"*was* Richard Henkel. Forty-four years old, no family, current address in Windsor, Ontario."

"And?" Zoe was sure from the way McKenna was speaking that there was an *and*.

"And he used to be a cop."

"'Used to be' as in before the train turned him into meat paste?"

McKenna shook her head. "As in five years ago. He was fired from the Windsor police service over an excessive-force complaint. He's had a few jobs since then, most recently in private security."

Zoe and Brodie exchanged a glance. The news wasn't completely unexpected. The 138 killer had been very good at staying one step ahead of the investigation, even when they surprised him in Lebanon.

"So he's Canadian?" Zoe asked.

"I don't have that intel. He's worked north and south of the border, though. We're talking to the cops in Windsor now. Needless to say, this is a shock to them."

"We need to talk to them," Zoe said. She turned to Brodie. "I think we should go out there now. If he was acting alone, fine. But if not, this could lead us to accomplices."

"We're on it, Zoe," McKenna said, smiling in a way that Zoe found a little patronizing. "But there's something a little closer you might be interested in."

"Closer?"

McKenna nodded, enjoying drip-feeding her the information. "It seems Henkel had a base of operations here in Boston."

"What?"

"We found a set of door keys on the body. They were stamped with the logo of a property-management company. Long story short, he rented an apartment in Roxbury under a fake name a month ago. Do you want to—"

"Of course I do," Zoe said. "Let's go."

57

ROXBURY, BOSTON, MASSACHUSETTS

The apartment rented by the recently deceased Richard Henkel was a one-bedroom on the second floor of a modern building on Norfolk Avenue. Zoe, Brodie, and McKenna were the fourth group to arrive. The Boston PD got there first, followed by the bomb squad, followed by the FBI forensics team. The door was splintered and hanging from one hinge where it had been smashed in.

McKenna showed her identification at the doorway and the three of them entered the apartment. Zoe could hear the forensics people in the living room murmuring technical jargon in short, efficient exchanges. Brodie went in there while she checked out the bedroom and the kitchen. There wasn't much to see in either. The former contained an unmade bed and a bare nightstand and nothing else. The latter suggested the occupant hadn't done much in the way of cooking, given that the dishes and utensils were neatly stored away and the trash was full of pizza boxes and stained Chinese food cartons.

She moved to the living room, the main focus.

There was a worn couch, a small television, and a desk in front of the window, which looked out onto the park across the street. In clear plastic evidence bags were a Dell laptop, a printer, notebooks, and newspaper articles. Zoe cast her eyes over those. They were all either actual clippings from newspapers reporting on 138 Main cases or printouts of stories from media websites. Several maps were pinned to one wall, covering almost every inch: a big one showing the whole of the United States and a series of smaller local maps. Zoe felt a rush of exhilaration when she saw there were pins in the maps. Some were in locations where there had been killings, but some were new. Brodie had already spotted it and was standing by the map, muttering under his breath.

"New Mexico . . . California again . . . Idaho . . . holy shit."

"We're alerting the teams at every one of these Main Streets," Agent McKenna said. "Just in case he wasn't acting alone."

Zoe didn't take her eyes off the map as she spoke. "And was he?"

"Acting alone? Too early to tell. But I'd say it's pretty clear from all this that he was involved."

With her fingertip, careful not to touch the map, Zoe traced a path from California to Alaska, then back to Kansas. Had Henkel really plotted this insane scheme alone and orchestrated it from this unassuming one-bedroom apartment? The anxious knot in her stomach told her that couldn't be so, no matter how much everyone wanted to celebrate.

A Boston PD detective with a pale complexion appeared in the doorway and spoke to McKenna. "How's Agent Walker? Any news?"

McKenna shook her head while Zoe fought back a lump in her throat. She was trying not to think about Walker. Focusing on this was the only thing that kept her mind away from it. She closed her eyes for a second and then opened them again.

McKenna had moved toward the man in the doorway. "What have you got?"

"It looks pretty good so far," he said. "Guns, knives, materials to make IEDs."

"IEDs?" Zoe repeated. All the killings so far had been executed by blade or firearm. If he was planning to escalate to bombs . . . "Can we tell if he actually made any?"

The detective shrugged. "If he did, they're not here. But he was planning to."

Zoe turned to Brodie to tell him to call the people at Principal's apartment, but McKenna already had her phone out and was heading for the door. "On it."

"What's this?" Zoe asked the nearest tech, pointing at a stack of papers neatly laid out on a surface.

"Travel receipts, hotel bookings, car-rental agreements. They match up with some of the one thirty-eight Main killings. Check this out." The tech held up a plastic bag containing a crumpled ferry ticket from Port Anthony, Alaska.

Zoe surveyed the travel reservations and crumpled-up receipts. Organization, dedication, investment.

"Who was this guy?" she asked.

"Nobody special," Brodie answered, glancing at the phone in his hand. He looked up at Zoe. "Just got preliminary background, though."

"Priors?"

A headshake. "Just the disciplinary with Windsor police. No details of early life, but he was with the police for ten years, then had a couple of odd jobs, most recently as a rent-a-cop out at some gated community in Toronto. Quit two years ago."

"So how did he fund this?" Zoe mused aloud. "None of those jobs leave you flush with cash, and he had no pension if he was fired from the police."

Brodie eyed the apartment disdainfully. "I don't know. Apparently he was living pretty cheap."

Agent McKenna appeared at the doorway. Her expression was unreadable. "Zoe, you got a minute?"

"What is it? Is it—"

"Still nothing on Walker." She motioned for Zoe to step out into the hall. "No news is good news, though, right?" McKenna said with a thin smile. "How are you doing?"

"Fine," Zoe said. "I'll be a lot finer if we can establish why Henkel did this and whether he was acting alone."

"That was pretty ballsy, going after him on your own."

"It's the job."

McKenna looked at her thoughtfully but didn't comment on that. "Chapman wants to see you tomorrow morning, unless you need a little time off."

Zoe shook her head. "I'm good."

"Okay. We have six seats booked on the eleven o'clock to JFK if you want one of them."

58

While they were waiting at Logan for the red-eye, the news came in via email: The investigators searching Cally Principal's place had found an IED fixed behind the aging refrigerator in her kitchen with enough explosive to kill whoever was in the apartment and perhaps demolish the building in the bargain.

"Why didn't Henkel just set it off remotely?" Zoe asked out loud as she scanned the email.

Brodie had seen the message a moment before her, so he was a little ahead. "The detonator was damaged by coolant leaking from the fridge."

"Lucky for Principal."

"Lucky is right," Brodie agreed. "It could have gone either way—the damage could have set the damn thing off early. Anyway, I think this explains a lot."

Of course. The killer hadn't wanted this phase of his campaign—the escalation from blades and guns to bombs—to be discovered yet.

"So that's why Henkel was trying to beat us to the punch," Zoe said. "He was going to kill her, then remove the camera and the bomb. Get away clean, like the other times."

"Right, but we interrupted him. The bomb's dismantled and the components are at the lab being tested. Maybe we'll get lucky too and there'll be prints or DNA."

Zoe heard the optimism in Brodie's voice and wished she could share it.

They landed at JFK a little before midnight. Traffic was minimal on the drive into the city. McKenna and Brodie discussed a viral video posted by some influencer explaining that Richard Henkel was actually a misunderstood martyr who had given his life for a cause.

"How do these idiots have time for this shit?" McKenna commented. "Don't they have lives?"

"This is their life," Brodie said. "After a while you probably forget what your real opinions are and just count the click money."

Zoe suddenly felt overwhelmingly tired. She knew it was her body's reaction to the adrenaline leaving her system after the chase. She fought the fatigue. She had too much to think about to sleep.

Brodie had been checking the news feeds and getting updates on the online work channels since they left Boston, giving Zoe a running commentary whether she wanted it or not.

Henkel's old apartment in Windsor, Ontario, had been searched. It was now owned by an elderly gentleman who had been bundled up and moved out to a hotel. More information was emerging about Henkel's background. Lots of red flags that suggested he wasn't quite a straight arrow. He had been fired for using excessive force in restraining a suspect, but there were other black marks on his record. He was questioned in relation to some unsolved break-ins on his turf, but there hadn't been enough evidence to make a case against him. Zoe was betting they would look a lot harder for evidence now and probably find it.

So far, they hadn't managed to uncover any details of his life before a stint in college in the late 1990s. Brodie said that wasn't so unusual. Lives weren't as meticulously cataloged before the spread of the internet and social media.

The suggestion of a briefing with Chapman was now firmed up to a formal meeting at eight sharp tomorrow morning. Zoe got the sense this wasn't going to be a congratulatory get-together. But she was tired enough that she didn't care too much.

McKenna dropped Zoe off outside her hotel. She went up to her room, undressed, and lay down on top of her covers.

Henkel was dead. It was over, wasn't it?

Despite all the evidence, she found it difficult to be confident about that.

59

138 MAIN STREET

GRENVILLE, PENNSYLVANIA

"This must be a big relief for you," Officer Semple said, standing on Patrick's doorstep. Patrick thought Catherine Semple—Cat, as she kept reminding him—looked pretty relieved herself. "That it's finally over, I mean."

"It's a weight off," Patrick agreed. "I've been watching it on the news all evening."

Semple took her hat off and rubbed the side of her head. "Crazy thing, when you stop to think about it."

"How certain are they that they've got the right man?" Patrick asked.

"Listen, officially they're playing it close to the vest, but . . . we're pretty sure this is the guy."

"Well, thank God for that," Patrick said. "And, frankly, thank God for you. I can't tell you how reassuring it's been to look out the window and see you guys down there, night and day, rain or shine."

"Hey, easy gig for me. Beats breaking up bar fights and frisking junkies, you know?"

"When you put it like that, I suppose so." He opened the door wider. "Would you like to come in for a drink? We should celebrate."

She held a hand up to decline. "I'm okay, thank you. On duty."

"A cup of coffee, then?"

"No, it's fine. I'm over-caffeinated as it is."

Patrick looked beyond Semple to her car, parked in its usual position. "I guess they won't need you out there anymore, huh?"

"We're staying in place for now while they dig into this Henkel guy's background, but I wouldn't be surprised if they pull us sometime tomorrow. My guess is we'll check in with you regularly for the next few days at least, just to be safe."

Patrick nodded. "That's good to know."

She looked at the car, then back at Patrick. She bit her lower lip, as though she were weighing something.

"Listen, I know you don't like to go out, but maybe I could come by another night. We could have that drink when I'm off duty?"

Patrick smiled. "I'd like that, Officer Semple."

Semple grinned. "*Cat.* Great. I would too. Anyway, on an official level, we'll be outside for the time being. You need anything, give me a holler."

Patrick told her that he certainly would do that and closed the door as she walked down the steps.

It's finally over. That was what Cat had said.

She almost sounded like she believed it.

PART 4

Monday

60

NEW YORK CITY

Zoe was in the line at a coffee place a few blocks from the FBI building when the phone buzzed in her pocket. But when she took it out, she saw it wasn't her phone. It was Walker's. In all the excitement, she had forgotten she had it from last night. There was still a speck of Walker's dried blood on the corner of the screen. There was no caller ID.

"Hello?" she said warily.

"I just killed a man at one thirty-eight Main Street, Daytona Beach, Florida. You'll hear about it in two or three minutes, I expect."

Zoe felt like somebody had poured a glass of ice water down the back of her neck. She steadied her voice: "Who is this?"

"You know who this is, Zoe. Just like I knew you were the one most likely to be answering Walker's phone. How is the old man, by the way?"

The voice. She was certain it was the same voice she had heard on the recording Walker played for them the other night. She forced herself to keep calm, even though her mind was spinning like an out-of-control carousel. "He's doing pretty good, considering. Should be out of the hospital before we know it. Maybe even before we get to you."

There was a short laugh. "You're not going to get to me. Henkel's a dead end. A cutout. You won't find anything that takes you anywhere you want to go. I made sure of it. Remember this, Zoe: I made sure of *everything*."

She gritted her teeth and said evenly, "What the hell do you want?"

"Straight and to the point. I think I like you."

Zoe said nothing, waited for him to continue.

"I want Wall Street shut down for one day starting tomorrow morning."

"What?" The word came out as an involuntary laugh. Her mind had been anticipating a rational answer to her question: amnesty. Free passage to a non-extradition-treaty country. A hundred million dollars. Something achievable.

"You heard me. The New York Stock Exchange shuts down for twenty-four hours. Let's see how the system you're so devoted to holds itself together."

"Listen, pal, even in the unlikely scenario that you are who you say you are, I'm not the one you—"

"I know that. But you can pass the message on to the right people, and they'll pass it on to other people, and eventually it'll reach someone with the authority to do what needs to be done. Close trading on Wall Street for one day and it all stops. You can take this deal to your superiors so they can start making arrangements. Tell them I'll call this number again in one hour to discuss the rest of the terms."

Zoe's head was reeling. Could what this nutcase was asking for even be done? If it could, what would be the consequences? Trying to sound confident, she said, "I'll tell you right now, it's not happening. The FBI does not negotiate with terrorists."

"Oh, please. You sound young, but you weren't born yesterday. Of course they'll negotiate. They'll do what I ask, because otherwise the people will hold them responsible."

"What people? How am I supposed to—" Zoe stopped when she realized the line had gone dead.

And now her own phone was buzzing. As she dug it out, she saw everyone else in the coffee place had stopped to look at the wall-mounted television.

It was showing helicopter footage of a neighborhood with a big smoking hole in it. In the center of the screen was a partly demolished and burning building; a thick black trail of smoke drifted with the wind. The burning hole had once been a house. A fire truck was arriving; police cars were already parked at diagonals across the road. The breaking-news graphic at the bottom of the screen said *Daytona Beach, Florida.*

61

Brodie's phone went to voicemail both times Zoe tried it while running to the office, weaving between the joggers and the sharp-suited, coffee-toting Monday-morning commuters on the sidewalk. As she crossed Broadway, she saw a crowd of people outside city hall holding placards and chanting and setting off red flares. Another 138 Main protest.

The security guard at the turnstiles narrowed his eyes and stepped into her path as she burst into the foyer of the Jacob K. Javits Building. He took longer than he needed to to check her credentials but eventually let her pass.

She tried calling Brodie again in the elevator, to no avail. She gave up and watched the numbers creeping up to her floor, seemingly at 10 percent of their usual speed. When the car stopped, there was a moment of calm before they opened on the chaos. She ducked between people moving hurriedly back and forth and made straight for Brodie's desk. She found him still on the phone. He saw her and told whoever he was speaking to he would call them back.

"Zoe, did you hear?"

"Yes, is Cally Principal still—"

"It's okay, they moved her. They're checking over the whole building in case there's anything else."

"I think there are bombs elsewhere. Come on."

Brodie looked confused as she practically hauled him out of his chair. "Come on where?"

"We have to go see the AD," Zoe said, heading toward the opaque glass door of Billie Chapman's office.

Chapman was on the phone as Zoe entered without knocking. A slim, blond-haired agent in shirtsleeves was sitting across from her desk, a legal pad balanced on his knee, a pen in his right hand.

Chapman raised her eyebrows in surprise at Zoe's appearance and put a hand over the receiver.

"Officer Hill, I'm afraid our meeting will have to wait. I—"

"This can't wait," Zoe said firmly.

Chapman blinked as if Zoe had slapped her across the face rather than interrupted her.

"Maybe you haven't heard the news, but we had a bombing in Florida ten minutes ago. I don't have time for this." She snapped her fingers at the blond agent. He looked from Chapman to Zoe, obviously trying to decide if the finger snap meant he had been promoted from note-taker to bouncer.

"He called me."

Chapman was apparently about to add another admonishment when she registered Zoe's words. "Who called you?"

"Lewis. The guy who's doing this," Zoe said, raising her voice. "He called on Walker's phone five minutes ago, told me about Daytona Beach before it hit the news. He wants us to shut down Wall Street."

Everyone in the open-plan office stopped moving. Zoe was aware that the people at the desks outside Chapman's door were all staring at her. A wave of silence rolled across the room.

At exactly 9 a.m. Walker's phone buzzed again. It had been hooked up to the speakers in the conference room. Chapman, Zoe, Brodie, and two other agents were present. Chapman said she didn't want a crowd. Elsewhere in the building, every resource had been directed to pick up as much intel as they could from the call. The location if possible, of course, but also background noise, vocal identification, anything that might be a giveaway. The work on all that would begin as soon as the call ended. Here in the conference room, they would focus on the words.

The phone rang once. Chapman gave the nod for it to be answered.

"This is Assistant Director Billie Chapman. To whom am I speaking?"

There was a long silence. No one in the room moved a muscle. Five pairs of eyes stared straight ahead, waiting. When the voice spoke, it had the same distortion Zoe had heard earlier. It sounded all the eerier amplified by the speakers in the conference room.

"This will be our only communication, so listen carefully. You know what I've done. You know what I can do. I can strike whenever I want, wherever I want, and there's nothing you can do about it. You know this to be true."

"I'm glad we have this opportunity to talk, sir," Chapman said.

Sir? Zoe couldn't help shooting Chapman a *What the hell?* glance, but if she noticed it, she gave no sign. She was utterly absorbed in the call.

"We'd like to talk about the reasons you believe you have for doing this."

"Reasons? Well, I could talk to you all day about my reasons, but I don't think that would be a particularly good use of your time or mine. I take it Agent Hill has passed on my message to you?"

Agent Hill. So he didn't know everything, Zoe mused.

"Well, that's the thing, sir. The FBI does not—"

The volume of the voice went up a notch: "The FBI *does not* ordinarily find itself utterly humbled by an opponent. And that is what has happened, what *is happening* here, isn't it, Assistant Director Chapman?"

Chapman was silent. Zoe noticed the two other agents in the room studiously avoiding eye contact with her.

Finally Chapman said, "The FBI does not negotiate with criminals or terrorists."

There was a short laugh. "Are you particularly new to this job or just particularly naive?"

Chapman's eyes shifted nervously to the side and then back to the screen. "The FBI does not negotiate with criminals or terrorists," she said again, raising her voice for emphasis but sounding even less convincing. Zoe found herself wishing that Walker were here.

There was a long pause. Then:

"I want you to listen very carefully. I've killed thirteen people, the last one an hour ago. You can't stop me. You can't even slow me down. But I'm offering you an opportunity. I'm the only person who can resolve your problem. Don't think of it as making a deal—you're doing what it takes to end this. You have no choice."

Chapman cleared her throat and seemed to rally. "Part of the reason we do not negotiate is that there's no way for us to know if the other party will honor the terms of a deal."

Zoe raised an eyebrow. Whether Chapman knew it or not, she had opened a door.

After a moment, the distorted voice spoke again. "You don't have to worry about me playing ball." Even through the distortion, the tone of mild amusement told Zoe that he knew this was going the way he wanted it to. "The game will be over. I'll take the ball and go home."

Chapman looked around the table, her eyes questioning. Glances were exchanged. A gray-haired agent in a navy-blue suit chewed on the end of his pen.

"It will be easier than you think," the voice continued. "You have until midnight to confirm publicly that Wall Street will not open for business tomorrow morning."

"Listen, Mr. . . ." Chapman stopped when she remembered she didn't know the name of the person she was addressing. "Even if we did consider your demand, I don't have the authorization to make any deals."

"That's all right. This is going to be very simple. I'm going to tell you everything you need to know, everybody you need to talk to, to put things in motion."

"We're prepared to listen, but that's all."

"How gracious of you. By midnight tonight, eastern time, someone with the requisite authority has to go on television and confirm that Wall Street will close for twenty-four hours. I'd like it to be the president, but I know he's a busy man; I can be reasonable. The secretary of the treasury will do. If the clock strikes twelve with no announcement, people will die. A lot of people this time."

Zoe thought she saw a panicked look in Chapman's eyes for a moment. She rubbed the bridge of her nose, and her face was composed again when Lewis continued.

"It might be the pizza-delivery guy getting back to his apartment in Danville, Virginia, after his shift ends. It might be the amateur landscape artist sitting in her garden studio in Rocheport, Missouri. It might be the little old lady in that cute clapboard house in Lancaster, California. It might not be any of them. But it will be someone unless you follow my instructions to the letter."

As the spookily distorted voice spoke, Zoe could see Brodie out of the corner of her eye frantically typing, scanning the screen, then typing again.

"To be clear, we are not entering into any deal here," Chapman said, looking significantly less confident than she sounded.

"This is the way it has to be," Lewis responded immediately, a fervor and certainty in his voice that chilled Zoe's blood. "This is the only way to save the country. And what are we talking about, really? Some rich people might lose some money? Is that really more important to you than saving innocent lives?"

Chapman opened her mouth but was at a loss for words. Eventually she managed to get out, "Uh . . . I don't think . . ."

"It's nine oh seven," Lewis said, sounding disappointed. "That means you have just under fifteen hours to save these people. And save all of us."

Before Chapman could respond, the call ended, and dead air filled the room.

62

Every one of those locations he named checks out," Brodie said as soon as Lewis had terminated the call. He was staring at his laptop screen. "We have them all on record, and none of the residents are staying elsewhere."

Chapman signaled to one of the two agents in the room. "Get them out now. I don't care if they're stayers, I don't care if they've glued themselves to the floorboards."

The agent, a burly guy in a navy suit, was out of the door practically before she finished speaking.

"Was he serious?" Chapman asked no one in particular. "Can that even be done? Shutting down Wall Street?"

"It would be absolute carnage," Brodie said. "He might as well have demanded we stop the sun going down tonight. This is not a rational demand. You'd be talking massive turmoil, volatility spikes in Europe and Asia. Wild price swings and massive margin calls across the S&P 500. If the dominoes fall the right way it could be an extinction-level event for the US economy."

"I mean, the suggestion alone could . . ." Chapman said, searching for the words.

"Chaos is exactly what he wants," Brodie continued. "Blow it all up and hope something better emerges from the ruins." He looked out the window. "And I'm worried he's not the only one who thinks that's a good idea."

Zoe turned to Chapman. "What are we going to do about the deadline? Can we stall somehow?"

Chapman considered for a moment, then said, as though making her mind up, "*We're* not going to do anything. I think you need to take a step back, Officer Hill."

For a moment, Zoe wasn't sure if she had heard Chapman correctly. But the look on Chapman's face said she had.

"What do you mean? We can get this guy, I know it."

"I'm afraid our planned meeting was preempted by events, but what I was going to say to you still stands. I read the report on what happened last night. You were ordered not to go after the suspect."

"He was running, I had to—"

"You had to do what your superior ordered you to do. I don't know how they run things down in Scranton—"

"Granton."

"Wherever. But in the FBI, you follow orders. The reason for that is that if you don't follow orders, people get hurt. Like Mr. Walker, for example."

"Hey, come on," Brodie said, his voice a little uneven. "That's not—"

"I don't recall soliciting your opinion, Mr. Brodie." Chapman turned her eyes back to Zoe. "You shouldn't even be here right now. You need to complete the after-action report and take a few days' leave. If we still require your services, we'll let you know."

With an effort of will, Zoe forced the frustration out of her voice and said calmly, "I can help. You can use me."

Chapman shook her head. "Walker took you on because we had to look like we were playing nice. That's all. We got what we needed from you." She added an ironic half smile after the last comment that was probably intended to be conciliatory. "Sorry, kid. You're on the bench."

Zoe narrowed her eyes. A hundred competing reactions soared through her mind. So many reasons to be frustrated, pissed off. When she spoke, she did so without thinking. And she had no idea why, but she picked the least important of a thousand reasons.

"Don't call me a fucking kid, Billie."

Chapman blinked. Her jaw tightened and her eyes moved from Zoe to the agent next to her. "Escort Miss Hill out of the building."

The man stood, and Zoe felt a tentative hand on her upper arm. She roughly shrugged it off, not taking her eyes off Chapman.

"Hands off. I'm leaving."

Zoe had almost reached the crossing on Worth Street when she heard running footsteps catching up with her on the paving slabs of the plaza.

"Not now, Brodie," she said without turning or breaking stride.

Brodie drew level with her and matched her pace. His face was red, and he was out of breath from the sprint. "You think that was a good idea?"

"To tell you the truth, I wasn't thinking much of anything. Don't you have to be in the next meeting?"

"You think they want *me* in there?"

"Why not? You're one of them, after all."

"Come on. That's not fair."

"Isn't it? I've never been one of you, not since the start of this. I'm just the small-town hick along for the ride. Even Walker thought that."

"That's bullshit. He wanted you right from Main Street, Granton. Chapman tried to get him to take some dick from the Long Island scene. Walker fought to get you."

Zoe stopped walking.

"Really?"

"Really."

She took a second to absorb that. She had assumed that her involvement was thanks to a rushed decision, but she could tell Brodie wasn't just spinning her a line. She turned and looked up at the building. "You think they're going to consider doing this? Shuttering Wall Street?"

"Your guess is as good as mine, Zoe. I think they'll follow this road a little way, anyway. Maybe this can get us close enough to nail him."

"You think he would be doing it like this if he thought we could get close to him?"

"We got close to Henkel. We *got* Henkel."

"Yeah. And how much usable intelligence did that provide us with?"

Brodie seemed to be at a loss for words. It was such a rarity that, despite everything, Zoe had to suppress the urge to smile.

"Exactly. Henkel was a cutout. A pawn. Maybe we were even meant to catch him, to take the heat off Lewis in the media and let him cut a deal. This guy is a cold-blooded son of a bitch, but he's smart."

"We catch smart bad guys all the time. Everybody fucks up sooner or later."

"Well, seems like it was sooner for me."

"You didn't fuck up."

"I got Walker shot. Maybe killed."

"No, you didn't. I was there, remember? If Walker were here, he'd say the same thing."

Zoe said nothing. An open-top tour bus was moving slowly past, the tourists on the upper deck snapping pictures of the FBI building. On the sidewalks, groups of garishly dressed people of varying ages and backgrounds were moving north. Many of them carried signs, some with paranoid slogans, others emblazoned with the killer's symbol: the digital map pin. The protest at city hall was breaking up. Zoe drew an aggressive glare from a skinny guy with a green 138 Main baseball cap. She stared back until he looked away and started muttering to his companion.

"What the fuck is the matter with these people?" she said, hating herself for keeping her voice low.

Brodie followed her gaze and watched the protesters for a moment. "They want a revolution, and this is the only one on offer this week."

"They can't seriously be buying this shit."

He shrugged. "I haven't had a lot of time to plumb the depths of social media the past few days, but he actually has some support out there. People think he's fighting the system. Targeting rich bankers where they live—literally. And cop killers can always find sympathy these days."

"Archibald Bowman wasn't a rich banker," Zoe snapped. "What about the Furmans? What about—"

Brodie held his hands up. "Whoa, easy there. I'm with you. They're idiots. They'll find another cause next month."

Zoe watched as the guy with the green ball cap got into a yelling match with a cabdriver stopped in traffic. She shook her head. If Lewis really wanted to bring down society, he wouldn't have to do much more than leave it to its own devices.

"What are you going to do now?" Brodie prompted after a minute.

She took a deep breath and blew out a puff of air, trying to expel some of the rage that was coursing through her at the way Chapman had dismissed her.

"I guess I'm going to take some time off, like your boss said. And then I'll be heading back to Granton to write up speeding tickets."

"We still need you. They'll want to talk to you about last night."

"Oh, sure, I'll get some long and boring debriefing sessions. Maybe some juicy paperwork if I'm really lucky."

Brodie was about to say something, but stopped when his phone buzzed with a message.

"Duty calls, huh?" Zoe said.

Brodie looked sheepish as he searched for the right words to say.

"It's okay," she said. "Go. We can catch up later."

He gave her a relieved smile. "Give me a call. We'll go for a drink, I'll cheer you up with news of how badly it's going."

Zoe laughed despite herself. "You're on. I don't have anywhere to be for the next few days."

Brodie tapped her shoulder and jogged back toward the building, his blue tie fluttering over his shoulder in the warm breeze. Zoe watched as he vanished inside the main doors, swallowed up by the monolith.

She let her gaze continue to travel up the skyscraper. She could see people moving around on the twenty-third floor. She felt as though she were watching a new chapter in her life end prematurely.

63

Zoe felt a little better after a long hot shower in her hotel room. She dried off and dressed in her spare suit and looked out the window at the buildings lining the opposite side of Canal Street. She barely even heard the muffled traffic noise from below now. She closed her eyes and tried to push down the burning frustration rising in her chest. It wasn't just that she had been the one to chase down Henkel; it was that she knew more about this case than most of Chapman's people. She had actually spoken to Lewis, one of only two people to do so before he delivered his ultimatum this morning.

She wondered what Chapman and her superiors would do about the demand. They couldn't give him what he wanted, surely? Then again, Lewis had been right about one thing. *We don't negotiate with terrorists* was a PR line; it wasn't real life. If the US government would openly negotiate with the Taliban, who was to say the FBI wouldn't secretly negotiate with the Main Street killer?

And then what?

What if negotiating, finding something that he would accept as a compromise, really was the lesser of two evils? Maybe it was, if it would make it stop.

No. Because they couldn't be sure it would stop. And people like this couldn't be allowed to get away with their crimes, even if nobody else found out about the negotiation.

A breaking-news notification popped up on her phone and she steeled herself for the report of yet another murder. But it wasn't that.

Once again, their adversary had made the decision about whether to go public out of their hands. He had posted an audio clip of this morning's phone conversation with Chapman, including his demand, on the same website that hosted his manifesto. The markets were in meltdown already, and Chapman's inept handling of the call made her look awful. Zoe wasn't proud of herself for briefly reflecting that every cloud has a silver lining.

She called Brodie. He was already up to speed.

"Well, at least we know one thing," he said.

"What's that?"

"It definitely isn't about money. This screws everybody equally, right?"

Zoe laughed and there was a pause. She was about to tell Brodie to stop wasting time talking to her and go back to work when he cleared his throat.

"You know, I was thinking . . ."

"Yeah?"

"After this is over, assuming you haven't sworn off speaking to everyone connected with the FBI . . . I was wondering if . . . well . . ."

"If I'd like to go out sometime?" Zoe finished, smiling.

She could picture his stupid face blushing, but he did his best not to make it obvious in his voice. "Well, that's very presumptuous, I must say."

"But is it wrong?"

"No."

"Then that would be nice. You can buy me dinner when this is over. Assuming money still exists."

"Hey, I know a place in Tribeca that's so hip, it probably already accepts barter, so we'll be—" He stopped.

"What is it?"

"Sorry, I need to take this call, do you mind?"

"Take it, we'll talk soon."

Zoe hung up, wondering what could possibly be happening now. The welcome interlude of lightness, normalcy, was already being swamped by the anxiety over what was coming next.

She was seized by an overwhelming urge to get out of the city, leave all this behind. But go where? She wasn't ready to go back home yet. Her phone illuminated again with a message from Brodie, and suddenly, her mind was made up.

Walker is conscious, doing okay, he says to give him a call.

Less than an hour later, she was in the back of a taxi on the way to Newark, a seat booked on the one o'clock United short hop to Logan. She wanted to talk to Walker, and maybe doing it in person would come as a welcome surprise. But the decision to head north was motivated by more than that.

She had been in a daze after all that happened in Boston last night: the killer at Cally Principal's apartment, Walker being shot, the chase, Henkel getting hit by a train. And on top of that, this morning's phone call.

It was too much to process. She had allowed herself to be whisked back to New York, only to be unceremoniously dumped from the case. But she couldn't help feeling she had unfinished business in Boston. Walker first, and then, if she could get anyone to tell her where Cally Principal was, she would check in on her. Maybe that would give her some closure. Then she could forget all about the FBI, about New York. She could fly straight home from Boston.

With your tail between your legs, a voice in the back of her mind said.

The traffic on the Williamsburg Bridge was like swimming through molasses. She was cutting it fine. She made it through security with five minutes to spare and joined the end of the boarding line at the gate.

When she got to her seat, she took her phone out to see if she could find the address where Cally Principal had been moved. Her apartment was an active crime scene, and nobody wanted to let people back in there until they had confirmed there weren't any more explosive devices. They were searching the other two apartments in the building too. But when Zoe tapped into the FBI work channel, there was a short message:

> You do not have permission to access this channel. Please contact an administrator.

She tapped through to the shared online workspace where she had been able to access her notes and the rest of the task force's reports on the investigation and got a variation of the same message.

She bit her tongue instead of vocalizing the curse, but the old lady next to her still asked if everything was all right.

"Fine," she said. "Bad breakup."

64

BOSTON, MASSACHUSETTS

The flight time from Newark to Boston was under an hour, but it gave Zoe a chance to process the events of the previous evening. She was getting used to flying now; she barely even felt anxious as the wheels left the tarmac.

She thought about Richard Henkel, a nobody who had drifted in and out of police and security jobs. She thought about Lewis, the voice on the phone. He had said Henkel was a cutout. Did that mean there were others like him, dotted around the country like sleeper cells?

The plane landed a little ahead of schedule just after two. When she turned her phone on, there was a message from Brodie. She called him as she walked through to arrivals.

"The lab's done with the device in Cally Principal's apartment."

"And?"

"And they recovered DNA, but only Henkel's."

"Shit."

"In a way this is good news," Brodie said.

"How is it good news? I'm sure this would be helpful if Henkel was in one piece to stand trial, but how does it help us catch the others?"

"This is the first time there's been any trace evidence on anything. Assembling these things is delicate work; it's very difficult to do it and not leave a print, a hair follicle, a skin flake. Of course, usually that doesn't matter because any evidence is destroyed with the bomb. But if we can find another one . . ."

"Big *if*," Zoe said. "Listen, can you do me a favor?"

"Name it."

She told him she had been locked out of the system and asked if it was possible to get her the address of the place Cally Principal had been moved to.

Brodie sounded hesitant. "I'll see what I can do."

They talked a little longer. Brodie told her to give Walker his best. She made him promise to keep her posted.

She got into the cab at the front of the line and gave the driver the name of Walker's hospital. The afternoon traffic was light and the trip to Massachusetts General through the perma-night of the Sumner Tunnel took less than twenty minutes. She squinted against the sudden daylight as they emerged from underground and saw old Boston redbrick buildings on either side of the highway, modern towers in the distance.

The driver pulled to a stop outside the glass front of the hospital entrance. As she closed the door of the cab, she caught a glimpse of her reflection in the back window and remembered she was dressed for the office. It was hard to shake the feeling of Walker being her boss. She guessed she would have to get used to that not being the case, though, even if neither of them wanted it that way.

The receptionist at the front desk said she had to call up to Walker's floor to speak to the charge nurse. After making the call, she told Zoe what floor he was on. Zoe followed her directions to the elevators, then went up to the sixth floor.

The doors opened onto an empty corridor. It was almost completely silent, save for the distant sound of a PA announcement on another floor. Zoe stepped out and paused for a moment, taking in the alien quiet. For the first time since she had answered the call from Walker in her mom's backyard, she felt as though she had stepped off the ride. The action was elsewhere. The story was unfolding without her. Maybe, after the initial anger and disappointment, she was all right with that.

Walker had a private room. The FBI probably had gold-plated health insurance for agents who were shot in the line of duty. She knocked on the door and entered. Walker looked up from a copy of the *Globe*, breaking into a grin when he saw who it was. Zoe remembered to reciprocate the grin, but only after a beat to get over her shock at the sight of him. Barely twenty-four hours had passed, but Walker looked as though he had lost ten pounds and aged ten years. Even his hair seemed more shot through with gray than it had yesterday.

He said, "I hear you didn't listen to me."

Zoe shook her head. "Nope."

"Worked out worse for the other guy, though."

Zoe tried to smile, but she wasn't feeling it. "Listen, boss, I just wanted to say I'm sorry. I think it was my fault that you—"

He waved a hand dismissively and winced as the movement jostled his wound.

"Son of a bitch," he said between his teeth.

"Oh, jeez, I'm sorry, I didn't mean to—"

"Quit saying you're sorry. You didn't make that asshole shoot me. And it was my call to go in there." He settled back on his pillow, wincing again.

Zoe's gaze fell. No matter what he said, she knew others held her responsible. And she knew her inexperience had played into how the situation unfolded.

"This stuff happens," Walker said quietly, as though reading her thoughts. "You know that better than anyone."

She looked up abruptly.

He nodded in confirmation. "I know about your dad. I guessed it was something like that when I saw how you reacted in Nebraska."

She thought about asking him if he had called up Yelich or somebody else at Granton PD, then decided it didn't really matter. Her father's murder was a matter of public record. Googling her last name and hometown would have been enough.

"It's not why I do it, you know."

"I know. That's not what makes you a good cop."

She turned away from him for a moment to wipe the tear from her eye with the back of her hand. She cleared her throat.

Walker pretended not to notice. "Anyway, Principal was okay, huh?"

Zoe nodded. "But she wouldn't have been if we hadn't gotten there at that second. She was dangling from a window ledge. Said she was close enough to the bastard that she could tell he was grinning underneath his mask."

"You interviewed her?"

"I talked to her at the scene afterward. One of your guys was doing the official stuff."

"You're one of my guys too," Walker said, catching the note of resentment in her voice.

"Not according to Chapman."

"What do you mean?"

"I'm done," Zoe said simply. "She thanked me for my time, gave me some constructive feedback about procedure, and told me to hit the road."

"Let me talk to her, I'll set her straight."

"No, don't. Anyways, maybe she's right. Maybe I'm not a fit for the feebs." She remembered she still had his phone and dug into her pocket. "Here you go. Almost forgot."

Walker weighed it in his hand. "Brodie told me Lewis called you on this."

"No, he called you; he got me. Chapman let me sit in on the next call, but maybe it was a parting courtesy," she said, unconvinced.

Walker wasn't convinced either. "More likely she wanted you there in case Lewis wanted you there."

"Well, he didn't even notice. He just gave us his demand and hung up."

"What are the details?"

Walker listened as Zoe told him. She updated him on the discovery of the bomb in Cally Principal's apartment and the theory that Henkel had wanted to beat them to it so they couldn't recover the faulty device. She told him about the call in Chapman's office. An impossible, quixotic demand and a promise that more people would die.

"You think they'll try to evacuate all the residents?" Zoe asked.

Walker shook his head. "From what you said, it sounds like he was being deliberately ambiguous. Maybe he blows up a bunch of houses on the stroke of midnight, but we can't know that. Sooner or later, people have to go back home. It's the same problem we've always had. And we would never get everybody out, not in that time frame. If Chapman was going to try, we would know about it by now."

"Well, I hope she's got *some* kind of plan. At least Brodie is still on the team."

Walker was lost in thought for a minute. When he glanced up, he looked almost surprised to see Zoe still there. "So what are you going to do?"

Zoe raised her eyebrows. "Weren't you listening to the story? They're going to decide whether to nuke the economy or let a terrorist keep killing people. Meanwhile I'm supposed to cooperate fully with the investigation into Henkel's death while taking some not-at-all-punitive days off and then go back to Granton."

"I didn't ask what you were *supposed* to do," Walker said. His expression was entirely deadpan, but then she saw the twinkle in his eye. "I asked what you were *going* to do."

Zoe smiled.

"I knew you were too much like me to be one of them. Well, to answer a question with a question, what would you do?"

Walker considered carefully. "I would take great care to support the task force in any way I could and not impede their efforts."

"But?"

"But it wouldn't do any harm to take a look from a different angle, would it?"

Zoe thought about it for a moment. "Where would you start?"

Walker turned from her with another small wince and turned his gaze toward the window, with its view over the Charles River. The river was the same stone-gray color as the sky. From this distance, the water appeared completely still, like a trench of poured concrete, but Zoe knew up close it would be ceaselessly churning, moving ever onward toward the bay and then on to the Atlantic. The case was a little like that. It seemed like a perfectly engineered grand design. But if you looked closer, there were flaws, evidence of the artist's capacity for human error, if not humanity.

"That old case you found," Walker said, still contemplating the river.

"The thing in Detroit?" Zoe asked.

"Yeah, the numbered streets. That kind of stuck with me. I don't know why. You do this job long enough and you encounter a lot of coincidences. But something about that . . ." He looked back at her. "But you don't need any advice from me. Go to it."

Zoe picked her coat up from the back of the chair and turned to the door. "You got it, boss."

"And, Zoe."

She turned, ready for the inevitable *Be careful.*

"How do I look?"

She kept her face straight. "Fucking terrible. What the hell do you expect? You got shot yesterday."

Walker laughed so hard that he hurt himself again.

65

On the way down in the elevator, Zoe checked her phone and found Brodie had messaged to say he was still working on restoring her access. In the meantime, he had sent over the address where Cally Principal had been moved: a serviced apartment in a complex in Beacon Hill, less than a mile from Massachusetts General. Even better, he had contacted the agent on duty and told them that Zoe would be visiting.

Less than twenty minutes later, she checked in with the concierge at the building. A security guard appeared after a couple of minutes. He was built like a linebacker, his gray suit straining across shoulders broad enough that he probably had to go through doors sideways. He gave Zoe a brief appraisal, glanced at her ID, then beckoned for her to follow him. They took the elevator up to the second floor, then walked down to the end of the short corridor, where the big guy knocked on a door and waited.

For a second, Zoe thought the guard had taken her to the wrong apartment. The woman who appeared looked a little like Cally Principal. If she had aged fifteen years while being dragged through shrubbery. She had the same straight brown hair, but it was duller and more wispy. She wore shapeless sweatpants and a gray UMass T-shirt.

Then Zoe remembered the wide-eyed woman who opened the bathroom door yesterday. "You're Cally's sister." What was her name again? Mary? Michelle?

"Mm-hmm," the woman agreed, glancing behind her. "Cally? It's a cop." She turned back to Zoe and squinted at her appraisingly. "At least, I think it's a cop."

"It's a cop," Zoe confirmed.

She heard approaching footsteps and Cally appeared behind her.

"Thanks, Melissa."

Melissa. That was it. The sister turned around and moved back into the apartment. The security guard, evidently satisfied that he had done his due diligence, tipped one finger to his temple in a little salute and shuffled off toward the elevator.

Cally's face was drawn. The relief of last night had been well and truly damped down. "I saw about Florida on the news."

Zoe nodded. "I'm afraid he's still out there."

Cally took a moment to absorb this; she looked like she was physically forcing down a swelling of nausea. Perhaps that was exactly what she was doing. She turned and walked farther into the apartment.

Zoe followed her along the hallway, passing a small bedroom where the sister was lying on a queen bed watching a talk show on an iPad.

Cally led her into the living room. It was stylish but austere. Lots of sleek gray furniture. A square-edged couch that looked uncomfortable. The room felt resolutely inoffensive, a contrast to the pleasantly cluttered, lived-in feel of Cally's apartment in Charlestown.

"Take a seat," Cally said, waving at the couch. "Can I get you anything? I don't even know if we have coffee but—"

"I'm fine," Zoe said. "How are you?"

Cally sat down and looked at her hands. She rubbed them together like she was applying hand sanitizer.

"Is he . . . is he going to come here?"

Zoe sighed, wondering what she could say to reassure Cally a little without bullshitting her. "I think it's unlikely. These crimes are as impersonal as it gets. He . . . *they* . . . were never interested in you, only your address. Matter of fact, it could have been anyone in your building."

"But it *was* me. And, forgive me, Agent Hill"—Zoe didn't correct her—"but that's real easy for you to say. I was sleeping twenty feet away from a bomb. They tried to kill me. Did any of the other victims survive?"

"None. Which was why we thought it would be sensible to move you, even though I know you wanted to stay put."

"I didn't need to be there anymore."

Zoe remembered the file. Cally Principal wasn't one of the stayers who was plain stubborn or thought the whole thing was a deep-state hoax. She had a real reason to stay put: her missing sister.

Zoe gestured at the other room. "Your sister's sticking around so far, I see."

Cally raised her eyebrows in the manner of someone intimately familiar with the phrase *Be careful what you wish for*. "She's stayed sober today. I'm going to try to keep it that way."

"There was one thing I wanted to ask you," Zoe said.

"What's that?"

"The power-company guy you called into the information line about, the one you saw outside your building. Was it the same person you saw last night?"

Cally thought about it. "It's hard to say. I didn't really get that good a look at him that day. And last night, the guy was wearing a mask. I suppose he could have been the same man."

Zoe took out her phone and tapped into the photo app. She swiped past a few gruesome shots of the aftermath of the train strike. She wouldn't be showing those to Cally. She found Henkel's DMV photo and held it up for her to see. Henkel had a distinctive appearance. Tall, with dark, almost black hair and a thin white scar two inches long on the left side of his forehead.

Cally stared at it for a long time and then looked up at Zoe, shaking her head apologetically. "I'm sorry, I just can't say." She touched a finger to her own forehead. "I don't remember the scar. He was wearing a hat, though."

"It's okay. We know he was working with someone else for sure."

Cally gestured over at the bedroom where her sister was ensconced. "She doesn't get it. That man would have killed me and it would have been her fault and . . ." She threw up her hands. "I guess guilt is for other people, right?"

"Right," Zoe said. "Listen, thanks for your time. We'll keep you posted."

She took the stairs back down rather than wait for the elevator. She felt better having spoken to Cally, though she hadn't learned anything she didn't already know. As she descended, she took out her phone and found she had two missed calls from Brodie. She waited until she was outside to call him back.

"What is it?"

"Something big, I hope," Brodie said.

"What? You found another bomb?"

"Not yet, but somebody contacted us about the manifesto. We have a name."

66

Zoe felt her hand reflexively grip the phone tighter. At the last count, they had over four thousand leads on the manifesto that were flagged for potential follow-up. People from coast to coast were convinced the 138 Main killer was the creepy janitor who worked in their local library or somebody they went to high school with or even a spouse. Many of the reports were easy to dismiss; some of them were added to a long list to follow up on. If Brodie was calling her about a specific tip, it meant it was something they hadn't seen before.

"Spill."

"This is strictly—"

"Skip it."

Brodie took a breath. "Do you remember we talked about the Bible quote that wasn't a Bible quote in the manifesto?"

It took Zoe a minute to filter through her memory and find the conversation that had taken place a couple of days ago. It seemed more like eight weeks ago.

"Right, that thing about the Wide World Church, the commune, or whatever it was. But you said it was kaput?"

"The *New* World Church. And that was correct, it isn't operating anymore."

"But you found somebody *from* the church?"

"The name we got is Jacob William Mendius. He was a professor at some backwoods Christian college in Northern California in the seventies. Then he was fired and dropped out of society. He and his wife joined the New World Church. His wife eventually ran away, and he either left or was excommunicated from the church. He's been off-the-grid ever since."

"So you think this Mendius guy could be Lewis?"

"We found a tip in the pile that turned out to be from the ex-wife. Her name these days is Amy Devereaux, but forty years ago, in her church-going days, she went by Ruth. She moved to Europe twenty years ago, but she saw a report about the manifesto on the news and thought it sounded familiar."

Brodie told Zoe that Amy Devereaux had looked up the full manifesto online. By the time she finished reading the first ten pages, she was convinced she knew who wrote it. She had heard the ideas and the concepts in the manifesto before—while studying philosophy at Springfield College under Professor Jacob W. Mendius, the man she later married. She lived to regret that decision.

"Did they have any kids?"

"Two, but we don't know what happened to them. They were born in the church, and they weren't big on officially registering births."

"Okay, but what do we know about Mendius? Is this out of no-where, or—"

"No. Turns out he has a file with the FBI, but I had to blow the cobwebs off it. He was some kind of radical in college back in the late sixties, big fan of direct action. He stuck around the college as a grad student and calmed down a little, and eventually they gave him a job. You know the type: If the work's good and he doesn't ruffle the wrong feathers, these places like to have a maverick around."

Zoe didn't know the type, and she was amused that Brodie assumed she would, but she let him continue.

"Anyway, he pushed his luck too far. The college suspended him over a lecture he gave praising the actions of various revolutionary terrorist groups. He might have weathered that, but he followed that up by kidnapping the college president's eight-year-old son."

"Jesus, did he—"

"The kid was okay. Mendius picked him up off the street and just drove around with him for a few hours. After everybody had started to panic, he appeared at the president's house with the kid and told the guy he should be more careful about who he crossed in the future. Somehow he avoided jail, but that was it for his career. Anyway, I can send you a link to the transcript of the lecture." Brodie paused a moment for effect. "It was called 'The Civilized Case for Terrorism.' "

Zoe felt a chill down the back of her neck. Those very words had appeared in the manifesto.

"How did we miss this?"

"It wasn't online; I got the college to scan and email me the hard copy they had kept from the disciplinary hearing."

Zoe's mind was racing. "If it really is him, how do we find him? It sounds like the trail is so cold, you could skate on it."

She heard the smile in Brodie's voice. "That was easier than I thought. Amy Devereaux left her husband and her sons—and the church—back in 1986, but she remembers Mendius talking about an old farmhouse that had been owned by his grandfather. Before she left, he talked about moving on from New World, starting his own church there."

"And you found the place?"

"She remembered the farm had been named after his maternal grandfather—Henman—and that it was somewhere up north in California. It didn't take us long to track down a Henman farm a couple of hours northeast of Sacramento. No record of anyone living there since 1978, but the roof looks like it was patched up recently, and the dirt road on the approach has been in use, from what we can see. We've got eyes on the house right now. Chapman wants to be sure before we go in, but if Mendius is there, he's cornered."

Brodie told her he had to go. Before Zoe could wish him luck, she was listening to a dead line.

She took a moment to process everything she had just been told. Could Brodie really have tracked down the mastermind behind the Main Street killings? And then she realized something—even if this Jacob Mendius was their guy, it was likely Henkel wasn't his only accomplice. There would be others out there, poised to strike.

They were still racing against the clock.

67

Three blocks from the apartment building where Cally Principal was holed up, Zoe found a quiet bar. It was an old-fashioned Boston Irish pub, traditional to the point of cliché. Dark-varnished wood, green neon signs, U2 playing on the jukebox. It was quiet, even for a Monday afternoon. There was a sign warning *Occupancy by more than sixty-five persons is dangerous and unlawful.* They were safe by about sixty-one persons. Once again, this time more acutely, Zoe was hit by the feeling of being thousands of miles from the action.

But there were loose ends to tie up. Perhaps she could help find Mendius's coconspirators before it was too late. She ordered a soda at the bar and picked a table as far away from the two other customers as she could manage. She opened her laptop and logged in.

Brodie had worked his magic. Her access to the online workspace had been restored.

Remembering Walker's suggestion from earlier, she started by pulling up her notes on the Luther Wheeler killings from the 1990s. The numbered streets in Detroit. Walker was right about this one sticking out. In the snowstorm of data she had plowed through in the past week, there was something about that case that had stayed with her. What was it?

She read through the summaries and scanned witness statements and court transcripts as her soda slowly warmed to room temperature. She combed through photographs and psych reports and the minutiae of the case. What the hell was it?

Frustrated, she turned her attention to the big picture, opening up the master map in a new window. She zoomed out so that the whole continental United States was visible along with every one of the ten colored pins, each one denoting at least one death.

She ran the time-lapse version so that the pins appeared in order, three seconds for each day. First Mississippi, then Colorado, then Long Island. Then the pace quickened.

What was the pattern? In the early days, the killings were as widespread as possible. More than once she had heard reporters and even fellow law enforcement officers describe the choice of victims and locations as random, but in fact they were anything but. Impersonal, yes, but not random.

The first few had obviously been chosen to cover a wide area. The selection of a California target one night and one in Alaska the next was designed to demonstrate reach. As the case hit the headlines and resources were poured into protecting victims, the pool of suitable targets diminished, and they would have had to be chosen with even greater care.

That was the key—it had to be. There was a master list of prospective victims somewhere.

The selected targets weren't truly random. There was a design; it just wasn't apparent if you weren't privy to the blueprint. But the more pins that appeared on the map, the greater the chance of finding a pattern.

Zoe looked at the full map of 138 Mains, looking for clusters, tight groupings. Then she scanned the list: the towns, the zip codes, the names of residents where those had been established. Nothing jumped out.

She went back to the map again, feeling like she was staring at one of those Magic Eye pictures, trying to see the pattern. She found her own hometown pin, Granton. The murder that had pulled her into this case. She put a finger to it and traced it east across the screen, toward the Long Island killing. Then she stopped halfway.

There was nothing in Michigan. Nothing anywhere near Detroit, where Luther Wheeler had carried out his murder spree in the 1990s.

She zoomed in on Detroit and its suburbs. Oddly, there was no Main Street in the city itself, but what about the suburbs?

At first, she paid most attention to the areas north and west of the city. To the east was the blue expanse of Lake St. Clair, and the area to the south, on the other side of the Detroit River, wasn't part of the playing field, since it wasn't even America.

And then it was like a light went on. Like everything in this case, it was all about the location.

Richard Henkel had worked security in Windsor, Ontario, which was just across the river from Detroit. She hadn't put the two pieces of information together before because they were in separate countries; she hadn't thought about how close the two cities were.

She had to google the name of the gated community in Windsor to check, but when she zeroed in on it on the map, it was less than five miles from the location of the first of Wheeler's murders.

Could that just be a coincidence? She had wondered if Wheeler's numbered-street killings could have served as the inspiration for the 138 Main killer, even if the perpetrators were different.

There was a document mapping Henkel's known movements over the past six months. He had been careful, so it wasn't anything close to a full picture, but working backward from his identification, the trail was there. Ticket stubs in his apartment showed car rentals in Mississippi and Colorado. The bookings had been made with IDs and credit cards bearing the name John Newman.

So far, geographical tracing had placed Henkel in or near the locales for four out of the eight Main Street attacks that occurred prior to his death. It wasn't a surprise to see the gaps. It had always been likely that more than one person was carrying out the murders. Was the other killer the man on the phone? Or someone else?

She didn't know what she was hoping to see. A lot of time spent around

Detroit, perhaps, but in that she was disappointed. Only one visit to Michigan, in April.

Zoe was about to move on when she spotted a location that wasn't tied to a murder. Or at least, not yet. The timeline showed that Henkel had been in Philadelphia twice the last week in May, just before the onset of the 138 Main killings. The previous weeks had seen him all over the country, presumably casing targets, perhaps setting up cameras and other nasty surprises like the bomb in Cally Principal's kitchen. If he had chosen to visit a single area twice so soon before the grand project got underway, chances were there was a reason.

The reminder on her phone to leave for the airport sounded. She ignored it, staring at the screen.

"What were you doing in Philly?" Zoe said to herself.

She checked the notes. The analyst who had added the file had left a brief note on the second date, the twenty-eighth, speculating that Henkel had caught a connecting flight in Philadelphia on his way from Boston to Durham, North Carolina, where he had showed up the next morning. Maybe, although that would have involved an eight-hour layover. But it didn't explain the visit on the twenty-fourth.

Zoe pulled up the nationwide Main Street map and zoomed in on Philly. Main Street in Philadelphia ran north–south in the Manayunk neighborhood of the city. There was no number 138. The numbering started at 3000 for some reason lost to history.

She widened the scope. There was a 138 Main in Darby Township, a few miles north of the city. That didn't look right either. She pulled out again. Five pins surrounded Philadelphia in neighboring towns and suburbs.

She went back to the list of Henkel's financial transactions. He hadn't used any credit cards in his own name, but the financial team had tied two pseudonymous cards to him so far. She checked the list against the two dates. He had used one of the cards to buy coffee on the twenty-fourth and gas on the twenty-eighth, both at businesses in one particular town.

A town with a Main Street.

Both purchases had been made at vendors within a mile of 138 Main Street, Grenville, Pennsylvania.

68

BOSTON LOGAN INTERNATIONAL AIRPORT, MASSACHUSETTS

By the time Zoe arrived at the airport, she knew she wasn't going home tonight.

Her laptop was low on juice and her phone was lower, but she tapped out a quick message to Brodie saying she might have found something. She could elaborate on a call. The charge on her phone had dropped to 2 percent when she hit Send. She knew exactly how that battery felt.

At the airport, she bought a cup of coffee and found an unoccupied counter near a charging outlet. She plugged her phone in, just rescuing it from oblivion at 1 percent. After giving it a minute to recover, she tried calling Brodie. He didn't pick up. Probably working flat out on the California connection. She left a brief message, then opened her laptop.

There was no phone number attached to the file for 138 Main, Grenville. Just brief details of the resident, a Mr. Patrick F. Massie, and a couple of updates from the check-ins. He had received his security visit on June 19, although as Daytona Beach and Charlestown showed, the security checks left a lot to be desired. There was nothing in the report submitted by officers C. Semple and R. Blatch that made it stand out from the thousands of others. No suspicious people watching the area, like the power-company guy at Cally Principal's place. But just because no one was spotted didn't mean no one had been there.

Massie was a stayer at the last update. The file mentioned he had some kind of mobility issue, an injury, though it didn't go into detail. The officer filing the report had also speculated he might suffer from PTSD, as he was reluctant to go outside. If the 138 Main killer had eyes on him, he was a sitting duck.

Henkel had been close to his address twice in the week before the killings. He had spent time in the area at what must have been a period of feverish activity. Suddenly, Zoe was sure of it: This was the lead she'd been seeking.

She clicked on the additional information file on Grenville. There was a picture of the front of the house—a storm door painted burgundy with the number above the doorbell in brass. There was a real estate agent's listing from the last time the house had been on the market. The floor plan showed all four stories of the property. There was also a map and a satellite image of the area with the house at the center.

Her eyes went to the front-door picture again.

If she knocked on that door, she was betting she would find that Patrick Massie was one of the potential targets. Perhaps there would be another camera or another bomb hidden somewhere in that house. Perhaps these could yield forensic evidence that could lead to the people behind all this.

She searched the number of the Grenville PD and then changed her mind before calling. They wouldn't give out information to her over the phone, not when she couldn't play the FBI card anymore.

Zoe squinted up at the departures board, just close enough to read. There was a flight bound for Philadelphia International. Gate closing in twenty-seven minutes.

69

HENMAN FARM, EAST OF LOYALTON, CALIFORNIA

Agent Joseph Marciano of the FBI's Sacramento field office edged in front of the other two men on the SWAT team as they approached the house at the end of the dirt track.

The house was a split-level, the copper-sheeted roof stretching out over the walls and casting the upper windows in deep shade. Below the top floor was a wide porch roof held up by four pillars spaced equally across the front of the structure. Between the shadows and the tall grass in front of the house, it was difficult to get a clear view of the door. He glanced to his left and right to check that the other two men were in position on his flanks.

"You getting this?" he said into his mic to Matt Brodie.

From three thousand miles away, on the East Coast, the analyst replied, "Crystal clear. Be careful."

Marciano kept chewing his gum instead of answering, but in his head his answer was *Okay, Mom.* There hadn't been time for much of a briefing, but there didn't need to be. Every man on the team knew what this was about, and they had all seen the pictures from Florida. Still, he kept alternating his gaze between the front of the house and the tall grass he was moving through.

"The place looks like it's been abandoned for years—you sure about your intel?"

"I guess we're going to find out."

They advanced until they were just in front of the door. Marciano paused and took a moment to pan the camera attached to his helmet from left to right along the porch. There were two weathered deck chairs out front. The door had a dirty glass panel in it. Above it was a hand-painted sign faded to almost nothing.

"Wait a sec, what's that over the door?" the voice in his ear said.

Marciano glanced down at the stairs and moved up onto the porch, hearing the wood creak beneath his weight. He squinted and tried to make out the word.

"Looks like it says . . . *Gehenna*? Name of the house?"

"It's a valley in Jerusalem," Brodie said. "And the biblical name for hell."

Marciano waited for the other two men to join him on the porch and looked back out at what had probably once been a grassy front yard but was now indistinguishable from the unkempt fields beyond. The rest of the team was stationed farther back, two black-and-whites and the tactical truck waiting. There were another four men around back. If there was anybody in the house, he was boxed in.

Marciano stood back while one of the other men examined the door. He took his time before straightening up and nodding.

"All good?" Marciano said.

"Looks clean."

Marciano stepped down off the porch as the other man attached a small charge to the lock. The door didn't seem like it would need much more than a gust of wind to blow it open, but they weren't taking any chances.

Marciano hunched down in the grass, watching the windows. Above them, the helicopter hovered sixty feet up, the rotors drowning out everything but the occasional voice in his ear as Brodie or one of the guys back at the perimeter made a comment.

The agent who had attached the charge stepped away from the door and backed down the steps. He moved ten feet from the lowest one, yelled, “Clear!” and tapped the button on the detonator.

There was a small flash and a crack as the tiny explosive he’d fixed to the lock did its job. The door moved inward but jammed on something, and the smell of smoke filled the air.

They moved forward.

Marciano peered through the gap and saw a pile of magazines keeping it from opening, some of them scorched from blowing the lock off. He put a shoulder to the door but it stayed put. It took him a minute to kick enough of the stuff out of the way to get the door open. The rest of the hallway was also packed full of junk, with a narrow channel allowing access to the rooms beyond.

“It’s going to take us all day to check this place out. Could be a fucking football team hiding under all this shit,” Marciano said to himself as much as the other two.

He narrowed his eyes and tried to filter out the visual noise to look for threats. There was no movement, and from the musty smell of the place, he doubted there had been any movement for a long time. But the mounds of clutter made it impossible to quickly assess the space.

He nudged a door open and saw a room filled with more junk. A calendar on the wall with a watercolor painting of a snow-blanketed forest: *December 1998.*

“You getting this, Brodie?”

“Yeah. Maybe the maid’s on holiday this week. Wait a second—what’s that in the far corner?”

Marciano looked up.

“Far right corner, near the ceiling.”

It took him a second to focus, and then he saw it. There was a tall bookcase at the back of the room, its shelves warped under the weight of stacked books and periodicals, but the space on top of it was atypically clear. No, not quite clear. There was a small gray box.

“Is that a camera?”

"Give me a second, I'll get closer and—"

Brodie's voice was urgent in his ear. "No, fall back. Let's think about this."

Marciano had already started climbing over the pile at the door. The box was in the corner of the room; it would take five seconds to get it and get back outside. There was an almost clear channel of worn carpet between himself and the bookcase. "Give me five seconds and I can get it."

As he moved forward, he saw some kind of black marking on the floor, partially covered by an empty cardboard box. He nudged the box aside with his foot, revealing a circular symbol that ended in a point. It looked as though it had been blowtorched into the carpet.

"Wait one," Marciano said as Brodie started yelling in his ear.

He had reached the bookcase. He could see that the gray box contained a camera. But when he closed his gloved hand around it, there was a blinding white flash.

GEHENNA

It was late, and the Professor had barely looked up from his desk since five o'clock that morning.

It had been a long and fruitful day. The finish line, seemingly so distant just twenty-four hours before, had been crossed. It was done. Everything was in place. He sat back in his chair and read the last lines.

> How does it end? It ends in the only way it can end. With creative destruction. The walls of Jericho must fall. The city on the hill must burn.
>
> Something better will rise from the ashes.

He pulled the last sheet of paper from the typewriter, a long breath escaping his lungs in sympathy with the whisper of the paper leaving the mechanism. Carefully, he placed the final sheet atop the stack and turned it over. It was done. Soon it would be time for the world to know the truth. But not before the sacrifices began.

He raised his eyes to the map on the wall, picking out the first few sites.

Mississippi, then Colorado, then east all the way to the coast. Long Island or Connecticut. Both were home to ideal targets, so he hadn't quite made his mind up there. And after that, back to the Midwest, and then, just as the world was waking up to what was happening, it would be time to widen the scope.

The rumble in his belly reminded him that it was long past the time for more fuel. There was just enough space in the kitchen to prepare his daily repast: plain ramen and a glass of water, no more than was necessary to keep him going. Spending time buying fresh food like eggs wasted energy that had to be put to a greater purpose. This was practical, but it also felt correct. His existence had taken on the purity of the ascetic, particularly in the past few years, since Noah had finally followed in his brother's footsteps and made the decision to leave.

He hadn't thought about either of his sons for a long time, but he did so now.

Lord, it had been more than three years since Noah left. And even longer since that hazy morning in the summer of '91 when Noah had woken his father to say that his brother Aaron had vanished in the night, taking nothing but the battered Walkman his mother had left behind.

Looking at the completed manuscript, he thought about how long it had been since he began. The years had scattered behind him like pages torn loose by the wind. It was 1988 . . . no, 1987 when he started work.

Aaron and Noah. They would be men now, both of them. Aaron had always disappointed him, always had far too much of his mother in him, but he thought Noah must be somewhere out there doing good.

Perhaps Noah would help him with the recruitment. He didn't think it would take many, not if they were the right people. Castro once said he could have begun his revolution with just ten men.

He pulled the quote from the fuzz of his memory—it was getting harder to do it now—and when he had recalled it, he recited it out loud.

"'Ten or fifteen men, and absolute faith. It does not matter how small you are if you have faith and a plan of action.'"

He moved to the living room, having to climb in an ungainly fashion over the boxes he had left in the hallway. The effort required seemed to be so much greater since the last time, and he was out of breath and sweating when he reached his destination. The television was still on in the corner, the screen mostly obscured by stacks of books. He couldn't remember the last time he had turned it off. The voices from the news channels were almost like company, dispatches from the Old World.

The news anchor was talking about the president. The current one, not Reagan or Bush. The House was voting on impeachment. Something about an affair with an intern.

Such pathetic, trivial concerns. They had no idea what was about to hit them. Something was coming to wake them from their lotus daze. Something was coming to—

The pain was like a sudden electrical current shooting up the left side of his body.

The Professor clutched his shoulder, fighting for breath.

No. Not now. Not when he was so close.

The telephone was in the hall. He could call for an ambulance and go outside and wait. The Professor stumbled out into the hallway, the edges of his vision already blackening. He felt as though all the energy were draining out of him. Or, rather, all his energy was being siphoned to focus into the pain that was exploding in his chest.

The telephone was beyond the stack of papers. He stumbled toward it and his foot caught the loose file on top. It slipped out from under him and he fell headlong to the ground. His outstretched arm knocked the table over, and the receiver tumbled from the phone's cradle and fell among the accumulated detritus of a life.

He heard the dial tone, an unbroken monotone drone. It sounded like a flatline.

The darkness was closing in quickly; what remained of his vision was blurry. The pain wasn't so bad now. The buzzing dial tone seemed to grow in volume until it drowned out everything else.

Not now.

Not—

PART 5

70

NORTH OF PHILADELPHIA, PENNSYLVANIA

The rain rolled in from the east, sudden and fierce. The inclement weather kept the traffic on the interstate light for most of the drive from the airport to Grenville. Zoe left the wipers of her rented Nissan on full, nudging the car's speed up as fast as she dared when she had to overtake a truck but otherwise staying in the slow lane.

As she reached the western outskirts of Philadelphia, she passed a sign for US Route 1. Days of immersing herself in American geography and infrastructure had made her feel like she was ready to take an advanced test. She knew Route 1 started up at the Canadian border and wound its way more than two thousand miles down the coast to Florida. She thought about something Brodie said about the northeastern megalopolis, how the geography and history of the Northeast had combined to create this long strip crammed with tens of millions of people. In a way, US Route 1 was the ur–Main Street for the whole country.

The rain showed no signs of abating, but she was becoming more accustomed to it. She allowed her foot to press down on the gas a little more, nudging the needle up to seventy, seventy-five. Finally, *Grenville* appeared on a road sign, below *Conshohocken* and *Bridgeport*. Twelve miles.

She thought about all the moving parts in this investigation, the manpower and the resources arrayed against a small band of determined people. The millions of pieces of information and evidence that needed to be processed and analyzed. The advantage to the other side had always been law enforcement's overload of information. Seven thousand Main Streets had just been the start of that. And then two seemingly disparate pieces of information had seemed to rhyme, and she was the one to hear the rhyme. Sometimes it happened like that. Chance. Coincidence.

If 138 Main Street, Grenville, was one of the upcoming targets, it might be ready to yield its secrets.

She reached the town limits of Grenville a little after ten. South Ridge Pike became Main at the boundary sign, which read *Welcome to Grenville, the Heart of Montgomery County*. She passed a gas station, a shuttered café, a pool hall lit up for business. West of Morley Street, Main became residential, cutting through the historic district. The street was lined with imposing three-story brownstones. Once again, she was struck by the way every Main Street was different. No dollar stores or dilapidated public housing here.

Her headlights lit up the familiar shape of a police car parked a hundred yards ahead. She pulled over to the curb, turned off the engine and the wipers, and stared out of the windshield as the downpour quickly turned it into a waterfall. She pulled up the hood of her coat and got out, then hurried across the street to the partial shelter of the trees.

She had thought long and hard about what she was going to do when she reached her destination and had decided she would not be approaching the cops outside the building.

Maybe they would have listened to her, even though she had no official standing or reason to be there. But if not, she would have blown her chance. If they didn't believe her, she would have no way of getting near that house tonight.

Zoe knew that a week ago she would have tried anyway. One cop to another was usually the very best way of getting what you wanted. But she had noticed a strange vibe with almost every local cop she had interacted with since joining the task force, from Yelich to that jerk spoiling for a fight in Nebraska. There was a distance now. She wasn't one of the guys anymore. She was one of *them*. She guessed the intention, insofar as there was a conscious intention, was to shame her into remembering where she came from. It had done the opposite. It made her never want to go back. Which, she supposed, meant she no longer belonged in either world.

If Cally Principal's apartment had taught her anything, it was that you had to know the lay of the land. Zoe knew from examining the map earlier there was an access alley that ran behind the buildings on Main. Before she committed to taking that route, she stood in the shadows beneath the trees for a while, watching. If she was lucky, there would be only one officer assigned to the stakeout. If she was unlucky, there would be someone guarding the back too.

Three minutes passed. Zoe was about to move when she saw a bobbing light at the end of the row of buildings. She held her breath as she saw a figure emerge from the alley carrying a flashlight. She could see that he was a cop. He continued along the sidewalk, giving a tired wave to the parked police cruiser as he passed.

Not the luckiest, not the unluckiest. It looked like there was one officer in the car and one circling the block. She had a window of opportunity.

Zoe hurried to the corner, turned left, then turned left again, following the narrow weed-strewn alley until she reached the rear of the town house at 138 Main. In contrast with the ornate frontages, the rears of the brownstones were spartan and undecorated. A few of the windows were lit on the other buildings, offering glimpses of bedrooms and kitchens, but at 138 every window was dark.

There was a six-foot-tall brick wall with a locked wooden gate. Zoe climbed over the wall and dropped down into the yard, which was landscaped simply but elegantly. Lots of fine gravel and a little pond. She took a moment to scan for anyone looking down from one of the windows above, conscious that what she was doing was a great way to get shot.

The back door was securely locked, but there were always other ways in. On the plane, she had read every word of the security review of the building, and she had a pretty good idea where to go. She cast a glance back at the alleyway just in time to see the bobbing flashlight appear at the far end. She shrank back into the deep shadows at the corner formed by the wall and the boundary fence and kept her head down.

She heard boots squelch on the muddy path, and the beam of the flashlight swept over the yard. The light moved back and forth as Zoe held her breath. Was he just being diligent or had he seen her? She waited, counted twenty seconds in her head. Why wasn't he moving on?

But then the light disappeared below the wall and she heard the sound of the boots on the mud continuing down the alley. She breathed a sigh of relief. She had a few minutes to find her way inside.

It took her less than sixty seconds to find it—the small window, only about two feet square, three feet from the ground. This was the one that had been flagged on the report by an Officer Semple, with a recommendation to install bars. The recommendation had not been followed.

The window was locked, but she could see there was a simple catch on the other side. She gritted her teeth and used the butt of her gun to smash the glass. The rain was coming down hard enough that the noise wouldn't be audible around the front, but for anyone inside it might be another story. Zoe waited for a second, poised to duck down if she heard a door open or saw a light come on.

Nothing.

She reached through the hole in the glass and undid the catch, then pushed the window up. She pulled herself onto the ledge and crawled through headfirst. She only just squeezed through. A larger person would have found it almost impossible.

She slid down until her palms reached the floor, then gently pulled her legs in. She got to one knee and listened.

There was no sound but the rain.

71

138 MAIN STREET

GRENVILLE, PENNSYLVANIA

Zoe used the flashlight on her phone to take a quick look around and found that she was in a small laundry room with an old washer and dryer and a dusty sink that likely hadn't seen a drop of water in years. The floor was concrete. The air smelled old, musty.

There was a steep set of stairs. Zoe turned off the flashlight and climbed them, steadying herself on the rough brick wall, straining to hear any noise that might be lost beneath the sound of the rain outside. The door at the top was ajar. Zoe waited by it for a moment, listening, then gently pushed it open.

She found herself in the high-ceilinged hallway. The front door was at one end, a sweeping staircase at the other. It was like the foyer to a particularly nice apartment building, except that this was all one dwelling. The house was entirely still. She could hear the rapid patter of rain outside. The water slowly running down the outside of the stained-glass panels flanking the door cast shifting shadows down the hall. There was something wrong about the place. It felt too empty.

The house was even larger than it appeared from outside, which was bad news. It meant there were a lot of places where a bomb could be hidden. Then Zoe thought about it again. Perhaps she was wrong about that.

The town house was a lot bigger than Cally Principal's apartment or the house that had blown up in Daytona Beach, but that just meant the device would have to be more carefully placed. If the aim was to kill the occupant at night, then it was a no-brainer where she should start looking.

She moved slowly up the stairs to the second floor.

The landing had four doors leading off it and an arched window looking out over the street. The streetlights cast a blurry sodium glow into the darkened interior. Zoe could hear the rain hammering off the skylight above. She was conscious again of how big this place was, how much space there was. She moved from room to room, checking to see if each one was clear. Once she was confident the building was empty, she could take more time to search the place.

Whoever lived here seemed to be getting ready to move. There were boxes packed up in each room. Furniture had been dismantled; mattresses leaned against walls.

Something about the emptiness unnerved her—it was like she had turned up at a party to find everyone had already left. Suddenly, she regretted her decision not to talk to the cops outside. What the hell was she doing here in the middle of the night alone?

The resident, Patrick Massie, didn't appear to be home. Perhaps he had overcome his reluctance to go outside? He certainly had a compelling motivation.

But if this was indeed one of the target addresses, the killer would have installed his cameras and might be aware of her presence already. Perhaps he would decide a lone intruder was as good a victim as any for this Main Street.

She jumped when she heard a sudden buzzing noise before realizing it was her phone. She took it out of her pocket and saw Walker's number on the screen. She tapped to pick up the call.

"What is it?" She kept her voice low.

"Are you near a television?"

"No, I'm—what happened? Brodie told me about the place in California. Did they go in?"

"It's a mess. The farmhouse blew up. Killed one of the tactical team, injured two others. Too early to say if this Mendius guy was there. They're looking for body parts for the ID. Brodie's trying to get out there now. I just spoke to him."

"Jesus," Zoe said, her mind filling with questions. She knew she needed to get out of the house. If she was standing on top of another bomb, she didn't want to find out about it the hard way. "Boss, I'm at one thirty-eight Main in Grenville, Pennsylvania. I'm going to—" She stopped; something had caught her eye in the room across the landing. The one room on this floor she had yet to clear.

"You're breaking up," Walker said. "Did you say Grenville?"

She spoke without taking her eyes off the room. "See if you can raise Brodie—tell him to call me back in five minutes, okay?"

She hung up while Walker was still talking. She put the phone down on the desk in front of her and took her gun out.

She moved across the landing to the room opposite. It, too, was in darkness, but a beam of light from the streetlamp outside had illuminated something on the wall. As she stepped through the door, she saw that she had been right. It was a wall-size map of the United States. Pins pushed into it in ten locations so familiar, she could see them in her sleep. But there were five more pins in this map. All around the Northeast: New York, New Jersey, Connecticut, Maryland. And one right here in Pennsylvania.

She took a deep breath and tore her eyes from the map to scan the rest of the room.

It hadn't been packed up yet. There was a desk and a laptop with three monitors attached. The screens displayed columns of numbers. They all seemed to be in flux, ticking up and down. She moved closer and noticed the photograph.

It was an old Polaroid taped to the corner of one of the monitors, the edges curling up from the bottom. It showed two boys in their early teens standing in front of a ramshackle farmhouse. Both were dressed in white clothes that were almost like linen pajamas. Their hair was long and unkempt. She thought the older boy resembled the man in the file photograph of Patrick Massie. But the younger boy was oddly familiar too.

As Zoe moved closer, she noticed a thick red line painted on the floor. She took a step back. Encircling the desk, maybe six feet in diameter, was the map symbol, the color of dried blood.

Taking a sharp breath, she recoiled and stepped back from the image. She had to call Brodie. When she turned around, she saw she was not alone.

"Drop the gun, please."

GEHENNA

June 18, 2020

The radio stations were all talking about the only thing anyone was talking about: daily fatalities, the governor's new mask mandate, banana bread. The man who had been known as Aaron until the age of fifteen decided to eschew talk. Instead, he switched to a country music station as he pulled out of the eerily deserted airport parking lot. He had no particular taste for country, but it was one of those DJ-less stations that were essentially one long playlist, so there was no extraneous chatter to break up the ads and the songs.

West of Cold Springs, he scrolled through the stations again and landed on a Christian one whose host was talking about the same thing all the other talk-radio hosts were, albeit in more Old Testament language. That cut a little too close to the bone, so he turned the radio off completely and drove the rest of the way in silence.

The traffic had always been sparse out here, but now he imagined this was how it would feel to drive through a dead world. Not for the first time, it made him think of the Rapture. The Bible stories they learned by rote in the damp town hall in a childhood where every day was Sunday school. This was back before his mother left, never to be seen again, and before their father took them away and embraced his own new religion.

He wondered if he would have responded to his brother's request for a reunion at any other time than this one. On balance, he thought probably not. If the airlines had not resumed service, the question would have been academic. This was a long way from home.

Slowing for the turn off the highway, he saw that the remains of the old signpost were still there, the one that had pointed the way to Henman Farm before his father had ripped it down and changed the name of the house. He slowed again so that the rented BMW's suspension would be just about able to cope with the rutted dirt track. He saw that some of the long grass had been flattened recently, which meant the rendezvous was on.

A moment later, that was confirmed as he saw the dark blue pickup parked outside. The house he had known as Gehenna since the age of eleven stood alone in the dead landscape under the endless blue sky. The roof was sagging on the east side, the paint peeling. More tall grass stretched up, almost obscuring the ground-floor windows. It was as though the land were slowly reclaiming the house.

He pulled to a stop, and as he got out, the driver's door of the truck opened and a man wearing jeans and a loose cream linen shirt emerged. He was wearing sunglasses. Noah was a little wider around the waist, his hair a little thinner on top since the last time they had crossed paths.

The two of them stood ten feet apart, each one silently appraising the brother he hadn't seen in more than twenty years.

"It's been a while," he said, finally breaking the silence. *A while* was an understatement. More like a lifetime.

Noah—or Richard, the name he went by these days—turned and looked up at the dormer window on the top-floor space that had been their bedroom. "Funny, I was just thinking it doesn't feel that way, now that you're here. Feels like you just left."

He wondered if he should step closer and offer his hand but decided to stay where he was. It was more than just fear of the bug that was keeping them physically distanced.

"It is good to see you, Aaron," his brother continued. "I wasn't sure if you would come."

"Don't call me that."

There was another stretch of uneasy silence. He thought about just getting back into the car. Perhaps nothing good could come of returning to this place.

"Come on around back," Noah said, beckoning for him to follow. He started to walk toward the fenced-off yard. "There's too much junk in the hallway to get the front door open. He basically barricaded himself in, before . . . well, before the end."

He watched as his brother slid a key into the new padlock on the gate, unlocked it, and walked around the side of the house. He hesitated a moment before following.

The backyard was a yellow-green sea of grass, tall enough to hide a man if he crouched down a little. More than tall enough to completely obscure the small wooden cross that marked the spot where Noah had buried their father more than twenty years ago. He remembered the detached way his brother had described finding their father's almost mummified corpse in the hallway. They could date his demise to the month and year thanks to a calendar on the wall, but no more accurately than that.

"You're living here?" The incredulity was more audible in his voice than he intended.

Noah found the door key in his pocket before he answered. "I guess so. World was falling apart, so I decided to come home."

Home. When he thought about it, it sounded like he was repeating a foreign word that was naggingly familiar.

Noah opened the door into the kitchen and they stepped inside. The damp, musty smell teased his memory. He remembered a summer day long ago. Sticky blood on his brother's face from the rock the kids had thrown. He had taken care of Noah that day. Was that bond still there?

Noah stood for a moment, with the air of a man delaying an arduous task. He opened the ancient refrigerator, which, surprisingly, still seemed to be working, then closed it again and turned back to his brother.

"You want something to drink? I don't have any beer or anything. Didn't seem right."

"Why don't you tell me why we're here?"

Noah nodded. No—*Richard* nodded. That was his name now. Given how much he hated his old name, perhaps remembering that was the least he could do.

Wasting no more words, Richard turned and walked through the narrow trench that had been excavated out between the piles of magazines and tomes and journals.

There was dark staining on the carpet. That must have been the spot where Richard had found their father, years after he could have helped him.

They went on down the hallway, where the piles of flotsam and jetsam were almost stacked to the ceiling, past the front door, all but obscured by more detritus, and into the one room in the house where some space had been cleared.

Richard stepped aside, pressed back against the wall to allow his brother to squeeze past, and watched him as he entered the room.

His first impression was that it almost felt like a historical attraction. Thomas Jefferson's old house, with his study preserved as it would have been in seventeen-whatever. Only this wasn't preserved as it had been when their father died. This had been what lay undiscovered under piles of useless papers and books for years.

Richard stepped in behind him as he took it all in: the desk with the Remington typewriter. The manifesto carefully placed alongside it. The gigantic map of the United States that covered one wall.

Patrick Massie turned to his brother.

"What the hell was he doing?"

72

138 MAIN STREET
GRENVILLE, PENNSYLVANIA

There was a man in the doorway aiming a gun at the center of Zoe's chest. For a moment, she considered raising her own weapon and firing, but she could see that he was already way ahead of her.

"Don't think about it. You'll be dead before you can pull the trigger. And no jury in the country will question the shooting of a home invader, not at this address. I'll ask you again: Drop the gun."

Zoe grimaced and let her fingers go limp. Her Glock dropped to the floor with a heavy thunk.

The man in the doorway wore a dark-colored blazer over a white shirt, but she couldn't see his face. He was outside the reach of the haze of light the streetlamp cast through the windows. Then he took a step toward her and she had confirmation. She recognized Patrick Massie from the picture in his file.

Patrick Massie wasn't a potential victim. Patrick Massie was Lewis. He was the Main Street killer.

"Who are you?" Massie demanded. He didn't sound at all rattled, just irritated. "How did you get in here?"

For a split second, Zoe wondered if she should play dumb. But that would be pointless. She was armed, creeping about in the dark, and in a room with all the evidence she needed to know whose house this was. She opted for the truth.

"I believe we spoke on the phone this morning," she said, her voice sounding calmer than she felt. "Zoe Hill."

Massie froze for a second, then adjusted his aim. For a second, Zoe was certain he was about to pull the trigger, but he didn't.

"Surprised?" she asked.

"Curious."

Zoe said nothing. She sensed she had a little leverage here. He might let her live long enough to answer his questions. It wasn't much, but right now, anything was better than nothing.

Massie gestured with the barrel of his gun, quickly pointing to a corner of the room and then back to Zoe. "Take a seat."

Zoe glanced in the direction he had indicated and saw an overstuffed armchair beside a standing lamp.

Not hurrying, not making any sudden moves, she sidled over to the chair, keeping her eyes on the gun and the man in the doorway. When she sat down, Massie quickly moved around the perimeter of the room to the spot where Zoe had dropped her gun. He picked it up, glanced at it, and put it in the pocket of his blazer. She could see a little more of him now. It was still dark, but she could make out a receding hairline and the fuzz of a beard. One of those artfully unkempt looks, the kind of scruffy facial hair that requires more effort to maintain than simply shaving.

He glanced at the clock on the wall. "We have a little time before midnight, Agent Hill. Why don't you tell me what brought you here?"

"The Luther Wheeler case," Zoe said. "Detroit, 1998."

He raised an eyebrow. "Interesting. Go on."

"You're going to kill me, aren't you?"

"Not necessarily. You can't interfere with this thing now, it's a done deal."

That was a lie. But Zoe knew that if she clammed up, she was probably more likely to hasten the bullet. As long as she was talking, she wasn't dead yet.

She cleared her throat. "I was assigned to identify similar historical crimes."

He snorted. "Similar? I bet that was a short list."

"You're right, in a way. Wheeler's numbered-street-victim profile was the only thing that stuck out. A killer targeting people because they lived on a specific street, not just in a specific locale. Of course, you didn't stick to one city."

"That wouldn't have been much of a challenge, would it?"

"Henkel told you about the Detroit murders, didn't he? He was a cop just across the river, in Windsor, would have known about the case. How did you know him?" she asked.

Massie smiled enigmatically. "We go back a long way. A very long way."

"The professor in California tonight. Jacob Mendius. You did that too?"

He laughed. "I blew up the house, yes, but I didn't kill the old bastard. He's been dead for twenty-five years. That one was natural causes."

Zoe was trying to catch up. If the manifesto was Mendius's work, then that explained the old-fashioned feel of the writing, the way most references to the modern world were concentrated in the chapters Brodie had identified as out of place. But did that mean . . .

She remembered the Polaroid of the two boys taped to the corner of the screen and knew why the younger kid was familiar. The scar on his forehead was fresher in the photograph.

"He had two children. Sons. Mendius was your father. You and Henkel . . . were brothers?"

"*Very* good." Massie looked mildly impressed. "I knew they would find the old California homestead eventually. Kind of disappointed it took this long, to be honest."

Zoe's mind was racing. Nobody knew what she knew, because she herself had pieced it together only when she saw the map and the photograph on the desk. Massie had to know she wouldn't be here alone if anyone else had figured it out. All he had to do was kill her. What he had said earlier was true—he had the best excuse in the world to shoot an intruder.

Her eyes went to the map on the wall. Carefully, she raised a hand and pointed. "Those are the next targets? If the FBI and the government don't make your deadline?"

"Whether they make my deadline or not. They're all set for midnight."

"How do you benefit from this? If you bring down the financial system, it doesn't help anyone, including you."

"The people who have inside knowledge about what's going to happen never lose out. I never told my brother. He would have found it all a little distasteful. But, uh . . ." He nodded at the computer screens. "I've made a killing. If you'll excuse the pun."

Now she got it. All of the numbers on that screen translated into stocks, which translated into money. Big money. The chaos in the markets was creating a lot of losers and one big winner. So much safer, so much less traceable than demanding a ransom.

Zoe narrowed her eyes. "That's why you wanted all the attention. That's why you leaked the call with Chapman. You never expected them to go through with it, but the threat was enough. You knew the markets would panic, because you had already proved what you could do."

"It's nice to have your work appreciated by a professional. That means a lot."

"They'll find you sooner or later. Someone will make the same connection I did. They'll see that Henkel visited this town twice."

Massie stared back at her with faux innocence. "And why would that matter? Just another target they were too late to save."

It took Zoe a second to catch up, and then she wanted to kick herself. Of course. There had been a pin in the map in Pennsylvania also. "This place too?"

He nodded. "Wish I could be around to see it. It's going to be impressive. My brother, who was very talented at these things before his passing, wired it up. He said it would bring the whole house down. Maybe a couple of my neighbors' homes, too. And thanks to a jittery stock market that I was in a unique position to predict, I've got everything I need to start a new life with a new name. It won't be the first time."

Zoe could barely hear him over the thudding of her pulse in her temples. They were sitting on top of a bomb.

She had told Walker where she was. Had he heard? Even if he had, he had no way of knowing she was in danger. And then she remembered she might have a chance. But she had to keep Massie talking for a while longer.

"Why did you do it? It can't just be about money."

"You know why. The country needs a shock, a new start."

"Bullshit. Your father was crazy, but I don't believe you are."

"Crazy," Massie repeated, and for a moment, Zoe wondered if she had pushed him too far. Then he broke into a smile. "You're right. The old man was a fucking fruitcake. But he was a genius too. I think he might have been right."

"*Might* have been? You're doing all this just to see what happens? You killed fourteen people. You've led the cops and the FBI on a wild-goose chase. You didn't have to go to all this trouble, all this planning."

Massie shrugged. "My brother believed in it. I think he halfway convinced me, even as I realized there was a way I could benefit in a more . . . earthly sense. Once we started talking about it, about putting our dear departed father's grand plan in motion, I got a little hooked."

"Hooked?"

Massie had an amused gleam in his eye. "It was fun. Have you ever had the pleasure of having of a true mission, one that you can plan and control yourself? A mission that has the potential to affect millions of people?" He laughed. "I guess not. Not many people do. It's a *rush*. The money is a nice benefit, but it's not the be-all and end-all."

"You seem very proud of yourself."

"Oh, I am proud of myself. Nobody has done anything like this before. It's the only thing anyone's talking about. I hear I have T-shirts, baseball caps."

The look in his eyes as he spoke, the glee in his voice, told her that the money wasn't the most important thing. It wasn't even about his father's crusade. Patrick Massie was making the nation dance to his tune, and he was having the time of his life.

But she didn't have a moment to waste thinking about the precise motivations of a psychopath. She took advantage of the dim light to look around the room for something, anything, she could use as a weapon. Perhaps she should have risked moving when he first appeared. He had been a reasonable distance away, and if he wasn't a marksman, it would have been difficult for him to hit a moving target under these conditions. Not so difficult now. He had closed the distance and had his own gun on her and her gun in his pocket.

Massie moved a little closer, keeping the gun pointed at her. "Why are you here alone? Feds usually come in a crowd, don't they?"

"I'm not FBI. I'm a cop."

"Of course. You must have been an addition to the task force from one of the early jobs," he continued. "Long Island?"

"Granton."

"That was one of mine. Bowman. It was the weirdest thing." For a moment there was a faraway look in his eyes. "He was awake when I entered the room, but he didn't fight. Just lay there like he'd been waiting for me all his life. Strange."

That made her think of the painted symbol in Bowman's bedroom. The thing that had brought her into this case to begin with. She glanced over at the matching symbol on Massie's floor.

"What's with the logo?"

"You like it? I came up with that. It tied the whole theme together. My brother thought it was unnecessary, but people have short attention spans these days. Branding is everything."

Zoe listened as Massie talked. She did not make any sudden moves, but her attention was focused on a pile of cardboard boxes ten feet from her. It was stacked precariously. If she could only cover the distance, assuming she was given the chance . . .

Massie paused. Had he detected that her mind was elsewhere?

"Am I boring you, Zoe?"

She swallowed. "Not at all. I'm just a little worried about what you said. How long do we have left?"

Massie's gaze didn't waver from her. "There's a clock on the wall—why don't you tell me?"

He didn't even seem to be blinking. He wasn't going to give her an inch. She just needed some kind of distraction. Just for a second, just for—

The sudden buzz came from the room across the landing. Walker, or maybe Brodie, calling back, her phone lighting up on the desk where she had put it down.

Massie glanced in the direction of the sound for a fraction of a second. It was enough.

Zoe moved without even thinking about it, giving the pile of boxes a shove as she ran past. Massie fired, maybe not even on purpose, but Zoe was already halfway across the room. By the time he aimed and squeezed off a second shot, Zoe was through the door.

73

Zoe heard a muttered curse and running footsteps behind her, but she was already thinking about the next two moves.

Every instinct told her to run downstairs, but she knew that would be a mistake. The door was locked. Even if there was a key, she would never be able to get the door open before Massie shot her in the back.

She took the stairs three at a time, gaining the next landing and taking the corner fast so as not to present a target if Massie stopped on the landing.

There were four low-ceilinged rooms and the large skylight above. The dull light from the moon cast shimmering waterfall projections on the walls. Zoe pushed open the first door she reached, caught a glimpse of a leather couch and a small side table, then continued to the next one, went in, and closed the door quietly behind her as she heard Massie's running footsteps on the stairs. He spoke, and his voice was calm. The voice of a man accustomed to authority:

"You've cornered yourself, Zoe. No way out from up here."

Zoe scanned the room. Like the others lower down, it was packed up. Stacks of boxes, bare bookshelves, a sheet hanging over some kind of dresser.

Why hadn't they thought of this? It was like Ferrera's theory about hiding a book in a library. Only the killer wasn't hiding his true target among the victims; he was hiding *himself*.

Lurking among thousands of Main Street residents must have amused him, but there was a more practical reason for him to be there too. Being one of the potential targets had given him a front-row seat for the investigation. He was privy to the techniques the authorities were using to protect targets, able to keep tabs on what they *hadn't* thought of.

Zoe didn't have much time. Assuming Massie checked every room in turn, it wouldn't take him long to reach this one.

74

Patrick knew he had time on his side.

This wasn't so different from a standard kill-or-capture mission in his old career. There was a ticking clock. He knew the territory. There were four rooms on this floor and no way out. He would clear each room one by one and when he found his target, he would kill her. No more conversation.

He had to admit to being impressed. So many thousands of cops and FBI agents working this case, and yet she was the only one to pick up the link to Wheeler. She had put the rest of it together quickly too when she worked out who he was.

He thought back to that pandemic summer, when he had heard from his brother for the first time in years. In the email, Richard had addressed him as Aaron, even though both of them had long since shed their New World names. Aaron and Noah had become Patrick and Richard years ago in the process of creating a facsimile of the ordinary lives their parents had denied them.

Two boys going out in the world trying to escape their father's shadow; both, in a way, finding themselves serving a country their father had always hated. Law enforcement for Richard, the military for Patrick. Both independently verifying the truth their father had known all along: This world will take all it can from you and, in return, offer you the familiar certainties—death and taxes.

When Richard showed him the map room at the old farmhouse, Patrick had been confused. When he read their father's manifesto, he understood.

Patrick paused halfway up the flight of stairs to the top floor. He took a folding knife from his pocket, keeping his eyes on the landing just in case his prey decided to go on the offensive. He found the wire that ran along the baseboard, slipped the blade between the wire and the wall, and severed it with a twist of his wrist.

Maybe it was just that everyone had gone a little crazy that year. Or perhaps it was the realization that they had a unique opportunity. Either way, he and his brother had chosen the moment well.

Richard was the true believer who trusted implicitly that their father's plan would result in a fundamental societal change. Patrick was attracted by that idea too, if only because he wanted to pour gasoline over this world and strike a match. He didn't much care what came after.

But the more involved he became with the planning, the more he saw how he could kill two birds with one stone. Striking a hammer blow against the system was attractive enough; making a hell of a lot of money on the side was even better. After all, the world did owe him a living.

Jacob Mendius's original plan had been straightforward: target Main Streets in small towns, shoot a few people—passersby, maintenance workers, whoever—and make a getaway before anyone could react. With so many targets to choose from, the authorities couldn't possibly safeguard each one, and after a few killings, no one would feel safe undertaking the most everyday of activities: walking down Main Street.

Patrick had understood at once that the plan would need fine-tuning. Mass shootings might have grabbed media attention in the mid-nineties, but they were beyond passé two decades into the twenty-first century. How would their attacks stand out from every organically occurring mass shooting?

And then Richard told him about Luther Wheeler, and Patrick knew how to make their campaign stand out.

He put the past out of his mind and focused on the present as he reached the top floor.

He paused and listened, waiting for his prey to give herself away.

75

Zoe held her breath and waited as she heard Patrick Massie's footsteps getting closer outside the room. There was a clock on the opposite wall. It showed 11:27. If Massie had been telling the truth, in thirty-three minutes this building, and at least four others on the East Coast, would be reduced to rubble.

Massie was being smart, methodical, carefully checking every room. He had her gun. Her phone was downstairs. There was no way out. No one was coming to her rescue. It was just a matter of time until he found her.

Damn it. The gun was one thing, but if she hadn't put her fucking phone down . . .

And then she thought about the first door she had opened on this level. She had never intended to go in, was just using it as a way to buy herself another thirty seconds while Massie checked it first. But in the split second before she moved on, she had seen a couch and a table. And on top of the table, a lamp and an old landline phone.

Did it work? Most likely it did, right? The report said this was a rented property. You don't rent out a house with a busted phone. Not at this end of the market, anyway. But that room was across the landing, and Massie was out there.

Zoe straightened up and considered for a second. She thought she had heard him go into one of the rooms at the front of the house. Could she get across the hallway without him hearing?

She moved through the room quickly, realizing how creaky the floor was. She knew the creaks would be harder to hear from outside the room, especially with the rain coming down on the panes of the skylight like that, but that did little to reassure her. She made it to the door and opened it a crack, caught a glimpse of Massie going into the room across the landing.

Zoe flattened herself against the blind side of the door. He would be coming this way in a minute.

She would have to try and jump him as he came through the door. Not ideal. He clearly wasn't an idiot. He knew she was in one of these rooms, and he wouldn't walk through the door unaware. She tensed as the footsteps got closer.

And then a stately doorbell chimed.

The footsteps stopped.

It felt like the house was holding its breath along with Zoe.

Ten seconds, twenty. Massie resumed walking. On the second footstep, the doorbell rang again, followed by the sound of someone banging on the door. It didn't sound like someone who was about to go away anytime soon.

Muffled through the door and the sound of the rain, Zoe heard a female voice: "Mr. Massie? Patrick? Are you in there?"

Zoe heard Massie take another step, and then there was a creaking sound. He must be leaning over the banister, peering down the drop. She didn't hesitate. She ran through the doorway and across the landing into the next room. She heard a short gasp of surprise from Massie, but as she had been gambling on, he didn't shoot. He couldn't fire without whoever was downstairs hearing.

She rushed into the room, grabbed the phone, then pulled it down with her behind a large couch. She jabbed 911 and gripped the handset, waiting for Massie to come running in. If she could blurt out the address in time, she might be able to hold him off until help arrived.

The doorbell rang again; there was more banging on the front door.

Was he in the room? Had he crossed the floor and was looming over her even now?

The room's door slammed and she heard a key turning in the lock.

She peeked over the top of the couch, then stood up. It hadn't been a bluff. The door was securely closed, and beyond it she could hear Massie's hurried footsteps descending the stairs.

She looked back down at the phone, wondering why she couldn't hear the voice of the operator yet. She put it to her ear and heard nothing. Frustrated, she stabbed at the disconnect button again. Nothing.

She went to the window. It faced out onto the backyard. She tried to push up the wooden sash but it was securely locked. Even if it hadn't been, there was nothing outside but a three-story drop to the backyard. *Fuck.*

How long did she have? That depended on how long it took Massie to get rid of the unexpected visitor.

76

Patrick hurried down the two flights of stairs, cursing under his breath. There was still time to right the ship, but he would have to deal with this interruption fast. He unlocked the door and pulled it open a few inches, keeping his gun out of sight.

It was Officer Semple, bent under the porch roof so that she was just out of the rain. Individual raindrops on the waterproof fabric of her jacket glinted in the light.

"Sorry to bother you, Patrick, but can I come in?"

"It's . . . uh. It's not really a great time, I was just about to—"

"It'll only take a minute. Somebody called from the FBI, said something about one of their people being in the house?"

Patrick affected a puzzled expression. "There's no one here but me. I haven't left the house all day."

Semple glanced at the car, then back to Patrick. "You mind if I take a look anyway? Everybody's on edge tonight. I don't know if you've been watching the news, but there was another bombing. A house in California this time."

Patrick grimaced. The longer this took, the more likely it was that Zoe Hill would find a way to attract his visitor's attention. Patrick hesitated. He couldn't hear anything from upstairs. He opened the door for Semple.

"Come on in."

Cat Semple stepped inside and stamped her feet on the doormat. She peered at him in the dim light. "Are you okay, Patrick?"

He swallowed and forced himself to be patient. He would find a way to get Semple out as quickly as possible, but he wasn't going to do that by making her more suspicious.

"I'm sorry, it's just been a lot. I thought we were out of the woods, and then this."

Patrick took a step back so that he was standing against the wall, the gun behind him. "So the FBI thinks somebody was in the house?"

"They said it was one of their people. Which I don't really understand, but we need to—" She noticed something. "Where's your walking stick?"

Patrick tried not to let the stab of irritation show. Richard had warned him that he had a habit of being too clever by half. Perhaps he had been right.

"I'm getting a little better. Trying not to rely on it."

Semple opened her mouth again, then closed it and looked at something beyond Patrick. Patrick didn't want to move and risk revealing the gun, so he didn't turn.

"You haven't been out of the house all day, you said?"

Patrick kept his eyes on Officer Semple. "That's right."

"So who left the footprints on the stairs?"

She looked at Patrick. Then, wordlessly, she moved for the stairs, taking her gun from its holster.

Patrick turned and saw what she was talking about. Zoe Hill had left a trail of wet footprints on the polished wooden stairs, glistening in the streetlight from outside. Inwardly, he winced. He liked Cat Semple. He was surprised by how much he liked her. In another time, another place, things might have been different. But there was only one course of action open to him now.

She turned around as he approached. "Could somebody have—"

Patrick was three steps behind her, pointing his gun at her head. There was the briefest flicker of emotion in her eyes—surprise, and something like betrayal.

Before she could move, he shot her three times.

77

Standing with her ear to the locked door, Zoe heard the three gunshots and instantly knew that the cavalry wasn't coming.

It could be that whoever was there had shot Massie, but deep down she knew that wasn't what had happened. Three shots, almost certainly one weapon. And only one of the parties would have had the element of surprise.

She retreated deeper into the room when she heard unhurried footsteps climbing the first flight of stairs. That sealed it. It was Massie.

Running out of options, she looked around the room again. There was a small desk with a heavy oak chair over by the window. Zoe pushed the desk over, sending a lamp rolling across the floor. She picked the chair up and smashed the glass, then used the chair leg to clear the shards from the frame. Beyond was a sheer drop to the darkness of the backyard. It looked like a bottomless void, and she knew there were no soft landing spots there. She leaned out and looked from side to side. The wind cut into her, the rain pouring out of the gutter above her. There was a drainpipe ten feet away. It might as well have been in the next state.

The footsteps on the stairs were getting closer.

78

Patrick checked his watch as he climbed the last flight of stairs. Eighteen minutes to midnight. Still plenty of time to put a bullet in Zoe Hill's head, grab his laptop and documents, and get the hell out of here. That would make two cops he killed tonight. An unexpected development, but to his surprise, he hadn't found it any harder to kill Cat Semple than the others. It had to be done, and so it was done. Perhaps his father would have been proud of him for the first and only time had he been alive to see it.

He stopped outside the locked door to the room and listened. There was no sound from within. He'd thought he heard something breaking a minute ago, but it had been muffled by the rain hammering on the skylight above. He turned the key and waited again, then quickly opened the door, braced for Hill lunging at him. But the door swung inward and bounced off the wall, revealing an apparently empty room.

The window at the far end was smashed, the heavy oak chair on its side, the table overturned. An insultingly obvious distraction. The only way out was down, so there was no escape there, not unless she wanted to try her luck with a long drop.

Moving slowly and deliberately, he approached the leather couch in the opposite corner. When he spotted the phone lying on the floor, off the hook, he knew it had been worth taking five seconds to cut the wire. There was space between the couch and the wall. More than enough to conceal a slight woman.

But when he drew level with the couch, he saw there was no one behind there. He turned and surveyed the room. It was sparsely furnished. There was nowhere else to hide.

He took another look at the window. Perhaps there really was a way out, if you were desperate enough.

Slowly, Patrick approached the broken window. Jagged shards of glass still clung to the frame. The pane of glass was probably original to the house, had been there over a hundred years before being unceremoniously smashed. Then again, the house in its entirety would be treated just as disrespectfully in a few minutes.

As he reached the window, he listened. There was no sound but the patter of raindrops on the ground far below. He hesitated for a second. Then he raised the gun. Holding it with two hands, he leaned out, being careful not to cut himself on the shards.

He looked down, ignoring the downpour soaking his hair and the collar of his shirt. Glistening raindrops fell, disappearing in the blackness before they reached the ground. He could see nothing below.

Could she have jumped?

Cautiously, he leaned out a little farther.

And then felt a sudden stabbing pain in his right shoulder.

He yelled out in shock and surprise, losing his grip on the gun. He stumbled back, pulling a dagger of glass from where it was embedded between his arm and shoulder blade. He dropped the glass and reached for the wound to stanch the bleeding.

She hadn't jumped. He had been wrong; there *was* another way. She had climbed *up*, onto the edge of the roof.

As Patrick was still clutching the wound, Zoe Hill launched herself back through the window.

79

Massie was staggering backward, clutching his bloody wound. Zoe had missed his carotid artery, but she saw with satisfaction that he was still bleeding badly, blood dripping all over the polished floor.

She climbed back in from the window, knowing she had to get to him before he remembered he still had her gun. But when she dropped from the windowsill, her foot came down on the edge of the chair she had discarded earlier, making her stumble. It provided enough time for Massie to recover.

He reached into his pocket and pulled Zoe's gun out.

Zoe grabbed the lamp from the overturned table and hurled it at him as he took aim. The gun went off as the porcelain base of the lamp thumped into his stomach, hard enough to knock him off-balance. Zoe heard the bullet smack into the ceiling above her as the lamp base crashed to the floor, the porcelain splitting in two.

She rushed him as he fell back and the gun, knocked from his hand, clattered on the floor.

She tried to land on top of him with her knee on his chest, intending to pin him, but Massie managed to twist at the last second. She collided with his side and rebounded off. He took a wild swing with his left arm and got lucky, his fist connecting with the side of her head hard enough to knock her over. Massie scrambled to his feet and hit her twice more. She blocked the first strike, but he got her square in the face on the second one.

She stumbled to the side. Massie wasn't young—he had two or three decades on her—but he had a big advantage in weight and strength. She needed to get to that gun.

"You fucking bitch!" he yelled, rushing her. She moved out of the way and seized his arm, tried to twist it behind him. He forced his arm free, grabbed the back of her head, slammed it against the wall.

Zoe saw stars. Her legs folded under her and she went down. This was so unfair. He was going to beat her because he was bigger and stronger.

The realization crystallized her anger, cut through the fuzziness in her head after the two blows. She rolled onto her back as Massie was lunging toward her and kicked him, aiming for his groin. She got lucky, connected perfectly.

Massie grunted in pain and fell back, allowing Zoe to scramble to her knees. He came at her again, swinging wildly, but the pain and the rage made him sloppy. Zoe easily ducked under the swing and gripped his belt, then used his momentum to hurl him forward. Massie crashed onto the floor as Zoe got to her feet and dived for the gun. It was slippery, coated with Massie's blood. She fumbled it, then got her hand around it just as Massie slammed into her, knocking the gun across the floor again.

He came down on top of her. She rolled as he lost his balance momentarily and managed to pull herself out from under him. He grabbed for her shoulders, trying to restrain her, grunting something furious and unintelligible. Zoe felt a small stab of satisfaction. At least if he beat her to death, she had succeeded in fucking up his perfect plan.

Out of the corner of her eye, she could see the larger fragment of the base of the lamp she had thrown earlier, just out of reach. She tried to grab it as she felt his fingers close around her neck. He squeezed hard, and she started to see blackness around the edges of her vision.

Her fingertips slipped on the lamp, pushed it an inch farther away. Then his weight shifted and she closed her fingers around the jagged edge of the lamp base. Blindly, she swung it hard in the direction she knew his head must be. It smashed the side of his face, and she felt sticky blood on her fingers.

Massie yelled out and his fingers withdrew from Zoe's neck. She kneed him, striking the side of his lower torso this time, pushed him off her, and kicked him again as she scrambled to her feet. She ran out the open door and into the hallway, hearing his footsteps already behind her. She grabbed the doorjamb, swung herself around into the landing. If she could just beat him downstairs, maybe the front door would still be unlocked from the unexpected visitor.

As she reached the turn on the landing, Massie slammed into her again, grabbed her, and threw her against the wall. She heard the plaster crack as she bounced off it. She turned and ducked a punch and hit him in the stomach. It had no effect. He grabbed her and pushed her until the small of her back was pressed against the polished wood of the banister.

One of Massie's eyes was jammed shut against a stream of blood from the cut on his forehead. It made Zoe think of the scar on the forehead of the little boy in the photograph, the other son. His visible eye burned with hatred. The cool, urbane schemer of a few minutes ago was gone, replaced by something more animalistic.

"You couldn't keep your *fucking* nose out of this, could you?"

He was still pushing, one hand gripping her left shoulder, the other across her neck. He wanted to push her all the way over, force her down that long drop.

She felt herself tipping over the edge. She let go of the banister and grabbed the lapels of Massie's blazer, her grasp tightening with grim determination. The fabric was good quality, heavy wool. His face contorted with the effort as he kept pushing her. She was over the tipping point now, but she was holding on. Massie leaned forward, perhaps hoping gravity would do the work for him, but she held fast, gritting her teeth and staring into his eyes. If she was going down, he was fucking coming with her.

Massie grunted and brought a hand up to try to pry her fingers away, but then something shifted and Zoe heard a loud crack, like an ancient oak branch splitting in a thunderstorm.

The banister gave way and the two of them fell into the void.

Midnight

80

138 MAIN STREET

On Main Street, Woodbridge, New Jersey, the apartment on the ground floor of the three-story building at 138 explodes, scattering glass across the street and igniting a blaze that quickly spreads to the upper floors.

—•—

At 138 Main Street, Queens, New York, a single-story clapboard house goes up like a Roman candle, sending a pillar of orange flame into the clear night sky.

—•—

In the family home at 138 Main Street, Danbury, Connecticut, a device concealed in the attic detonates, blowing a hole in the ceiling and bringing the roof and the top floor down through the rest of the building in a lethal cascade of timber and concrete.

—•—

A three-story Victorian on Main Street, Chestertown, Maryland, erupts and then collapses, one-hundred-and-fifty-year-old architecture transformed into a heap of rubble in the space of fifteen seconds.

—•—

At 138 Main Street, Grenville, Pennsylvania, the windows on the bottom floor of Patrick Massie's town house turn from dark to blinding white before exploding outward, followed almost simultaneously by a series of explosions on the upper floors. After a brief instant where the building seems to have withstood the assault and held its ground, it folds in on itself, dissolving in a billowing cloud of black smoke and dust.

—•—

Zoe Hill felt the heat on her face where she was crouched behind a police car a hundred yards along the street. She clamped her hands over her ears and jammed her eyes shut. She felt the car rock on its tires as the blast wave washed over them.

After the initial thunderous explosion, there was a longer, heavier rumble as the building collapsed, raining rubble across the street. When the rumble finally subsided, Zoe risked straightening up. She looked over the roof of the police car and saw the street had changed utterly.

Patrick Massie's town house was gone. It was as though someone had simply erased that building from the row. Black smoke and dust were still billowing up into the air and across Main Street, a dull orange glow from the flames behind it.

"Holy shit, you weren't fucking kidding."

Zoe only just heard Officer Blatch's exclamation over the ringing in her ears. She turned and looked around at the assortment of neighbors cowering behind cars and in doorways of houses a little farther down. Blatch had done a good job of evacuating everyone near the town house. Perhaps that would make him feel a little better about being on foot patrol and out of earshot when his partner was killed. She doubted it, though.

Zoe just hoped the teams at the other locations had done as well.

She reached for her phone when it lit up with a call from Brodie.

"Did you get through to the other scenes?" Zoe asked breathlessly.

"Are you okay? Did the—"

"The building's leveled, but I think everybody's okay. What about the other Main Streets?"

"I don't know. We got through to everybody, told them to move fast."

Zoe closed her eyes, replaying the past few minutes. She had grabbed her phone, made it out of the house, and stumbled over to the police car outside with ten minutes to spare to alert the other five locations. She could only pray that had been long enough. The pain in her left arm seemed to increase in intensity with the aftermath of the explosion. It was probably broken. Better an arm than a neck.

She had lucked out. As they fell, her upper body had glanced off the banister on the next floor down, pinwheeling her over the rail and onto the landing. Patrick Massie hadn't been so fortunate. He took the most direct route to the ground floor, hitting it headfirst. His body was under several tons of rubble now.

She would get her arm checked out when the paramedics got here, assuming the elderly lady from the house at 126 didn't need the attention more urgently. She looked like she was about to keel over. Brodie's voice in her ear reminded her she was still on a call.

"Zoe?"

"Yeah?"

"You mind telling me what the fuck just happened?"

Two Weeks Later

81

138 MAIN STREET
GRANTON, ILLINOIS

Zoe stood outside the house at 138 Main, absently flexing her fingers to kill the pins and needles in her arm. The grass was a little overgrown, but lookie-loos trampling over it had tamped it down so much that you couldn't tell.

There was a shiny new real estate agent's sign outside. The listing on the website had said *Priced for quick sale*. She wasn't surprised. Brodie had told her that over two hundred 138 Mains had been put up for sale in the past two weeks. Walker had half joked that maybe one day there would be a hipster revival, like with vinyl—people actually seeking the places out.

Zoe doubted it, and even if that happened, she doubted many buyers would be fighting over this particular 138 Main, where a man had actually been killed. One of the more troubling effects of the terror campaign was the way it had gained support from the darkest corners of the internet. The analysts were concerned about copycat attacks, and she thought they were right to be. The online conspiracy theorists were already out in force with a million suppositions about what had happened in that house on Main Street in Grenville, none of their theories anywhere close to reality.

Fifteen victims, not counting Massie and Henkel. A trail of bodies from coast to coast. And all for what? She had been thinking about that. On the surface, it was about the money for Massie. Inspired by his father's deranged scheme, he had come up with a perfect way to use terrorism to hold the country for ransom. But he had enjoyed it too. It wasn't just about payback in the financial sense. It had been kicking back against a world he felt owed him. Zoe wished she could say she thought the brothers were monsters, aberrations, but the truth was they were terrifyingly ordinary. Massie had just come up with a more creative arrangement to set his dance of destruction to than your garden-variety psychopath did.

She turned away from the house and walked to where her car was parked, at the corner of Maple Avenue. She drove the half a mile back to her mom's house on Pine. The house she had grown up in, the place where golden childhood memories mingled with the trauma of receiving the news of her father's death.

Her mother was in the yard, pruning the roses. She looked up as Zoe pulled into the driveway.

"You were right about cutting the bushes back," she said in lieu of a hello. "Makes it a lot brighter in the living room."

Zoe surveyed the newly exposed front of the house. The siding had been repainted. It looked fresh and new.

"I'm glad."

"How's the arm?"

Zoe ran her other hand along the rough surface of the fiberglass cast. "Doing okay. This comes off in a couple of weeks, then I can resume my pro tennis career."

"You shouldn't be driving with it."

"It's fine. I barely even notice the cast anymore."

There was a long silence, punctuated by the occasional clip of her mother's pruning shears as she snipped away deadheads. Both of them knew what they had to talk about next. She had no idea what her mother was going to say. In truth, she had no idea what *she* was going to say. She had made her mind up. Nothing Mom could say would change it, she knew that. But that didn't mean it wouldn't take its toll. When her mother cleared her throat, Zoe braced herself.

"You should take the good skillet."

Zoe's brow knotted.

"What?"

Her mother straightened up and gestured in the direction of the kitchen. "To make French toast. You know I can't have dairy anymore. It should be with someone who can use it."

"I . . ." Zoe began, at a loss for words.

Her mother said nothing, a hint of amusement in the corners of her eyes. "I know you're going."

"You do? How?"

"I don't know the details, but of course the FBI will offer you a job. New York or Chicago?"

Zoe took a deep breath and said it out loud for the first time. "Chicago."

"And you already decided to take it."

There was no point sugarcoating it. "Yes."

Her mother looked at her a long time, her expression impossible to read.

"Mom, I know you're worried about me, but despite"—she raised her cast—"the immediate evidence, you don't have to be. I can handle myself."

Her mother closed her eyes for a moment and nodded. "I know. I guess I always did know." She stepped forward and pulled her daughter into a hug. Zoe was too surprised to react at first, but then she returned the embrace.

"Just try to visit when you can, okay?" she said, her voice muffled because her mouth was pressed tight against Zoe's shoulder.

Zoe pulled away from the hug and smiled, wiping a tear away.

"Are you kidding? Who else is going to make me French toast?"

Her mother laughed and told her to come inside and she would make some right now.

They ate French toast and bacon and drank coffee. There was more talking, lots of it. And planning for the future. And remembering the past.

Zoe stayed until it was dark, then she walked back out to the car and waited there to make sure her mom double-locked the door.

She got into her car. Her work phone was still on the charger where she had left it. Two messages had come in. One was from Brodie, complaining that the job he'd been promoted to was more boring than he had anticipated. The other was from Walker.

Good luck for tomorrow. And be there on time, Banner isn't as soft as Chapman.

Zoe smiled and started the engine. She waved at her mother, watching her from the window, her straight posture betraying neither apprehension nor dismay. Zoe turned the corner onto Maple, then drove the four blocks until she reached the intersection with Main.

She waited at the stop sign for a few moments even though there was no traffic. The engine idled in the July evening air. She looked up and down Main, at the lights in the houses, the dozens of stories unfolding within. She thought about all the Main Streets across the country. All the thousands upon thousands of stories that had been interrupted, disturbed, and, in some cases, ended over the past few weeks.

Easing her foot down on the gas, Zoe turned the car left onto Main and drove north. One hundred forty-three miles to Chicago. She hoped the hotel room was nice. She already had viewings lined up for three apartments. She rolled the window down to breathe in the night air as she passed by the darkened windows of 138 Main. She thought about the long, wide road that cut through the heart of her hometown and every hometown and how it didn't stop at the boundary. It kept going.

She followed the road.

Acknowledgments

This book has had a longer gestation period than most. I began writing chapter one on a sunny April morning in 2021 and finished reviewing the page proofs on a cold February night in 2026. Hopefully, all that time means it's beautifully aged rather than overcooked. Either way, like George Foreman said, I like it enough that I put my name on it.

138 Main Street was the first novel I've written on spec in over a decade. The first time since I got started that I had written a book no one had asked for and no one was waiting for, for no other reason than it was the book I wanted to write. I'm incredibly grateful to my agent, Luigi Bonomi, for finding it a home, and so pleased to be with my new publisher, Simon & Schuster.

My UK editor, Katherine Armstrong, made some fantastic suggestions, which were complemented by the equally fantastic notes from my US editor, Alison Callahan, ably assisted by Taylor Rondestvedt. Thanks also to the brilliant PR and marketing teams on both sides of the pond who are already doing an amazing job of making sure the book looks great and gets to readers.

I'll sign off by thanking Laura, Ava, Scarlett, and Max/Oliver for putting up with me, and all of the booksellers, librarians, reviewers, bloggers and . . . oh yeah—**you**, the reader . . . for keeping me in a job.

About the Author

GAVIN BELL has written a number of crime novels under different names, including as Mason Cross and Alex Knight, and has also worked as a highly effective ghostwriter for bestselling authors in the genre. His debut novel as Mason Cross, *The Killing Season*, was longlisted for the Theakston Old Peculier Crime Novel of the Year in 2015, and his second novel, *The Samaritan*, was a Richard & Judy Book Club pick. He lives in Glasgow with his wife and three children.